Praise for the Tempes

TEMPEST BLADES
THE MAGICK OF CHAOS

By

Ricardo Victoria

ISBN: 978-1-951122-60-7 (paperback)
ISBN: 978-1-951122-61-4 (ebook)
LCCN: 2023934305
Copyright © 2023 by Ricardo Victoria

Cover Illustration: Salvador Velázquez
Logo Design: Cecilia Manzanares & Salvador Velázquez
Album Cover Illustration: Salvador Velázquez
Cover Design: Ricardo Victoria & Salvador Velázquez

Shadow Dragon Press
9 Mockingbird Hill Rd
Tijeras, New Mexico 87059
www.shadowdragonpress.com
info@shadowdragonpress.com

Follow Ricardo at: https://ricardovictoriau.com/

Content Notice:
This book contains scenes and descriptions of mental and physical abuse of minors. In addition that are descriptions of war and battle including injury and trauma. Some readers may find these scenes to be disturbing.

Acknowledgments

To the people that have helped to make this project a reality and allow me to keep working on it: my wife, my family, my friends, my publisher and more important, the readers.

Timeline

The Heroic Age (from 180 years ago to current time)
Year 1820 After Death of the Dragons (ADoD) to Present

1820: The magick field regenerates. Powerful Magi are born. The Society of Wanderers is created. Yokoyawa (Yoko) is born in the Samoharo Hegemony.

1844: Fraog finds the Silver Horn and takes it to the Humbagoo Forest deep into the Mistlands to stop a reopening of the Gates containing the Wyldhunt. Siddhartha (Sid) is born in the Samoharo Hegemony.

1850: Fraog meets Hikaru the Demonhunter.

1852: Fraog meets and marries the Freefolk Dawnstar, the last of the Wind Tribe.

1855: Izia is born in Skarabear.

1856: Fionn is born.

1861: The remaining members of the Wind Tribe of the Freefolk are chased away from their ancestral lands by the Silver Fangs. Fraog dies, Dawnstar settles her family in Skarabear with the help of Hikaru.

1863: Ywain is found as a baby, later to be adopted by Castlemartell. It's later found that he was born a Gifted. Hikaru trains Fionn and Izia.

1866: Hikaru disappears during a Demonhunter mission.

1868: The Blood Horde attacks Ionis. The Great War begins.

1872: A scouting party of the Blood Horde attacks Skarabear. Fionn finds and reclaims Black Fang and kills every member of the scouting party.

King Castlemartell of Emerald Island plans the counterattack of the Blood Horde. The dreadnoughts start their construction at the behest of the newly formed Free Alliance between the Emerald Island and Portis.

1873: Fionn joins Castlemartell's army by killing a succubus. Izia joins the army a few weeks later. They are placed under Byron's command.

1874: Byron is corrupted by the Golden King's treasures, using his soul as avatar.

1875: The Great War hits its apogee. The Twelve Swords are created. Joshua destroys the last weapon stored in Carpadocci.

1879: Fionn and Ywain destroy the Onyx Orb. Fionn becomes Gifted.

1880: Signature of the Free Alliance Charter in Sandtown, including most of the city states of the Ionis continent and part of the Freefolk tribes. Fionn marries Izia. Together they travel the continent.

1887: Ywain discovers Byron's treachery. They fight and Ywain is presumed dead. The Secret Rebellion begins.

1888: King Castlemartell falls ill, Byron is ready to take the throne.

1889: Byron kills most of the Twelve Swords. Izia sacrifices herself to save Fionn and separate Byron's soul from his body. Fionn sleeps for a century.

1959: The Foundation is created.

1969: Harland is born.

1955: Korbyworld is built in the Coyoli Archipelago. The Dark Father secretly returns.

1979: Gaby is born.

1980: Alex is born.

1981: Kasumi is born.

1984: Sam is born.

1989: Harland's finds Fionn. Fionn finds and adopts Sam after the death of her parents.

1992: Gaby becomes Gifted and escapes the Sisters of Mercy.

1994: Sid is banished, starts building the Figaro.

1995: Alex becomes Gifted, first major demonic incursion takes place in *ages*.

2003: The A.I. 'Wanderer' is developed by Esai, Alex's friend.

2005: The Withered King adventure takes place.

2007: The Cursed Titans adventure takes place.

2009: The Magick of Chaos adventure takes place.

Track List

1. I Remember
2. Holding Onto Our Memories
3. Not Everything You Are
4. Raised Darkness
5. If Only We Could Run
6. Urban Legends
7. The Ballad of Haunted Beings
8. Beautiful World, Wicked Games
9. Wrong End of the Sword
10. Moonglow
11. Against all Odds
12. Crossroads
13. Tears of Blood
14. Bound to Survive
15. Make Destiny Our Own
16. Magick Lights
17. Who I'm Meant to Be
18. Bonus Track: Twenty Stitches

Chapter 1
I Remember

You can choose who you are.
Seventeen years ago.
Manticore Island, home of the Sisters of Mercy Academia.

✝✝✝

THE ISLAND, WITH ITS WARM climate and soothing sound coming from the waves caressing its cliffs, was a paradise.

On the surface at least.

Beneath it, a different kind of horror brewed every day. Such were the ways of the Sisters of Mercy.

"Who are you?"

"I'm Gaby," the thirteen-year-old girl replied, a tremor in her voice between sobs to the voice that came from inside the caves and at the same time, from no place at all. Her dirty brown-blonde locks hid a precious face covered in blood and dust. In contrast, clear blue eyes betrayed an immense amount of pain, for her small body was broken from the fall. Better said, due to being unceremoniously dropped into a chute that connected the Academy of the Sisters of Mercy with the maze of caves below the hills that made up Manticore Island. Gaby lay bleeding out in a dark cave, with only a faint light at the far side of the corridor. It was a miracle, or perhaps a punishment, that she hadn't lost consciousness after the long fall from the Rectorship's special chamber. Then again, the piercing pain of a broken leg and broken arm would do that to you. She had been cast away—no, discarded—shoved into the chasm below the building by the Superior Mother and the Elder Council for refusing to murder her defeated classmate, after the special combat exam they had been instructed to present that night.

She is beaten, Madam, Gaby remembered saying. *Isn't it mercifully to forgive a beaten opponent? Livia is my friend, why I should have to kill her just for winning a stupid fight?*

You misunderstood the kind of mercy we offer, child; the Superior Mother had sneered. *It seems that your training has been flawed, for while you are able to summon the Ice State, you lack what you need to join the upper ranks.*

If I'm lacking that training then I count my blessings, I don't want to be one of you, Gaby had replied, defiant, as she measured every member of the Council, wondering if she would be able to beat them all and escape. Unfortunately, the collar she wore shocked her before she could jump toward even one of them.

Your defiance won't be tolerated, child, and you are showing us that you will never bend to our rules. Thus, we have no use for you anymore than we have for the weeds that grow on the shores of this island. Maybe the beast below in the maze will find you worthy as a snack. Take her away. We will give her father the usual reply for when a student fails to graduate.

The last thing Gaby remembered before awaking amidst the waves of pain caused by the broken bones and open cuts, was of being snatched up, carried toward an open chute and dropped as if she were a bag of trash. The darkness yawned around her, seemingly elongating her fall, yet she still hit the ground with enough force to jar the breath from her lungs and break bones. It was a miracle she had survived, and that she remained conscious. She cried now out of pain, fear, frustration. She was just a kid, a few weeks shy of her thirteenth birthday, and she was going to die—either from her injuries or being eaten by a monster.

"I want my mom." It came out a strangled whisper as she tried to scoot away from the point of impact. "I don't want to die here."

"If you want to live," a voice whispered into her head, *"I can help you."*

† † †

"Poor thing, broken, discarded," the voice said.

"Who's there?" Gaby asked. She was unable to see anything in the darkness. Aside from the hard rock and the damp air, there was no other reference to where she actually was. The darkness was all encroaching, disorienting, frightening.

"Be at ease," the voice replied. Gaby turned her head, desperate to see anything, to banish the fear. A tiny glow appeared in the darkness and she had to force her eyes closed and reopen them to make sure she wasn't seeing things. The light got closer becoming a tiny ball of light floating in the air. The ball shifted into a translucent humanoid silhouette, which changed shapes constantly. For a brief second, Gaby saw the shape grow wings in the back.

"I'm a friendly spirit and mean no harm. A prisoner like you, trapped here. And I see that you are dying, you are entering into shock. So, I will ask you once: Do you want to live?"

"Yes," Gaby said instantly.

"Then I have a deal for you."

"What is the deal?"

"You let me merge with you and I will heal your body, save your life. And then we will escape from here, together."

3

"Will it hurt?" The waves of pain from her broken body threatened to overwhelm her mind.

"I think so, but not for long."

Gaby's heart was slowing, her breathing was shallow, and a heaviness invaded her. She didn't have long.

"Do it."

Before she closed her eyes and her breathing stopped, Gaby saw the spirit kneeling beside her and touching her forehead.

"I see you are an old soul," the being whispered.

What does that mean?

"Just something I haven't seen before. But I can feel her blessing upon you."

"It hurts!" Gaby cried as the pain increased. If she could move, she would have embraced herself to ride the waves of pain.

"Don't worry, all will be well. It will end soon."

The spirit's hand entered her head and a jolt of energy rocked Gaby's body, causing a seizure that shook her with convulsions, one after another for what seemed to be an eternity.

† † †

Gaby was floating in space. Or what she imagined was space. It was more like a strange dimension, not unlike those depicted in a videogame. It was neither cold nor warm. She tried to make sense of the surroundings. Wherever she was, there were drifting derelict ships, massive planets, and asteroids.

Below her, she saw a labyrinth. A random memory from her literature class told her that it was the same as depicted in an old poem from the times before the Warring Kingdoms. That labyrinth was the infamous entrance to the Infinity Pits.

"Maybe I'm going to Hell," Gaby mused to herself. "I

guess I skipped too many masses."

She felt herself being pulled by an unseen force toward a verdant planetoid full of light. She landed in a grass field in front of the same energy being as before. They looked more solid now, an androgynous humanoid shape with wings, wearing a strange, almost high-tech armor with running lights across it, covered by a toga. They were sitting on a big limestone rock.

"I didn't expect that the afterlife resembled a science fiction version of a classical poem from five centuries ago," Gaby noted. While she was seated, she couldn't move her body below the neck. "I guess even here my body is too damaged to move. Weird."

"Hello, Gaby," the spirit said.

"Hi," Gaby replied. She was surprised at the calmness of her own voice.

"You know? I will never understand the contradictions of the Sisters of Mercy," the spirit said. "I mean, look at the whole concept: The cave was below the Sisters of Mercy Academy. Centuries ago, it had started as a religious organization of nuns that attended the injured and moribund from the battlefields, in a time where the kings and queens of the continent had decided that killing each other with more terrible weapons and tactics was the way to go. Of course they didn't do the dying, for the most part that was the fate of the poor souls that were forced to serve as their armies. And the Sisters administered their merciful teachings, trying to save as many of them as they could. Until one day, something changed, for their superior mother decided that the best mercy at the time was to deprive the warring kingdoms of their soldiers by releasing them from their mortal coil. When that didn't stop the 'noble' heads, the Sisters of Mercy decided to solve the problem from the root, thus becoming the premiere spies and diplomats of the political scenes of Ionis, creating bridges between the different factions. *Soon they managed to get 'gifted' their own land, Manticore Island, and became a school for the daughters of the privileged, with the aim of stemming conflict by manipulating the agenda of rulers.*

"Of course, if you think about it, all roads to the Pits are paved with good intentions, for the step from diplomats to assassins is just the small one that it takes to a push well-hidden dagger into someone's chest. And thus, the training of said daughters turned them into assassins of high caliber, equally versed in the finer forms of protocol and the finer forms of killing someone. Because for their leadership, it was equally merciful to stop a war through diplomacy as through killing someone before they got ideas in their head. Which it might be a good point, if it weren't for the way the training of these little girls from early ages went, with many dying in the process, from gruesome training to failing to pass the final test only a few were selected to undertake... which was showing actual mercy to a defeated enemy, as you have realized before your enforced fall."

"Now that you put it that way," Gaby conceded, "it is pretty contradictory. Like their grove, where they take pride in keeping a sample of every flower of the island, but they refuse to take the small Hildebrandtia of the stony shores, because they think they are worthless."

"No flower is worthless," the spirit said. *"It's just that not everybody understands their purpose until is too late."*

"Kinda like me?" Gaby asked. "Am I dead? I must be because I was badly injured. Am I'm going to the Pits or to last Heaven?"

"You're not dead. You're not alive either, not at least for a while. You are in a state of uncertainty. And this place is... let's call it an extra dimensional space folded between upper and down dimensions, where magic, souls and hyperspace converge. Some called it the Tempest. In here, I can talk with you with my voice, rather than through your mind."

"Why are we here?"

"To protect your mind and spirit while your body heals. As the Gift rebuilds your body, the pain can overcome your threshold and seriously damage your psyche. It will take some time until you can move back."

"Like an operation without anesthetics?"

"Exactly. So, we will be here for a while. Don't worry, you can still feel your body if you notice, it just feels like it is numb. Again, it's to keep you sane from the healing feedback and for when you go back to being alive. The shock is quite intense for mortal beings."

"One would think that magickal healing would be painless and faster," Gaby mused.

"Magickal healing is one of the most difficult things to do in the mortal realm, because not only does it require a lot of energy, but all-encompassing knowledge of how a body works down to a molecular level. That's why magickal healing beyond curing minor wounds is usually done through divine summoning or requires an advanced medicine degree on top of being able to use magick, otherwise you might end up causing more damage. And also depends on your own body wanting to cooperate with the process and in which way, and to keep going despite the trauma it causes. That's why to receive the Gift, a mortal being has to have an unshakable will to live against all odds."

"You are confusing me."

"Ah, right, I forget that you are still a child for your species. And yet you have gone through a lot."

"So, what are you? Who are you?"

"I'm a spirit from ancient times, who had been trapped in the cave since the Academy was built. Waiting for the right person to help me get free."

"And I'm that person? Because I don't think I'm the first to be punished like that."

"I'm browsing through your memories and your very

soul and yes, you are the right person. And you are right, you are not the first person to unfortunately be sent here. You are the first, however, to survive the fall for several hours."

"Why?"

"My guess? Because your will to live is stronger than anyone else before. And thus, you are a perfect recipient for the Gift."

"The Gift?"

"It's what I'm doing to your body. I'm healing it, but also changing it to enhance it, to allow you to sense and interact with reality in a way that no mortal can achieve, even with aids or centuries of spiritual training. My core will be your core. My being will be your being. And through this merger, the Tempest—where magick and souls dwell—will become a part of you. Through this, your connection to reality, to the world at large will become immense. And with time, you will be able to do things that no mortal can do or survive."

"This might be a bit late to ask but ... does the merger affect who I am as a person? My personality, my beliefs?"

"No. You will remain you. That's a promise. I will be there just for the ride, as your kind say, a part of your psyche, which in reality is an amalgamation of various factors, including how you see yourself and how do you think others see you. Plus, whatever was already here before I got inside, which by what I can see, it's something old."

"What is that supposed to mean?"

"I'm not sure either, She left out many details."

"Who?"

"The one who created the process to bestow the Gift. One of our leaders. Some of your mortals call them gods, although that doesn't define them right either."

"And are you happy with this?"

"Oddly enough, yes," the spirit smiled, looking above. "I thought that I wouldn't, but with my physical body hav-

ing been destroyed aeons ago, before your kind were put into this world and nothing to do here since the first Sister trapped me here for her own purposes, I could only reflect. And now I understand why She asked us to accept this. It's a second chance. An opportunity to fix our mistakes, and through you, leave a better legacy."

"Will it hurt you?"

"I can't be hurt anymore. My body doesn't exist anymore. This one you see is one created to allow your mind to understand what is happening without going mad at facing an n-dimensional being. The only way I will be hurt from now on is after you and I become truly one."

"How long will it take?"

"The initial part of the process is almost done; I have repaired your dying body to make you healthy enough to move and get out of here. The injuries will heal completely in a few days. The mental process will take longer, years perhaps. And the Gift will be constantly growing and evolving, it might even give us supernatural abilities. And that can take even longer. Or be done in a few days. The Gift acts on its own once we are merged."

"What abilities?"

"Of that, I can't be sure. I can't even remember which ones I had when I was a physical being. Probably something that amps, reflect or complements something you have or need."

"Will I remember this conversation?"

"I doubt it. I mean, you could remember snippets. But once we truly become one, my memories, my personality will fade away, maybe mixing a bit with yours, but nothing more than vague dreams."

"It sounds sad," Gaby said, looking downward.

"Perhaps. But it's my destiny now and I accept it. Okay, I think we are ready to move."

"I feel it," Gaby said, as a tingling ran across her body.

"Even if it's not here."

"Move your legs and hands." The spirit indicated. Gaby did something better, she stood up. As sensation returned, she stared at her own hands. They were part of her but not hers at the same time, the same applied to her whole body, as if it belonged to someone else.

"Okay, we are ready to leave this space," the spirit said, taking Gaby's hand. *"I want to congratulate you Gaby, you are taking this with aplomb and calm rarely seen."*

"As I see it," Gaby replied with a shrug. "Getting anxious won't change anything. And you are the first one to compliment that. Most of the adults in my life find that either annoying or unnerving. That and that I'm too defiant."

"Must be part of having an old soul," the spirit said as they expanded their wings and took to fly into the open space, pulling Gaby by her hand.

† † †

"I can't believe it," Gaby said, mostly to herself as she stood up. Her bones still hurt, as they were mending, but she could stand on her own. Her muscles felt heavier, denser. As if they were made of braided steel cables. Yet her body didn't seem to have gained significant weight. She took a deep breath and realized that she breathed in at least twice the amount of air as before. She looked around the cavern, taking in the damp walls and then realized that there was no light—she could see in the dark now. Not very well like it would be with the aid of a light source, but if she were to compare it to something, it would be to one of those old, night vision cameras with grey displays. It beat walking around in the darkness. The pain was subsiding. Her bones, while they ached, were reminiscent of growing pains rather than fractures.

Gaby jumped and reached the ceiling of the cave with ease. After landing, she threw a few kicks in quick succession and was amazed at the speed she could do it now. "This is amazing! Weird, scary, but amazing!"

"*I know. But here we are. Now, before we leave the island, we need to help two more captives that have been trapped here for long, long time.*"

"Why?" Gaby asked, even if she knew it was the wrong thing to say. She had just received a second lease at life. Then again, couldn't she be a bit selfish for a while? She wanted to get home, her real home, with her grandparents as soon as possible. "It will just make our escape more complicated, guiding others to get out."

"*Because it is the right thing to do, and you already know that. Besides these prisoners won't be hard to take with us. And they will aid you with further danger ahead.*"

"Fine, then we leave," Gaby replied. As she looked around the cave and saw the bones of previously discarded girls and she realized that she was fortunate because she would make it out of here alive. If she could help others to do the same, instead of dying here, then it was her duty to do so. "No one deserves to be left alone here in darkness to die."

† † †

The spirit guided Gaby through the maze of caves below the island. Even far from the place where she had fallen, close to the entrance below the Superior Mother's Rectory, people's bones lay scattered on the ground. Some showed fractures that one might get from a great fall. Others had signs of having been gnawed upon by sharp teeth. Gaby realized then and there that if wasn't for the spirit, she would have died really fast. But then again, there was a lingering doubt in the back of her mind.

"*I know what you are thinking,*" the spirit said. "*Why didn't I offer the deal to others before you got here?*"

"I was wondering that, yes. Why me?"

"I already told you, your will to live is the strongest I have ever seen. In the other cases, I offered the same deal to some, but they didn't take it, they were too scared, or too gone, unfortunately. Others wouldn't have been a good fit, I'm afraid. There needs to be some compatibility between our souls. And not everyone would have survived the process with a sound mind. My kind saw it before, when something similar to the Gift was granted to extraordinary beings to protect mortals and they ended up being corrupted by their own mind or others, submerging the world in a time of darkness that only certain individuals such as the Storm God and his demon hunters could dispel after much sacrifice."

"So, you didn't leave them to their own?"

"No. Of those I couldn't merge with, I offered the next best thing, to ease their suffering until they passed away. Of those I couldn't reach before the manticores, I could only pray for them."

"Now that you mention it, for an island being called Manticore, I haven't seen a manticore before."

"I can assure you, they are here. But they are keeping away for some reason. Maybe the same reason that has kept me trapped here as well. There is old magick on these rocks, one that became twisted when the Sisters arrived here. It became corrupt. That's another reason that kept me from going through the deal with others. It was as if the Sisters were actively keeping me from reaching someone."

"You did it with me."

"Whatever that dark spell is, it feels weaker than before, not enough to free the manticores, but enough to allow me slip through the cracks. That's why I believe it should be possible to take the other two prisoners with us. Their prison must be wearing out as well."

"Their location, is it far?"

"We are there."

Gaby found herself at the entrance of a grotto. It was huge, full of smaller alcoves and platforms that looked natural at first, but on a second look Gaby realized all of them were perfectly level. The more Gaby looked, the more she was inclined to believe that the grotto had been shaped to combine the organic growth of the stalactites and stalagmites with a well-designed plan in mind.

Some ancient magick? Gaby wondered.

As she stared at the stalactites, Gaby realized three things: one, some of the stalactites were made of glowing crystals, which provided the cave with colored light in green, blue and purple tones. Two, from time to time, when a particular crystal stalactite increased its glow, a chime-like sound echoed through the alcoves, creating some sort of natural music. And finally, the grotto didn't look like a prison cell, nor were there people inside.

"Where are the captives?" Gaby asked.

"They are there."

Gaby looked again. "No, they are not. There's nobody in there."

Gaby thought she felt a sigh in her head.

"Look again, behind the large pillar."

Gaby leaned to her right and looked behind the large pillar in the center of the room. Behind it was some sort of altar upon which lay two objects. It took her a moment to realize they were two short swords, identical to one another in nearly every aspect.

"The swords are the captives?" Gaby asked again, trying to make sense of it. A weapon couldn't be a prisoner because it was an inanimate object. Also, given how lax the security and the protections seemed to be, it seemed weird that no other Sister of Mercy had attempted to take them previously.

"Yes."

Gaby thought she detected a tone of exasperation in

the word. "But they are just swords," Gaby replied. "How can they be prisoners? And how come no one took them before?"

"They are not just swords. They are Tempest Blades," the voice replied. *"They can't be taken. They choose their wielders, for they are alive."*

"I thought they were a myth!" Gaby exclaimed, the words echoing across the grotto. She hadn't paid much attention to her classes on classic lore and mythology of the Core regions, but she recalled the myth of a legendary sword—or were two?—that had been wielded by legendary heroes across time and that could cut pretty much anything. But as no one had actually seen one in ages, aside from rumors of it being used during the Great War of the past century, they had been discarded as fanciful stories.

"They are real."

"Is it true they are alive?" Gaby asked as she approached the pedestal and examined them. She now noticed that they were not identical as she had thought, as each had different engravings on their blades. They were around 45cm long and had no cross guard. They resembled knives or some sort of Freefolk blade weapon. The grips were covered by skin of a kind Gaby couldn't identify—but given that regular skin couldn't have lasted long in the humidity of the grotto, nor for ages if the myths were true, the only remaining option would be dragon skin. And given that the last dragon died a little more than two thousand years ago, the blades must have been at least that old, if not older. And yet their keen edges gleamed as if they had been forged last night. The engravings on the blades were in an iconographic language she didn't recognize. But all in all, they were beautiful.

"In a way. The engravings are their names: Heartguard and Soulkeeper. Be sure to take both with you. They are a

team and haven't been separated in all their existence." "Being alone here must be a terrible thing," Gaby mused. "Okay, let's take both."

"Just one thing I forgot to tell ..." As she grabbed the hilts of both blades, a shock ran across her body, shaking Gaby to her core.

Waves of pain shot through Gaby's body. Her mind flashed with hundreds of memories and feelings at the same time. A sharp pang hit her heart. Another in her head forced her to her knees.

Who are you?
What have you done?
Are you worthy?

A new pair of voices echoed through Gaby's head, joining the already existing cacophony. It was as if the swords she had just picked up were examining her body, her mind, her heart, her very soul.

Images flashed through her head so fast that they were but a blur and each sent waves of pain, like a hot ice pick stabbing into her skull. Everything in her life, up to this very moment, even things she couldn't remember from the time she was a baby, or that seemed to belong to another person in another life, raced through her mind.

I just want to get you out of here! she cried.

"Please stop!" Gaby gasped. "Once you are out of here you are free to find someone else to take you. I just want us to get us all out of here."

Gaby released the two blades and they dropped to the ground, with a metallic clink that echoed through the grotto. The barrage of images ended, and she collapsed onto the platform and grabbed her knees, sobbing. She wasn't sure what had happened, other than she'd been forced to relieve all of her memories—good and bad. All at once. The experience left her shaken. Shaking. No wonder no one had taken these swords before, they weren't keen on someone taking them.

Something rumbled nearby.

Gaby stared down at the weapons through tear-streaked eyes. The blades glowed with their own light now. The one called Soulkeeper glowed blue, while the other, Heartguard, glowed red.

"*I think you passed their test,*" the voice said. "*The last time I saw someone trying to take them, she ended up in a coma.*"

"Well, the Gift could have helped me to avoid that fate."

"*Trust me, their will is so strong that if a Tempest Blade doesn't want you to hold it, you won't do it. But go on, try to grab them now.*"

Gaby slowly reached for both, unsure if she would get another shock. She closed her eyes as she grabbed them and ... nothing happened. She opened her eyes and lifted the blades. Oddly enough, they seemed to be lighter than before, as if they were made of pure air.

As Gaby stood up something moved from the recesses of the grotto, charging straight at her. In under a second it was on her, and Gaby barely had time to hold up the blades to try and deflect the attack.

It was the worst thing she could face in such an enclosed space: a manticore.

† † †

The manticore's attack had such force behind it that it sent Gaby flying. She landed roughly several meters away on the ground. The impact barely registered. As she stood, the manticore closed the gap between them and tried to slash Gaby with the razor-sharp claws on its paws. Instinctively, Gaby used the Tempest Blades to defend herself, slashing deep cuts on the manticore's front legs. The manticore growled in pain, hesitating.

Gaby stared, for the manticore's hide was known

to be near impenetrable. She glanced at the blades, and then moved to evade the random attacks of the creature. She ran across the grotto until she was standing opposite what seemed to be the creature's nest. The manticore ran to put itself between Gaby and the nest. The manticore stood about four meters away and growled as the high-pitched noises of a smaller manticore—which was showing its face above the nest—echoed through the grotto.

They stood like that for a minute or more, both opponents catching their breath.

Manticores were dangerous beasts, but a handful of books mentioned that they weren't without intelligence. And it seemed, without maternal instinct.

It dawned on Gaby that the manticore wasn't guarding the swords, it was protecting its hatchlings and it perceived Gaby as a threat to them. The harder Gaby fought the creature, the harder it would fight back, and any animal backed into a corner would fight to the death. A frontal attack would only end in the death of one of them, if not both.

This is not the way, Gaby thought. The manticore stood back, covering its hatchlings, growling at Gaby, ready to pounce once more. Gaby, calming herself, breathed slowly. Inside her body, the warmth increased, and in her mind, she could see a glowing ball of energy growing with each breath, infusing her body with energy. Every fiber of her muscles became stronger, increasing by tenfold, as a rush of adrenaline kept her at the ready. But there was another change as well, in her senses. It was impressive how much detail around the world the Gift allowed her to detect. It was as if the world around became denser, more solid and tangible, but at the same time transparent. The increase in her senses allowed her to notice things she hadn't even known were there before.

17

As her hearing became enhanced, she could hear tiny drops of water falling from the stalactites in a passage near where they were, a different one from where Gaby had entered the grotto.

She focused her hearing there, while keeping an eye on the manticore. Gaby noticed that her eyesight became keener despite the poor light conditions, as she could see the subtle shifts on the manticore's muscles. Holding Soulkeeper and Heartguard in a defensive stance, she tried to indicate to the creature that she wasn't planning to attack it. A subtle change in the air let her know where the entrance to the other cave was located. A few meters to her right. A side glance let her know that the cave was wide enough to let her enter, but not the manticore, who remained in its position, ready to pounce.

Gaby gave a last look to the manticore, licking its wounds, tending to its babies. Hopefully that would be enough to keep her from chasing Gaby and if the legends were true, the manticore would heal from the wounds she had inflicted, no worse for wear. She backed away slowly until she was out of sight of the creature and its young. As she looked toward a cave that might be a potential exit, Gaby was hit with a vision.

The voice had told her that every mortal that had been bestowed the Gift received abilities well outside the ordinary. Beyond the changes in physiology and biochemistry. Abilities that were superhuman. The vision didn't fade there. It became a glimpse of the future. Mere seconds. But that was enough to show her what would happen next. She would run toward the entrance she had found, with the manticore taking that as a sign of aggression and would pounce after her, slashing at her back. Gaby would evade that attack by millimeters as she ran with all her strength. Her evasion would cause her to trip on a small rock causing her to fall face first. She would turn to see the widening maw of the manticore close over her arms and then her face, bringing the vision to a grim darkness.

Okay, let's be careful with where I step, Gaby thought. *Because I can't see another way to get out of this without risking it.* She took a few more deep breaths, allowing the Gift to engulf her whole being, powering her body.

Here it goes.

And she took off.

She ran toward the entrance, with the manticore pouncing after her, slashing at her back. Gaby evaded that attack by millimeters, pushing her legs and lungs. As she came close to the cave entrance, she jumped over the small rock. The manticore slashed again but Gaby dodged that with only a scratch as result. She reached the entrance of the cave and leaped forward, with the manticore crashing into the walls of the entrance, too small for its wide body. The creature growled in pain, while Gaby fell to the ground, but instead of turning, she pushed up with her hands, still holding the swords, getting her feet under her and increasing the gap between her and her persecutor.

When she was sure the manticore was not following, she stopped and turned back. The entrance was quite far, but she could still see the creature. The manticore stared at her, licked its paws and turned back, walking toward its hatchlings.

† † †

The entity's voice was becoming quieter, speaking less as the hours passed. Random comments were the only thing the entity said when it broke the silence inside Gaby's head, and every time it was with a soft voice, eventually becoming a whisper. The integration the entity had mentioned was well on course. The thought of the changes her personality and body would suffer scared Gaby, but the idea of staying trapped, or dying, inside this maze-like cave scared her even more. And so far, the entity had fulfilled its end of the bargain and had left her memories alone, guiding her with a gentle touch through the endless passages, helping her to evade pitfalls.

Gaby walked for what seemed to be endless days. Her body continued to heal, faster than she ever imagined, and the pain soon diminished. The path toward the cave's entrance became a steep slope. Gaby gazed up, her body weary, her mind exhausted, and knew that it would require everything she had to climb. She didn't have a lot left. But the faint rays of sunlight shining in gave her hope that her journey was almost over.

Gaby considered using the swords as some sort of pickax to help her get a better grip on the surface, but she discarded the idea. She thought the blades would do the job, but she felt it was wrong to use them this way. Legendary blades or not, Gaby knew little about these 'Tempest Blades' as the entity had called them. She thought it was better to learn more about them before abusing them like that.

She shredded the hem of her shirt into two strands and tied each to the hilt of each sword, then she tied the other ends to her waist. Breathing deeply, she mustered the courage needed for the final part of the trip.

You can do this, you are almost out of the proverbial woods, the voice whispered inside her head.

Gaby started the climb, digging her fingers in where possible, looking for pockets and holds. Despite her bones having been mended, her legs were soon in pain from the effort of the climb. The muscles in her arms threatened to give out from the exertion.

No matter what the Sister had decided, I will leave this place alive, she thought.

Cramps spasmed in her hands. Yet she persevered

through gritted teeth.

All these years of pain won't be for nothing.
Every meter she left behind was a meter getting her close to the increasingly shining open entrance of the cave.

I'm going to free myself forever.
Dust fell on her head, making it difficult to breath, to see, yet she persevered through the dirt in her mouth and nose.

Once I'm out, no one will tell me what do to anymore.
She got new cuts on her arms and face as she climbed, and they itched as they healed themselves. Whatever this Gift was, it wouldn't let her die from her injuries now.

"Are we in the clear yet?" she muttered to herself again and again. The closer she got to the entrance, the slipperier the slope became. Gaby lost her grip, scrabbling for purchase as she slid, barely catching a pinch of rock that kept her from falling over the edge. Her eyes welled up with tears from the pain and frustration. Yet she persevered.

Get up, Gaby, you are not a failure, you can do this.
The swords hanging from her waist clanged as they hit the rock on her way up. It took all her remaining strength to hang onto the rock, let alone climb. Then her vision took on a blue tint and she realized that her eyes were glowing with an intense blue light. The climb up suddenly became easier.

The light became brighter as she reached the entrance.

The only monster is in my head, I'm almost there...
"In the clear yet? Good," she muttered as she hauled herself out of the cave. As she did, she noticed a tiny plant. It was a weed, that's what the Sister had called it—a bindweed. Yet from the stem emerged flowers shaped like trumpets, as if they were shouting their worth to the world.

We exist, tiny plant, because we can, Gaby thought,

letting her fingers run along the stem. *Contrary to what others say about our value.* Hildebrandtia. The plant twined around others nearby, digging itself into the earth, refusing to be moved. Stubborn, beautiful, and willing to do whatever it takes.

Like the humble blue Hildebrandtia, breaking through the harsh soil of the stony beaches, Gaby broke free from the maze below the island and into the wide-open world. The area around the cave's entrance was carpeted with Hildebrandtia flowers.

And yet we stood a chance.

Gaby untied the swords to stop them from banging and held them tight in her grip. She kept close to the rocks, being careful not to slip and to keep out of view. Gaby knew the Sisters had members patrolling the island. It took her a moment to realize where she was—the Sisters had not encouraged a lot of outdoor exploration. Gaby did know there was a small cove nearby that was secretly visited by fishermen. She had seen the boats early one morning when she had been punished by running a lap around the island before breakfast. They arrived with the morning mists, caught their fish, and then hid out in the cove until dusk when their vessels would be harder to see as they sailed home. Gaby just had to wait and be alert for a little longer.

As she sat on a rock, waiting for the boats, she took deep breaths, inhaling as much as she could of the clean, salty air. The other voice was no longer there. Or at least Gaby couldn't feel it anymore as a separate being. So when the voice did speak as Gaby sat waiting, it did so with her own voice—but it felt like echoes from a distant past.

I remember who you were, but who do you want to be?

It was the last thing Gaby heard, but it rang with promise. Hope.

† † †

It took a while, but the fishermen arrived and dropped the anchor of their small fishing boat in the swallows of the cove. Two men were on the deck of the boat. One of the men was tall with a thick, bushy beard. The second carried a bottle of wine, which he opened by prying the cork with his teeth. Bracing herself, taking a deep breath, Gaby walked toward them with a smile plastered on her dirt-covered face.

"Hello there," Gaby said as sweetly as she could.

"Where did you come from?" the first fishermen asked with a start. The second man gave a yelp and dropped the wine bottle. It broke as soon as it hit the rocks on the ground.

"Apologies for scaring you," Gaby replied. "I was sitting there at the back of the cove. I escaped from the cave on the northeast side of the island. Look, I want out, I'm not here to hurt you. Please, help get away from this place."

"You are not the first one to ask us for help to escape," the first man replied. He gave Gaby a hard look, as if he was measuring her. Gaby knew she was a mess between the dirt, the scratches, the dried blood and the missing teeth. "Although you are the first one to claim to have come through the caves. Legends say that no one makes it out alive of those caves, for monsters gather there. How did you do it?"

"Luck, I guess," Gaby looked at the incredulous faces of the men gathered there. She would have doubted her story too. "You think I'm a spy for the Sisters, but I assure you, I don't want anything to do with them. Never again. I just want to go home."

"How can we trust you?" the second fisherman asked. "That you won't report us as soon as we reach port?"

Gaby nodded, acknowledging it was a fair question. "Trust goes both ways, though. How can I trust you that you won't take me back to the Sisters? I'm willing to trust you and put my life in your hands if you are willing to do the same."

The fishermen stared at Gaby for a while, until the man with the beard broke the silence with a hearty laugh. "This girl has more guts than you, Hertford,"

"What about payment, Marek?" Hertford asked. "We should take those fancy swords of her as payment for our troubles. You know we won't be able to return here for a couple of weeks at least."

"That's true," Marek said as he scratched his beard.

"You are welcome to try," Gaby said, her eyes narrowing at the second man. "But I promise you, these swords won't leave my hands till the day I die."

He took an involuntary step back, remembering that despite her age, Gaby was probably trained by the Sisters.

Gaby smiled, "If what you want is money, I promise you, I will give you a reward worth the risk I'm asking you to take, once I'm safely home."

"Promises are worth the air in which they float away."

"I can give you a blood promise if you want," Gaby replied, remembering a bit of sailor's lore. They took oaths with an iron-clad seriousness, for they believed the gods could actually enforce them. And while Gaby hadn't encountered a god and since her mother's death, she wasn't exactly religious, her experience in the cave and the entity had proved that there was something else somewhere. She held out her hand. "I'll swear an oath under the names of the Mother Goddess Kaan'a, the Trickster Goddess of the Freefolk, the Storm God, and the Sea Lords below the waves that if I don't fill my promise before a year from today, I will submit to their judgement with no complaint."

"Not many are willing to take such an oath."

"I'm unlike many. Do we have a deal?" Gaby asked, as she prickled her thumb and extended her hand toward Marek.

"Fine," Marek agreed, as he returned the handshake. "Told you, Hertford, she has more guts than you. And you, girl, you will follow my exact instructions, okay?" "Yes, captain!" Gaby smiled. A peculiar smirk formed by her upper lip.

† † †

Thankfully there were no surprises on the trip to the port town of Alcaraz. Gaby had to hide beneath the deck, inside a hold that must have at one time carried smuggled barrels of orange rum. The smell of the spirit was so strong that she could barely smell the salt water of the open seas. She wondered if she could get drunk on the smell. It took the best part of the afternoon and the night to return. Gaby passed the time listening to the songs of the sea that Marek sung with a booming yet melodic voice. She couldn't be sure if he was doing that to keep her entertained in her restricted seclusion, but she was nonetheless thankful.

When they arrived at the port and after they had unloaded their catch, Marek finally let Gaby out of the hold. Hertford had put a cloak over her shoulders and they led her to a small hostel on the other side of the docks.

"You can stay with Sybil until things calm down."

"Do you trust this Sybil?" Gaby asked.

"We have trusted her with our lives, more times than we can count," Hertford said.

"She will keep you hidden for a while. After that, you will need to find somewhere else to stay."

"I have that solved," Gaby replied, "Thank you both for your help."

"No need for thanks, kid," Marek said. "You needed help. If more people helped each other the world wouldn't be such a shit place."

"That's a good point, "Gaby said. "That's why I want to

ask you another favor."

"What?" Marek asked, confusion visible in his face.

"If you can keep helping girls to escape that insane place, I will make sure you will have the funds and the resources to do so. And to live more comfortably. You and your crew."

"Big words for a small child," Marek said.

"I'm not a child," Gaby replied.

"You are not a normal girl either."

"I know." *Not anymore,* she thought. "Do we have a deal? Do you want me to swear another oath?" Gaby extended her hand toward the captain a second time.

"Heh, no need for that kid," Marek said. "The first oath is good enough. And something tells me that you don't backtrack on your promises."

† † †

Sybil received Gaby through the back door of her hostel. She had whispered something to Marek, which made him laugh. It sounded to Gaby to be a halfhearted complaint for waking her up, but she couldn't be sure. The Gift had warned Gaby before of dangerous situations, but this didn't seem to be one of those.

"Come on, child, let's get you to where you can have a good rest. Do you have in mind where you can go? Because I can only keep you hidden for a few days, I'm afraid."

"Yes, if you give me a piece of paper, I can give you the phone number of my grandparents."

"Grandparents? Usually, the girls that escape the Sister of Mercy want to stay away from their families as well, what makes you sure that they won't turn you back to the school?"

"Because my grandparents, my mother's parents, never wanted to send me there and they fought tooth and nail to stop it. But my *father,*" Gaby replied, with a scornful tone, "is a resourceful man and got me there before my mom's funeral ended. I'm sure they won't let that happen again."

"For our sake, I hope you are right, child," Sybil replied. Skepticism colored her voice and expression both.

Sybil took Gaby to a small room on the third floor of the hostel, near the attic. There were no other rooms around and the place smelled of dust and wood. There was a twin bed, a nightstand with a lamp, a few books and magazines piled on a table under the window. On the far corner, there was a small bathtub and a sink.

"Here," Sybil said, as she left a bottle of water, two wrapped sandwiches and a cookie on the nightstand. "It's not much, but for now it should be enough, I will try to get you something more nutritious later on, and some clean clothes for you to change, when the other guests are asleep. I suggest you stay here a couple of days while I make the calls you asked me for, just in case the Sisters are looking for you. Once I'm sure it's safe for you, we will send you on your way."

"Thank you, for everything," Gaby said.

"We rejects have to stick together," Sybil replied with a wink, as she closed the door.

"Why am I not surprised?" Gaby muttered. Of course, Sybil would be a former student at the school. Marek *had* said that it wasn't the first time they had helped girls to escape the place.

Grumble.

The noise from her stomach echoed in the room. Gaby sat on the small bed and devoured the sandwiches. It may have been a humble meal for others, but for Gaby it was a feast. She realized that she must have spent at least a week without eating anything. At least the cave and the boat had water.

I guess the Gift won't let me die from starvation, she

thought. *I will never take food for granted again.*

After she finished the meal, Gaby scrubbed her face and arms, then lay on the bed, while waiting for the clothes Sybil had mentioned. She turned off the lamp and stared at the night sky she could see through the window. The mattress was surprisingly soft and comfy. It would be the first night in a while she could sleep that wouldn't make her back ache. As she lay on the bed, she dreamed of possibilities and planned how she would reach her maternal grandparents' estate in the Montsegur region. How to get emancipated from her father so she would never be sent back to that hellish place. How to change her last name to that of her mother.

As she drifted off to sleep, she promised herself that she would always use her newfound abilities to help others, to prove that she had worth. And she would remember all of the people that had helped her and pay them back as soon as possible.

While she wasn't exactly religious, she had a sneaking suspicion that she wouldn't like to get on the bad side of the deities she'd sworn by, especially the Trickster Goddess.

Besides, the best way to make the world a better place, she thought, *is through random acts of kindness.*

Chapter 2
Holding onto Our Memories

THE MORNING WAS COLD WHEN they started their daily run. Since Gaby had moved to Saint Lucy years ago, living first with Alex and Sid before they moved to Mercia, she had made a habit of running every morning around the city. These days, Fionn ran with her. After settling into some sort of home life after the Chivalry Games, and the short tour promoting her band Hildebrandtia's first album *Wrong End of the Sword*, their days were now only interrupted by Gaby's recording sessions of the second album *Unconscious Serendipity*, or Fionn's secret projects. Of course, those projects were only secret for others seeing as she had been involved in at least one of them. While the original plan had been to go their separate ways and attend to their respective plans, it didn't last more than a month. Gaby and Fionn realized that the time they might have together would not be much, so they made a point to spend as much time as possible as a 'normal' couple. This arrangement had served as well to give Fionn a cover for his projects.

After running several blocks from her penthouse, they arrived at the spit of land that joined the marina with the small peninsula park known as Habiger Park, where the Crystal Towers rose above the tree line. It was where Sam had died and been resurrected as one of the Gifted. They didn't talk, sharing each other's company in companionable silence.

Fionn wore a green jogging suit, which made Gaby feel envious, as she had to wear a puffy winter jacket and a knitted cap on top of her purple and silver skin-tight exercise suit. Her nose was half-numb and red from the breeze while Fionn seemed unperturbed by the early spring weather. Fionn attributed it to the fact that he was a northerner Freefolk and the Skarabear was famed for getting really cold most of the year. But it could be Fionn's Gift as well: he kept regenerating the frozen bits of skin and therefore barely noticed it.

Lucky bastard, she thought, adjusting her earbuds and turning up her music.

As they ran alongside the ten-kilometer-long seawall around the park, the rising sun slowly revealed the beautiful skyline of Saint Lucy, with the impressive planetary ring crossing the sky in the background. The aurora borealis was also visible, an uncommon morning sight, and Gaby reflected on the series of fortuitous events that had led her to being here, running alongside the love of her life, listening to her favorite song—"I Remember"—from her own album.

She and her band had just finished recording it and the entire album was filled with memories. Her escape from the Sisters of Mercy. Returning to her grandparents' estate—to their surprise and relief. Getting a lawyer that fought for her right to be emancipated from her father and who got her back her mother's inheritance. Moving to the Straits to study high school away from the bad memories. Using her Gift and her blades to help the odd kid from her class and a samoharo outcast to save the survivors of an incursion by extra dimensional beings. Graduating high school and buying her own home, the two-story penthouse in Saint Lucy. And becoming housemates with that odd kid, Alex, and the Samoharo Sid, while she and Alex attended college.

As they reached the end of the circuit, she nodded to Fionn, pointing to the longer Dragonwolf Gate Bridge that connected both sides of the Breen delta that split Saint Lucy from the northern forested area where Firefly Park was located. Few people from the city traveled there on foot, due to how far it was from the city center. However, she and Fionn usually ran there and back, amidst the maple and redwood trees. Thanks to the Gift, the twelve-kilometer run was barely a warmup jog for both of them. Staying in shape while possessing the Gift was tricky, as it required three times the effort a regular human needed to be in shape. It meant that they had to run longer distances, lift heavier loads—like a trike or a small car—and train for longer hours before they actually felt tired and sore, forcing their muscles to regenerate stronger than they already were.

Fionn shook his head and pointed to the clock tower at the train station. The distance wouldn't be an issue, but the time would. They needed to go back now so they'd have time to get ready. Alex was presenting his doctoral dissertation later today and if everything went according to plan, which included Alex not blowing a fuse or a hundred, would mean he would have finally obtained his degree. That had taken longer than the rest of their friends due to Alex's convalescence after almost dying fighting the Creeping Chaos. It was a huge milestone not only for Alex, but for the family they had become.

Fionn and Gaby changed their route to a shorter one, which would take them through the grounds of Saint Lucy's University—Gaby's alma mater—and it's Trianthropology Museum, with is collection of Human, Freefolk, and Samoharo artifacts. As they ran students and others would recognize them and then wave. Being a celebrity after the past two years was still a new experience for Gaby.

So many things had happened, and not just in the past four years. The rhythm of her feet mingled with memories that the University grounds seemed to conjure as they ran. Coming to terms with her mother's death from that tragic car accident. Changing her major from psychology to musicology. The fight with Alex that resulted in him transferring to Mercia. Sid joining Alex as he worked to finish building the Figaro. Patching things up with Alex and meeting Professor Hunt. Then trying to warn the Professor about her visions of the future. Meeting Fionn and Sam and fighting Byron and the Bestial. And then the Chivalry Games and the rise of the Cursed Titans. And then the heartmate ceremony that made official her relationship with Fionn.

All of that was history, as Alex was fond of saying. That would quite literally be the case, too, if Harland got his way. He was writing an account of all the recent events, asking all of them for help to recall the details. Alex was helping Harland, which was a bit of a problem as Alex, never one to be good with dates, had given Harland some wrong information about her.

I need to fix that mistake, she thought. *So at least the timeline is correct among all that embellishment. How had Sam agreed to that? Right... Sam...* Gaby gave a glance toward Fionn as they ran. *That's an awkward topic for later.*

All those memories and thoughts in the front of her mind couldn't silence the noise at the back, the one about her deepest fear, which had been exacerbated by recent events: How could you be sure that your choices are your own? Especially if you suspected you might be someone else, or in this case the reincarnation of someone else? More so, who might be trying to regain the lost time with her husband and children. It was... confusing to say the least and something she hadn't mentioned to anyone except Alex. She knew it would be a sore issue for Fionn.

"Penny for your thoughts?" Fionn asked her with that big, goofy smile he sported when they were together. Most of the time it would have been endearing, but right now, it filled her already confused heart with sadness. She took off her earpods, not breaking her pace. Gaby mustered a faint smile, which Fionn clearly noticed.

I hate how he is so observant of every detail, she thought.

"Just worried about Alex's exam," she lied.

"You know it's not that," Fionn replied. "That guy can run circles around his examiners at this point. If he prepares more, he will punch a hole in reality. I'm more worried about his temper. But I suspect that's not what's bothering you."

"I hate that you can read me so well," Gaby lied again, a pang of guilt striking her. "He and I haven't patched things up. I feel guilty that he had to spend his recovery and physiotherapy alone and the trip to Korbyworld was really short and too hectic to really talk."

"I think he understands why we couldn't visit right away. He has a big target on his back as it is right now, and us being at the hospital would've put him at risk by revealing where he was. And he wasn't alone, he had Kasumi and Yoko, occasionally Sam, to keep an eye on him. And the trip, from what I heard, was pretty fun. Sorry for not being there, you know I had something to do."

"I know," Gaby said, smiling at him. "I still feel like we have to talk before something happens."

"'Something happens'? Did you have a special dream again?"

"No," Gaby punched him in the arm, and Fionn responded by feigning hurt. "But given our line of work and how our lives tend to go, it is too bad that these moments of peace are short lived. I mean, with what's going on down south and all..."

Fionn's expression turned somber. "I know. And no, you are not wrong for wanting to fix things with a friend. Heaven knows I know how fleeting the time with your loved ones is." They jogged, rounding a corner, as they began the return trip. "And about the thing in the south, don't worry," Fionn said with a smile at Gaby. He was trying to reassure her. "Harland and I have been working on that."

"The same way you have been working on polishing that special technique that Alex used and almost killed him?"

Fionn stopped. Gaby walked a few more steps, turned back and smiled at him.

"How did you..." Fionn muttered, caught by surprise.

"I can hear the sonic boom all the way from the park to the apartment when you sneak out at dawn to practice," Gaby replied, patting his arm. "The fact that you are still alive and healthy as usual means you managed to make it work."

Fionn shook his head, stifling a laugh.

"There are some small kinks to fix, but the visit to the oracle below the Shimizu Water Temple helped to clarify things."

"Ah! The infamous trip you made—without me, I might add—that you promised to tell me all about that, the same way you promised to finish packing? If we're gonna move to Skarabear anytime soon, you have to finish packing and send them."

"You are one to talk," Fionn said, and laughed. "You haven't finished either."

"I did, last night," Gaby replied. "What I have left is the clothes I'm taking with me to Mercia and a few mementos I still need to sort out. But they will have to wait because I have to take a shower and catch a warptrain. Alone."

"I will be there, I promise," Fionn said.

"You are the most unpunctual person I know. Remember our first date?" Gaby prompted, staring at him. They were almost back at their starting spot, at her apartment building.

"I already apologized for that," Fionn said, with a rueful smile. "And I *will* be there to celebrate with everyone. I'm travelling there with Harland and Kasumi. You are the one that wants to get there earlier than needed."

"And I already told you, I want to talk with Alex before his exam."

"Are you sure it's the right time to do so?"

"Knowing him, he will be thankful for the distraction."

"I can't argue that." Fionn slowed to a walk as they reached the end of their run. "You are very secretive about those mementos; can I know what they are?"

"No."

"Why? Are they from any ex?" Fionn teased her.

"Oh, you really don't want to go there," Gaby replied with a devilish smirk on her face. She put her earpods back in and ran toward her apartment. "Don't be late!"

"What's that supposed to mean?" Fionn said.

† † †

The ride on the warptrain had been relatively quiet for Gaby. Aside the delay on departing—warptrain companies prided themselves of always being on time and a five-minute delay freaked them out—and the occasional traveler that was a fan of her band's first album, or of the Chivalry Games, asking for her autograph, most of the time she was left alone to her own thoughts. Warptrains couldn't go full speed close to populated areas due to the residual energies, so they had to travel at half speed, which meant that it took an hour to reach Mercia. It was almost noon when she arrived. Alex's examination wouldn't start for another two hours so odds were that he was doing something to keep his mind distracted instead of fretting like he used to do. Gaby took a small bus to the campus; she didn't fancy walking in heels and formal attire, with a backpack, uphill on cobbled streets.

She texted Alex. *Where are you?*

The reply took a while, but it arrived as the bus reached the entrance of the campus.

Playing hoops? Gaby thought, confused. *He hasn't played hoops in ages.*

She got off at the closest bus stop to the gymnasium and walked toward the entrance. The campus was quiet as the term had ended a few weeks before and most undergrads used the winter break to visit their families. Only postgrads remained, plus the few being examined. She entered the gym and saw Alex and Sam playing two-on-two hoops against Yokoyawa and Sid, who seemed to be having difficulty understanding the simplified rules from the official six-on-six game. Sid threw the ball toward the hoop and Yokoyawa intercepted it, dunking it with such force that for a moment Gaby thought he would break the whole backboard.

"Three pointer!" Sid exclaimed.

"No! I already told you," Sam replied. "That is an assist, you only scored two points, because Yoko caught the ball and dunked it. It's only worth three points if you shot from behind that line."

"Which I did," Sid pointed.

"Yes, but Yoko grabbed it midair, that makes it an assist," Alex clarified, exasperated.

With such small patience, I hope he doesn't go into teaching, Gaby mused as she waved at him.

"Do you have this, Sam?" Alex asked.

"Yeah, we'll be there in a minute or two, if someone actually plays attentions to the rules," Sam replied, staring down at Sid.

"It's not my fault this ancestral hooman game has such complicated rules," Sid said. "Samoharo Phitz is easier, you just kick and hit a ball with a stick toward a goal and that's all."

"That's all?" Alex exclaimed as he walked toward Gaby. "The ball is on fire! That's not all."

"It makes for a beautiful night spectacle," Yokoyawa said.

Alex shook his head as he gave Gaby a hug. Gaby let out an "oof", clearly Alex's strength was back. After his long recovery from the battle with the Creeping Chaos she was glad to see he was back to normal. He had even gained a bit of weight and had cut his hair short since she'd last seen him, yet the top remained a mess as usual.

"Missed you, Lucky Charm," Alex said. He let go of Gaby and they walked over to the bleachers.

"Missed you too, Bed Hair" Gaby said as she ruffled with his messy hair.

"You look nice, though more business-like than I expected from our favorite rockstar."

"Of course, I look nice. I always do. And I wouldn't come to an academic event dressed as if I was going on tour," Gaby side eyed Alex, while her trademark smirk grew on her face. "You could use a shower though. Please tell me you are not planning to attend your own examination in shorts and a t-shirt?"

"Of course not? Who do you think I am?"

"Do you want examples of your previous crimes against fashion?"

"Point. But no, I have a change of clothes in the lockers. I needed to let go of some stress. Playing here while its empty means no one will see us using you know what to dunk the ball from half court."

"The Gift," Gaby asked. "Why do you insist on keeping

it a secret now of all times?"

"It's been a bit awkward here lately between the people that saw the Games and the people that actually prayed to that... thing as their personal god. Believe it or not, it had quite a following. So, Sam and I decided to keep it on the down low."

"With two samoharos in tow. Sure," Gaby replied with a sarcastic tone.

"Actually, only one, Yoko," Alex said. "Sid arrived just last night. Anyways, I'm so happy you are here, I thought you would still be on tour, but knowing that my best friend-slash-lucky charm was coming really helped to ease the nerves."

"We couldn't continue with the tour, with everything that is going on down south," Gaby replied with a somber tone. "And talking about lucky charms. I brought you something that you can have to help you while facing down those vicious examiners. And to remind you that no, you can't punch them in the face."

"Aww, why not?" Alex pouted. "One of them is known for being a big academic bully, Friend of my supervisor, but a bully. And you know I don't like bullies."

"Be nice, Alex," Gaby said. She opened her backpack and shifted aside her Tempest Blades to pull out a small box. "Here."

Alex took the box and opened it. Inside was a bracelet made of black beads threaded through by a leather strap. Replacing one bead in the middle of the chain was a small golden lucky charm, a bow with an arrow. Alex lifted it out.

"It's a Kuni bracelet for protection against bad vibes, with a lucky charm I know for sure is for good luck."

"I know this charm" Alex examined the bracelet. "I gave it to you when you went with me to graduation."

"And I have kept it till now." Gaby said, taking the

bracelet and placing it on Alex's left wrist. She noticed how it was still stiff at the joint, after the multiple fractures his arm had suffered on that grueling day at Kyôkatô. Even with the Gift and the aid of magick and scientific healing, some injuries still took longer to fully heal. Gaby's chest felt tight. She felt guilty for what had happened to make Alex feel like he had to do things alone. But not anymore. They were in this together. "But I want you to have it back. Not because I don't like it anymore, but because I want you to have something to bring you good fortune and support during your exam."

"Aww thanks. Although I would appreciate it if all of you, especially you, stopped treating me like I'm going to break. I get it, but none of you need to feel guilty about my choices. And I'm getting better each day, so everything is fine." Alex winked at Gaby, then examined the bracelet. "Man, this brings back memories. I still can't believe that you waited a whole year until I graduated so you, Sid and I would move together to Saint Lucy. Or that you would go with me to that party."

"At that moment, my two best friends were still living there, and I didn't want to be anywhere else, so of course I would wait. And of course, I would be your date for that party even if I was plan B."

"You are never gonna let me live that down, are you?" Alex grimaced.

"Never," Gaby smiled at him. A long pause fell between them.

"Talking about memories..." Gaby took a deep breath. "Alex... do you remember that hoops game? Your last year in high school?"

"My final game?" Alex looked up, as if he was trying to recall the day.

"Yes, that one. I have always wanted to ask you one thing. Why?"

"Why what?" Alex stared at Gaby, frowning.

"You barely played that season. It was a championship game; the team was losing badly..."

"Correction, the coach barely played me, I was reserve, and we were losing by forty points by midtime."

"And you got in, you stole a ball on your first play, fell down and then you got up, ran, scored and you keep scoring until you deleted that difference almost single-handedly. Forty points!" Gaby exclaimed.

"I actually only scored thirty. The rest were my teammates," Alex replied, scratching the back of his neck. "It was a team effort."

"Yeah, but you carried the whole team for the second half until you failed your last shot when you blew out your knee," Gaby said, pointing at Alex's right knee.

"A very unfortunate injury. I still don't get the question." Alex replied, narrowing his eyes.

"Why did you decide to play that way in that particular game when you didn't do it the whole season? By then you already had the Gift so you could keep playing even with an injured knee. You could have won the game on your own the way you were playing and yet you still lost by one point. Why did you choose to do that?"

"That's a loaded question," Alex replied with a sigh as he stared at the ceiling. "When we were losing at midtime, I talked to the coach, and I asked him to let me in. I mean with us down forty points; a reserve playing wouldn't make a difference to his plans, the game was lost. And I had decided that it would be my last game because I wouldn't be able to play again, not when during that term the Gift started to become more noticeable. I broke a finger, and it healed in two weeks. I mean, is not Fionn's level of self-healing, but still pretty noticeable. So, I got in, and when I fell on that play, I considered staying down, because hey, I'm just a reserve, no one expects anything from me. And then it hit me. *No one expected anything from me,* and that was a liberating thought! So, I got up, ran for the ball, and crossed the court and scored. And it felt so good, and I just kept doing it. Because I realized I didn't want my last game to be a beat down. Win or lose, I'm ok with that."

"Right," Gaby replied with sarcasm in her voice. "Come on, you are very competitive even in boardgames."

"I know," Alex replied sheepishly. "I don't mind losing, if I know I did everything possible to win. Forty points against is not having done everything possible. So, I decided that I would push and do everything possible to win the game. And somehow the coach and the rest of the team agreed with that by the time I scored twenty points and the other team almost none. It was exhilarating."

"And the injury? Did you fake it? It was your last game."

"Hey! Now that's kinda insulting." Alex crossed his arms in front of him. "I didn't throw the game. The injury was real, I damaged my right knee badly when I took that last jump shot and the other guy pushed me. I fell wrong and tore my ligaments. I still have the scan the physician took. I could barely stand afterwards."

"But you technically still could play a minute more if you wanted. It was just one point of difference."

"True, but I actually couldn't move. Now? I could have done that easily, I mean, I stopped a train with a broken arm. Back then neither my pain threshold was as high as now, nor the Gift so strong. I knew I would heal in a few weeks, opposed to the months-long recovery everyone expected. And I wanted to trust my teammates to rally and finish the job. As you said, it was just one point more."

"Yet you still used crutches for what? Another four months? At least until after graduation. You had to watch the final from the bench. That they lost, although not as bad as everyone predicted."

"Oh, I know, those were the two most frustrating

hours in my life," Alex sighed. "Knowing I was healthy enough but had to continue to fake it because I didn't think it was a good idea for everybody to know that I had the Gift. Still, knowing that I could do that inspired me to do other things later."

"Do you regret any of those choices? And every one of those choices was your decision? You didn't have a voice in the back your head telling you that you were expected to do such and such?"

"No, the voice in my head usually tells me that I suck. That's why I go to therapy." Alex smiled. "And I don't regret anything. Why the emphasis on choice?"

Gaby sighed as her arms fell limp at her sides. A painful lump formed in her throat. She looked to the ground, defeated.

"You can tell me," Alex said, taking her hand in his. "We have been friends for years. We have gone through a lot. You know you can tell me anything."

Gaby looked up and met Alex' gaze. He smiled at her. Yes, she knew she could tell him anything. But in this case, she wasn't even sure what was really bothering her. The visions, the fleeting thoughts, the cramped memories. Maybe when she sorted out her thoughts, she would be able to tell him what was going on in a clearer way.

"It's nothing, I'm just having some doubts about recent choices lately. Sometimes I wonder if the choices I've made are actually mine or if there is something else leading me. Some days I feel like I'm a different person from who I think I am. It's confusing."

Out of the blue, Alex hugged Gaby. He didn't ask more questions, just let her rest on his chest. Gaby let some measure of relief sink in, as if the burden on her shoulders and heart had become slightly lighter. The doubt was still there, but not as pressing as before, at least for now.

"It's okay," Alex said. "With all that has happened lately,

I think is normal to wonder whether we have free will or we are playthings acting under the penned commands of a capricious god."

I was thinking more on reincarnation and that kind of stuff, but yeah, Gaby thought.

"I dunno what's bothering you or why you are second guessing yourself, but for what it's worth, you are my best friend, an excellent singer, one of the best people in this world, a hero in your own right and that's because you have the kindest, hugest hearts ever. And a will of steel. To me, you are Gaby, and you will always be," Alex said.

"Thank you," Gaby whispered, as she broke the embrace. "I'm sorry for breaking the moment, but you need deodorant. You are all sweaty."

"Hey, that's what friends are for, to ponder the heavy questions of life and go nowhere. But you are right, I do have to hit the showers and change for my exam," Alex said as he stood up and walking back to the court.

"One last question, Alex," Gaby said, making Alex turn back.

"Yeah?"

"I have always wondered, was your original date for the graduation Kasumi? Or was it a lie. Why did she cancel?"

"Yes, it was Kasumi, I never lied about that," Alex grinned. "And she called a few days earlier to tell me that her operation to fit her a new set of hearing aids had been rescheduled and she wouldn't be able to make it. Which is totally understandable. Now I really have to go. Have fun with your number one fan and the two bickering samoharos. I'm sure Sam will ask you to sign her copy of your album. Or maybe ten."

Right, Sam. Gaby thought. *I really need to talk with her too.*

†††

"Do these examinations usually take so long?" Gaby asked Sam. They sat at the tables of a closed coffee stall on the promenade of the examination building. "How long has it been?" Sam asked, lifting her eyes from the signed copy of Gaby's album. As Alex had predicted, the first thing Sam had asked her was to sign a copy... or two... or three.

"Three hours," Kasumi interjected. Her face was the perfect portrait of boredom.

Sid and Yoko stood against the wall, each in a separate corner.

Harland and Fionn sat next to Gaby. Fionn was idly playing with the silverware, while Harland kept checking messages on his phone.

"It's quite common, actually. I heard of one guy whose exam took a whole week. And didn't even pass," Sam replied with a wave. Small flicks of light came from her hand, but Gaby wasn't sure Sam had noticed.

"That sucks," Fionn said.

"Do you think the restaurant will respect our reservation?" Gaby asked.

"I already texted them," Harland said, "I booked the whole place, so they are not going to cancel us."

"That's very generous of you," Yokoyawa said from his corner.

"That's the least I can do for him after the Games" Harland shrugged.

Suddenly the lights flickered on and off several times and everyone stopped to stare at them.

"Someone is getting angry," Sid noted.

"Let's hope he doesn't blow a fuse," Kasumi added.

"Or the whole power grid," Fionn said as he stood up. Gaby noticed the subtle changes in the tension of his muscles under his leather jacket. He was getting worried. "Did his Gift recover?"

"Yes, but not to the levels he had before," Sam

explained with a sigh. "Long way still to get there. He can't even use his bow now. He doesn't generate enough charge to extend the bow, much less to electrify the arrows."

A heavy silence fell on the room. Despite their best efforts to help him, Alex's Gift was almost totally burnt out. It had taken the best part of a year to get him to a level where he could actually have the physical aspects back—speed, strength, stamina—but the special abilities with the electromagnetic control were all gone, aside from the occasional flickering light from an emotional outburst. Fionn had theorized that it would take a decade for Alex to build back his power level, and no one was sure they would have that much time, given how things were going down south with the resurgence of the cult of the Golden King and its insidious takeover of the city states that had left the Free Alliance. Gaby sensed that the whole group felt guilty for what happened to Alex during and after his fight with the Creeping Chaos avatar. He had won, but at what cost?

The noise of a door opening broke the silence. Alex's supervisor came out, talking with the other two supervisors. A minute later, Alex came out, loosening his tie and looking exhausted.

"I think they finished," Sam muttered, as Alex's supervisor gave her a thumbs up with a smile. "And he passed."

"Is it finally done?" Sid asked.

"He may have to correct some stuff, but it's done," Sam said.

"How did it go?" Gaby asked Alex.

"Believe it or not, I don't recall what just happened. Can I change now, and can we go to eat? I'm starving," Alex begged.

†††

Harland had chosen a small restaurant close to the

place where Alex and Sam were staying for a few more weeks until everyone moved to Skarabear. Fionn had quietly asked each of them to move to his hometown, 'just in case,' but nobody wanted to talk about that tonight.

The environment was relaxed, everyone was happy and talking loudly. Alex had changed into his usual outfit—a comfortable hoodie and sneakers—much to Gaby's chagrin, as everyone else had gone for more formal attire. But Alex's look of exhaustion stopped her from saying anything. He'd earned a night to celebrate the way he wanted.

Fionn remained silent, taking in the whole scene. Deep down he was feeling guilty for wrecking their lives.

"You should propose a toast," Gaby whispered to him. "You are kinda the head of the family."

"Now I'm the head of the family?" Fionn replied with a whisper. "Since when are we a family?"

"Since you gave me this." Gaby gave him her trademark smirk and pointed to the heartmate silver bracelet embossed with a dragonwolf holding an iridescent pearl in its mouth. "And since you decided to take care of all of us."

"Fine," Fionn said as he stood up, took his glass and gently tapped his fork against it. Everybody became quiet. "Gaby asked me to make a toast. And you know how much I suck at this because I don't like to speak in public like Harland. Or stand on a stage in front of fans like Gaby. But she made a good point. All of you—including Joshua, who is not here—are more than just my friends, you are my family. And families should celebrate when one of them achieves something they have been working hard to get. Just like we celebrate Kasumi's championship or Gaby's album release, I want us all to raise a glass and congratulate Alex for finally finishing his postgrad. I'm really proud of you and—"

A ringtone echoed across the room, interrupting

Fionn's speech. Everyone looked around, for no one had their phones at hand. The ringtone was a tune based on a song by Hildebrandtia, Gaby's band, which made her face turn red as a tomato. Harland looked at the side table and saw his phone shaking.

"Apologies, I'll turn it off," he said. As he went to grab it, his face fell when he saw who was calling. "Excuse me, I better take this."

Harland left the room to take the call with some degree of privacy, even if the door was open.

Fionn saw Harland out of the corner of his eye. His friend was getting agitated as he listened to the call, pacing in circles in the other room. Whatever was happening, it wasn't good. His mouth went dry. He had a bad feeling about this. Harland returned in a rush.

"Fionn, we better go back to Saint Lucy. Fast," Harland said. There was an edge to his voice.

"What happened?" Fionn asked.

"Your oldest friend wants to see you, she is dying," Harland replied, crestfallen.

Everyone remained silent, as it was clear who the oldest friend was. The only other person as long-lived as Fionn, and his only friend from his past: The Queen.

"You won't find a warptrain at this hour," Sid said. "I will take you in the Figaro. Just get me permission to land on the palace grounds and you will be there in a blink."

"Do you want me to come with you?" Gaby asked Fionn.

"Always, but will Alex be okay? It's his party," Fionn replied, nodding toward Alex.

"Don't worry," Alex said, "we can finish here and go back to Saint Lucy tomorrow. You go."

"See? We will be fine, Dad," Sam offered him a smile.

"I will make this up to you," Fionn promised.

"Just go, old man. I will put more food on Harland's

tab," Alex grinned.

Fionn picked up his jacket and grabbed Gaby's backpack. Sid was almost at the door already, opening it for Harland.

"This is a momentous thing," Fionn heard Alex say to Sam and Kasumi.

You have no idea, Fionn thought.

Chapter 3
Not Everything You Are

"*Airship designation FG-Twenty-Nineteen* requesting permission to land on the grounds," Sid asked through the comms as he approached the royal castle on the outskirts of Saint Lucy. From the cockpit he could see few lights turned on inside the castle. This was in stark contrast to the Saint Lucy skyline, which seemed to be filled with thousands of fireflies. As Sid initiated the landing procedures, the castle security service, probably a Solarian knight working graveyard, replied.

"Permission granted. Please be careful with the bougainvillea."

"I don't know why they bother with a designation for the Figaro," Sid mumbled, and he pulled the yoke to aim the nose of the Figaro toward the designated landing area. "It's not like there are more than two ships around, and the other one is still in the test stage at the Foundation."

"It gives them a sense of control," Harland replied as he turned a few switches. By now, he was familiar with the Figaro's systems and was effectively Sid's copilot. "And right now, I think they deserve some slack in that regard."

"Point," Sid said as he looked toward the back seats, already empty. "I guess they are ready to disembark."

As soon as the Figaro touched the royal grounds of the castle's inner garden, Fionn and Gaby jumped out of the cargo bay and ran toward the queen's bedchamber. Sid's hand automatically went to the switch to activate the ship's emergency defense systems.

"You don't need that," Harland said, stopping Sid's hand. "Aside from saying goodbye, I don't think anything portentous is going to happen tonight."

"I suppose?" Sid sighed. "Sorry, force of habit."

Sid and Harland took their time to disembark the Figaro. They would have a long night ahead of them. Sid looked around the grounds, thoughtful. He hadn't visited since the Battle for Saint Lucy. The Queen had offered to let them stay in the castle while they recovered from the battle in a safe and secure location, something Sid had been grateful for. She seemed a good person, which saddened him, for the lifespan of a human was short compared to that of a samoharo, even for a human with the Gift.

That the Queen had lived more than a century out of sheer will to steer the Alliance into a hundred years of peace through what Sid surmised had been the cost of her life, spoke well of her. The only hope remaining once she left toward the stars of her ancestors—as per samoharo's beliefs—was that the Alliance survived. Too many organizations crumbled not long after their founders were gone. Sid knew that under the current circumstances in the southeast of the continent, with the Golden King's cult growing strong and taking over the separatist regions, the challenge to the Alliance was greater than ever. Sid glanced at Harland, his friend and business partner, and knew that the man was concerned about the succession, for while Prince Arthur was a capable warrior, he would need to be a diplomat as well to keep the Alliance together.

Sid couldn't shake the sense of foreboding that stalked him, tension knotting his neck and shoulders to the point of pain. Contrary to what Harland wished for, this would prove to be a portentous night. A crack echoed through the otherwise clear night sky. Sid looked up and saw the northern lights shimmering with unnatural intensity. Worst of all, the Long Moon, which should have been visible in the sky, was nowhere to be seen. Sid turned to Harland, who was staring at the aurora borealis with open concern on his face.

"You were saying?" Sid asked, his voice trembling.

This is not good, the samoharo thought.

† † †

Fionn and Gaby reached the entrance to the Queen's chamber. Outside the door, there were two Solarian Knights Fionn didn't recognize alongside Prince Arthur.

"M'lord," Fionn bowed before Arthur, while Gaby curtsied, as was protocol. What was not protocol, however, was the prince hugging Fionn.

"I'm glad you are here," Arthur said, as he released Fionn. "I know this doesn't seem too regal but..."

"With all due respect," Gaby interjected. "You deserve to act normal right now."

"She is right," Fionn said, placing a hand on the prince's shoulder. "Get it all out, for tomorrow you won't be able to. Right now, you are among friends."

"Thank you," the prince whispered.

Fionn could understand how the man who, sadly, would inherit the crown in a few hours felt. The Queen, his great-grandmother, was his only remaining relative as most of the other Castlemartell had died or disappeared in ways that made it feel like they were cursed. Given what happened to Byron, Arthur's great-grand-uncle, wouldn't be too far-fetched. Long after he was 'unfrozen' Fionn only had Sam as his only living relative, so the thought of losing her like he had lost Izia, or their time with their daughter, had affected him deeply. He considered himself lucky, for now he had the whole gang, but more importantly, he had

Gaby. Though, she had been acting weird lately, as if something weighed heavy on her mind.

Gaby thought he was oblivious to what was worrying her. What she didn't know was that Fionn did have an inkling of what was happening, because Gaby talked in her sleep. She once sang her full album as if she had dreamt she was performing at a concert. Fionn hadn't yet broached the subject with Gaby because he respected her privacy. And, quite frankly, because he had no clue how to address the whole 'reincarnation' thing that plagued her dreams. Freefolk afterlife beliefs didn't generally include reincarnation. The Freefolk believed that once you died your soul joined nature as an ancestral spirit, similar to the Kuni kami belief. The one Freefolk belief that did discuss the topic was vague enough to leave Fionn confused.

The door opened, as Doncelles, the First Thain of the Emerald Island and the Queen's right hand, came out of the chambers. For the first time in years, Fionn saw the man's usual imperturbable façade fracturing into a rictus of pain. He, like Arthur, was about to lose someone close.

They are lucky to have the opportunity to say goodbye on their own terms, Fionn thought. *I know how rare that opportunity is.*

"Glad you made it here on such short notice," Doncelles said with barely a whisper. "She wants to see you now."

Fionn looked at Gaby. He didn't move, not wanting to enter. His only living friend from his youth lay dying in the other room. He knew he would be in tears the moment he entered the room.

"Go on, I will wait for you here," she replied with a gentle smile, as if she knew what he was thinking.

"She wants to see you *both*," Doncelles said.

† † †

The chamber was big, probably larger than Gaby's

whole flat, with a wine-colored carpet that covered the whole floor. For some reason, Gaby expected the Queen's private chambers to be full of colorful knick-knacks after such a long life. But the room was sparsely decorated. Not even her combat armor or her personal sword were anywhere to be seen. Aside from a few personal items on a dresser, some comfortable chairs and a bookcase, the only other piece of furniture was the bed where the Queen was currently lying. It was large, but it seemed so small and weary in the large, empty room.

As Fionn took a chair next to the bed, Gaby stood behind him. She noticed that on the bedside table, there was an old photograph in a simple frame. In it, there were eleven people, though it looked like the photo had been cut to remove one person. Gaby recognized Fionn as a young man, the Queen herself, a small child of no more than sixteen, with her tooth gap, Ywain, who looked like a more athletic, but shorter, younger version of Alex. And Izia.

Izia stood next to Fionn, almost as tall as him. There was a certain family resemblance to Sam, which was to be expected. She had been a fit, beautiful woman, a powerful summoner and caster. Nothing like Gaby, and yet, the more she stared at the picture, the more she felt like it was a picture of herself. If Gaby looked closely, Izia's smile resembled her own crooked smile. Like staring into a mirror. A lump grew in her throat.

The Queen looked at Fionn with a smile, her tooth gap showing.

"You came."

"I wasn't planning on leaving my best girl alone in this moment," Fionn replied, taking hold of her left hand and caressing it. "Remember the oath of the Twelve Swords: together till the end, bound to survive against all odds."

Gaby gazed down at the Queen, studying her. Long

gone were the youthful features on her face. It was as if the last years, since the awakening of her elder brother Byron as the Withered King, had robbed her of her energy, had depleted her Gift.

"Gabriella, bring a chair here. I want to talk with both of you," the Queen ordered, then she turned her attention back to Fionn. "You look like hell," the Queen said.

"Yeah," Fionn chuckled, as his eyes began to tear up. "It has been a couple of tough months."

Gaby approached with the chair and sat next to Fionn.

"You are always carrying the weight of the world," the Queen continued. "That's unfair, you have earned a rest."

"You know very well, Sophie," Fionn replied, "I can't do that. Not right now."

"This... the restless hero... this is not everything you are. You are fortunate to have a second chance. Not many do." The queen looked to Gaby with a kind smile. "You should be embracing her with all your strength. Take it from an old lady that has lived long and buried many of her family. Time is precious because it is the only thing you can't regain once it's used."

"I know." Fionn lowered his head.

"Don't be sad for me, Fawn Fawn," the Queen said to Fionn, using his childhood nickname. "In retrospect, I lived a good life. I loved, lost love, and found it again. I had a family. I saw that my father's sacrifice wasn't for nothing."

"And I missed a lot of that." Fionn stared at the floor, avoiding her gaze. "Although I didn't miss that nickname."

"But you have earned much now," the Queen looked at Gaby and extended her hand to touch her heartmate bracelet. "Gabriella, I wanted to thank you for taking care of my good, dumb friend here. I know you haven't made it public and official, but you have my blessing."

"Thank you, Your Grace," Gaby replied, not sure of what else to say.

Gaby felt the Queen's eyes on her. Gaby tried to smile and had the odd sensation that the Queen was piercing her soul, looking into the depths of her very being. It lasted for more than a couple of minutes, to the point that Fionn stared at both of them quizzically.

"I think I know what troubles you," the Queen said, taking Gaby's hand. The touch sent a current of energy into Gaby. "I won't presume to know how it feels, but just know that you are you. We are the sum of our history, our choices, and yours, for what I've seen, is one of a kind woman that fights against all to protect others. You choose who you are."

"I... I..." Gaby stammered.

"It's okay. That's why I just gave you my—"

The conversation was interrupted by the sudden breakout of the nightjars' sounds, a monotonous series of noises, which sounded like someone was knocking on wood. As the Queen took a deep breath, the nightjars synchronized their song—for lack of a better word—to her breathing.

"The psychopomps have been waiting for me for days," the Queen said. "They are waiting for my soul. They did the same with my father. Fionn, do you recall that night with the succubus that you killed?"

"There were similar noises that night," Fionn replied, with a somber tone.

"What's going on?" Gaby whispered.

"My family," the Queen replied, her breathing becoming more erratic. "Have always attracted these... beings. Fionn... saved my father from a succubus... when the war was starting. But they got his soul after Byron..."

"Take it easy, Sophie," Fionn said, nodding to Gaby to check the window. Gaby stood and moved toward the windows without making a sound, as if she were a shadow. She peeked through the window, but the gardens below were empty. The guardians in turn were nowhere to be seen. The only thing Gaby could notice were the nightjars perched on the tree next to the window, their small eyes reflecting the light like shiny black beads. She nodded to Fionn.

"They want mine now, a Gifted," the Queen continued. "For their crown of souls. But I want to rest... don't let them take... me."

"As I told you the first time we met, I swear that no one will hurt you," Fionn replied.

"Thank... you... for being... my... friend," the Queen whispered. "Be free."

The room's drapes swung as the breathing of the Queen became more labored. Gaby couldn't recall what happened to a Gifted when they died from old age, perhaps because there had been so few in history. Most died violent deaths.

"You can... let me go," the Queen said to Fionn, pulling her hand from his grasp.

Her body shook as if jolted by an electrical current. She opened her eyes and mouth wide as beams of light shot out from them. A strong gust rocked the whole room. The light condensed above the bed, forming a silhouette of a young woman, made of pure light. The silhouette floated toward the ceiling. Gaby wasn't sure if what she was seeing was real. It wasn't the first time she had hallucinated. Maybe it was the Gift. After all, it allowed their bearers to sense the entrance to the Tempest, like that day at Sandtown, after Byron had opened the rift to merge his airship with the Bestial. Alex had theorized that because they got the Gift during a near death experience, it left them susceptible to noticing the supernatural. That was useful when you had to fight incursions from the Infinity Pits and other creatures from the underworld. Kasumi had told her once that the demonhunters had also developed a special sense that allowed them to detect *yokais*—spirits—which in turn helped to fight them. Since the demonhunters had been founded for the Storm God, who may have been a Gifted, it made sense they would have learned this ability.

As Gaby watched the silhouette of light, she noticed a red light coming from outside the windows, aimed at the Queen's soul. The light seemed to be dragging her soul toward the windows, and outside. The Queen thrashed and struggled. Fionn ran toward the window, Black Fang already unsheathed. Gaby drew Soulkeeper, swinging it at the red light. As the blade cut the beam, a shockwave sent her and Fionn tumbling to the ground. The soul kept ascending to the ceiling.

"Thank you," the disembodied voice of the Queen echoed through the room even as it dissipated. Fionn recovered from the hit and helped Gaby to get up. As they returned to the bedside, the body of the Queen dissolved into thin air, leaving nothing but her clothes behind.

The door opened in a rush, as Doncelles, Arthur, several Solarian Knights, Harland, and Sid entered the room.

"What happened? Where is the Queen's body?" Doncelles yelled. "Did she escape them?"

"Her Majesty is finally resting with her ancestors," Fionn replied, eyeing the knights that blocked the door. His gaze cowed them into sheathing their weapons. "As for what happened, I'm not sure, but I have the feeling that you do."

† † †

"She had her fears, and her suspicions," Doncelles said, as Harland looked around at the people gathered in the small office the Queen used for her personal writing. Arthur was there, serious and calm, although Harland knew he was hurting. Knowing that a relative is near death still does not prepare someone to experience it. This would be his first unofficial act as King, until the coronation took place. Since the Chivalry Games, Arthur had been taking over more and more duties as the Queen's health had been in decline, but the ceremony would make it official.

Fionn and Gaby sat next to each other. They held hands, and on her left wrist she wore the heartmate bracelet. It was the first time Harland had seen her wearing it in public.

Sid was there as well, which surprised Harland, because Doncelles was not the friendliest person on his best days, even less so to strangers. Harland assessed that Sid's presence meant the meeting was an all-hands-on-deck situation. Given the recent restructuring that both the Alliance and the Foundation had undergone in the last year, maybe Sid's presence was warranted.

"Suspicions of what?" Fionn asked. His tone and the tension of his neck muscles gave Harland the impression that Fionn was reliving some unspoken horror. Flashbacks were never pleasant.

"That at her moment of death, someone would attempt to steal her soul, like what had happened to her father," Doncelles replied. "I thought you knew about that."

"I wasn't there when King Castlemartell died," Fionn said. "And I never asked her what happened. At first, I had assumed that he had died of old age after fighting a long war. Later we found out Byron might have had a hand in his death. But no one mentioned anything about soul stealing."

"What about the succubus thing?" Arthur asked. "You were there for that."

"Succubus?" Sid asked. "I'm sorry, but you know I haven't read any of the multiple biographies about you."

Fionn sighed, and his shoulders dropped. Gaby

caressed his hand.

"After I got Black Fang and beat those marauders in Skarabear, I went in search of the King to join his army. When I found him and his entourage, they rejected me. Which was to be expected, if I think about it. I was just a scrawny half-Freefolk kid from up north with barely any combat experience. I trailed the King's entourage for a while, and it was then when I noticed that something was trailing him as well.

"One night they stopped at an abandoned inn. I stayed at a nearby farm. The farmer told me that the inn was haunted and that in recent days they had heard the wailings of a woman coming from nowhere, which was a bad omen. He told me that I was lucky to not stay in the inn because last time that wailing was heard, all its occupants died in one night. I got up, ran toward the inn, with Black Fang unsheathed. I didn't know back then the meaning of the glowing green blade, but it was warning me that some creature from the Pits was there. When I opened a window to enter the inn, I found a succubus, draining the life force of one knight. The rest were dead, or frozen in some sort of open eye sleep, waiting to be murdered. The succubus finished the knight and moved toward the King. I fought the creature. How I withstood its spell I'm not sure, maybe it was the demonhunter training I had. I managed to kill it and free the King and the survivors from the spell and the rest is history. But I'm not sure what that has to do with what just happened?"

"In recent years, even before the Battle for Saint Lucy, Her Majesty had the growing suspicion that the attack that you stopped, and later events in the King's last days, were related. That his soul was somehow stolen at the moment of his death to use for some nefarious purpose," Doncelles replied.

"Nefarious purpose?" Harland asked. Mostly, he

wanted to confirm a growing suspicion he had. After all, his father had made him learn by heart pretty much every folktale, myth and legend from the Ionis continent, most of the Core regions, and even what they could find about the ancient myths of the Akeleth in the Grasslands.

"Have you heard of the Crown of the Dead?" Doncelles asked.

"The trinket which can control the fate of a battle?" Sid replied. "Isn't that just a human tale from before the Warring Kingdoms period?"

"You have been listening to those podcasts again," Gaby said. "I thought you didn't like them."

"Not at first, but they are addictive and very hilarious."

"Ahem," Harland cleared his throat. "It is not just a human tale. There have been recorded sightings even in Freefolk texts. I thought it was lost."

"Excuse me, Harland," Gaby interrupted, "but I don't know what it is. Not my field of study."

"The Crown of the Dead was an iron crown with rubies inset in it. Legend says that it was forged sometime between the Hunt of the Titans and the Fall of the Freefolk Kingdom of Umo, so it could be at least as old as Black Fang. The crown was said to be able to steer the tide of war by providing the wearer with the insight of every tactic and strategy possible, to the point of granting some level of precognition. With time, it can drive the wearer mad. It was rumored that King Castlemartell used it during the most difficult part of the Great War to gain an edge over the four generals of the Blood Horde."

"So, it is a magickal item."

"I would say it is more akin to a Tempest Blade," Harland replied. "You see, the dirty, bloody secret of the Crown is that within each ruby is trapped the soul of a famous tactician. How this happens, no one knows, but it could be because they wore the Crown and it took their soul, or the wearer somehow trapped the soul of a rival king. The insight is the memories and experiences of those souls trapped in there. The legends say that there are six rubies already filled, with a seventh free to be used."

"Why is that everything surrounding these weapons and items have this morbid bent?" Sid muttered.

"And let me guess," Fionn said. "The ruby when used emits a red beam that drags the soul into the stone. The same beam you interrupted Gaby."

"You are correct," Harland continued. "I guess the Queen suspected that someone did that to her father and was trying to do the same to her."

"Exactly," Arthur confirmed. "And with... Byron back, she thought one of his surviving followers might try that. That's why she had been studying the crown, souls, psychopomps, and reincarnation for the past few months."

Harland noticed that Gaby shuffled on her seat, clearly uncomfortable at the mention of reincarnation.

"Byron didn't have it. Of that I'm sure," Fionn said. "And I never saw the King using it if he had it. I do recall discussions about tracking an item that could help the war effort, but I always assumed Byron was referring to the Orb."

"A good thing he never got ahold of that," Arthur said with a nod toward Fionn.

Fionn ignored the complement.

"So, if the King had it, which I sincerely doubt, he probably returned it to where it was originally after the war ended and never spoke of it," Fionn said.

"The Queen suspected as much. She wanted to find the Crown before it could be used on her. And to free her father's soul, if her suspicions were right. The Crown poses an existential threat to the Free Alliance. Our intelligence services discovered that the army of the Golden King and its southern allies have sent one of their generals, Edamane, to find the Crown. If they get the Crown first, who knows what damage they can do on top of the scourge they have already committed," Doncelles explained. "We... outsourced a specialist to find it but haven't heard from her in a few weeks."

"You did that behind the Queen's back?" Harland asked. "What for? Do you want it for yourself?"

"No, in this matter, believe it or not, I wanted to follow her wishes," Doncelles replied, looking exhausted. "I wanted to find that crown and destroy it. I'm glad they didn't get her soul. Heaven knows how powerful that cursed thing could have become with her inside. For protecting her soul, Lady Galfano-Estel I thank you."

"I didn't do much, just cut the red beam," Gaby corrected Doncelles. By the way she changed her posture, becoming stiffer within the chair, she wasn't happy to be referred by her new title.

"That, m'lady," Doncelles smiled—Harland thought it was the first sincere smile the man had ever had—and said, "might have proven the difference."

"What we want to ask of you," Arthur continued. "As an official but secret request, is to find that crown and destroy it. Unlike my ancestor, I have no desire in having such a cursed item in our possession, the risk for it being misused is too high. It's better if we get rid of it at once. Like you wisely did with the Orb."

"When do you want us to depart?" Fionn asked.

"As soon as possible," Doncelles replied. "I know you would prefer to attend the funeral, to even be a pallbearer, but as you understand, this is a time sensitive matter, and state funerals take some time to carry out, more so if we have to hide the fact that there is no body to bury."

"I'm sure my gran... the Queen would have understood. She always said that you understood that carrying on one's duty came with sacrifices," Arthur added.

"Fine," Fionn said as he stood up, anger and sadness warring for dominance on his face. There was no clear winner between the two. Gaby followed him, clenching his hand tight.

Duty, Harland thought, withholding a sigh. Fionn couldn't escape it. *The perfect excuse for lack of empathy.*

† † †

"Why did he leave the Figaro so far away?" Fionn complained as he and Gaby covered the twenty kilometers to Firefly Park.

"Well, you told him after the meeting with Arthur and Doncelles to take it some place far away to not attract attention," Gaby replied as she drove her car into the park's parking lot. "And the Figaro is as much a celebrity as we are by now. Also, there is more space to land there than in Habiger Park."

"Hang on, I have an incoming call," Fionn said as he answered his phone. The Figaro came into view in a clearing near the park entrance. "Culph? Thank you for your condolences. A case? No, I'm sorry, I won't be able, but call Samantha… yes… I'm deputizing her as of right now… yes, she is more than capable. And Alex is with her so she will have excellent help."

They reached the Figaro and boarded the airship.

"They will be there before the end of the day, if you don't mind waiting. I get it, the weirdness won't go anywhere, hopefully. Just keep the place cordoned off till they get there."

"Who is he talking to?" Sid asked as he flipped a switch to close the cargo hatch.

"Culph, about a case," Gaby replied. She looked at Harland who was also on his phone. "And Harland?"

"Kasumi," Sid replied. "Buckle up, we are about to lift off."

"I'm sure," Harland was saying. "I will be more at ease if you keep an eye on Alex and Sam. They need someone that can keep them calm if something happens, and right now, we are entering difficult times. Besides, I'll be safe. I'm going with Fionn, Gaby and Sid, and no place in Theia is safer than this or your side... Sure, if I get some info about him, I will let you know. Be careful."

Harland hung up. He turned to see Gaby already seated. Fionn was pacing around the tight space of the cockpit as he talked with Culph.

"Kasumi takes her job very seriously," Gaby whispered to Harland.

"She even keeps track of my meals, so yes."

"Between her and Amy, they basically run the Foundation. They only keep us around to be the public face," Sid laughed.

"Why, oh why, did I name you co-director of the Foundation?" Harland complained.

"Because you know you need help with the airships project."

"Airships? Plural?" Gaby asked.

"The logical step after the Figaro," Harland said. "We might need another one sooner than we expect. We even have Scud, your drummer, training as pilot after the tour got cancelled."

"So that's where he had been hiding, and not taking my calls," Gaby muttered.

"Okay, we are ready to go," Sid said. "For the last time, Fionn, take your seat."

Fionn kept talking, so Sid just flipped a few switches and pushed the yoke, making the Figaro lift up. The sudden movement threw Fionn to the ground.

"Hey!" Fionn yelled.

"I told you to take your seat," Sid said. "I take it we need to pick up the others on our way to... wherever is our next stop."

"No," Fionn replied. "There is a case near Mercia. It's strange enough that Culph wanted me to look into it. But we are pressed for time as it is, so I suggested that he call Sam to look into it. It will be a good way for Sam and Alex to get back into shape. If it turns out to be nothing major, then we can pick them up after our next stop. Although Sam will never forgive me for not taking her there."

"Where now then?" Harland asked.

"Ravenhall," Fionn replied.

"I was afraid you were going to say that," Sid replied.

Chapter 4
Raised Darkness

"*I hate Sunday afternoons,*" *Alex* said as he drove the truck into the narrow streets of the town of Velcarra. The town was located in the hills between Mercia and Saint Lucy. "Nothing good happens on them. It's a bad omen. Just look at the sky."

"I thought you didn't believe in omens," Sam replied, anticipating another tangential chat from Alex. They were driving toward the address Agent Culph had texted her. She was nervous as this would be her first official case as Justicar and wanted to make a good impression. She wondered how her dad and Harland managed to keep so many things in check at the same time, while she was having trouble just keeping Alex from diverging into some rabbit hole every other hour. Yokoyawa was pretending to be asleep in the truck's back seat, but Sam heard him chuckle. Kasumi, seated next to Yoko, was looking out the window into the darkness of the forest.

"This town is a maze," Kasumi said. "So many small streets crisscrossing these hills. And the forest. The yokai and kami that live here are unsettled."

"Unsettled how?" Sam asked. Alex's outlandish ideas, she could dismiss. She'd learned to appreciate them, but he cycled through those ideas so fast that it was hard to follow all of them. But Kasumi, who usually was friendly and even chipper, had been oddly quiet. And when a demonhunter tells you that the spirits are unsettled, on your way to a peculiar Justicar case, you better pay attention. "Aggressive, you mean?" "No," Kasumi replied. "They are scared; some seem to be leaving the whole zone. I've only seen them doing that when an incursion takes place. He is right, something is off." "See?" Alex added. "On whose side are you, Kasumi?" Sam turned back and looked at Kasumi, who smiled at her. "On the one that makes the most compelling argument." Kasumi replied "As he said, look at the sky, aurora borealis nonstop for three days. When was the last time that happened? Add the death of the Queen and what's happening in the south. Now this case you were asked to look into. And as I already told you, yokai and kami alike are unsettled." "You are always siding with him," Sam said, not believing it herself. She took a deep breath. "Although, you are right about things piling up." "Told you, bad omen," Alex replied. "And by the amount of people standing outside that old house straight out of a horror movie indicates anything, it's a bad omen. That and the buzzing in my ear."

They had arrived at a hill on the outskirts of the town. The house was one of a group of old, abandoned two-story houses on the hill. It was substantial, big enough for a large family, but not exactly a mansion. The style was relatively modern, from the post-war period at the very least. Their destination was situated was at the end of the lonely road. The whole hill was its own microcosm of a ghost town. And as much as Sam rued it, she had to agree with Ale: there was something off in this place.

"Yes, this seems to be the place. Stay here, let me do

the talking," Sam said, looking at both Alex and Kasumi. "If I need your help, I will come back for you."

"I wasn't planning to stand up," Yoko said from the back, while Kasumi and Alex traded knowing glances.

††††

"Good afternoon, Agent Culph," Sam said as she approached the officers gathered outside the house. She wiped her sweaty palms on her black leather jacket and extended a hand, trying to look professional. "I'm glad to see you are back at work."

Culph looked at her and offered a calm smile that contrasted with the scar on his upper lip he'd gotten some years ago, around the time Fionn and Gaby had met. "Thank you Miss Ambers-Estel." Culph returned the handshake. "I understand that your father is busy, so I thank you for agreeing to help us. Although I'm not sure about the weirdos."

"What weirdos?" Sam asked. Culph pointed with his pen toward the brick wall that served as fence for the old house. There, in all their 'glory,' standing atop the wall, were Alex and Kasumi, both decked out in their superhero gear. Which consisted mostly of the special shock absorbent vest, kneepads and back scabbard with the sword Yaha in it for Alex; and Kasumi's demonhunter garb, the black and blue open long robe, and including a new white cat mask that covered the upper half of her face. She had Breaker, her naginata in her left hand. "Really? You two?"

Sam strode toward them, trying to ignore the snickers from the officers.

"I get that she is a demonhunter, but what is your excuse?" Sam asked, pointing at Kasumi first and then to Alex. "You haven't recovered yet."

"A job is a job."

"That's true," Yoko said, with his deep, booming voice,

from behind her. His sudden presence made her jump. To this day Sam was unable to explain how the two-meter-tall and almost two hundred fifty kilogram samoharo with a long tail could move so fast, and so silently. As Alex had put it once, in his gamer jargon, "...it was like watching a mountain trying to be stealthy and rolling consecutive critical successes to make it happen."

After recovering her breath, Sam said, "Please don't do that again. And you are enabling them, Yoko?"

"What can I say? I'm curious as well," Yokoyawa said. The large samoharo stared at the old house, the nostrils on his large snout twitching. "There is a faint but unpleasant smell coming from that place."

"I guess that's three out of three," Culph said, then he looked to his men. "And you better stop laughing. Unlike you, they are willing to go inside that... place."

"Something we should know before going in?" Alex asked as he came down from the fence. Yoko and Kasumi remained in their positions, almost like statues. Whatever was inside had caught the attention of the two more experienced members of the group. Now, Sam was thankful they had tagged along. While she was more than capable of holding her own in a fight or in academia, detective work on supernatural cases was her father's province, not hers. *Heck, maybe even Alex might prove useful with his vigilante experience*, she thought.

"What he is trying to say," Sam interjected. "Is what happened here?"

"The report says that these houses have been empty for at least a decade. They've been a canvas for local graffiti groups and according to local rumors, in the past year, it was host for a group that performed strange occult rituals. The town council had decided to transform them into a hospice for the homeless, but never got the funds to do it. Then three days ago, neighbors reported loud bangs, strange lights and screams coming from here. This happened at random times during the following three days. The local officers were called as the noise became so loud it reached the town center. When they arrived and entered the house, they found a single body," Culph explained as he took out a photo from a folder.

"Before you see this, be warned, the scene is pretty gruesome," Culph warned.

Sam exchanged a look with Alex. She took the photo.

In it, there was a body of a man whose top half of his head was gone. The wall was covered in blood and a black ichor. The kind of ichor Sam and Alex had seen before. Aboard the Bestial.

"This is pretty gruesome, but that's not all. The body is glued to the wall because of that black gooey stuff. And then the noises started all over again. Look, last time something remotely like this happened, things got out of control. I got this scar, half of my men got injured by a gang of cultists, and you ended up fighting that flying thing. That's why I called your dad, because I learned my lesson."

Alex looked like he was about to say something, but Sam placed her hand on his mouth.

"Thank you for your trust," Sam quickly replied. "We will look into it and will let you know what we find. C'mon, Alex."

Sam dragged Alex away from Culph and went toward Kasumi and Yokoyawa.

"Why did you shut me up?" Alex asked her.

"Because it was not the moment for one of your smartass comments," Sam replied. "You don't know dad's and Culph's history, but I do, so for him to be this agreeable with us, it required a lot from him."

"I wasn't going to make a joke, I have learned my lessons too," Alex replied. "I was just going to ask about those scorch marks on the walls. They don't look like anything I've seen before. Can I give you one piece of advice though?"

"What?"

"Relax. I'm not the enemy. I'm just here to help you. If you don't relax, you will miss things that you should be able to detect. And even then, we are here to watch your back."

Sam looked at Alex, who smiled the dumb smile she hated to love so much. She could feel the rush of blood creeping through her cheeks and ears. She was glad to have him at her side.

"Sorry, you are right. I've been taking it out on you because arguing used to be our dynamic. I guess I'm falling back on that because... I don't know."

"Because you don't want to disappoint your dad, I get it. As I said, relax. We are a team, we have your back, fearless leader."

"Therapy has really helped you to mature, you know?"

"That, and a brush with death."

"Very funny," Sam gave him a weak punch on the arm. Unlike the previous months, this time she could feel the muscle beneath the skin. He was recovering fine, at least the physical part. But if his Gift remained erratic, and with weakened capacity, he would be helpless against some of the beings they might face in the future. And unlike Kasumi, Alex had fewer years of training, which he'd compensated for with the Gift. Sam hated to admit it to herself, but she was worried about him and to some extent, Kasumi.

"So, are we ready to enter there?" Sam asked them. "Last time to back away."

Yokoyawa just chuckled, which in the case of a samoharo his size, sounded more like a bark. Alex and Kasumi exchanged glances and replied in unison.

"Nah!"

Heavens, I really love those two, Sam smiled.

††††

They walked along the path that separated the fence from the entrance. Sam noticed the scorch marks Alex had mentioned earlier. The grass was burnt as well as the stumps of trees that had been burned away. There was no rhyme nor reason to it. Whatever had caused them had been released at random, like when one of the younger Freefolk kids at Ravenstone lost control of their spell and sent energy beams all over the place. The teachers sometimes had to deflect those beams with shield spells to avoid someone getting injured.

"Those were deflections," she commented.

"That would explain the randomness," Alex replied. "I was wondering if they were caused by magick, but the marks... they are straight beams. Not sure how common those are from spells."

"They are not. Not with this level of narrowness. Maybe an energy weapon?"

"Nah, energy weapons create fire. Fire leaves electromagnetic traces on the ground, even for centuries. While I'm not one hundred percent back, I can still sense electromagnetic shifts. And I can tell you I sense none."

"How do you know that?" Kasumi asked, as she studied some poor unfortunate birds, which had been cut in half. A few of those birds were ravens.

"It's a somewhat recent archeology technique, like a decade old at most. Andrea explained it to me three years ago when we were working on her and Birm's thesis. I never expected to use it for forensic work, but hey, there is always a first time."

"Well, that would be consistent with the ground, and those birds," Yoko said as he picked up one. "This poor creature wasn't burned. It was disintegrated in half."

"Now, that's a worrisome thing to say," Sam replied, looking at the bird. What was left was a charred mess of mud and dust. "Because I can't recall a regular spell that can do that."

"I take it there are some special spells that can," Kasumi said. She opened the door by gently pushing it with the tip of Breaker, whose cold blade was glowing with a phantasmagoric white light. "Which kind?"

"The divine kind. The one you ask a god to use to smite someone," Sam said.

The door opened with a creak. At that moment the aurora borealis flickered with intensity. A sudden chill crept across Sam's arms. There was magick in the place, of that, she was sure. But while magick per se had no alignment, the one she could detect had a malevolent intent, and had been infecting the house.

"Aw, crap," Alex whispered. Sam had to agree with the feeling.

The four of them stood in what should have been the living room. The photo Culph had showed them didn't do justice to the scene. Amidst the old, rotting furniture a man was glued to the wall by crystalized black ichor. He sat with his legs spread open, his back resting against the wall, while his arms lay limply at his sides. What was disturbing, though, was the silly smile plastered on his face, which contrasted with the fact that everything above the eyebrows was missing. And where his brain should have been there was only black ichor.

"Assuming this guy died three days ago," Kasumi said as she knelt to examine the body. "It is odd that muscular stiffening hasn't set in."

"Lucasian time," Sam said. "Magick of certain kind tends to alter the passage of time. Like the gravity well of a star or..."

"Inside the Scar and Ravenhall," Alex added. "Hey, you

remembered what I told you."

"Contrary to what you think," Sam said with a smile at him, "I do pay attention to you."

"The ichor is not coming from the walls," Yokoyawa said as he examined the crystalized goo. "It seemed to flow from his head, which could explain how this guy got his head blown off. But I can't identify the smell."

"Murcana," Alex said.

"What's that?" Sam asked.

"It's a psychotropic drug, made from bone peyote. Aside from it being illegal, it is highly dangerous. When you consume it, you open your mind to other dimensions, like y'know, the Pits." Alex shrugged his shoulders and twisted his lips into a scowl.

"How do you know all that?" Sam asked, looking at him. She hoped he knew that for some other reason than from using it.

"Because sadly the only place where you could find bone peyote is north of the Straits. And Ywain and my great-grandma Zyanya met when they faced a shaman that used this stuff. They destroyed all the known bone peyote."

Alex's reply calmed Sam's quick-beating heart.

"I have heard of that," Yokoyawa said. "Which would explain why it smelled familiar, yet novel. It's similar to some traditional medicine made from a more common and less dangerous peyote species, used for treating neurobiological ailments."

"Like memory loss and cognitive degeneration. I think Ywain suffered from that after his fight with Byron," Alex explained.

"The thing is," Kasumi interrupted. "How did a lost drug from the other side of the ocean, end up in the hands of a junkie that got his head blown off?"

"Good question," Sam said. "There is something off

here. I mean, aside the bone peyote thing. This place is hiding something."

"Like a mirage?" Yoko asked.

"Fionn mentioned that something similar happened when Professor Hunt disappeared," Alex said. "That his house was under some sort of curse."

"I guess I better use the same trick as Dad did back then," Sam replied, grinning. She rubbed her hands together. The friction caused tiny specks of light to float from her fingertips.

"Let there be light." She pushed her hands outwards and countless light specks floated away. The house creaked as the door swung wildly, there was a faint rumble under their feet and... everything remained the same after a few seconds.

"Nothing happened," Kasumi said. "Maybe Fionn used some aid. He is not a spell caster right? Some demonhunters use blessed ofudas to dispel magick."

"My dad used a lamp for that," Sam replied. She took out her silver pendant from under her shirt. The pendant itself curved like a dragon claw, expert craftsmanship allowing it to hold a lilac quartz-like crystal. It dangled from a finely threaded silver-orichalcum chain. Sam raised it to her eye and looked around. The faint light that entered through the windows refracted in odd ways within the crystal. "Something is off. The magick energy in this place is off its axis by several degrees. Dad's lamp wouldn't have worked here either. I guess it's time for plan B."

"Are you sure?" Kasumi asked. "We know how much you don't like plan B."

"What's the point of having the Gift if I can't use it as my own source of magick?"

Sam closed her eyes. Alex and Kasumi had helped her to train her Gift to use it as her own independent magick battery instead of drawing the energy from the local energy fields. Gaby had taught Sam how to summon the Gift at her command. But it still made Sam feel uneasy. Nausea grew as she focused on the energy core at the center of her soul, of her very own existence. She could feel a ball of energy begin to pulse inside her, then it exploded through her body with the intensity of a thousand stars. As she opened her eyes, her irises turned from her usual green into lilac, the same color as her hair. As she generated her own version of the radiation expelled by the thaums that composed the magick field that surrounded the planet and was constantly generated by the sun's astral form— her 'allergy' to magick showed, a side effect relatively common in freefolk spellcasters—a silver fox tail grew from her tailbone, through a well-hidden hole in her jeans. The transformation wasn't painless, but Sam had learned to tolerate it. Before the Gift, her allergy only manifested as purple hair. But since she got the Gift, it manifested this way. Some of the freefolk elders said she'd been 'touched by Asherah,' the legendary freefolk matriarch and hero who was the first to use magick. She had undergone extreme changes that had left her looking like a human girl and no longer able to shapeshift.

Sam was, in a word, insecure about the transformation. It was difficult not to feel like some object of ridicule. Sam felt her cheeks redden in embarrassment.

"I think the tail suits you," Kasumi said, smiling, trying to assuage her insecurities.

"For what's worth," Alex added, "I totally agree."

Sam smiled and rubbed her hands together. This time it wasn't just specks of light floating away. Her hands were glowing. Sam pushed them outwards once more. "Let there be light!"

The house creaked and shook once more, but this time did so with such force that Alex and Kasumi lurched and lost their balance. Yokoyawa shifted behind Sam to help her maintain her footing while the spell destroyed the mirage around the place. As the illusion collapsed, it revealed the actual form of the walls, with scorch marks and three humanoid bodies nailed to the walls by their hands and feet. The bodies looked human, but were mostly featureless, without hair of any kind, but covered with deep gashes and scars. They were sexless. And their eyes were missing.

"Geez, gross," Alex said. "What the hell happened here?"

"A summoning ritual gone wrong?" Kasumi asked.

"It went well, actually. Look." Sam pointed at the three humanoids.

"What the Pits are those things?" Yokoyawa asked. "Were they human?"

"Wait, let me check," Kasumi said. "I never expected to use my biosciences degree this way. But it helps for forensics."

Kasumi approached one of the bodies and looked around. Whether she was disgusted or scared, it was hard for Sam to tell.

Which I guess is the purpose of the mask, not good for the civilians to see a demonhunter scared, she thought.

"This is odd," Kasumi said. She knelt to pick up a pencil from the ground and used it to open the corpse's eyelids. "They didn't lose their eyes. They never had them in first place."

"What do you mean?" Sam asked. She moved closer to Kasumi. Her tail swayed from side to side, hitting Kasumi in the leg. "Sorry, still getting used to this one."

"The orbits are closed, no remains of an ocular globe. Even if it was boiled away, it should have left remains of the optic nerve. But aside from these scorch marks on the edge of the lids, there is no sign they ever had them. Which makes me wonder what else they are missing."

"Are you planning to cut them open here?" Alex asked.

"Just one," Kasumi replied. "Give me some space please."

Sam stepped back, with Alex and Yoko behind her, as Kasumi spun Breaker in her hand. With a quick slash, she made a perfect horizontal cut on the belly of the corpse and another vertical, from where the bellybutton should have been to collarbone.

"I'm still amazed at the precision of the cut with such a large blade," Alex said.

"Practice." Kasumi replied. "Yoko-san, could you help me crack open the ribcage?"

Yokoyawa walked back to the body and cracked open the ribcage with such ease that he could have been opening oyster and not a humanoid body. The organs spilled onto the floor. Except for a white mucus covering them, there was no blood or any other fluid.

I guess I know where the old adage, 'Let the samoharo win' comes from now, Sam thought.

"Interesting," Kasumi said. She was examining the organs. "Their lungs are bright pink and not inflated. There are no liquids in the other organs. It is if as they were never used. These bodies weren't born. They were created somehow."

"Aw, crap," Alex said. "That can only mean one thing,"

"Like they are avatars for some spirit?" Sam mused.

"Hence the 'aw, crap'" Alex replied.

† † †

Yokoyawa's nostrils flared once more. This time the smell was different. Underneath the whiffs of bone peyote and rotten corpses, there was a familiar smell. He had smelled it once before, when Mekiri had made her appearance at the elders gathering after the Chivalry Games and the return of the Titans. It smelled of petrichor mixed with hildebrandtias and copal. It was a unique smell, and while faint, it was noticeable enough to him. The skills he had honed as a tracker had more than one application. While the others examined the bodies, he wandered toward the back of the room, looking around. The whole place was covered in dust and cobwebs; all except one spot: a line on the ground of no more than forty centimeters. While Sid was the one that had consumed more human media, Yoko had been catching up while performing Alex's therapy. He remembered one movie about a treasure hunter finding a secret passage to a temple, beneath one of the walls of his room in an old castle. Yoko tapped the wall above the floor, and he heard a hollow echo behind it.

"Secret door," he muttered. He looked for the edges of the door and once he detected them, used his claws to grab them and rip the door open. Yoko expected to find a cultist or a cowering wizard. Instead, he found a young woman lying on the floor of the cubbyhole. She had long, fiery red hair with jet-black strands that framed a face with olive skin and a smattering of freckles. Yoko couldn't help but to be reminded of Sam. But the woman was also very awake, and sported a friendly smile alongside with big turquoise eyes of such a deep color that it pulled one in. She was also naked, and exuded a scent that Yoko associated with Mekiri.

"You look familiar," she said. Her voice seemed older than time itself.

"Hey!" Yoko called the others. "I think you should come and see this."

The others approached Yoko and the woman, and proceeded to stare at her in silent befuddlement.

It was nearly a full minute before Alex broke the quiet that had settled over them. "Doesn't she look like...?"

"Mekiri. But in her true form," Sam replied, somber. By now they were familiar enough with Mekiri to recognize her features regardless of her shape.

"You all look familiar," the woman said. "Do I know you? Because I feel like I do. I have memories coming back but they are fuzzy."

"If she is here, in this state..." Alex continued.

"I better get some spare clothes from the truck," Kasumi said as she hurried out of the house. Sam took off her jacket and covered Mekiri with it.

"*Mierda*," Alex said. "I better get Culph to evacuate the place. This might get worse than the Battle of Saint Lucy."

† † †

Kasumi and Alex returned with the spare clothes.

"I mostly brought your clothes, Sam," Kasumi said. "She is taller than me so I doubt mine will fit."

"It's okay," Sam said as she helped the woman to stand.

Yokoyawa was seated in front of them, his back toward them to offer some cover and a semblance of privacy with his width. Alex was examining the scorching marks once more.

"What about Culph?" Sam asked.

"He looked at me weirdly for a second, then ordered his men to start evacuating the place. I'm surprised how well he took the suggestion."

"He is not dumb. I hope you didn't tell him that we have the human avatar of the Trickster Goddess here, with amnesia," Sam said.

"Heavens no," Alex replied as he continued examining the room. He avoided the bodies. They didn't look like any kind of incursion he had seen before, and he had seen his share. Usually, incursions were marked by terrible creatures from the Pits that looked nothing like any native species on Theia. Only godly avatars like the Creeping Chaos and what Fionn suspected was this self-proclaimed Golden King currently causing strife down south, resembled a human or a Freefolk. But these things... they looked too human, almost perfect aside the eye thing. His mind wandered to the worrisome implication of incursions coming from Last Heaven, the supposed realm of the gods. If that was the case, how had it come to be? And what happened to Mekiri—if that was her real name, the humanoid avatar of the Trickster Goddess of the Freefolk—to end up in a place like this, naked and amnesiac?

While Alex tried to be less negative after undergoing therapy and working on his depression, he couldn't avoid thinking about the possible answers to those questions. None of them were good. If murcana was involved, it meant that somehow it had been used to open a gate to the other side and trap Mekiri here. But why? And by whom? It couldn't have been the Golden King. So far, he had avoided direct confrontation. And Alex was sure that he and Sam had destroyed the avatar of the Creeping Chaos, at great cost to himself and half of the city of Kyôkatô. The options that remained were few and even those, as Fionn had once told him, had to answer the question of: who benefits?

Alex reached a side room. He could still see the others helping Mekiri get dressed in Sam's clothes, as the room he had reached was missing half a wall. He pushed the switch and the sole light in the ceiling turned on. It barely lit the room, generating shadows that increased the creepiness factor by tenfold.

Sometimes a shallow light is more dangerous than total dark, Alex thought, remembering a saying that his great grandma Zyanya used to say. *At least there is still power in this room.*

Next to the damaged wall sat an old TV. It seemed to be intact, although covered with dust.

At least is not covered in ichor, I wonder if it will work?

Alex turned on the TV. The sound was off and the image unclear, so he worked the knobs to adjust the settings. Most channels were empty static, until he clicked on Channel Eleven, which was used for news and emergency broadcasts, so it was transmitted using more powerful emitter towers.

"...in another news, telecommunications are experiencing massive outages," the news anchor was saying.

"Well, that explains the static," Alex muttered to himself.

"The wrap train services have been suspended until further notice..." the news anchor received a sheet of paper from an aid. "And this is just in, some Freefolk magi have been reported having troubles with their spells..."

"Sam, you need to watch this," Alex crouched to keep working on the screen.

"Wait," Sam said from the other room. "I'm helping her get dressed. And my phone is blowing up with messages."

"You better check those messages now," Alex told her, raising his voice.

He tried other channels, and as the news anchor said, they were down. Static wouldn't have normally caught his attention, but he noticed a strange repeating pattern every time a line of dead signals scrolled up the screen. The pattern had regular intervals of different lengths, like those old telegram messages.

I should have paid more attention to learn the code, he thought, as he tried to decipher what it was saying.

"It... it can't be!" Sam yelled from the other room.

Alex started to get an idea of the message. It was a warning, telling him to escape. He drew Yaha by instinct. Without his ability to use his electric bow, Yaha had become his main weapon and thanks to Fionn and Yoko's teachings, he had gotten pretty good at swordplay.

A new smell invaded the room. Alex stood up and looked around. The wall behind him was glowing with a strange, pure white light, and it was actively eroding, bit by bit. The buzzing in his ears became unbearable. He darted toward the other room, where only Sam and Mekiri waited.

"Where are Yoko and Kasumi?" Alex asked.

"They went back to the truck," Sam replied, not looking at him. He guessed it was logical, after all, if the woman really was Mekiri in her true avatar form. It meant that Sam was in front of one of, if not the main deity, of her species' pantheon. And no matter how many times you have crossed paths with said deity, the realization that something or someone had left Her in such a state must have been frightening. Alex looked back once more. The glow was increasing as well as the feeling of danger.

"Sam," Alex repeated, more urgently. But she was still scrolling through her texts, concern visibly mounting with each new message. "Sam!"

She looked up from her phone. "What?"

"Get down!" Alex shouted as he tackled Sam and Mekiri to the ground, shielding them with his body. Two solid light beams vivisected the room. Narrow, focused—and above all—perfectly visible despite the lack of a medium to see them with the naked eye.

"How is *that* possible? Solid light beams?" Alex mused. Still using his body as a shield, Alex rolled over as he positioned Yaha in front of himself and the two women. He hoped that Yaha would be able to withstand the disintegrating beams that were getting dangerously close to his face.

The beams bounced off a shimmering energy shield that looked like a honeycomb: Sam's True Spell, the most powerful protection bubble ever known to mortal kind. Against an unmovable force, the beams soon dissipated.

"Someone or something is messing up the laws of magick," Sam said, breathing heavily. Her True Spell, especially when drawing from her Gift left her exhausted from altering her heartbeat.

"We better get away from here, now!" Alex said as he lifted Sam. "Follow us, Mekiri!"

Alex carried Sam, Mekiri in his wake; the avatar with a bouncing skip in her walk and thousand-watt smile, as if she was having a grand adventure. Alex walked past Yoko and Kasumi and placed Sam in the back seat, then pushed Mekiri inside the front of the truck.

"What happened?" Kasumi asked. Two more beams cut through what was left of the house as a pair of the humanoids, similar to the ones that were still nailed to the walls, stalked towards them. Those beams came straight from where their eyes should have been. It was painful to look at, and would have been worse if Alex hadn't called up what was left of his Gift to increase his speed and reaction times.

"That!" Alex pointed at the creatures while he got into the truck. Yoko jumped into the bed and Kasumi scrambled into the front passenger seat. Without missing a beat, Alex started the engine and pushed the accelerator to the floor. The wheels squealed for a few seconds until they got enough grip to launch the truck into the road at full speed. Alex's irises were glowing with a subdued golden hue.

"You shouldn't be using your Gift," Kasumi said. "You will get tired soon."

"I'm just using enough to help my reflexes as we escape from these things!"

"What are they?"

"I guess family of the guy you opened up."

"I didn't hear you complaining."

Alex took the truck off road, expertly weaving between the trees as they crossed the forest around the town. His reaction times and reflexes synchronized well with the gear changes and the brake, allowing him to lead the truck through very narrow spaces, as the humanoids moved at a fast pace behind them, their beams slicing through entire trees willy-nilly.

"They are gaining on us," Yoko said from the rear seat.

"I know!" Alex replied.

The radio on the truck exploded with static noise. Alex could hear the same pattern he'd noticed on the TV. He looked at the rearview mirror. The only thing breaking the pitch darkness from the forest were the humanoids he had nicknamed 'Headlights,' for they reminded him of the trucks and cars at night. The aurora borealis were flickering with increased intensity.

"It's Tapping Code. It says, 'river jump'", Yoko said from the back. A beam passed very close to his head. Too close.

"Well," Alex said. "There's a river in front of us. And I don't think we can fight those things right now so..."

"You are not thinking what I think you are thinking," Kasumi said.

"Oh yes, get ready to get Mekiri out of here. Yoko, grab our bags! We are going for a swim!"

"I thought you weren't suicidal anymore!" Kasumi yelled as she kicked open the passenger door and grabbed Mekiri.

"I'm not!" Alex said as he pushed the accelerator and sharply turned the truck toward the river. The river had dug a deep channel into the rock, so the bank was a steep cliff. Alex steered the truck to a small mound of dirt from which it jumped just as two beams hit the tires. They exploded with a bang. Time slowed for him as he used all his remaining Gift to increase his speed. He ripped open the door and pulled Sam toward him.

He, Sam, Kasumi, Mekiri, and Yoko fell into the icy water of the river as several beams hit the truck and it exploded into a fireball.

† † †

"*That* was your plan?" Sam sputtered at Alex. They exited the river, clambering onto a sandbar. "You are lucky I woke in time to cast the bubble spell, you moron!"

"You can yell at me later. We need to keep moving."

"I have never seen you so scared before, Alex," Kasumi said as she helped Mekiri to get up. Yoko walked out of the river with all their bags and without a hitch. He was a tank.

"I was scared because those are not normal incursions. I don't have enough power to fight them, Sam is having problems with magick."

"And Yoko and I are regular mortals compared to you, that's it?" Kasumi said, a hint of anger in her voice.

"You three should breathe and clear your heads," Yoko said in his soothing therapist voice.

"No," Alex replied to Kasumi. "You two can fight titans. I would never doubt your abilities. But all of us right now are out of our depth against the Headlights guys..."

"Headlights guys?" Sam raised an eyebrow.

"That's the name I gave them, anyway," Alex explained. "We don't know what they are or how to fight them. We can't get close to them because of those beams that don't follow the laws of physics. *And* we have the freaking Trickster Goddess trapped in her amnesiac avatar self. We need to regroup."

"When you put it that way," Yoko replied. "You are right. Let's take cover in that old metal shed and think about our next step."

"Thank you!" Alex said. "How are you holding up Sam? How are your aids, Kasumi?"

"My aids are fine," Kasumi replied, still hot under the collar.

"I'm cold, I'm tired, and I can't get dry because of this stupid tail!" Sam replied.

"But at least you got us out of there alive," Mekiri

pointed out with a smile. She moved towards Alex and boped him on the nose. "I think I told you once that you can't live this way all the time, silly bunny in a river boat."

"Great. *That,* she remembers," Alex said, ruefully.

"What *is* she talking about?" Sam asked.

"A dream I had before the wyvern attack. Which makes me sure that she is indeed Mekiri."

The five of them entered the shed. Yoko and Alex barricaded the door, although Alex knew it wouldn't help much if those things found them. But the metal walls of the shed were thick enough to buy them some time. The truck had exploded because the beams must have hit the power batteries, but the beams didn't disintegrate it right away, unlike organic tissue or materials derived from a living being, like wood.

"What now?" Sam asked as she and Kasumi wrung her tail to dry it. "I'm not using magick or the Gift, why doesn't this damn thing disappear!?"

"I can teach you how to move with a tail," Yoko offered.

Alex was sure that was not the answer Sam wanted to hear. "We have to get away from here without leaving a trace that allows them to track us."

"And how do we do that?" Kasumi asked, somewhat less angry now.

"I have a very stupid idea that you are not going to like," Alex replied, staring at Sam. Her eyes opened wide as she realized what he was planning.

"Oh no, no, no, no. You know that spell is super-dangerous," Sam replied, waving her hands in front of her to push Alex away.

"What spell?" Yoko asked.

"A teleportation spell," Sam replied. "But he knows, since the day we met, that the spell is highly dangerous, complicated, and the number two cause of death for many practitioners of magick."

"May I ask why?" Kasumi asked. "I have seen you cast some pretty hard spells, aside the healing ones. What makes this one difficult?"

"One: you need to know where to go and have a clear picture of your destination in your mind. Two: you need to be able to make the calculations in your head to compensate for stellar drift and all your components, or you end up floating in space or inside a rock when the planet moved. Or with your body split into tiny pieces all over the continent. Now try to do that with five people, with the magick field not working properly. And I'm not familiar with samoharo biology beyond my high school biology class," Sam explained.

"How do other magi do it?" Yoko asked. "How can we help?"

"They do it by using already known equations engraved into special crystals that activate when they cast the spell. Others just let their instincts do the math. But while I'm good at math, it will take me time and my pendant doesn't have the equation nor the spell."

"But you can do it if we have time," Yoko pushed. "Maybe the Gift can help you solve the equations."

"I don't want to end up all over Ionis," Kasumi quipped. "I have tickets for that illusion show."

"I could, but..."

"But you better hurry," Alex said. He pointed to two tiny white dots on the wall of the shed. "Because they're here."

"Oh shit!" Sam exclaimed. "Okay, okay, you can do this Sam."

Her irises glowed lilac as she whispered the spell. Alex, Kasumi and Yoko had their weapons ready, although Alex wasn't sure how effective they'd be. They stood protectively around Sam and Mekiri. If at least Sam and Mekiri could escape, it would be worth it.

"Good news: The beams are not piercing the metal, "Alex said. "Bad news, they are melting it."

"Sam, I don't think this shed will hold for long," Kasumi added.

"I'm working on it," Sam replied, with her eyes closed. She was making a real effort now. Three circles of white light grew from her hands to encase them. Each circle was actually two with runes arranged in a mathematical equation between them. One circle rotated horizontally at ground level. A second one rotated vertically from the ground to above Yoko's head. The third one moved freely around an imaginary globe that surrounded them.

"I don't want to annoy you, but you need to hurry," Alex pressed. The beams were almost through the metal walls of the shed.

"You know Sam doesn't like backseat spellcasting Alex," Kasumi said.

"Let me help," Mekiri said as she hugged Sam at the same time the shed exploded.

Time slowed to a standstill. Alex saw pieces of the shed being blown away and stopping midair. The Headlights were not moving. Their beams stopped mere centimeters from his face. The energy circles around the group moved at such speed that it looked like they were being engulfed in a ball of light. Alex saw from the corner of his eyes how the bodies of his friends started to turn into particles. He looked at his own hand and it dissolved slowly. It wasn't painful as he had expected.

Then both Sam and Mekiri opened their eyes, and everything exploded around them, leaving only scorched marks on the ground.

Chapter 5
If Only We Could Run

*"**Why is the Figaro's movie** database full of Luna Revaria movies?"* Fionn complained as he scrolled down the list of entertainment stored in the Figaro's memory banks. To say that Fionn hated to fly was an understatement. He didn't suffer from vertigo, but the way Sid flew always made his stomach twist. Sometimes Sid forgot that not everyone was a samoharo, and thus their bodies hadn't evolved to handle the extra Gs. For that reason, Fionn wondered if commercial flight would ever be available. He also wondered why the memory banks where Sid stored his 'in-flight entertainment' were full of old mystery movies.

"Because the Figaro's A.I. loves them after Gaby, Sam, and Kasumi had a girl's movie night at the hangar and used the projection system of the ship to see the movies," Sid explained from the pilot's seat. "The A.I. blocked my rights to delete them, so I might just add more memory banks later."

"Those are expensive," Harland mumbled from the copilot's chair.

"It's not my fault that my flat was without power that night," Gaby replied from her seat next to Fionn. "Besides, those movies are good."

"In any case," Sid said, "we are almost there, so please

put your trays in place, fasten your seatbelts and get ready for the bumpy ride."

Fionn felt the ship descending into the World's Scar, a landmark of a canyon that crossed more than half of the planet's surface. It owed its creation to the time when the Trickster Goddess decided that it would be nice to experience the mortal realm but forgot that her divine form was too powerful for the planet. Due to the amount of magick energies inside it the descent was bumpy, as the Scar was full of gravitational waves that in turn created a gravity well that effectively altered reality. They were lucky that Sid had become an expert on navigating the Scar by now.

"You really have improved," Fionn acknowledged. "I didn't feel a bump."

"He better be," Gaby replied, trying to stifle a laugh. "He has been traveling here *a lot* to visit his girlfriend."

"Are you telling me that he is dating Vivienne?" Fionn asked. "How does that work? I get human-freefolk, but samoharo-freefolk?"

"It works perfectly, and we have been talking about settling down, thank you very much. As much as I don't appreciate you using my personal life as an explanation for why the flight is so smooth, this is not my doing."

Sid gave a worried look to Harland, who was busy checking the sensors. "The gravity well is no more..."

†††

It was midafternoon when the Figaro touched down. Fionn was worried about Sam and her team. The case seemed relatively simple for her skill level. Yet Fionn couldn't shake off the sensation of dread permeating his bones, the knot in his stomach. It was as if something had disappeared from his very being, but he couldn't pinpoint what, for everything was the same.

The Figaro rested on a clear spot at the bottom of the

World's Scar, not far from Ravenstone, the academy where the Freefolk learned to practice magick in a safe... safe-ish way. It was the probably the only place where blowing up stuff wouldn't be considered an act of war, and therefore the best. And while the bottom of the canyon that crossed half of the planet could be a dangerous place due to the Lurkers—critters that feed on the natural magick of the place and preyed on the Freefolk pilgrims traversing the Scar—the place was oddly quiet. It seemed to be bereft of any activity beyond the lizards scurrying along the canyon's limestone walls.

"This place is giving me the creepies," Sid muttered as the group stood in front of a wall, staring at it. "A different kind of creepies this time. Like whatever inhabited this place is gone."

"And it gives you an existential dread about the nothingness?" Gaby asked.

"Pretty much," Sid replied. "You know that sensation that Alex described after therapy, about walking on a tightrope over a dark chasm, without safety net? Like that."

"I recall that," Harland added, clutching tight at his arms. "It makes you feel that your heart has been hollowed out. Except that instead of coming from the inside, the feeling comes from all around us. An uncaring cosmos."

"Are you sure this is the correct place?" Fionn asked. He was well acquainted with the sensation they were describing. It was the same he'd felt over a century ago; the first time he'd faced Byron at Lemast. This was wrong.

"Dude, please," Sid replied, somewhat offended. "Who are you talking to? Of course, it is the place. I make it a point that the Figaro's AI records every stop in the log, in order to calculate more efficient routes. And while visiting Vivienne I brought Sam to The Door once last year. Of course, it is the same spot."

"The Door should be here," Gaby added. "But it is not."

"Maybe we are not doing what we should be doing?" Harland said. "Last time we were here the Scar felt... alive? Even if it was dangerous."

"Whatever is going on, it would explain the readings I got as we descended," Sid said. "Or better said, the lack of them."

"What do you mean? Why didn't you say anything?" Fionn asked.

"Me muttering that something is off wasn't enough to catch your attention?" Sid asked. "You should have paid more attention to that instead of asking questions about my love life."

"To be fair, you complain all the time. It is hard to know when you are being serious," Fionn said, smirking at Sid.

"Good point. Anyway, when we were descending, I didn't notice any of the feedback I got last time I flew here. Nor did the AI detect any gravitational wave. It was as if whatever mystical presence was here altering the reality of the place was just gone."

"What do you mean by gone?" Gaby asked this time. "That doesn't sound good."

"It is not," a voice echoed through the canyon, startling them. From the shelter and shadows of a recess within the unforgiving rock, a man emerged. Broad, stocky. His dark brown hair nearly blended with the canyon wall until the light hit it. Beneath his clothes, several markings and tattoos in black and blue ink could be seen. They indicated his rank as an elder of the oldest tribe, that of Fire, also known as the Children of the Fireflies, Asherah's original tribe.

Alongside him there was a tall freefolk lady, mid-thirties to early forties, lean and fit. She wore a statement piece in knee-high heeled green boots, black leather trousers, a white blouse, thin frame glasses, and a green magi robe with golden embroidery. The hefty backpack that she carried promised an interest in more than just fashion, weighed down by odds and ends that one could only come across in a profession like hers. But her more remarkable features were her green hair styled in a wild pompadour and pixie ears that contrasted nicely with her fair skin and the freckles that peppered her face.

"Stealth!" Fionn exclaimed, and he went to embrace the man. "I'm so glad to see you."

"Ah, my favorite Freefolk engineer," Sid added, offering his hand to Stealth. Then he ran toward the freefolk lady, took her hand and kissed it. "M'lady Vivienne"

"M'lord," Vivienne replied with a courtesy, kissing Sid on the cheek. She gently wiped the samoharo slime from her green lips and took Sid's hand.

"What are you doing here?" Sid asked. "Not that I'm not delighted to see you."

"Now I'm the Freefolk Master Librarian," Stealth explained.

"And as much as I would love to say that I wanted to see you Sid, I'm here by orders of the Elders on official business," Vivienne added matter-of-factly.

"Elders' orders?" Fionn looked at her quizzically. "What's going on, Vivi?"

Vivienne exhaled. "Since you pulled your trick of becoming an elder and reforming your clan, they decided that you needed closer supervision from someone that you—but more importantly, they—trusted. Given who the other options were and that Ravenstone is still a year into being repaired, I offered. Trust me, better me than Twig Golring; you know, the guy that almost expelled Sam from school three times. He really doesn't like your family."

"Those old folk, they still think they can manipulate us as their predecessors did with Asherah," Fionn replied, rueful.

"That means that you're coming with us?" Gaby asked. "Yes," Vivi replied and looked at Sid, who was staring at her with clear concern in his face. "Don't look at me that way, Siddhartha. I can take care of myself, even if magick is not working anymore."

"What do you mean by not working anymore?" Fionn asked sharply, tension visibly tightening the muscles of his neck with the rising pitch of his voice. Without access to magick, the freefolk were in a precarious situation. Especially with the Golden King amassing an army and annexing territories to his cause.

"As of this morning, the magick field collapsed into itself. We can't cast magick," Stealth replied. "The Aurora Borealis have been visible all day over our lands and there are sights of the Wyld Hunt. Which I believe you and your dad Fraog were well acquainted with."

"Fu....," Fionn was about to say, when Gaby put her fingers on his lips.

"Okay, hon, I know what you are thinking," Gaby said. "But let's focus on one crisis at a time. If we find the Crown first, then we can stall the Golden King till this situation fixes itself or we find out what's going out."

"Besides," Harland put in. "It's not the first time the magick field went out of service. It's happened before and regenerated itself. Probably a solar flare overcharged it."

Gaby glanced at Stealth and Vivi, who traded worried looks.

"We thought you were coming here to find out what happened," Stealth said.

"No," Gaby replied. "We are on a mission to find the Crown of the Dead. The Golden King is looking for it and someone tried to steal Queen Sophia's soul before she passed away."

"She passed away?" Vivi asked, then she turned to Fionn. "I'm so sorry, I know you were close. We didn't know. With the magick field gone, communications are failing as well."

"Warp trains are next," Sid said matter-of-factly, crossing his arms. "Too much of a coincidence."

"As I said, one crisis at a time," Gaby replied. "We wanted to access Ravenhall, but..."

"But without magick, we can't," Fionn observed. "Where is the Tricks... Mekiri?"

"She went into the Mistlands on a meditation journey, I haven't been able to contact her," Stealth replied. His body language suggested that he was lying, and that he was concerned, for his shoulders slouched and his lower lip trembled. But Gaby didn't want to push it. Fionn was already enough on edge. "But I can tell you, you are not the first to come looking for undisclosed information about that Crown."

"You mean *aside* the usual folklore tales mentioned on those crappy TV shows about lost relics on a channel that is not about history anymore?" Harland asked.

"She came a couple of weeks ago. But the library of the academy is still being sorted. You know how tricky it is to keep regular books with magickally infused tomes that have their own personalities and space requirements and can transform you into a rabbit without any warning. That's what I've been helping with, to design a safer storage."

"And this person, what did she find?" Harland asked. "Do you think it was Doncelles hired expert?"

"She said she had come with the province of the Emerald Island government. And aside from a location, no, she didn't find anything else, because I wasn't comfortable with a Sister of Mercy looking around our records. No offense, Gaby."

"None taken. Sister of Mercy? Do you recall her name?"

"Olivia... Livia... Lixia? Tall, curly hair in a ponytail."

"I know her," Gaby smiled. "She is a good person, a bit stiff when it comes to historical preservation. Did she introduce herself as a Sister of Mercy? Because last thing I knew, she left the order a few years ago."

"No, but she moved the same way you do, speaks several languages, and lifted a heavy tome with ease. It's not my first time dealing with the Sisters," Stealth explained. "And there was something... odd in her demeanor. So, I went with my gut and kept her from accessing some of the most obscure tomes. But she wasn't concerned. It was not as if she was looking for some info, but more like trying to confirm something she already knew."

"What?" Harland asked.

"The last known location of the Crown, as per those shows, is a red herring. There is an actual last known location," Stealth replied.

"Do you know it?" Sid asked.

Stealth pointed to his head.

"I memorized the info before disappearing the book. It's in the Tower of Salt."

"That's down south of Orca Bay, far from the disputed lands, closer to the Seven Watersnakes Delta, the territory of the old Montsegur kingdom," Gaby replied. "With the Figaro at full speed we should be there before sunset, correct?"

"Should be doable," Sid said, sulking next to Vivi, who grabbed his arm.

"Okay, less chat, more flying," Vivi said. It was both funny and endearing how Vivi, who was at least one meter seventy-six, almost as tall as Sam, quite close to Fionn in height, towered over the one meter fifty samoharo. It was more noticeable with the high heeled boots.

"But Vivi!" Sid complained as she dragged him toward the Figaro.

They actually make a cute couple, Gaby thought as her

crooked smile appeared. She was happy for her friend for having finally found someone to share his already long life. Both samoharo and freefolk could have long lives, under the right circumstances, so it was good they could share the time together.

"Vivi nothing, I'm not asking you. I have my job, you have yours, and for now they intersect, so come on. Besides, I'm wearing the boots you gave me for my birthday, so you better appreciate that."

"Who would have suspected that Sid would be henpecked," Harland whispered to Gaby.

"Alex won't believe me when I tell him." She then turned to Fionn. "Are you coming or not? You are the leader of this mission."

"Yes," Fionn replied, then he whispered something to Stealth.

He reached Gaby and Harland, and the three of them entered the Figaro. The engines roared as the cargo bay hatch closed.

"Remember," Gaby said to Fionn. "One crisis at a time. We will get through this together."

Fionn offered a weak smile as a reply. This day was proving to be a long one... and it was only noon.

† † †

"We are arriving at the Tower of Salt. I will circle around to find a spot to land," Sid said. "I will wait outside of town, because that Tower doesn't seem sturdy enough to hold the weight of the Figaro and I don't think the good folk of Riverol will appreciate the Figaro blowing dirt into their houses by landing there."

"We won't take long," Fionn replied through the comms, as he, Gaby, and Harland, wearing their gear, were already in the cargo bay. "The place seems empty, so it should be easy."

"Famous last words," Sid whispered as he pushed the switch to open the cargo bay. The Figaro touched down and the engines went from their full throttle roar to a murmur. Once Sid saw them leaving the Figaro, he closed the hatch.

"Are you not planning to go with them?" Vivi asked, making herself at home in the copilot's seat.

"Why? I'm more comfortable here," Sid replied, covering the console with a plastic shell and placing his feet on top of it. He grabbed a magazine from below his seat.

"What about your sense of adventure?" She was still trying to figure him out. "Don't you want to participate?"

"Knowing them," Sid replied, thumbing through the magazine, "the adventure will follow them and reach me here, whether I want it or not. Odds are they will need a quick pick up, hence why the Figaro is in suspension mode, not turned off. So, I will read this magazine while I wait for them to screw the pooch and I will have to save them. Again."

"You make it sound like this happens frequently."

"Remember the day we met, when your workplace got blown up by Byron and his dreadnought?"

"Hard to forget."

"Wello that was just the first of many, including Sam skydiving without a parachute, Alex blowing up a demonically possessed energy core. I had to fly out of a sentient hurricane to save those two from themselves. And that's just a sample. Trust me, it will happen again. So, relax. Candy?" Sid offered some fruit-flavored sweets. He never shared the candy with anyone but her. Vivi rolled her eyes, but she smiled and took one from the bag.

"Fine. Do you have another magazine to read?"

† † †

Gaby, Fionn, and Harland walked through the main

street—actually, the only street—of the small town of Riverol. The small houses, derelict and old, hinted that the place was close to being a ghost town. Perhaps sooner than even the remaining few inhabitants realized. Those residents that peeked through their windows and out of doorways remained silent as the trio walked by, mere glimpses of gaunt faces betraying their unspoken belligerence. Their group soon reached the bridge that would take them to the Tower's entrance.

"Seems that the secession hit the economy of this town bad," Harland said. "A lot of trade must have collapsed. And was just me, or did the locals seem hostile?"

"It not just you," a voice said from behind the bushes that covered the cliff's edge. It was a steep fall into the sea from here. "They don't like outsiders, especially when they are armed and decked out in what I assume is some kind of prototype armor and heading toward the Tower. The only reason they didn't stop you is because they know who you are and what you are capable of. Like half the planet."

A young woman came out from the bushes. She was in her late twenties, dressed in beige pants and a brown leather jacket with a sheathed sword tied to her belt. Her black hair was pulled into a tight ponytail. She smiled as she walked toward Gaby, opening her arms.

"Gabs!" the woman called.

"Livia?" Gaby smiled and ran toward the woman, hugging her. "I'm so happy to see you! So much time has passed."

"Look at you," Livia broke the hug and looked up and down at Gaby, beaming with pride. "A bona fide hero."

"You're exaggerating," Gaby blushed.

"I knew you would do great things when I heard you had escaped. You inspired several of us to do the same and forge a life away from the Sisters. And you are here with the legendary Greywolf and the leader of the Foundation, such distinguished company." Livia offered a curtsy. "I'm Livia Junipero."

"She was my best friend and roommate many years ago at Manticore Island," Gaby added.

"Nice to meet you," Harland replied, offering his hand. "Seems that you were expecting us."

"My current employer called me before communications went down, telling me that I should be here to help with the search of the Crown."

"Why am I not surprised?" Fionn muttered.

"Shall we go in?" Livia pointed toward the Tower.

† † †

The four of them, led by Livia, headed up the stairs of the tower. Fragments of light shone through the cracks in the walls and what few windows there were, keeping their ascent from taking place in total darkness. Cobwebs and lichens blanketed most of the walls and steps. The place smelled of a combination of salt water, a vague fungal odor thanks to the lichens, and the weight of accumulated centuries. On their way up, the stairs stopped at times on large platforms that were the entrance of empty, darkened rooms. And yet, Gaby couldn't shake the feeling that they were being observed, followed even. In one of those rooms, Gaby caught a vanishing glimpse of pale, unblinking yellow eyes. When she was about to say something, she noticed Livia's eyes were that same shade of yellow—or so she thought. A trick of light?

"Are you okay?" Livia asked her with a warm smile.

"Yes," Gaby replied. "Just thought I saw something... but probably I'm imagining things."

"With the things you have seen and experienced, I don't doubt your mind might get confused at times," Livia said. "But don't worry, you probably saw some vermin skulking around. As I was saying, the locals are very protective of this place, despite its haunted reputation. No one is sure when it was built, but the foundations seem to dig deep into the ocean bed. The locals hold it in the same esteem as a guardian spirit, keeping attackers and fae alike away. That's why they don't like outsiders."

"This place feels... sad. Not just cold, but sorrowful," Gaby pointed out.

"It is said that centuries ago, a group of warriors used this place as a headquarters, for an organization whose aim was to maintain the peace at the start of the Age of Strife," Livia explained.

"And what happened to them that gave this place such an aura?" Gaby asked. Fionn was uncharacteristically silent.

"They were betrayed and killed to the last, or so the locals say," Livia replied. "They also believe their cries can be heard at night, and those cries protect the town."

"They revere a haunted tower?" Harland retorted. "Isn't that odd?"

"Is it? I would say it's not that different from those who hold in high esteem the fabled Tempest Blades. Rumors of how they came to be are widespread now, after the Games," Livia said. "I didn't expect you have a pair, too, Gabs. Where did you get them?"

"It's a long story..." Gaby replied, distracted as she saw again the pale eyes peeking from beyond the darkness. "Where are we going?"

"The main hall, two floors more up," Livia looked up. "That's where they held their gatherings, so if there is any clue to the Crown's whereabouts, that's the place to check."

As they reached the entrance to the main hall, Livia entered first, followed by Gaby, who suddenly found herself alone in the empty room. There was nothing aside a darkened archway that led to another room, a stone table in the middle of the circular room, and a wooden door opposite the archway.

"Livia? Where are you?" Gaby asked as she turned around to look for her friend.

"I'm here," Livia replied, appearing out of nowhere, making Gaby jump. "Relax. What happened?"

"I keep seeing something. I think we are not alone," Gaby said.

"The corridor seems to be empty," Fionn said as he entered the room with Harland. "Same as the back room, it probably was a cupboard."

Though unsettled, Gaby wandered the main hall to get a better feel of the place. As she did, a sudden, sharp pain exploded behind her eyes.

†††

Gaby stopped in her tracks near the stone table at the center of the room. She shook her head, as overlapping, ghostly images appeared before her eyes. These images had a strange quality. Unlike her dreams and brief glimpses into the future, these had muted colors, as if they were old photographs decolorized by time. It didn't make sense.

Fionn approached her, placing his hand on her shoulder.

"Are you alright, hon?"

"I think I'm having a vision," Gaby replied through gritted teeth.

"Something is going to happen?" Harland asked as he moved closer to Gaby.

"No," Gaby replied, holding her head with both hands, her knees almost buckling due to the intense pain in her head. "Something already happened. I think it's a vision of the past. And it's giving me a heck of a migraine. Stop!"

"I have seen this before," Fionn said with a sorrowful smile. "I think Sophie passed to you her psychometric power, as a parting gift. Hold on tight to my hand. When we did that during her first visions, the pain lessened as it was being shared, then with time the pain never returned. I promise." He took Gaby's left hand. Her migraine receded in part, as Fionn threw his head back, gritting his teeth for a moment, until he regained his bearings and looked at Gaby once more, with loving eyes.

"Hold on to mine, too," Harland said, reaching for Gaby's right hand. The shock of the pain made his eyes briefly clench shut, but he regained his composure and smiled at Gaby. As Fionn had promised, the migraine lessened.

Why on Theia did the Queen give me her Gift power? And how? Gaby thought before all went white.

"What's going on?" Livia asked, but her voice got lost as the room changed before their eyes.

† † †

The room became a blurred image for Gaby, Fionn, and Harland. They were unable to move, as if their bodies were made of stone. The only thing any of them could do was watch as the room spun. It was a vision of the distant past, for Gaby couldn't recognize any of the people in the room. They were human warriors dressed in armor and garb from different cultures, most of them wore titanarmors, a few demonhunters, all with strange weapons that somehow gave Gaby a sense of familiarity. She glanced at the faint red and blue glow her Tempest Blades were emitting, their light bouncing from Fionn's shoulder.

One of the warriors placed a burnished black-bronze crown in an intricate design. The metal was twisted to resemble a ribcage crossed with protruding spikes that looked like temple spires, while intertwined throughout were vines and thorns. Metal flowers, a mix of roses and carnations, dotted the crown and each had at their center open-mouthed skulls. A couple of the skulls held large rubies in their mouths, while the other jaws gaped empty.

A girl—not older than sixteen, wearing red and gold armor, her hair coiffed in a tight ponytail—approached the table to stare at the Crown. Her face was full of sorrow and anger, and she exclaimed in a language that Gaby didn't understand, but the meaning was clear: She wanted the artifact destroyed. The girl unsheathed a broadsword with an odd-looking hilt that reminded Gaby of Yaha. Another warrior pushed her away as an argument sparked between them.

Idiots. They must be fighting to decide who gets to use it for some cause they think is just. Fionn's thoughts went straight into Gaby's mind. Perhaps he understood the language, or more likely, he was used to such arguments. Byron had tried the same with the Orb, before Fionn and Ywain destroyed it.

Thunder rocked the place, creating a momentary period of darkness. As light returned, the warriors stood befuddled before a floating figure, opening his arms in front of them. One of the warriors strode toward the table, grabbed the crown and delivered it to the floating figure, declaring "All hail the Golden King!" in a common tongue before he bowed and walked back with a devious smile.

He turned his head toward them and met Gaby's gaze, staring directly at her. The warrior gave off an oddly familiar aura, but Gaby couldn't remember where or when she had felt it.

The Golden King appeared as a floating man, dressed in tattered red robes with golden trim. From his head, two stag antlers grew, glowing like the embers of a dying fire. A golden aura or halo surrounded him, conferring on him a quasi-angelic appearance, through which he fooled his followers. But the most disconcerting feature, the one that would remain etched in Gaby's mind, was the Gold Mask that covered his face, or at least, *should* have, for behind it there was a darkness akin to an endless pit that threatened to suck your soul into it, only broken by the two glowing points that passed as his eyes. The very eyes that had swayed so many to fall under his thrall. The King laughed, followed by the warrior, whose body transformed into that of an Asurian priest, wearing their ceremonial toga.

The tower shuddered, walls creaking. The air took on a red haze. The room, perhaps the whole tower, was transported by a dimensional rift, temporally into the Infinity Pits. The walls were overgrown by ruddy. leathery material—akin to fungus or lichens, but shot through with pulsating black veins. Their roots dug deep into the ground, connecting the place to the deepest levels of Hell. A few of the gathered warriors reacted immediately, breaking free from the King's spell, and attacked. Their efforts were for nothing. The fungus had grown on the floor as well, infecting them like a virus and rendering their bodies marionettes on strings. Worst of it, they were clearly conscious of what was going on, but unable to act. All except for the girl with the ponytail. Her sword glowed with a fuchsia light.

It's a Tempest Blade! Gaby thought. Fionn grasped her hand tightly, and all the while she could sense Harland's revulsion.

The weapons of the other warriors bore a fading luminosity, but their glow winked out as they fell to the ground, connections to their wielders severed. With a flick of the Golden King's left hand every weapon but that of the girl exploded into clouds of dust that clogged the air.

The girl in the ponytail pushed back at the sweeping wave of dark energies that destroyed the other blades. She continued slicing at the encroaching fungus in attempt to keep it at bay. At the same time, the transfixed warriors were going rancid at the feet of the Golden King. The Tower subsumed their rapidly decomposing bodies and even their armors into a mass of organic matter, leaving only their contorted faces and their scared eyes, probably wondering what was happening to them.

Run! Gaby wanted to yell at the girl. But she knew it wouldn't change the outcome. *If only we could help her.*

The girl with the ponytail held on in spite of it all, fighting back the corruption creeping through her skin. Slowly, she advanced toward the Golden King as he and his aide mocked her, sneering, as her irises glowed in a mix of fuchsia and gold. She swung her Tempest Blade at the Golden King. The impact against his mask audibly rang with the crack that raced down it, the Tempest Blade arcing downward at the hand that gripped the Crown. The hand flew away as it was liberated from his body, but her Tempest Blade exploded into fragments upon contact with the Crown. The Golden King's laughter died, and without a word, his severed limb regenerated into a spike that impaled the girl in the chest, punching through her plate armor like paper. The girl, with the glow in her eyes flickering, drew a ragged breath and swung what was left of her Blade. It struck the Golden King's left antler at such proximity, black ichor seeping from the shattered bonde.

Dull irritation thrummed from the Golden King, and he flung the girl off of her impalement.

Her body made a sickening thud against the wall. And yet, she stood again. Blood poured from her wound, bubbled up in her mouth in a bright froth. Her last breath was spent in an inarticulate shout of defiance, pushing forward one last time even as her body gave out. She collapsed as she reached the stone table.

As the Golden King approached to steal her soul, the harsh, serrated cry of the onyx falcon, followed by the gurgling croak of the raven, and the booming sound of a trumpet interrupted him, stopping him in his tracks. The room flickered again as it returned to normal space, the Golden King and his tovainar aid nowhere to be seen. The girl, with her last breath, carved two words on the table with what was left of her Tempest Blade. The glow of her Gift faded from her irises as two winged humanoids appeared next to her. One was a man in purple and red armor, with black wings. He put his hand on the girl's forehead, muttering a silent prayer, while the other humanoid shape, that of a woman in silver armor with red and black feathers, who reminded Gaby of Mekiri, with tears in her eyes, kissed the girl on her left hand and closed her eyes. As the armored female stood, she held in her hand a ball of energy whose last tendrils came from the girl's body. Both figures lingered and argued for a moment before disappearing, taking the ball and the fragments of the broken Blade with them. The vision blurred once more as the flow of time resumed, bringing them to the present. They nevertheless witnessed the body of the girl being absorbed by the tower itself as the last of the vision evaporated.

Livia spoke, breaking the spell of the visions. "What did you see?"

The three of them mutely shook their heads. Harland, breathing slowly through clenched teeth to calm himself, walked toward the table and searched for the carved words, which he examined once he found them. Gaby bent over herself, her hands on her knees, trying to regain her composure. It wasn't just being physically taxed by having the vision, even sharing it with Fionn and Harland. No, it was the images burned in her brain that gave her pause. Her eyes welled up, and her heart filled with sorrow for the girl. A Gifted girl, not unlike her, of similar age to when Gaby and Alex faced an incursion and barely made it out alive. She glanced at Fionn who was standing, immobile.

He had unsheathed the Black Fang, and it glowed with

familiar intensity. Unflinching, he started at the shadows shifting on the walls. The fungal growth from her vision was making a reappearance, and rapidly so. His grasp of Black Fang's hilt was white knuckle, and his irises glowed green.

"Harland, finish what you are doing. This is not over." Gaby straightened, unsheathing Heartguard and Soulkeeper. Her companion blades glowed blue and red, as her own irises took on the blue glow of her Gift. There would be other time to mourn the unknown girl. For now, it was time to survive.

Livia's attention flicked to Gabby's face, lingering on her eyes. "You are a Gifted," Livia said.

"Surprise," Gaby replied. "Harland, get ready. It seems that the tower will play another trick."

"What do you mean?" Livia asked.

"This place is not haunted," Harland replied, memorizing the pair of scratched in words. "It's beyond cursed. It's damned by its connection to the Infinity Pits."

"What do you mean?" Livia asked a second time.

"That." Harland pointed at the shambling corpses coming out in droves, some of them wearing mockeries of the armors of the warriors they saw in the vision. Including the girl in the ponytail.

"How many do you think have been trapped through the years?" Gaby asked, readying her Blades.

"Too many," Fionn replied. "At least her soul got out of here instead of being trapped as well. When we are done, I will take this place down piece by piece."

"You can't destroy a piece of history, no matter how horrible!" Livia exclaimed.

Fionn didn't reply. Pent up emotion rendered him reticent as he went forward and unleashed a brutal series of attacks on the undead. Gaby had never before seen him so furious. Not even with Byron, despite their history.

"We can discuss that later, Liv," Gaby glanced at her friend. "Please, help me to keep Harland safe."

"Fine," Livia replied.

She couldn't say more, as she had to deal with her own share of the undead. As soon as she cut one down, two more regenerated. Their moaning and grumbling filled the air with a hateful cacophony.

The Infinity Pits on Theia, Gaby thought. She released all her sorrow, mixed with anger to increase the amount of adrenaline and energy the Gift granted her to stem the tide of corpses. But deep down she knew it wouldn't be enough, as it wasn't enough centuries ago. For this Tower had deep roots into Hell itself.

† † †

Gaby struggled to fend off the undead. Their numbers and their strength surprised her for being centuries old rotten corpses—comprised of fungus, no less. Behind the horde, in the dark archway, she glimpsed the pale yellow eyes again. They blinked at her as the white of a smile bared large canines that contrasted with the shadow, which started to move toward her group.

Now what? She thought.

The shadow moved at blinding speed for the rest of the world, but from Gaby's point of view, it was as if time was slowed down, her perception of time being altered by the Gift. The shadow became smaller, then changed into a shroud-like cape surrounding a man carrying a double-headed spear which blades emitted a familiar glow, but in orange hues.

The man jumped onto the stone table, as the shroud disappeared in his back, not before slicing four of the undead in half. As the shroud disappeared, a man in jeans, well-worn hiking boots, and a black shirt appeared. His most striking features were the fangs, the long red and black hair, and the pale yellow eyes that changed in color, the irises firing up in shining crimson as if they were made of red-hot metal. The man raised his head, smiled at Gaby—who returned the smiled, relieved—and jumped into the horde of undead, as his blade exploded with fury in flames. Flames licked off of the man's forearms and legs alike, pivoting amidst the undead horde, he turned more of bodies into ash. His skill with the fiery double blade was such that his strikes were unnatural, inhuman. He turned his back to the group and walked back to be on the same line as Gaby and Fionn, standing between them. Time resumed its regular speed.

"Missed me?" the man asked.

"I would be lying if I said no, Joshua," Fionn replied, dodging an undead that moved far too fast for a rotting corpse.

"Wanna join us in a very dangerous mission to stop the agents of the Golden King from getting the Crown of the Death?" Gaby asked as she cut a body in half with her twin blades. A rain of spiritual energy daggers came from behind her, hitting and impaling several of the remaining corpses. Gaby stared back at Livia.

That's new, she thought. One undead nearly hit her in the head, but Joshua caught the fist with his left hand and burned it to ashes.

"Yes, sure, why not? Once we get you guys out of here."

"Any suggestion to end the fight faster?" Harland asked from the back row.

Joshua spared Harland a glance. "One: Take cover."

Fionn and Gaby made a final push to send back the horde and then dragged Harland and Livia into the cover of the small room behind them. Fionn slammed the door and braced against it with his shoulder. Gaby did the same as she looked through one of the small slits between the petrified wood of the door.

† † †

Joshua concentrated, slowing his breathing. Small tongues of flame escaped his lips with every exhalation. The Beast went to sleep as he awoke the core inside him, the same Titan core he and the Beast had absorbed in their battle at Kyôkatô. He spun his own Tempest Blade, named the Fury, which augmented the intensity of the flames. The blade whispered in his head, with the voice of a young girl, confirming what he had suspected since he'd entered this place: This was where she had died, holding her own Tempest Blade centuries ago. Now Joshua and the girl were one by choice and fortune, and before them was an opportunity to close the circle, for one of the reanimated corpses approaching was originally hers.

Joshua still didn't know the name of the soul inside the Blade. In reality no one knew that about their own weapons, with perhaps the sole exception of Fionn. But he could understand the feeling, the unbridled rage, the burning anger at seeing her body desecrated in such a way. It was the same kind of rage Joshua had felt for more years than he could remember over being used by the Dark Father as the prototype for the tovainar. It was these shared emotions that had allowed Joshua to bond with the Fury when he reclaimed the weapon atop the Bedesala, the Damned peak.

Burn everything down, the voice whispered.

"Almost all," Joshua replied. "We still have friends here."

Burn almost everything down then, the voice agreed.

Joshua let go. An explosion ensued, filling the place with walls upon walls of fire, only leaving a small section between Joshua's back and the door behind which Gaby and the rest were taking cover free of flames. The fire was sentient, an extension of Joshua, who had left behind his tovainar past and had reclaimed the power of the Titan of Fire, with the aim of obtaining justice and redemption. The whole corpse horde was incinerated in a matter of seconds, leaving only mounds of ash. Joshua opened his eyes as the flames became smaller, absorbing all the fire inside his body and putting the titan core to sleep once more, living in the strange symbiotic relationship with Joshua and what remained of the Beast of Shadows.

Joshua rested the Fury against the wall. "You can come out," Joshua said, and wrenched at the melted door to let them out. The slagged metal gave an audible whine and snapped at the weak spots, leaving razor sharp edges for them to pick through.

"Do you know this guy?" Livia asked, astonished at the destruction around her. Even the stone table was half melted, any inscription on it utterly desecrated.

"Yes, an old friend," Gaby replied as she hugged Joshua.

"That was pretty impressive," Fionn said, gawking at the still red-hot melted stone. "I feel like I'm in a hot spring."

"And exhausting," Joshua said with an awkward smile, embarrassed. He wasn't used to anyone outside the Shimizu family complimenting his skills, and they usually referred to his cooking skills. "I'm still trying to get a good handle on it. Sometimes it's hard to gauge how much fire and heat to produce. If I'm not careful, there are unfortunate side effects."

"Said side effects include collapsing ancient structures?" Harland asked as he inspected the damage to the walls and the beams holding the upper floors.

CRACK!

The sound of stone breaking echoed through the tower as cracks appeared on the walls.

"Oh, not again!" Joshua said, rueful.

The upper half of the tower fell to one side, most of it collapsing over the cliff and falling into the sea below.

Fragments of molten rock and flaming wood fell on the bridge, taking it out as well.

† † †

"What in the Pits was that?" Vivi asked, as she looked through the Figaro's cockpit windows at the collapsed tower. The whole ruckus had attracted the attention of the town inhabitants. An inhuman scream, not from the throat of any living creature in this plane of existence, came from the crumbling tower.

"Told you." Sid sighed as he dropped his magazine, ignited the Figaro's engines and took the ship toward the tower, covering the distance in seconds. He pushed a switch on the console, opening the cargo bay hatch and lining it up with the floor where his friends and two new guests were standing, surrounded by piles of ash. "I guess the idiot is back."

"The guy with the double-bladed spear? Why do you call him an idiot?" Vivi was confused. She recognized the man as the one that had represented the Foundation at the Chivalry Games, alongside Alex and Kasumi, and that had fought the Titan of Fire. One would assume that should have earned Sid's respect, but the samoharo was very opinionated.

"Because he is an idiot who literally made a deal with the devil. Long story, I will fill you in later."

Harland, Fionn and Gaby were the first to enter the cockpit, followed by Joshua and Livia. All of them were covered in soot and ash.

"What happened?" Vivi asked as she changed seats, to leave the copilot's chair free for Harland, the actual co-pilot. Her concern for their wellbeing was replaced with a stifled laugh at how comical the legendary Greywolf looked all covered in dirt, as if he were a scruffy young kid.

"Vision from the past regarding the Golden King, undead former gifted warriors, unknown Tempest Blades destroyed and dead, a clue leading to the Crown's whereabouts, met Joshua," Fionn enumerated, closing finger by finger his right hand.

"Who I assume used his Titan of Fire powers," Sid muttered as he adjusted the static flying position of the ship, so he could turn to see the others.

"Yeah. That pretty much sums everything up," Gaby replied with a smile.

"Who's the new hooman?" Sid nodded toward the newcomer.

"I'm Livia Junipero."

"She is a friend from my days at the Sisters of Mercy," Gaby elaborated.

"They allow friends there?" Sid retorted, earning a soft slap on the shoulder by Vivi, who took the seat behind him.

"Funny," Gaby said, openly mocking Sid's expression. "She was my only friend. Now a freelance explorer and archeologist, who was hired by Doncelles to find the Crown too. We might as well join efforts."

"Ah," Sid said, noncommittal.

"What's that supposed to mean?" Livia asked, fixing her stare on the back of Sid's head.

"He is not fond of strangers," Vivi explained, waving her hand. "Apologies in his name."

"I hope you better have an apology for them, too," Sid pointed at the angry mob coming their way from the town. "Really angry people are coming this way. Why?"

"Probably because you destroyed their cultural heritage, one of their sources of tourist income. And maybe they were fond of the undead," Livia replied with a pointed look Joshua, who was silent in the farthest seat in the cockpit.

"Good riddance. If I could, I would obliterate what's

left of that place," Fionn growled with such vehemence that silence fell over the cockpit. Even his irises glowed an intense green for a moment.

"Undead? You know that is not possible, necromantic spells are unavailable," Vivi replied, only to wince at having caught herself saying something that no one outside the freefolk should have known.

"Why?" Livia asked, her curiosity paired with an unnerving smile.

"Just something we noticed with the magick field, surely an irregularity that will be fixed on its own. Sometimes certain spells don't work according to the season," Vivi said as Sid just shook his head, for an egg had hit the window.

"Great, that will take time to remove," Sid mumbled as he pushed the yoke of the ship forward. The noise of the Figaro's engines roared as it was being pelted with rocks, eggs, and vegetables by the angry inhabitants of Riverol. "We better leave this place now, before their aim gets better. Tight your seatbelts, this will get bumpy."

† † †

As the Figaro flew into the blue sky in the capable hands of Sid, and settled at a reasonable altitude from which the landscape below seemed to be a scale model, Harland looked at Joshua's spear.

"Does it have a name?" Harland asked him.

"Those weapons have names?" Livia interrupted.

"Every Tempest Blades has a name," Joshua replied. "It calls itself the Fury."

"A very appropriate name for what it can do. But I don't recall that name from the list of known Blades, nor the rumored Lost Ones," Harland said.

"As far as I know, it was reformed from the fragments of a previously destroyed Blade, which was owned by a

young girl whose soul resides inside now. Based on its reaction, she must have died at that tower," Joshua explained.

"The girl with the ponytail, the one that carved something into the table in our vision," Gaby prompted, turning
toward Harland.

"It was the name of a city," he said. "Mon Caern."

Fionn was barely paying attention to the conversation.
The vision had affected him more than he was willing to
admit. He was still grieving his last surviving friend from
before being frozen in time by Izia's spell. Gaby suspected
that the vision had resurfaced repressed memories from
when Fionn lost almost all his friends and Izia, trying to
stop Byron a century ago. The very friend and liege that
had betrayed them. But then she also remembered the
nightmares he often had. Fionn talked in his sleep about
being trapped in a hellish maze, made of stone and ruddy,
pulsating organic matter covered with far too many eyes.
The description seemed similar to what they'd just witnessed in the vision.

"If that's the case, how did it end up in Bedesala, deep
in the Grasslands. And who told you that it was there?"
Harland asked.

"You already know who told him," Sid said, through
gritted teeth.

Joshua had disappeared after Alex's surgery, and
Gaby recalled when they found out where Joshua had
gone. The shock that had accompanied the raven's message. Sid was the most annoyed that Joshua had made a
deal with the devil, after all the work Alex and Kasumi had
gone through to save Joshua from the Beast that had made
him a tovainar.

"Not sure how it ended up there. These Blades tend to
appear at their own will," Joshua shrugged.

"Maybe that's why so many unknown blades have resurfaced now, assuming they were not destroyed in the

events at the tower," Harland mused. "Bloody betrayal that was."

"What are you talking about?" Sid asked.

"We had a vision in the tower. We saw someone betraying and massacring a group of warriors, while momentarily teleporting the tower to the Infinity Pits," Fionn explained. The way his voice changed the moment he mentioned the Pits, confirmed Gaby's suspicions about Fionn's nightmares being visions of how the Infinity Pits were like. And yet, Gaby couldn't shake the feeling that those nightmares were actually repressed memories, for how real they felt to him. Part of his PTSD must have had that as root.

"They were not only murdered and suffered a fate worse than death, their weapons, which seemed to be Tempest Blades were destroyed. Only one girl lasted long enough to cause significant damage and her blade exploded into pieces. If we ever wondered about the Lost Tempest Blades, now we know the answer to their whereabouts."

"That's why you weren't so surprised that I had my Blades when we met for the first time?" Gaby asked Harland.

"I wanted to ask you where and how you got them, but it always slips my mind," Harland replied.

"To be fair, I find it more concerning that something can actually destroy a Tempest Blade," Vivi said. "Aren't they supposed to be indestructible? How old is Yaha?"

"According to Alex, at least ten thousand years," Gaby replied.

"So, anything capable of breaking, or at least damaging, a Tempest Blade should be an object of equivalent mystical or spiritual power in the hands of a being that can handle said power. That doesn't leave many options on this plane of reality," Vivi continued, thoughtful. She had been asking the right questions, as an academic who actually took her job seriously was meant to do.

Fionn broke his silence a second time. "Gods from the Pits. The tovainars, assuming they have roughly the same power level, would be the ones to do so with the right tool," he said, grim. "Truth be told, Alex and Sam really pulled all the stops against the Creeping Chaos and Alex barely made it out alive."

"But we only know of two tovainars, and one is dead, no one knows anything about the other three."

"One is the right hand of the Golden King, from what we saw, which is a massive problem unto itself," Fionn interjected. Gathering information and preparing a secret counteroffensive in case a new war began had been his main concern in the past year. And Gaby knew he hated being right about that. Fionn was tired of war. On top of that, this time he had new reasons to be worried. He was right, taking down the Creeping Chaos had almost killed Alex, left Sam with scars on her hands, and Yaha... how the sword held on and didn't break was a miracle.

"Correction, anything about the other two," Harland said.

"I was following the trail of one, but I lost it near here," Joshua explained. "I entered the tower in case they were hiding under the energy aura of the tower itself."

"I have always wondered how a tovainar came to be," Vivi asked. "Professor Hunt used to talk about them before his unfortunate incident. Aren't they some kind of boogey-people?"

"For what we know, they are some sort of twisted reflection on the Gifted," Harland explained. Gaby noticed that Livia frowned and crossed her arms. Joshua shifted in his chair, a sullen mood falling on his face.

"Can't talk about the others, but Byron became one because he was afraid of losing his power, both political and physical. I recall he never took well seeing the King being physically frail after the war. Which was to be expected after the whole ordeal. Byron had a vain streak, never accepted that someone was better than him, or that he eventually would get older and die. He often joked about living forever. I guess all of that combined gave him the motivation to become one," Fionn explained. After Hunt, he and Joshua probably were the people who had the most experience with them.

Harland's eyes widened in realization.

"I just realized something that fits with what little I have been able to piece together since we faced Byron, the bits here and there about the other tovainars you told me, what we know of the Asurian legends and stories. The difference between the Gifted and the Tovainar, is that the former were technically killed while protecting others. The latter killed others, sometimes by the thousands, to protect themselves. The process are reflections of each other," Harland explained, elated that he had figured it out. It could lead to find a way to defeat the remaining ones.

"That's a blanket statement, a product of the limited information you are working with," Livia interrupted, shaking her head and waving a finger at Harland. "Little is known about either of those groups, or the cultures they came from. We barely knew anything of those that died in that tower. How many supposedly good beings ended up causing many horrors upon the people of these lands, like the Titans? How many Gifted have been killed by the samoharo before they could become a danger to others like the Titans again. Oh yes, many people know about the little dirty secret of the samoharo. For all we know, maybe the tovainar were original beings that found a way to protect their people and a handful got corrupted. Assigning them a moral quality for just a supposition on how they came to be is callous and unprofessional."

"Can't disagree with Harland's assessment," Joshua

interjected. "He is right."

"How do you know?" Livia asked, her fingers clenching the arm rests of her seat.

"Because once upon a time, I was one of those tovainars. And while I don't remember all the details of how I became one, I do know it meant the death of a whole city. And then there is Byron, which no one here will disagree, was a huge danger. No offense, Fionn."

"None taken," Fionn replied, not bothering to turn around. His mind seemed to be elsewhere.

"Two of how many? Five perhaps? How many Gifted and Titans became a danger? The odds are in their favor. I think no one should be hastening to cast judgment without further research," Livia replied with disdain.

"Relax," Gaby said, trying to defuse the situation. "It was just a comment."

"I don't have time for wannabe posers passing as experts on folklore and history. I think it's embarrassing coming from the leader of the Foundation. I take my job as an archeologist seriously, not as a hobby by a dilettante," Livia replied, standing up.

"Archeologist or tomb raider? How many things have you stolen, sold, or been hired to obtain?" Sid countered.

"Easy—we are all friends, let's not fight, okay?" Gaby soothed.

"Yeah, tell that to your *friends*." Sid was unable to let go, for some reason. He was being too insistent, and the way he pronounced the word 'friends' told her that something was off, but Sid had been unwilling to say what was bothering him. Did he suspect someone? After all, Sid had been trained as a special operative to... well... take down super powered beings, including Gifted. That he had decided to not do that to Gaby and Alex, spoke of how much he trusted and cared for them, like an older brother. It was plain that he had been offended by how Livia had spoken to Harland. While Sid and Harland ribbed on each other, in reality they had a lot of respect for one another, to the point that Harland was the only one authorized to sit in the copilot seat, pilot the Figaro, and see the blueprints. On the other hand, Livia was the only former Sister of Mercy she trusted, after their harrowing shared experience, and Joshua had proved to be a loyal friend, or at least ally, during the Titan crisis.

Sid cut into her train of thought. "I will find a suitable place to land and then we will talk. Meanwhile if none of you want to be thrown out of their airlock, I suggest you keep your mouth shut, especially you two, idiot and new girl."

"I have a name," Livia said, indignant.

"I don't care. Shut it or airlock," Sid replied, not taking his eyes off the cockpit's view. He was being more irascible than usual.

"I will put on some music to calm the mood," Harland offered as he sulked in the copilot seat, hurt. Gaby placed a hand on his shoulder, which he grabbed. "Take it easy, Sid."

"You are the best at what you do, Harland," Gaby whispered in his ear. "Don't ever let anyone tell you anything different."

Harland smiled back weakly.

"Don't worry, I have heard that all my life: that I never made a good choice."

That was something Gaby could relate to. She wondered if it would have been better to keep with the band tour with some changes, instead of returning to her life as 'adventurer,' as Alex had put it once.

Facing the drunks at a concert is easier, Gaby thought.

Chapter 6
Urban Legends

"I THINK I'M GONNA BE sick."

The world spun for Sam so fast that all became a blur. It was easier to close her eyes than try to make sense of the quantum folding through which the teleportation spell worked, using the Tempest behind the Veil as a bridge to connect two distant points. For the shortest distance between two points is not a straight line, nor in the case of a planet, a curved one. It was zero. That's what the Tempest represented in this case.

Magick was hard to do. Probably the hardest thing to do this side of coming up with a humane, functional economic system, for magick had to ask the universe to bend itself to the will of the caster. And the universe could always say no. There were several ways to do magick though, depending on your training, nature, and beliefs. If you didn't have the natural abilities to draw thaums into your body but did have an intellectual inclination to learn and didn't mind the long way, you could learn to use sympathetic magick to alter the odds of probability through quantum entanglement to get what you want. Then again for that, alchemy would be a faster way. Or even faster, albeit far costlier in the long run, you could ask a favor of a patron, be it a god or some other powerful cosmic entity that could come from anywhere, including the Pits and the folds of the very universe. Most humans would do this. Even those trained by Freefolk Magi. Summoning the spirits is less dangerous but trickier, for spirits are fickle and if they don't like you, well, the least thing you could expect is a prank. Kuni magick worked like that, plus a few low-level cantrips powered by the spiritual energy of the body. Something like an auto summoning. There were other ways to empower spells and get the universe to help you, like the blood magick, which the samoharos use for their pathfinding and smiting way, albeit only they know how these small offerings to their deities worked. For the pact with the Great Spirit—or Kaan'a for the humans—that sustain such dealings was made in the distant past and no one remembered the details.

Freefolk don't have any of these problems, for they are the people of the magick. Since Asherah, during the Pilgrimage, tamed the natural force that is Magick and taught her people how to draw the thaums from the natural field generated by planets and stars. Doing so changes the very nature of the freefolk, from shapeshifters into near-human forms, but their blood, their very essence was that of magick. By drawing it through their bodies as conduits, by suggesting, sometimes imposing their will, they can reshape reality itself, as their brain works in an instinctive manner the equations required for such effects.

Of course, as Sam once explained to Alex—since she was in charge of teaching the younger apprentices the basic rules—this is not as easy as it sounds. Freefolk magick has rules: there is feedback from reality, the stronger the spell the more energy you use with the risk of burning out and so on. Thus, there are certain spells that are more difficult to make than others: healing magick—and in general, any magick related to the body—required an intimate knowledge of how the body works or it would have awful consequences.

Teleportation is another kind of spell that is difficult, for the user has to take in account several factors, like stellar drift, how your body looks and where you want to end up, or you will appear inside a rock or with all your body parts in different places. Transfiguration into animals has its own risk in terms of consciousness integrity. Resurrections and necromancy are out of the question, for they require too much energy, plus the willing cooperation of the subject's soul and permission from the guardians of the world beyond the veil. Time Travel is forbidden and nigh impossible to work out, mainly because there is no agreement on how time travel works, if it's possible at all.

That's the difference between a show illusionist and a magick caster. The former creates the illusion across the stage, through props and low-level mirage spells, that they can make appear or disappear, or cut in half, or impale, or transform their assistant into a panther. Magick casters actually try to do that, and sometimes, are successful. Not always. That's why freefolk are so feared—even if only a few in hundreds can cast magick—and that's why Sam had the most potential of all. Because she is the second freefolk with the Gift. And the Gift doesn't follow the same rules.

But Sam doesn't know that.

Which is why she is surprised that her teleportation spell has worked at all.

They landed on a lonely side road, barely lit by the *Paidragh* lamps that kept it safe from spirits and minor creatures. They hit the ground hard, as the spell sent them a meter above the ground, but otherwise intact, from what Sam could see. Which was not bad considering that Sam did pretty much a blind jump.

Alex was on the curbside, heaving. Not quietly, either. *No surprise there*, Sam thought. *He has vertigo and motion sickness.*

Mekiri was seated on the ground, smiling. "My legs feel wobbly," she said. "And my ears are floppy."

Sam hadn't noticed until then that, on top of Mekiri's head, were her usual rabbit ears she wore in her smaller form.

So, she did help with the spell, thank the Goddess... err thank her, Sam thought. She was confused, but suspected that Mekiri, memory issues aside, had helped her to cast the spell correctly by doing all the complicated math to get them here intact.

Yokoyawa was standing, imperturbable. The guy was a mountain.

Kasumi was kneeling on the ground, clenching her fists into her robe, breathing heavily.

Sam was dizzy, and her legs trembled from the effort of standing. Even her tail hung limply. But otherwise, she was fine.

"It worked," Alex said. He was pale. "I think we are in one piece too. Kasumi, are you okay?"

Kasumi, with some effort, extended her left hand, calling Sam for help.

"I'm gonna check on her," Sam said. "It's my responsibility."

Sam approached Kasumi and knelt beside her.

"Are you okay, Kasumi?"

Kasumi whispered something barely audible. But her blissful smile, the kind of slow heavy breathing, the moaning sounds she was making and the way she was clutching her sides told Sam everything she needed to know. Now she understood why Kasumi once had told Sam during a date, that when she was a teenager, wanted to be an illusionist's assistant. Kasumi, blushing, then had asked Sam if she knew how to do those tricks and if she could be Sam's assistant. It was the first time she had seen that kind of effect on a person being teleported.

"Take your time, Kasumi," Sam whispered to her and kissed her on the top of her head.

Sam walked toward Alex, still stumbling a bit due to the spell. Alex moved to catch her. "Are you okay, Sam? Is she okay?"

"I'm just tired, the spell was too taxing. As for Kasumi give her time, the side effect on her was... *peculiarly strong* and will take a bit to wear off," Sam replied with a wink at Alex, watching Alex's face turn red as a turnip with realization. "Now the question, is where we are?"

"Judging by that sign, in a road in the middle of nowhere between Carffadon and Saint Lucy," Alex replied, pointing to the sign near where they had landed.

"I'm sorry I couldn't get us into a safer place."

"We are each in one piece, safe and sound. And we are far from those things, so I would call that a win," Alex replied, fixing a strand of Sam's hair that had come loose.

"Do I still have the tail?" Sam asked. "Can't feel it. I don't like it."

"You look pretty with it," Alex smiled. Since the day they had met, Alex had always made her feel less uncomfortable regarding her 'allergies,' "which made Sam regret the way she sometimes treated him when it came to his half-baked ideas.

She gave him a kiss on the left cheek.

"I wanted to apologize for yelling at you earlier," Sam said. "I know you had to think fast, and I was kinda out of commission."

"No, no, you and Kasumi were right," Alex replied. "I need to learn to think faster and think through my ideas. We were lucky you reacted faster."

Kasumi only replied with a thumbs up, before collapsing with a faint moan. Alex ran to her side.

"She is fine. Trust me. I think the effect was stronger

than I surmised," Sam said. "Happens the first time at least. Then if you survive, you get used to it."

"I think we need some help to move around faster," Alex explained. "You put distance between them and us, but we don't know if they can track us. And with both Kasumi and Mekiri unable to walk for now, me dizzy and you unbalanced due the tail, plus the backpacks, we won't be able to move quickly."

"I can carry one of them," Yokoyawa offered. "And half of the backpacks. But that only solves our speed problem by half."

"I can't teleport us again. I'm exhausted to begin with," Sam said.

"In this case, Sam," Alex said. "I concede to your expertise. Any suggestions? I mean besides magick?"

"I could try to summon a creature or a wind spirit to carry us..."

"I can call my pet," Mekiri interjected, smiling.

"I'm confused," Alex whispered to Sam. "Does she or doesn't she remember anything of who she really is?"

"My best guess?" Sam replied in a whisper. "Whatever left her trapped in that state jumbled her memories and thoughts, so she can access them, but needs a prompt to do so to sort out who knows how much information she has inside. I mean she is the avatar of a goddess. I assume that even if the avatar holds a tenth of the power and knowledge of the original deity, is a tenth of a lot more than we can imagine."

"That makes sense with all we have seen," Alex said with a somber tone. "But I would hate to know that the thing we fought last time was just the tenth of the real thing."

"You stopped a god, or a godly avatar dead in its tracks, Alex. Helped to save a city, if not the world itself. You should..." Sam said when she was interrupted by a loud, sharp whistle by Mekiri.

A few seconds passed.

The wind started to pick up in strength as a howling echoed through the air in response to the whistling. Alex and Sam looked around, but the road remained empty. Footsteps of something big rumbled through the ground. A ghostly white smoke approached them, and with each meter it advanced, the smoke took the shape of a giant white dragonwolf. As it solidified, the dragonwolf walked gingerly toward Mekiri, while clinks came from the bags full of trinkets hanging from the side of the creature. It reached Mekiri and licked her with its large tongue. It tilted its head to the left and with its big, curious, kind, puppy-like eyes stared at Sam. The white dragonwolf panted as Mekiri scratched its left ear.

"Thank you for coming, Cookie," Mekiri said with a smile. "She can carry us."

"Well, that's a convenient plot twist to keep the adventure moving," Alex said with a shrug of his shoulders. "Then again, I guess it's kinda just, given that we have a godly avatar on our side."

"Don't ruin the moment, Alex," Sam replied as she punched him softly in the arm.

"Any suggestions on where to go?" Yokoyawa asked.

"I'm not sure if it's another coincidence, but if that road sign is correct and we are between Carffadon and Saint Lucy, I think we are close to one of the few people that know more about arcanotech, akeleths and myths in this island," Alex replied.

"Professor Hunt!" Sam added with a smile.

†††

The dragonwolf carried them swiftly along the road, fast enough to cover the distance in a short time, but not enough for her passengers fall.

"You said earlier that somehow the laws of magick are not working as they should. How come?" Alex asked, raising his voice. "I mean, magick comes from thaums, the manifestation of the fifth fundamental force. It's basically a natural energy field around Theia. How can it get out of balance out of the blue?"

"The field might be naturally occurring," Sam replied. "But accessing it and using it are not. Our teachings say that Asherah worked hard under the guidance of Mekiri to 'tame' the magick after the Pilgrimage, so it would be safer to use. The last time something like this happened was when Queen Kary burned out the whole energy field with a spell to stop the War of Thousand Tears between the Freefolk and the Asurian for good, just after the death of Black Fang the Dragon. And even then, the damage was not like this. The field was just reduced in power and had to build up to its current levels for centuries. Right now, the only explanation I can come up with based on Mekiri being here in her actual form, is that something sundered her avatar from her divine form inside the Tempest and without her to keep check on them, is rewriting the laws of magick."

"Is that possible?" Kasumi asked. She still looked groggy but sported a wide, peaceful smile.

"And who did it?" Yokoyawa added.

"It seems it is possible," Sam replied. "And no idea who did it, but this is a huge problem."

"Because our civilization's technology is dependent of that field?" Kasumi asked.

"It's worse," Alex replied. "That leaves the freefolk open for attack and the only thing that has kept things from escalating down south is the threat of the freefolk letting loose in defense of the Alliance and their territories. Don't worry, Sam, we will find a way to fix this, somehow."

"How? We don't know where to start!" Sam yelled.

"Well, we know murcana was involved. That's a clue."

"You don't understand," Sam explained "It's not just that. If I'm not being affected by this as the freefolk are, then am I one of them? And I can't say that I'm human anymore because of..."

"The Gift?" Kasumi said.

"Yes," Sam said as her eyes welled with tears. "Besides, if I'm the only one that can still cast magick... that means all of this hinges on me."

"I know no one can understand what you are going through right now," Kasumi replied. "I don't have the Gift, so I only know of it what you two have told me. And we are under pressure here, you most of all of us, but you are not alone. We have your back."

"We will help you, with all of this," Yokoyawa added.

"Besides, Sam," Alex said. "For whatever reasons, call it destiny, call it coincidence, call it the universe karma, things are happening for a reason. And Mekiri..."

Mekiri looked at them with a wide smile. It was clear she was enjoying the ride.

"...used to work in mysterious ways. So maybe we, you, are her back up plan. If someone can fix this, it's you. I believe in you. Fionn does, that's why he put you in charge."

"Nice speech," Sam said, sobbing and trying to smile. "But that makes me feel more pressured than before."

"Sorry, I'm not good at rousing speeches. That's Fionn and Harland's job." Alex shrugged his shoulders. "And we are here."

Professor's Hunt house was a closed gate affair, located on top of a small hill, overlooking the fields extending for miles below. The style of the brownstone house was classical, from pre-war times, making it at least a century old. The house must have been recently renovated because the paint seemed fresh. Alex could detect a faint glowing pattern coming off the walls, beneath the paint. He rubbed his eyes, and the glow disappeared. As he hadn't recovered his Gift to his usual levels, he was having trouble seeing energy fields like before. The house had four newly built towers, one at each corner. Not a mansion, but big enough to hold one of the best-curated book collections on obscure topics outside Ravenstone or even Ravenhall.

"I think we knock now," Alex said, as he jumped down from the dragonwolf, as it lowered her body to allow everyone to climb down.

"Time to go home, be safe," Mekiri said to her dragonwolf while patting her large head. The creature replied by wiggling her tail, which sent gusts of air all over the place. Mekiris' pet stood up on her four legs, howled, and then ran into the darkness, dissolving into a mist.

"That's convenient," Alex muttered, as the automated gates for the estate opened.

"No," Kasumi replied, "the gates opening on their own is convenient."

† † †

"Hi. I'm glad to see you once more, lads," the Professor said as he received the weary group into his home. Leo Hunt sat in a wheelchair at the entrance and had an accent that fit perfectly with the second most well-travelled man of the Core regions. He was also quite stubborn as well. For all the kilometers he had covered, he had not lost his grip on the accent he grew up with. And yet it had still picked up enough notes and inflections here and there that when he returned home, he sounded like a stranger. He belonged everywhere and nowhere, with a voice that began deep then rose into a high pitch of enthusiasm, but still held hints within it of the soft, rural lands he called home, and the kilometers under his feet ever since.

"Apologies for not receiving you at the gates," he said as he led them to his studio. The place had been refurbished to accommodate the recent needs of its owner. And while most of the weirdest artifacts were now safely secluded in a vault at the Foundation, the rooms were still filled with bookcases filled to the brim with books and binders. And the walls we decorated with framed newspaper clippings. "But as you can see, I'm still dealing with consequences from my unfortunate entanglement with the Withered King. And when I saw you standing at the main door through the security cameras, I asked my new assistant to open the gates."

"It's alright, Professor," Sam said. "I apologize for not being able to remain as your assistant. I too had to deal with some personal and large-scale consequences from the Battle of Saint Lucy. But I think you already knew that."

"Judging by your looks, Sam" the Professor replied, "I take it that you became a peculiar version of the Gifted. And that requires special training. I thank you for rescuing me. And to you, Alex. Although I'm not acquainted with the rest of you."

"I'm Shimizu Kasumi, pleased to meet you," Kasumi said, bowing.

Using the Kuni way of introducing oneself with the family name first gave Leo only the barest of pauses before he took it in stride with a nod. "Ah! Harland's bodyguard and the Chivalry Games current champion," Leo replied. "That means that you, sir, must be the legendary Yokoyawa of the Samoharo."

"That's right, Professor," Yoko replied with a bow of his own. "Although I think that from both of us, you are the more famous one."

"I'm not sure of that," Leo stared at Mekiri, who was looking at a nearby board which had tacked to it newspaper clippings from the past few days. The headlines on a few of the clipped articles read: "Aurora Borealis Blamed for Magick Failure," to "Artists Share Strange Dreams," and

"Psychics Admitted to Mental Health Clinics".

"And who might the lady in the back be?" the professor asked.

Sam and Alex exchanged looks. With a loud sigh, Alex replied. "That is Mekiri, the Freefolk elder and librarian."

"And also," Sam added, "the Trickster Goddess avatar."

"Now, this is someone my new assistant will want to meet," Leo said, his eyes as wide as saucers.

†††

"I can't believe you are his new assistant," Alex said to the tall, skinny man currently serving them tea in the studio, his longtime friend Quentin.

"After graduating, I had to get a job, like Birm and Andrea. Not everyone can go around the world having adventures sponsored by the Foundation, like you. And I can't believe that you know the Trickster Goddess and never told me," Quentin replied. "Although she seems to be too spaced out for you know... a deity in human form."

"One, it wasn't our secret to tell," Sam said, as she took her cup from Quentin. The tea smelled good, relaxing even. So relaxing that as Sam took her first sips, her tail finally dissipated in a cloud of light specks, with only her new hair color remaining. That was manageable with her knitted beanie hat. "Finally! I can sit properly. And as I was saying, we didn't tell in part because we weren't one hundred percent sure, until now. And two, given our line of work, it's not something you go announcing to the world."

"What happened to her?" Leo asked. Behind him, there were a couple of monitors showing what the security cameras around the property were registering.

"We found her naked, with her memories and thoughts scrambled, in a derelict house full of humanoid bodies that seemed to be born the day before. And then we were pursued by two of those humanoids that can shoot solid beams of lights from their eyes..." Kasumi explained. "In total violation to the normal laws of physics, I might add," Alex continued, rubbing the back of his neck. "Also, the place reeked of murcana."

"Are you sure?" Quentin asked, then he exchanged a look with the professor and then took a seat. "Are you sure that's the Trickster Goddess, and that there was murcana involved?"

"We are sure in the sense that she looks like the Mekiri we know, just taller," Sam replied, placing her cup on the table.

"This would fit the chatter we have found in the aethernet," Hunt said. "Since the aurora borealis started to act strangely a few days ago. Psychically attuned people having strange, vivid dreams, reports of warptrains experiencing malfunctions, now the freefolk reporting problems with their magick casting, the aethernet itself fluctuating, strange ghostly apparitions, incursion alarms failing, the fae staying close to the Paidragh lamps, despite how much they abhor them, as well as reports of odd looking people wearing shades at all-time prowling places known for being magick field convergence points..."

"Like those two odd men that camera three just caught?" Quentin asked as he stood up and approached the monitor. "Are those guys like the ones looking for you?"

"Yes, we need to move before they find us here," Alex said as he stood up from his chair.

"There is no need." The professor waved his hand, indicating for him to take seat again. "I installed mystical sigils and wards all over the place. This place is a blank spot when it comes to scrying or any other detection spell or technology."

"Magick is going haywire, so I dunno how those will work now?" Sam pointed out.

"They are not magickal, they are of akeleth origin,

written in what I believe is the divine language spoken at the start of the universe. And I also installed turrets and other defensive countermeasures," Hunt replied with pride.

"Not taking any chance, huh?" Alex asked as he stared at the monitors. His hands were itching to take out Yaha from its sheath, resting next to his seat.

"Not again," Hunt said with a smile.

"They left, the wards worked," Kasumi noted. She had been tightening her grip on Breaker, which was faintly glowing with a white light.

"For now. This is the third time this week we have seen the acolytes prowling around," Quentin said as he returned to his seat. "This house has been previously visited upon by strong magicks, so we assume the residuals are what attract them to the region."

"Acolytes?" Yokoyawa asked.

"Yes, that's how those beings are named in ancient texts," Hunt explained.

"I think my nickname of Headlights worked better," Alex said, crossing his arms and slumping in his chair.

"Let it go," Sam admonished Alex, before he could go into one of his long-winded ramblings. She turned to the professor. "This is the first time I've heard of them, what are they?

"I'm not surprised that you haven't heard of them" the professor said. "They are beings from the human religion and lore, not the freefolk one. And if I recall correctly, human religions were never your forte at grad school. They are minor angels in the service of one of the higher ranks. Some legends collected by Belger during his initial trip to the Grasslands tell of the Acolytes being sent to judge entire nations and erasing them from history with their holy lights.

"There was nothing holy about those lights," Alex

said. He was sweating at the memory of those beams. Sam knew he was worried about them, even visibly scared—a first for him.

"There are mentions of them from texts recovered from the Asurian Empire before its fall. They considered them the enemy, as their dark religion provoked them, since the being the acolytes served was some sort of deity overseeing karmic retribution and curiously enough, it seems that he oversaw creativity as well. I believe that was the reason the first tovainar came to be. Your friend Joshua was meant to kill the acolytes," the professor replied.

"And he is not here to do us the favor to get rid of those pests," Alex muttered under his breath.

"What kind of human deity could have beaten her?" Sam asked aloud. This was worrying news. Because Mekiri—well, her real self—was not only the patron saint of magick users and heroes, she was also a staunch ally and protector of the freefolk. And while Sam was technically only part freefolk, she felt deeply for her people, often ostracized by their customs and their ability to cast spells with ease that none of the other species had. "She is the Trickster Goddess! Only the Judge or the Guardian are at her level. None of the angels from human religions, nor their spiritual leaders like the Carpenter are known to be able to use magick as she does... did... no, does."

"If I may explain," the professor said. "Compared to some of the hierarchy of the Infinity Pits' beings, demons and deities, there's awfully little that we know about Last Heaven's hierarchy or how it works regarding the major religious beliefs of the three species. We know slightly more, but not much, about the Akeleth civilization, their relationship with the Freefolk Gods, the Samoharo Paths or even human religions. Some scholars compared them with the angels of myth that served Kaan'a as angels, others believe that the Akeleth are the Freefolk Gods that ascended aeons ago. We know even less of how deities' avatars are created. At this point, you are the foremost experts on these myths and folklore for the experience at hand you have. Because you have faced them. You have interacted with their manifestations."

"They are not that different to the incursions. So, your theory is right professor," Alex said. "They translate their state of matter from their dimension to matter from us that follows the rules of physics... to a point. Their matter is different to anything I've seen in the material labs. Other than the puncher ring or summoning spells to open a bridge, I can't see how the process works for a deity, because they are not using any tether. I mean, those acolytes had bodies that were similar to those of a newborn, they weren't using hosts, leaving the corpse all mangled up. And the more animalistic incursions disintegrate once their core is destroyed so I can picture how these 'deities' create their avatars, just that they are so damn hard to kill and—"

"The goddess decided to descend upon the world once more." Mekiri recited, interrupting Alex. *"However, this time she would take a different approach. The last time she used her true form and full power, she broke the world, leaving a scar that held reality warping anomalies. Thus, she opted to create an avatar as she came down. She first projected her personality and part of her wisdom and power into the world. Around that, using her divine powers, she invoked Kaan'a's light. Globules of light coalesced around the spiritual form.*

The goddess manipulated matter at quantum level first, then atomic, then genetic. She built from scratch a mortal body, one of a humanoid girl with long reddish hair and big black eyes. She walked across the Mistlands, naked, while she moved her hands, matter shaping around her, making clothes and shoes. It took her a while to readjust to the lessened mortal senses. Only a modicum of cosmic awareness remained, an ironclad thread to her real form tucked in the higher dimensions.

"It's so weird to have a physical body in this realm. Let's find that girl Asherah. I have a mission for her. But first, I need a name for this avatar." Mekiri fell silent and returned to playing with a crystal ball.

"What was that?" Hunt asked Sam.

"I think she is accessing random memories, as she tries to recover her mind. Perhaps what we are saying triggered this one. So, I guess the legend of the Trickster Goddess entering the world after cracking it and creating the World's Scar was actually real," Sam replied.

Hunt smiled, as her answer had confirmed something to him, something he'd had a suspicion of until now.

"As you know, that's how my original thesis evolved into my research on arcanotech," the professor explained. "What we call urban legends are reinterpretations of real events, told within a short time frame and modified due to communication mishaps. As time passes urban legends become folklore, then legends, then myths and from there they either get lost to history or become something else, like religious figures. That's how akeleths work. They were beings that reached a certain level of advancement that we mix up with deities and demons. Their advanced technology is not different from what we call magick, maybe it is even the same. Or a different interpretation of the same phenomena."

"So, are you saying that deities are not real? Because there is one sitting there right now, licking that rock," Kasumi interjected. "Mekiri, don't do that, please. You don't know where that was."

"Not exactly," the professor continued. "Rather, we need to change our concept of divinity. As we can see here, gods are real beings. But what we need to reflect upon is that those beings are advanced beings compared to us, at a spiritual level perhaps, maybe at an intellectual or technology level too, living in one of the multiple dimensions that conform reality, but not necessarily gods in terms of worship. If that's the case, they are not different from us. I believe that mortal beings contain a piece of Kaan'a, The Great Spirit, The Universe, chose the name you prefer. Each one of the three species, and even some of the minor, more primitive ones like the Felp orcs believe that there is a divine being that created us. But I believe that every being has a part of its divine spark. We are the universe trying to understand itself. And when these beings reach a certain level of understanding on how the universe work, they ascend to the next level of reality. I had my suspicions before, but now I'm sure this is the case because of you."

"What?" Sam asked, as her train of thought came to a halt, making her blink twice.

"Yes, you, the Gifted," Hunt declared with firm voice. Sam had never seen her former boss so sure of himself about something. It was almost as if he was proud of them, with the way he shuffled in his wheelchair. "What you can do is above what even the highest trained demon hunter can do. No offense, Kasumi."

"None taken," Kasumi replied with an offhand gesture.

"Or anyone, really, can achieve," Hunt continued. "And yet the demonhunter and to a lesser extent the titanfighters, the freefolk magi, the pathfinding warriors of the samoharo, can summon power from within or from the world, or Heavens, to achieve superhuman prowess for a brief moment, because the Storm God, or Asherah, who I believe was Gifted, taught them. The difference is that you, as Gifted, can do it at will, for as long as you want. You have fought tovainars from dark prophecies, titans that leveled the world, an avatar of the Creeping Chaos, if what

Harland told me is correct. No one else in history has done that since the Founders. If that's not proof of the spark of divinity, then I don't know what is."

"You are kinda right," Mekiri said with a cryptic smile. "And kinda wrong. But on the right track. Can I drink more tea while I stand on my hands? I want to test something."

"I don't think that's advisable, your grace," Yoko said, taking the cup from her hands.

"I wonder what will happen to your stories in the distant future," Quentin said out of the blue.

"What do you mean?" Sam asked.

"Do you realize that you guys are considered urban legends?" Quentin replied, excitement in his voice. "Because of everything you have done both at Saint Lucy and during the Chivalry Games? Of what you can actually do?"

"How come?" Kasumi asked.

"There is footage circulating around about what you can do, your powers. There are even rumors that you killed a god from the Wastelands, which we know are true. You can't get more legendary than that—aside from Fionn, of course. He is considered a living legend. There are chat rooms where there are mentions of him as if he were a minor deity like the Storm God and not a mortal anymore," Quentin explained.

"There are chat rooms?" Yokoyawa asked, surprised.

"Yes, that's what I was checking early today when the Aethernet went down. Some of those rooms mention a rare urban legend about Fionn taking down the Wyld Hunt on his own, two decades ago," Quentin said.

"That's no legend," Sam interjected, causing the chatter to disappear into a heavy silence. "That happened. That's when Dad rescued me from the sorcerer that sacrificed my parents to the Wyld Hunt and was planning to sacrifice me as well."

"You never told us that," Alex said, watching her with eyes that were trying to hide both a tinge of betrayal and of sorrow. She knew that look. Since his bout of depression, he had tried to be as open and honest with her to avoid making her worry about him doing something stupid, like challenging a god to a fistfight all by himself. And she knew she had not been fulfilling her part of a bargain that she had proposed.

"I don't like to talk about that. It's painful," Sam replied, looking down. Truth be told, even almost two decades later, she still had nightmares about that fateful day. Ever since then she'd looked for the signs that the Wyld Hunt would return for her, even after Fionn had defeated their champion—by beheading a ghost nonetheless—and freed her from the bonds of the planned sacrifice.

"I think you need something. Group hug!" Yokoyawa proposed, hugging Sam. Alex joined in with glee, while Kasumi did so somewhat reluctantly. Quentin and Mekiri exchanged a glance, shrugged their shoulders, and joined as well. For being such a large Samoharo, even by their standards, and a former prize fighter-turned therapist, Yoko was obsessed with group hugs.

"I can't breathe," Sam gasped from the center of the hug. Yoko broke it with some reluctance.

"Anyways, do you know what they call your group?" Quentin asked as everyone returned to their seats.

"I told you your silly competition with Joshua would have consequences you wouldn't like," Sam muttered to Alex.

"Is the name of the group something horrible?" Kasumi asked.

"The Pack," Quentin replied.

"Ugh, that's awful!" Alex, Sam, and Kasumi exclaimed in unison.

"There are others, some worse than that, but there is

another that is more popular," Hunt added.

"I'm afraid to ask," Sam said.

"The Band of the Greywolf," Quentin replied. Behind him the Professor was trying hard to keep from laughing.

"That ain't half bad," Alex said, restraining a smirk.

"There is more data about you and your actions. You are moving from urban legends to actual ones," Quentin said with a beaming smile. He was clearly proud of his childhood friend.

"No offense, but I don't want to know more about that," Alex replied, at that point beet red. "You and I know that murcana is an urban legend by now. Officially destroyed but crops up from time to time in hushed whispers. If your sociological theory about the evolution of legends is true, then murcana is still around. Do you know where we can get it? Because I don't think anything less strong than that can help a goddess' avatar to recover her mind and fix magick."

"There is only one place in the world that is rumored to still have the last remaining bone peyote and refined murcana: KorbyWorld." Quentin declared.

"Are you kidding?" Alex said, standing up from his chair with such haste that it screeched back. Alex had to snap a hand out to keep the chair from toppling.

Sam couldn't understand why Alex always got excited when talking about that theme park, and the cartoons that gave it origin. But she also found such childlike excitement coming from an adult endearing. It meant that the harrowing experience at the Chivalry Games hadn't changed him, and he was on the road to recovery with the aid of his therapist. She gave Yokoyawa an appreciative glance, who was sipping tea from a cup that looked decidedly tiny in his large hands while making small talk with Mekiri. "I have heard rumors that the frozen head of one of the founders was hidden in a secret lab beneath the Enchanted Fortress attraction. But never heard about murcana being related to Korbyworld."

"Well, the rumor is that one of the founders didn't imagine the characters and the stories for their cartoons, but got glimpses of them from the fabled Old Earth and its culture, by overdosing on murcana. And he kept doing that to the day he disappeared, leaving the whole thing to his partner. The crazier rumors..." Quentin replied.

"No offense, but we have taken long enough and need to keep moving. The longer we stay, the more we put you at risk. And the freefolk remain defenseless," Sam interjected. She toyed with the silver dragonclaw pendant as she bounced her right foot, just like her dad did when he was anxious. Every minute that passed was a minute that left the freefolk open to attacks from the cult of the Golden King.

"I will give you all my notes on the topic, if you promise to bring me back proof of existence and maybe more," Quentin replied, handing Alex a leather-bound notebook. "I don't trust digital backup anymore. I lost my thesis that way. I prefer to have physical copies now."

"Don't you want to come with us? We could use your expertise," Alex asked, hopeful.

"No offense, but I'm genre savvy enough to know that it will be extremely dangerous. I like adventure, but I'm just a regular guy," Quentin replied. "And right now, Yaha or not, you kinda are too."

"He's right," Sam added. Leave it to Quentin to be the voice of reason from the group of friends Alex had since high school. Sam loved them to pieces because they'd accepted her into their group after Ravenstone was destroyed. But they had the habit of indulging Alex in some of his hare-brained ideas, like the competition with Joshua to catch the largest number of criminals possible. Kasumi was often the same, but even she knew when to set limits. And Quentin was right, this was no place for an unpowered civilian. Sam didn't want to admit it, but she worried that Alex was closer to that category since almost losing his Gift. At some point he would get into a situation he wouldn't be able to get out of without his lost abilities. What Sam didn't want to admit, either, was that she was afraid of losing him. But leaving him behind wouldn't help. She was wondering what to do, when Kasumi, giving Sam a look that told her that she knew exactly what Sam was thinking, changed the topic back to what would be their next step.

"In any case. How are we going to get there? It's on the other side of the Lirian Ocean." Kasumi said. "We are close to hurricane season. A ship there would take days, if not weeks. I should know, I have done that trip from home to here once."

"That's a good point. If the Aethernet went down, the warptrains probably did as well, as both use the magick field to work," Yokoyawa noted. "Your species should really consider some alternate means to power them."

"I think we have to call Harland," Alex replied with a smile, stroking his chin. Sam knew the cues he broadcast when his mind came up with a plan.

"How? Phone lines are failing," Sam asked.

"Yeah, but the Figaro uses samoharo tech, remember?" Alex pointed out. "And as Sid told us once when he was drunk, they have something called satellites, orbiting or floating in the upper atmosphere from which the Figaro bounces the signal to our comms."

"Are you planning to ask them to pick us up?" Kasumi asked. "Aren't they in route to a secret mission and that's why Fionn asked Sam to help Culph?"

"Yes, they are. That's why I want to ask him to lend us his new pet project: The X-33 prototype. If you are okay with that course of action, Sam."

"The what?" Sam echoed, trying to make sense of what Alex was saying. She looked at Kasumi, whose eyes were wide and was shaking her head, as if she was telling Alex 'no'.

"The Figaro's little brother," Alex said with a wide grin.

Chapter 7
The Ballad of Haunted Beings

"*WHAT DID WE LEARN FROM* that clusterfuck?" Sid asked, rhetorically, as he threw another twig into the campfire. "Nothing. We never do. That's why these things keep happening."

The Figaro sat in a forest clearing thirty kilometers from the Tower of Salt, Riverol, and the town's angry inhabitants. The fuselage still had stains from rotten eggs and tomatoes, and one stone had knocked away one sensor antenna. Their whole group was sitting on blankets around the campfire, which Joshua had easily started, despite how wet the wood had been. The mood was sour, especially Sid's. Fionn had a suspicion of what was bothering the usually annoyed samoharo. He would be fooling himself if he didn't admit he shared Sid's concerns.

"Look at the bright side," Harland pointed out with a smile at the samoharo. "We got another clue, and we recruited two more allies."

"For heavens' sake!" Sid snapped. "You barely made it out alive. And not to mention how angry that mob got. For a second, I thought they would slay you right there, because they seemed to be very fond of those undead. And these two appearing?" The longer he ranted, the louder he got. Sid then pointed to Joshua and Livia. "No offense, but I don't believe in coincidences."

"What are you implying, samoharo?" Joshua stood up with a bolt of anger, but Gaby took his arms and gently pushed him back to his seat with a soothing smile.

"You know what I'm implying. You were gone for a year and half, you come back with a Tempest Blade, and you have a new boss, doing his dirty work in the Grasslands!" Sid shouted at Joshua. This time, Vivi had to hold him back.

And here I was thinking I'm the only one not fond of having a tovainar in the group... ex tovainar, Fionn corrected himself.

"How did you?" Joshua asked, befuddled. It was clear that Sid's revelation had taken him by surprise. Then again, the whole group already knew. Someone had let them know of Joshua's predicament, mostly, to assuage Kasumi's concern for her longtime friend's whereabouts.

"You know what?" Livia interrupted, getting up. "This is getting too heated for me and I'm not even part of your club, so if you'll excuse me, I'm going to sleep inside the ship, because unlike you, I'm being paid to find that Crown. I've already wasted too much time listening to your infighting and I don't like to sleep outdoors if I can help it. Goodnight, Gaby."

"Goodnight, Livia, thanks for all the help," Gaby said.

"Don't mention it, see ya later." Livia entered the Figaro. As soon as she left, everyone looked to Gaby.

"What?" Gaby asked. Fionn knew that look, she wasn't confused, she was sad.

"I think Sid has a point. If I were a betting man, I would say all of this will collapse before we reach the Crown," Fionn replied.

"Good thing I'm not a betting man anymore," Harland said. He did look confused. "Am I missing something?"

"Isn't it obvious?" Sid pleaded to Fionn. "Please tell me that you are not the only one thinking the same as me."

"I am," a guttural, deep voice replied from the darkness

of the forest behind the campfire. The flapping of a bird of prey rustled the tree branches and four pairs of eyes shone like red rubies, piercing the shadows. The shape of a large onyx falcon came into sight. It wasn't black, it was as if a void had eaten away every ray of light coming from the fire, casting a shadow over the whole place. The smell of sulfur filled the air. The temperature dropped several degrees.

Evil is cold, Fionn recalled.

"Who said that?" Sid glanced around nervously. Vivi stood up and made some gestures with her hands, until she remembered that magick was out of service.

"His new boss," Fionn replied, pointing at Joshua. "The stench of sulfur is unmistakable."

"I see my sibling can't keep her mouth shut, even with her silly riddles she says too much," the voice replied.

"Great, we are being visited by the devil now." Sid rolled his eyes. Gaby reached for her blades almost on instinct, but Fionn shook his head. She left them where they were. If the visitor wanted a fight, none of them would have much of a chance to act before it was too late. After all, this visitor had a twisted understanding of rules.

"The Judge," the voice corrected. "The Jailer if you prefer, Siddhartha. I'm here only because I have an alliance with your beloved goddess."

"We know," Fionn cut him off. He was not fond of that presence, having encountered it twice a century ago. And it was the same presence he felt in his recurring nightmares about being trapped in a labyrinth on the upper layer of the Infinity Pits, a nightmare that had haunted him the very moment he woke up in pain from the burns of the explosion that had bestowed him the Gift. It was a presence Fionn had unable to shake since. The vision at the Tower of Salt had only made the memory more vivid. He hated it because he suspected the Judge was doing it on purpose.

Gods and their games. I really hate them, Fionn thought.

"What do you want?" Gaby asked, standing up next to Fionn. She wasn't intimidated by the presence in the least, and that made him love her even more, if that was possible.

"Aside from congratulating you for dealing with the undead remains of Gifted people, blowing up the only thing that kept them from rising now that the Golden King is flexing his necromantic skills; I have to let you know that your only chance to reach the Crown is before the next lunar eclipse, tomorrow. Try not to get killed before that by being the usual goody two shoes you think you are."

"How do we know you are telling us the truth?" Harland asked, staring at the ruby eyes.

Fionn studied his friend.Harland wasn't afraid, either, but seemed to be exhausted if the slouch of his shoulders was any indication.

"I'm not a trickster like my sibling, I will tell you only what you must know. And as Joshua can tell you, I do honor my deals and alliances. See you in another moment, Joshua, if you survive... Ah, that's right, it doesn't matter. At the end, everyone faces the Judge."

The ruby eyes exploded in a flock of smaller onyx falcons that rustled the trees and flew away toward the north. The oppressive shadow that the presence held over the place lifted and the fire in the middle of the camp burst back to life.

"How nice of him to come in person," Sid replied, shivering. "And being so melodramatic."

"That was not him in person, it was just a projection," Joshua explained, releasing a long-held breath. "Ben Erra, his avatar, is nowhere near here. If he were, the smell and the coldness would be the least disturbing thing."

"I hate to say this, but the red glowing eyes were right.

A lesson you three need to learn, before you get us killed," Sid said, "is that you can't trust everyone, you can't save everyone. Especially those that don't want to be saved. And that goes double for those that see you with envy or contempt."

"That's a very cynical outlook," Harland replied.

"I know," Sid continued as Vivi took a seat next to him. He paused and took her hand. "But it is reality, as sucky as it sounds. At some point in life, you need to learn to triage who to save, or you risk burning out. And you, Fionn, know I'm right."

"I know. I don't like it, but I know," Fionn replied. He hated that Sid was right.

"But why?" Gaby asked.

"I agree with the samoharo," Joshua added. "They won't see you as an ally. At best, they will see you as a hypocrite, using your power to feel better about yourself. At worst, as a conqueror bent on taking away what they perceive as a peaceful way to obtain what they want. Why do you think Meteora is the mess it has been for centuries? Or why the Grasslands is not as unified as the Core? People are people, they have short sights. And it seems that the Southern regions suffer from that. For them, the Golden King is a better option for their own particular ends."

"Things shouldn't be that way," Harland interjected. The weight on his shoulders increased as much as his resolve.

"Maybe when you become President of Theia you can change that. For now, we need to focus on the mission to find and destroy that crown and then stop the Golden King. The rest will sort out in time, or it won't. But at least it won't be under the yoke of that abomination," Joshua concluded.

"That may be," Fionn said. "But I disagree. My old man used to say that the biggest problem in this world is that no one wants to help each other. And he was right. But that has to change. And being that change is how I lived my whole life and will keep doing till my last breath. And I believe, Sid, that you think the same, even if it's begrudgingly. You have showed me nothing but that since day one."

"Your personal code is like a contagious itch," Sid retorted with a sigh. "Alex is the same, probably got it from Ywain. And Sam got it from you. But, as I said, I hope it doesn't get us killed. I prefer the living legend part."

"I think we should rest," Gaby interjected. It was clear she was ending this conversation one way or another. "Calm down and keep our minds clear."

One of the handheld comms Sid had taken from the cockpit, which looked less like a cellphone and more like a turtle shell, began to vibrate. Fionn was confused how it was possible, since most communications used the magick energy field to transport the signal, and that field was apparently gone, yet the comms of the Figaro seemed to work.

Samoharo tech, most likely.

Sid flipped the cover of the comms handheld and answered the call. The way his face shifted from annoyed to worry and the haste he passed the comms to Harland, told Fionn everything he needed to know: bad news from either Sam or Alex.

"Oh boy," Harland said with a grimace.

† † †

"So, now we know why magick is not working," Vivi said as she dropped on the blanket that served as her seat, took off her glasses and rested her head in her hands, exhausted. "The Trickster Goddess is gone. The freefolk are defenseless."

Gaby empathized with Vivi. This put her people at risk with the Golden King on the rise. She was sure Sam was having similar thoughts. Worst of all, Fionn was most likely sharing those thoughts. Which probably compounded the inner maelstrom he'd been combating ever since Sophia had passed away. She loved the dunderhead, but good with processing feelings, he wasn't. That's why she hadn't been able to open up just yet about her other concerns, like she had done with her best friend.

"How is that possible?" Harland asked. "She *is* a goddess."

"Technically, Mekiri is an avatar, no different from the Dark Father," Joshua explained. "They are part of the god, the one they use to communicate with us. As Alex and Sam proved before, they are not indestructible."

"So basically, someone unplugged her from whatever the godly equivalent of the Aethernet server is for her," Sid surmised. "Just great. What now? Should we drop the search for the Crown and go with them? Split, rearrange? Fionn, what do you say? You are awfully silent. It's bad when you are silent."

Fionn bit his lip and stroked his chin, looking down to the ground. Gaby knew that look and had a decent guess of what he was thinking right now. His "papa wolf" instincts were kicking in. It was better to stop this before Fionn did something stupid and compromised the whole mission.

"Fionn, can I have a word in private with you?" Gaby pushed Fionn away from the campfire. The mood was too tense; tempers were running hot. And the call had done nothing to defuse the situation. If anything, it had made Fionn restless. And while Fionn usually kept a cold mind during crisis situations, things were piling up on him, which Gaby knew, would cloud his judgment.

"Look, I know that your first instinct is to go and interfere with Sam's mission," Gaby said, "but you need to let her do it on her own."

"I'm not just worried about her. I'm worried about

Alex, too; he is not in good shape. And I can't afford to lose more people right now."

"Alex will be fine. You are not thinking clearly," Gaby took his hand and squeezed it with enough force to crush a rock. "You know what, I have a story to tell you."

"We don't have time," Fionn complained. But she was not going to have any of that.

"Tough luck, because you are going to listen to me," Gaby dragged Fionn to the access ramp of the Figaro's cargo bay.

"You want to know why I trust Alex so much, as he trusts me, despite some of our latest fights? I will tell you why. It was back in high school. I was retaking physics because I had failed the subject the previous year. There I was: This skinny, braces wearing sixteen-year-old that could bench press a compact car, back at school after the whole incursion thing. After that, and given that I was still the new student at school, I tried to keep a low profile. I even dyed my hair a shade darker than it is now and wore an oversized stellar print hoodie.

"I had been back for two weeks, sitting alone in that classroom as everyone ignored me, when Alex entered the room alongside Quentin. Alex at that time was a bed hair, chubby, fifteen-year-old kid with anger issues trying to hold it together amidst the merging process and what was a clear mental breakdown. I'm not sure who, but someone threw a ball of paper at his face. And I swear I saw Alex's eyes glowing for a second, ready to let loose once more. But he kept it cool, on his own.

"Then our eyes met, and he smiled. A part of me prayed that he would stay away, I didn't want to be connected to the kid that despite having saved a lot of classmates during the worst incursion of recent decades, was still bullied. Even the teachers bullied him, the archery team dropped him because they thought he was a danger."

"What? Were they serious? Did he take Yaha to school? Or you and your blades?" Fionn's eyes were wide.

"Of course not!" Gaby replied. "What kind of irresponsible idiot allows a teenager to bring a weapon to school? It was already bad that we owned those Blades being underage. Anyways, he must have guessed what I was thinking, for he gave me a faint smile. And I just had to return the smile, because it was breaking my heart. He just needed a bit of empathy. To hell with what others might think.

"He took a seat next to me and spent most of the class staring at the wall behind me, his gaze lost as his head rested in his arms. The teacher was an asshole, he kept mocking him and all the other survivors. And he kept asking increasingly difficult questions, which Alex answered with ease despite not paying attention. Remember, this is a guy that is so bad at math that he can't keep straight how many years we have been friends. And yet every question he answered came with a slight flash on his irises, the Gift at work.

"The class ended and none of us moved from our chairs. Quentin went for food for Alex, as I tried to finish copying the equation on the whiteboard. I finished, picked up my stuff and once we were alone, I looked at him. His eyes were red as he had been trying to hold it together. He stood up and came close to me and told me the most heartbreaking thing I have heard to this day, 'Thank you for smiling back and not making me feel alone.' Every single classmate, even those that he had saved, had ostracized him, just because he was ill. I threw fear away and hugged him as hard as I could, as he sobbed. I noticed Quentin closing the door and telling someone that the room had a faulty fuse, so no one used it. And we stood there talking until the school closed.

"At that point, he and I were the only ones that could understand what the other was going through, the way the Gift messes with your brain, even worse at that age. Our bodies were still growing.

"He walked me back to my place, as I was living mostly alone, just with one aide sent by my grandparents, who wanted to keep me as far as possible from my father until my emancipation trial was finalized. And he stayed at my place, helping me with my physics homework and I helped him with his Core language one. Back then he could barely speak a word of Core and I was trying to teach him, with my accent and all."

"I knew about your family situation, but his?" Fionn tilted his head, looking at her quizzically.

"It wasn't as bad as he makes it sound, but it was not good either. Basically, his family blamed him for what happened and the legal mess that my grandpa helped to clean up, with a lot of bribes I have to say. He spent most of his time at my place, and then Sid joined in and the three of us became this sort of family. Sid was the older brother, and we became the younger siblings. Alex is the brother I never had and I'm more of a sister than his own has been. The only rule we ever had was to not interfere with our respective sentimental relationships unless we asked for it. And as he stabilized, and I became more open at school, joining the band, he applied for the hoops team and together he and Sid built my guitar, the one you've seen, for my seventeen birthday. I even stayed a year after graduating so I could watch Alex play his last tournament and I ended up being his date for prom.

"Every time I needed a shoulder to cry on, he has been there, no questions asked. He even threatened my father to get him away from me once at college. A man who is *known* for his shady deals. Alex didn't even flinch. And every time he has gotten his heart broken, or had family fights, or his mental health has been shaky, I have been there for him. That's why I felt so guilty last year for not noticing his depression, even if I know it's not my fault."

"And that's why when I needed help to decipher the disappearance of Hunt and the circlet, you took me to him," Fionn said with a nod, understanding.

"He was the one who convinced me to go and meet you at the Harris to travel with you after our adventure," Gaby said, and smiled at Fionn.

"I didn't know all of this," Fionn replied, pensive. "Just to think that you went through all that despite what you did for others."

"And I'm sure Sam went through her own issues while you were isolating every day because of your PTSD and you didn't notice. Growing up is not easy. Especially not for us. But we survived. And that's why I'm sure that whatever problem they might face in their mission, they will find a way to solve it. Sam is as stubborn and willful as you. And Alex has never let me down. Do I worry because his Gift is almost gone? Yes, he is my family. But I know him, he will always find a way. And with Sam at his side, those two are a team I wouldn't want to fight against. And they have Kasumi and Yoko as support. You have to re-learn to trust your teammates if you plan to lead us when things get difficult. Right now, we are fighting a war on two fronts, and both affect the Freefolk. I get it, but you know good and well that if the Golden King gets that Crown first that not being able to cast spells will become the second most important problem."

"When did you become so wise?" Fionn said, and hugged her.

"I have always been, you just are catching up." Gaby winked at him.

They hugged for a minute, until Fionn sighed and broke the embrace.

"You know what, you are right," Fionn said. "I'm too emotionally involved in this to think clearly. That's why I want you to lead this mission instead of me. I will follow you, no questions asked."

"Me?" Gaby pushed him back, her stomach fluttering, swallowing hard. "Why? I'm not a leader. I don't know how to make the right call."

"You do. Like when you decided to give Alex that smile back. If you think about it, that changed everything and that's why we are here, right now. I don't believe in things like destiny or fate, but I do believe in you. And I'm honest enough to know when I'm not in the right mindset."

"And if I have doubts?" Gaby pursed her lips. She was worried about what path to take, how to know which choice was the right one. She did not have the same amount of decision-making experience as Fionn did.

"I will always listen to them and if you want suggestions, you will have them. Because I'm your family too, now."

"I hope I don't disappoint you."

"You never will," Fionn said as he looked up to the darkening skies. The smell of rain hung in the air. "Let's rest for now, as you suggested. It seems like it's going to rain."

† † †

"We should have waited until the skies cleared," Harland complained.

Rain was down pouring as the Figaro flew northeast across the skies of Ionis toward the mountainous forests where Mon Caern was located. The clouds were dark, heavy with the water they carried. Sid had tried to take the Figaro above the clouds, but they were thick and seemed endless, with wind currents causing severe turbulence. Lightning cracked across the sky in a constant series of blinding flashes. They were still far from the Thunderplains, known for spectacular lightning displays, and from where the Alliance got part of their electrical power before the current conflict. Sid suspected that this weather was not a natural occurrence. With magick all wonky, that wasn't out of the realm of possibility.

"I'm surprised you can fly with this rain," Fionn said.

"After flying inside a sentient hurricane, this is a bite of a cupcake," Sid replied. At least this storm wasn't actively trying to crush the ship. It just slowed its flight with the heavy curtain of water that forced Sid to rely more on his instruments than on the visibility outside the cockpit windows. Lightning struck close to the Figaro, the resulting shockwave rocking the ship.

"That was close," Harland muttered, looking up. The lights in the cockpit began to flicker, followed by a shrill sound, coming from the console.

"What's with that alarm?" Gaby asked.

Sid flipped several switches and looked at the indicators on the console. He pushed the yoke to lower the ship.

"Power failure. We will have to make an emergency landing," Sid replied calmly. After the past three years, pushing the original Figaro and the current model to the limits of endurance, with crashes at least twice a week, a power failure where he still had total control of the ship and enough power to land has a walk in the park.

"Emergency as in proper procedure or as in frantic yelling and waving of arms," Gaby asked.

"The first one. For a change." Harland rolled his eyes as he helped Sid land the ship. As they dropped below the clouds a forest spread out beneath them, the tops of the tallest trees were just a few meters under the ship.

"What happened?" Fionn asked.

"I'm not sure, probably that last lightning fried something just by being close." Sid gave Fionn a knowing look. "One of those odd coincidences."

"How far are we from Mon Caern?" Gaby asked, already up from her seat, trusting the stabilizers to keep her from falling.

"A couple of hours by foot if we land around here," Sid replied, taking the Figaro parallel to a rustic road. There was enough power left to slow the ship to a hover, which would allow them to jump off the cargo bay and onto the road. "I will leave you here while I take the Figaro deep into the forest to hide it."

"Okay, everyone, get ready to disembark," Gaby said.

"You have enough power for that?" Harland turned toward Sid. As always, the man that was his partner was more worried about the integrity of the ship than anything else. At least it was a good sign that he trusted that Sid would be fine.

"The Figaro still has like five minutes of power, more than enough if you hurry up."

"I'm staying with you," Vivi offered.

"Don't forget your ponchos, it's pouring outside!" Sid exclaimed as the group walked toward the cargo bay.

† † †

The Figaro sat inside a large cave. Its mouth opened onto a small plateau on the side of a hill, tall enough to keep large animals away from the ship but still covered by the foliage of the thick forest. It was the kind of forest a sane person wouldn't wander through. But Sid was not worried about sane people. It was the insane ones that worried him.

"I knew it," Sid said as he opened a wall panel in the corridor of the Figaro. Several power relays had been ripped from their sockets by brute force. There were scorch marks, indicating that fire, or at least extreme heat had been used to damage the relays before being ripped away, which was not an easy task for a regular human. Which meant that no one aboard was a regular human and *that* meant...

"Sabotage?" Vivi asked.

"And a bad one at that. Ripping out those relays affects the energy flow and partially discharges the dragon core. But since the combat against the Bestial, I took the precaution of adding redundant energy backups, batteries to recharge the core, and hidden spare parts, just in case," Sid explained as he knocked on the middle of another wall and a secret compartment opened, with several spare parts neatly arranged. "This means Fionn might win the bet. He will be insufferable for the next week."

"You expected this to happen?" Vivi was clearly confused. "You suspect someone? So that's what that fight last night was about? I knew you were faking it."

"Not expected, but suspected, yes. No, I wasn't faking my annoyance at Joshua. I don't trust him, nor his new boss. To be honest, none of us wanted it to be true. But given the kind of mission and the kind of opponents we are dealing with you learn quickly to plan ahead. As we say, becoming adventure savvy. You get used to that."

Sid grabbed the spare relays, handing them to Vivi. He began to replace the torn ones with care. Inserting them into the connectors required a peculiar mix of finesse and just the right amount of strength to not snap the metal ends. Sid was so focused on the task at hand, the tip of his tongue peeked out in concentration.

"What happened at the Games really shook you all," Vivi said as she gave him back the relays, one by one.

"Yeah," Sid replied, closing the panel. He returned to the cockpit as the rain outside seemed to subside. He pressed a few buttons and grabbed a small metallic cylinder with a flashing red light that he pocketed. "Okay, I will leave the AI running the self-repair protocol to finish the calibrations of the new relays and the recharging of the dragon core. And set up the unwanted visitors' deterrent."

"The one you used that night at the park? And what's with the cylinder?" Vivi asked.

"Activating a beacon. Only Alex, Harland, an employee of the Foundation, and myself have a tracking transponder for it. Just a precaution. This is very advanced tech that shouldn't fall in the wrong hands."

"Sometimes I think you are in love with your ship," Vivi said, and rolled her eyes.

"My lawyer told me to never answer that." Sid replied, offering her a pair of flat sole boots. "These are spares from Sam, so they should fit you. We might be walking for a while and as much as I love you seeing you wearing heels, it will be uncomfortable. Let's go, the rest are waiting, and it will get dark soon."

"You don't have a lawyer." Vivi grabbed the boots and went into the medical bay to change.

† † †

"This is a part of the world I've never been to," Sid said out of the blue while they walked on a road that looked more like a well-worn trail. The ground was still wet from the rain that had just ended. Thunder could be heard far away, the clouds carried away by westward winds. The sun was beginning to set on the horizon. "And I hate awkward silence. It feels like something will jump from the woods and stab me in the back. Harland, what can our lore master tell us of our next destination?"

"Planning to produce another audio guide for the Figaro?" Fionn asked, stifling a laugh. He gave a knowing look to Gaby, who understood its meaning. The failure on the Figaro had been no coincidence. She sighed.

"Say what you want, Fionn," Sid replied with a huff. "But the guide for Kyôkatô was useful, so why not? I might as well earn some extra money from these crazy globe-trotting adventures. Financing the Figaro is not cheap."

Fionn laughed even harder.

"Why do you laugh?" Gaby asked him with a crooked smile. It was the first time in days she had seen him laugh that way. It melted her heart.

"Because Sid and Harland are more alike than any of them want to admit," Fionn explained.

"Uh?" Sid uttered, confused.

"I told him last week that I would like to write a world reference book of lore and culture, based on what I've seen these years," Harland replied.

"Then go on," Joshua said. Gaby noticed that he was keeping an eye on everyone, clutching the Fury. He seemed to be stressed out, more tense than normal. "I could use a good talk about the folklore of autumn to keep my mind occupied."

"Fine, fine. Mon Caern is famous for various reasons, you know, as cultural and commercial trading post in a privileged position. But what I find more interesting is the stories surrounding two of its most famous citizens that somehow got intertwined. And that I think, is important to our quest." Harland began to explain when Gaby could no longer hold back a yawn, stopping short. "Am I boring you?"

"Not at all, just the lack of proper sleep hitting. Please go on," Gaby replied, waving her hand in a circle to keep him talking. It was better than the unnerving silence of the forest surrounding the road, or the thoughts brewing in her mind, connecting dots across the history of the Sisters of Mercy and what she had learned in the past years.

"Centuries ago, during the Age of Strife, there was this King, by the name Matthias. He was the man behind the construction of Mon Caern as we know it today, growing it from a fortified trading post to a bustling mercantile city with the outer wall and the inner wall protecting the castle complex of Vitous. He was a fair and just king for the most part. But it is said that he committed two transgressions that cursed him afterwards. The first one is not well known, just that he had procured something that aided him to conquer and pacify the region in less than a year, for no army could oppose him, and no trap could take him by surprise, as if destiny itself was on his side."

"That doesn't sound like an easy feat to pull," Fionn interjected.

"It wasn't. That's the thing," Harland replied matter-of-factly. "Whatever he did was attributed to dark magick, a pact with a demon, or stealing a treasure from the Infinity Pits themselves, no text is clear on that."

The mere mention of the Infinity Pits caused visible shudders on Fionn. Gaby had grown used to his nightmares awakening him in the middle of the night, for they were too vivid to be just that, and yet he was certain he had never set a foot in the place. Gaby hoped he never would.

"In any case, that set in motion the second transgression: His marriage with a princess from a neighboring realm. Said realm had been his bitter enemy, and Matthias vanquished it by force, murdering through subterfuge its king, all the royal family, and stealing the princess. Texts are not clear if said princess was the daughter or the bride of the murdered king, versions vary from author to author."

"As long as they were not the same," Vivi shuddered.

"Personally," Harland continued. "I'm inclined to believe the bride version, for most texts say that the lady in question possessed an otherworldly beauty and presence, closer to the fae or the Akeleth themselves. And that her origins were neither entirely human nor freefolk. A few versions say that her first husband was the one that had stolen her from her people and that Matthias had rescued her."

"So much confusion and contradiction," Sid complained. "You are dumping a whole encyclopedia on us!" "Learning won't kill you, Sid," Harland laughed. "And that's the thing with legends and folklore, as time passes, the changes in versions start to pile up. In any case, this dark-haired beauty rarely uttered a word and was never seen smiling, not that I can blame her. All agree that Matthias was smitten by her and was for all purposes a dutiful husband. And she was nice to the people. That's why the curse hit hard when it arrived. The couple had a baby, but his birth caused such a stir for he was called a 'demon', which caused lean times on the population, until a saint convinced the king to build Mon Caern's famous Clocktower to atone his sins and a small chapel nearby to contain the demonic object. It is said that the King later on sent his builders to raise a second Clocktower in a far distant land. But it wasn't enough and eventually the king got ousted by a powerful, scheming nobleman, a duke. The former king was imprisoned and died, but due to his initial pact, he became a powerful wraith that eventually joined the Wyld Hunt both of us know very well."

"Unfortunately," Fionn added, ruefull.

"Who is the other person you mentioned before, the princess?" Gaby asked.

"No, the saint that convinced the king to build the Clocktower," Harland replied. "Sylvie Braneh was a famous astronomer who spent a lot of her life disguised as a man, in order to get her scientific discoveries about celestial measurements and dimensional rifts accepted. Once her identity was discovered, she was forced to become a nun. But by then, the Clocktower and the chapel had already been built and the demonic object contained, improving things for the population, as she predicted, which made the people of Mon Caern accept her back. She died at a really old age, her body was placed at the chapel, where it is said that kept performing minor miracles. The only person, aside Matthias, who came out for worse from this, was the clockmaker. Driven mad, the clockmaker took the ultimate revenge, throwing himself into his extraordinary work of art, gumming up the clock's gears and ending his own life in one stroke. In doing so, he cursed the clock. All who tried to fix it would either go insane or die. So, they just left it alone. It only works when there is an eclipse, lunar or solar. Like the one that takes place tonight."

"What about the princess? What happened to her?" Livia asked.

"No one knows. After the birth of her child, there are no more mentions of her. She might have died during childbirth or suffered some other tragedy. Maybe she returned to her people. Who knows? She might even have entered the Tempest itself. Back then, with the Wyld Hunt on the loose, that wasn't unheard of. That ended when Fionn's dad bound them with the Silver Horn," Harland explained.

"Fraog's tale? That's your father?" Joshua asked Fionn.

"Yes, but the tale widely exaggerates a lot of things. And is not respectful of my father's memory," Fionn said sharply, swatting at the air with disdain.

"Maybe something like that will happen to our adventures in the future," Sid said, and laughed.

"No thanks," Joshua said. "I concur with Fionn. I don't want my life turned into a child's fairy tale, or worse, a novel by some hack writer aiming to make it into an animated series."

"Going back to the task at hand," Gaby said. "Do you think the Crown is there? Let's assume that the object Matthias used was the Crown. How did it return here after the latest use, centuries later? And more importantly, why didn't we come here first? You could have saved us time!"

"I agree," Livia added. "We could have found the Crown by now and be on our way back to Saint Lucy."

Harland slowed and looked up to the sky, his breathing measured, as if he was arranging his thoughts. "To answer your first question, some mystical objects seem to have a will of their own and enough power to appear where they wish. Case in point: Yaha. Didn't you say once that Alex didn't have the sword before the incursion and yet somehow it went from his grandfather's house to where he was, hundreds of kilometers away?" Harland asked.

"Yes," Gaby nodded. "I still don't know how that happened. Alex doesn't know."

"Same case with Black Fang. The place where its draconic namesake fell is not the same lake that held it for centuries until Fionn fished it out. They are not even on the same landmass." Harland smiled.

Knowing him, he must be embarrassed for not thinking of Mon Caern first, Gaby thought, but she couldn't blame him. He and Fionn had much on their minds with that project of theirs and Harland had taken the southern region's split from the Alliance hard, despite all his diplomatic effort at the Games.

"Which takes me to your second question: all I just told you about Matthias is a legend, not verified. But we did know that the last verified sighting of the Crown was the Tower of Salt. We work with the information we have at the time."

"In any case, we are on our way there," Fionn interrupted as he unsheathed Black Fang. The Blade's glow ignited, providing illumination. Gaby suspected he had done that to spare Harland some embarrassment. When it came to these things, Harland had always said that he lived under the shadow of his father, who not only created the Foundation, but had been an explorer and sage extraordinaire. The comparison made him feel like a child again, he had once told her. And right now, Gaby could understand the feeling more than she had wanted to. "This trail is somewhat treacherous and light is dimming. I will take the vanguard. Sid, Vivi and Gaby in the middle, Joshua and Livia, the rearguard. Harland, come with me."

"How do you know this road?" Joshua asked.

"Because I remember this part of the trail. I walked it once with Izia," Fionn replied, sadness in his voice.

The mention of Izia made Gaby slow her walk, as her limbs and her chest seemed to acquire the weight of the world.

† † †

"You seem a little bit frustrated with travelling by foot," Vivi said to Gaby. Sid was walking between them, which offered an interesting contrast due to the height difference between the ladies and the samoharo.

"I have known you for more than a decade," Sid interjected. "You are not bothered by having to reach Mon Caern by foot. You are bothered because you are not good at dealing with memories and this is resurfacing something that happened not long ago, with him."

Sid nodded toward Fionn, who was walking alongside Harland, several meters ahead, in total silence, lost in his thoughts, as he led the group along the paved road surrounded by the Paidragh lamps. Fireflies flew closer to the lamps, attracted by their lights. But with magick haywire, their powers to ward off creatures of mystical nature were gone. Hence why Fionn was using Black Fang as improvised deterrent to the fae.

"I'm that obvious?" Gaby asked, her cheeks flushing a vibrant tomato red.

"As I said, I have known you since you were a teenager," Sid replied. "You can trust us, what's going on?"

Gaby sighed. "It might sound silly, or selfish, but... this improvised road trip reminds me of the first one I made with Fionn three years ago. It was fun, exciting, we got to know each other, but..."

"Things didn't always go as you imagined?" Vivi asked this time, with a knowing look.

"Please don't get me wrong. Fionn is... the love of my life and an awesome person. So nothing bad happened, just weird."

"Weird, weird? Or kinky-weird?" Sid replied with a sly smile, obtaining as a result a stern glare from both Gaby and Vivi. "Sorry, wrong question."

"For your information," Gaby replied, and she punched Sid on the arm before continuing, "it was the former. When you walk into a town where they still remember him from the war. Or the decade after that, when he was travelling with... Izia. They see him as a folk hero. A legend. They always ask him for help. And by extension, me. And I don't mind helping but..."

"And aside the issue of the comparison with his deceased wife, who was a legend in her own right, let me guess: He never says no," Vivi said, nodding.

"Exactly. No matter the risk," Gaby said.

"Maybe that's why they still remember him," Vivi said. "Because at the heart of it, he is that kind of person. That's a folk hero for you. And I guess, because I haven't known you for long, as Sam has, that's one of the reasons why you love him."

"Pretty much. I know, it sounds dumb."

Vivi and Sid exchanged looks. It was a curious thing to see the relationship between them. Gaby had been so busy for the past two years that she had never stopped to consider that her friends had a life outside the proverbial pages. And it was in that way that one of her closest friends had developed a relationship with the older woman—who he had met under very dangerous circumstances—to the point they could talk with just a look. There were questions Gaby had about how an interspecies relationship worked in this case, because unlike the Freefolk-Human relationships, where both shared similar genetic makeup, Samoharo were a whole different matter. Not to mention the cultural differences. But somehow they had made their relationship work to the point that they acted like an old married couple. Gaby was kinda jealous, wondering if she would ever have that with Fionn, considering how hectic their lives were at the best of times, and the whole reincarnation thing that kept popping up in the back of her mind. How much of their relationship was truly theirs and how much just happened that way because that was the way it had been if she truly was Izia's... Gaby shook her head, trying to push that from the forefront of her mind. Maybe she was overthinking things.

"It's not dumb," Vivi broke the silence. "If you don't mind me talking about this subject."

"Not at all, I could use the opinion of someone with a bit more experience. Female experience," Gaby clarified. "As much as I love Sam as family, she and I don't agree on some things. And Kasumi is a whole other issue. She is more like one of the boys."

"I would feel offended that my experience is worthless," Sid said, "but I'm mature enough to know this is not about me. And Vivi is a good listener."

"Ha!" Gaby laughed. "Mature?"

"More than Alex." Sid lifted his chin with pride.

"Anyone is more mature than Alex. Regardless, please continue, Vivi."

"Look, for you... Fionn is your heartmate, your friend, your lover, your partner, your confidant of most things. He's your safe place. Like you are his after you brought him back from his ennui," Vivi explained. "But for others, especially the freefolk, he is something else entirely, it's a folk hero, a figure larger than life, borderline mythical.

He is the one that always advocated for us before King Castlemartell, the one that finally got us most of our ancestral lands back after centuries. I would say that, aside from the elders, who don't like people they can't control, he is on the same level as Asherah, Mekiri the librarian, and probably below Ishtaru, the Trickster Goddess."

Gaby looked at Vivi, wondering if she should say something about Mekiri's actual identity. Vivi must have guessed her thoughts.

"I know about the dual identity. Most senior freefolk lecturers at Ravenstone knew, or at least suspected. She is not what you would call reserved."

"That's the understatement of the century," Sid said with a laugh.

"And there are records," Vivi added. "But I digress. My point is, for most of the world, he is *the* Hero. And from what Sid has told me, and from what I saw at the diplomatic talks during the Chivalry Games, that's a heavy burden on his shoulders. One, mind you, he never asked for, but is carrying anyways. And here is the thing: you are quickly becoming the same for our people."

"What?" Gaby asked, her thoughts grinding to a halt.

"Why do you think the elders asked you to represent us during the Games? You are the Goldenhart, the Lady-o'-war that helped to destroy the ancient enemy of the Bestial. Some of my younger former students had posters of you over their beds."

Gaby winced at that image, her cheeks flushing. She wasn't used to that level of adoration, even being a musician.

"You might be of human origins," Vivi continued, "but the Freefolk already consider you one of us. Damn, I even saw you with awe the first time I met you properly. And the last time that happened was with Izia, so comparisons between both of you will be, unfortunately, unavoidable.

But here is the thing you should remember: you are you. All of that fame, if you like, you earned it through your choices and actions. And for what little time I've spent with you, you are an awesome person that I'm glad to have met. You are an inspiration," Vivi finished with a smile.

"Which adds a burden on its own," Sid added. "So, no. What you are feeling is not dumb. But if we can give you some advice, this is something you need to talk with him about sooner or later. Because if life has taught us something, later arrives before you think, leaving you without the opportunity to talk. Just like almost happened to us with Alex. That was a close call and we almost lost him."

"You are right," Gaby said, with a deep breath.

"For now, enjoy your status as legendary hero, destroyer of the Titan of Earth. Your trading cards are pretty expensive in the secondary market," Sid continued, showing her one of the cards he was carrying in his pocket, framed inside a clear flexible resin. He had one of Alex and one of Sam as well.

"Trading cards?" Gaby examined the photo. "Oh, for Heaven's sake!"

Gaby was abruptly back to being that awkward sixteen-year-old girl trying to keep a low profile after being caught in the spotlight of recent events. The trading cards did not help ease that feeling.

† † †

The group crested a small hill and Fionn saw Mon Caern in the distance, coming to life as night fell. The tiny lights from houses and the Vitous castle complex at the center of the city appeared as fireflies. The wind carried the scent of ale, food, and fun. And yet, there was something else in the air that was making his legs restless and tightened his chest. He sheathed Black Fang and pointed to the crowd below, slowly moving toward the entrance of the city. They were coming from the nearby villages and small towns to participate in the local harvest festival. "Let's mix with them. I don't think it's advisable to call attention to ourselves. Mon Caern is near the disputed lands and their guards must be a bit tense right now."

As they advanced, Fionn noticed the pennants decorating the road, as well as the posters about the eclipse. Last time he had been here it was the start of the year, and the roads were covered in snow. Izia and he had had to drink mulled wine aplenty at an inn to recover their body heat. He was about to ask Harland, for he wasn't familiar with this celebration, but Sid beat him. The samoharo, always observant, had noticed too.

"Are all this people coming here for a festival about a lunar eclipse, something that happens with some frequency?" Sid asked. Samoharo took very seriously the study of the celestial bodies, for it was the basis for their 'path finding' techniques as well as their religious beliefs. And probably their particular blood magick as well, for they claimed that like the dragons, their species was born from a star. An eclipse for them was not that impressive.

"Yes. And now, it seems that the eclipse has coincided with the Harvest Festival of the region. I guess is a twofer," Harland replied with a shrug.

"Humans have the weirdest celebrations," Sid said.

"We are a few days from All Souls Night as well, and you celebrate that," Vivi pointed out.

"She got you there," Harland said, and laughed.

"Yeah, but that one makes sense. Souls come back for candies. Not for an eclipse."

The group had crossed the entrance of the outer wall and was moving through the main street toward the castle complex. The city of Mon Caern was a mix between ancient *striferal* and Post Great War architecture, with modernist abstract sculptures contrasting with the houses and buildings, most of them empty. It seemed that while the whole city was decorated for the festival, the actual celebration would take place inside the inner walls of the castle complex. As they reached the main stone bridge that would take them inside, a group of guards intercepted them, blocking their path.

"Fionn Estel," the captain of the guards said. She was wearing a more elaborate helmet than the rest. "The Duke wants to speak with you and Mr. Rickman."

"The Duke? What? How?" Harland asked confused.

"New surveillance system, installed a few weeks ago," The captain explained. "Please come with us. All of you."

The guards circled them in a tight formation, forcing them to follow them.

"I don't like this," Fionn murmured.

"And here we go again," Sid replied with a sigh.

Chapter 8
Beautiful World, Wicked Games

SAM WATCHED THE SMALL BLACK V-shaped ship taking off as it left them not far from the secondary entrance to the Korbyworld complex.

"Seems that Scud is in a hurry to get the ship back to the Foundation," Sam said, stretching. They had spent most of their time aboard the tiny, not so comfortable X-33 stealth scout ship asleep. It had been built by the Foundation, based on Sid's specs, and supervised by Alex's university friends, Birm and Andrea. Still a prototype, not many people could fly it. That was why after Alex's call to Harland, he had called the Foundation and ordered Scud to head to Hunt's house to pick them up and take them to Korbyworld. Scud was a Meemech samoharo, like Yokoyawa, and was related to him and Sid, and was also the drummer for Hildebrandtia, Gaby's band. Sam mused how their circle of friends and acquaintances was actually rather small. Then again, there were only three certified pilots for the human-samoharo airships, and all three of them were the only samoharos outside the Hegemony. And only two humans were on track to get that certification: Harland and, to Sam's worry, Alex. But given that Alex had helped to build the first Figaro, that was just matter of time.

"Why do you say that?" Alex asked, yawning. At that

point, Sam was wondering how Alex was still able to talk, with how tired he looked. With any luck, the cold sea breeze would keep him awake until they reached the hotel.

Seems that therapy hasn't knocked out of him that dumb habit of him pushing past his limits, she thought.

"Because he could have left us closer to the hotel, instead dropping us in the middle of an empty parking lot," Sam said.

"Scud is a young samoharo," Yokoyawa explained, picking up the bags. "He is still anxious about losing his job and being forced to return to the Hegemony, especially as the tour with Hildebrandtia got cancelled. That's all."

"Can they force him to go back?" Kasumi asked.

"Not really; once you are out, you are out. But again, he is young and new in the human-freefolk world," Yoko shrugged. "Besides, he has picked up too many human-freefolk habits to be functional in samoharo society again. I should know, I'm using sneakers now."

"Also, I don't think Harland wanted his secret project to be damaged or even exposed. He was very adamant about that," Alex added. "That's why he dropped us here, this early, far for prying eyes."

"I can't believe that you convinced the boss to lend us that," Kasumi said. "It's his new pet project. And you know how he gets with those."

"I can be persuasive when I want," Alex said with a sly smile. "Besides when it comes to Sam, he never says no. He is like her doting uncle. And this is your mission."

"And given the track record of the Figaro, his concerns about damaging the ship are not entirely unfounded," Sam conceded. "Yeah, it's better if Scud takes it back as soon as possible."

"Harland's concerns or Sid's?" Kasumi asked, stifling a laugh.

"Siddhartha has been oddly attached to that ship since we were hatchlings," Yoko mused.

"I can't get used to you calling him Siddhartha." Alex shook his head.

"I can't use his actual samoharo name, you wouldn't be able to pronounce it," Yoko explained. "Same with mine. You lack the tongue flexibility. People from the Straits get by with basic samoharo, but there are physical limits to the sounds you can pronounce. Besides..."

"Excuse me, but we are losing track of why we are here," Sam interrupted. "And as you said, this is my mission. So please, Alex get us up to speed with Quentin's notes."

"Well, as you know," Alex began, pulling out the notes to skim as he walked. Kasumi had to guide him by placing her hands on his shoulders, or else he was liable to walk into a lamppost. "Korbyworld was built by Korby Studios founders and lifetime friends Ray Korben and Wally Byne, after they secured funding from several sponsors, including a family name I've never seen in the masthead, the Zay family, to create the park based on the cartoons and characters they animated, starting one of the megacorps on par with the Galfano family, and the premiere entertainment provider of the Core regions. Korbyworld was planned as the city of the future first, then as a theme park. The Coyoli archipelago was chose for its location within the Lirian Ocean, the main warptrain lines crossing it, major trade routes, and the fact that the archipelago had been deserted for most of the previous century."

"Spare us the leaflet information, get to the point," Sam said, gesticulating with her right hand, indicating for Alex to move on.

"That's where I'm going. The location. The Coyoli archipelago is not that far from Albarrán Point."

"And?"

"That's where the most recent incursions this side of the world have taken place, including the one where I got the Gift, and met Sid and Gaby." Alex explained.

Sam bit her lip, wanting to kick herself mentally. *How could I have forgotten about that?* she thought. But if Alex had noticed her misstep, he was gracious enough to ignore it.

"It's not a coincidence it is near the samoharo hegemony territory either. That's why the Fraternity of Gadol tested the puncher here. The whole region is ripe with ley lines and energy wells, that's why it attracts *predacors* every time there is an earthquake. And here is where things start to get weird. Hear this out: the archipelago was once home to a pirate kingdom, related to the ancient realm of Mon Caern, people that had fled here after a plague hit the city."

"But Mon Caern is on the other side of Ionis, in the Northern Peaks, that join with the Jagged Mountains, far from to the ocean," Sam said. She was trying to make sense of how a landlocked kingdom from the Age of Strife, around the first century ADoD, was related to a pirate kingdom on the other side of the world.

"Apparently, the thing connecting both realms is the language, and the Clocktowers that both the major island and Staromac, the city state where Mon Caern used to be, have. They have similar design and construction techniques. Even the clockwork is identical and according to Quentin's notes, are synchronized."

"That's noticeable," Kasumi said, "But hardly weird."

"That's the thing." Alex kept reading. "After the fall of the pirate kingdom, of which no name has been found, nothing of the old infrastructure here survived but that Clocktower, which was believed to be haunted and cursed, for people disappeared inside, even after it was included into part of the hotel that was here before the park was built. The islands changed hands between the Straits, the Kuni, and many others, but no one managed to control most of the islands until the KorbyWorld project got started and an influx of immigrants joined the few locals to form the current population. The Clocktower is still standing."

"And where is that Clocktower now?" Sam asked.

"You won't believe it, but that's the best part." Alex smiled as his eyes shone with a glint of mischief. Sam recognized that smile. She had seen it only a few times, in this park actually, almost a year ago, when Alex made her take that ride over and over because it was his favorite and he always wanted to visit it. She had felt sick as soon as she'd put a foot on it. The place was full of magick energies, but she hadn't noticed at the time because Alex had been annoying her. Now karma was back.

"No frikking way," Sam said with nothing less than despair.

"Yeah, the awesome Haunted Clocktower Ride!"

†††

The room that Kasumi had gotten them through the Foundation's business account was not fit to be called something so... normal. It was almost a penthouse with two separate bedrooms, huge samoharo sized beds, a living room with a large screen TV, a half bathroom and a full one with shower and jacuzzi. The center table in the suite's foyer had wax candles in the shape of fruits as well as actual fruit baskets. There were an old bow and arrow hanging from the wall, probably only useful as decoration and not for shooting. The best part was the terrace, which overlooked not only the artificial lake that served as pool, but the actual parks in the distance. It was as if the room had been designed to see both the solar eclipse taking place the next day as well as the fireworks show for the

Eclipse Festival later that night.

As Yoko set the bags on the floor, Sam returned to her earlier conversation with Alex.

"So, what Quentin's telling us is that there is this urban legend about how Wally Byne didn't actually die in a car accident after the park's first year of operation after he overdosed on murcana, which he'd used to come up with his zany cartoon concepts, but instead got his head put in a jar, which is hidden in a subterranean room, below the Fairy Fortress. And the company still gets their cartoon ideas from him there, which is why there is still murcana there, but Byne's head is guarded by monstrous versions of the characters and monsters he created, produced by a hellish machine and made from ink?" Sam concluded, dropping herself into the comfy bed.

"Yeah," Alex replied. "That's a nice summary. Which, judging by your tone of voice, you think it is completely stupid?"

"Well," Kasumi interjected as she dropped onto the bed, where she grabbed Sam's right hand. Kasumi patted the mattress, indicating for Alex to sit next to her and took his left hand. "It does seem that way."

"Only fools know the hidden truths beneath the misinformation created to provoke mayhem," Mekiri whispered. Then she looked at them. "I'm hungry."

"What was that?" Alex asked.

"It seems another random memory resurfacing," Yoko said. "But I'm not sure what she is trying to say."

"She is right on both accounts," Sam said. "It's stupid enough to be real. Or at least, have some grain of truth. I hate to say this because I dislike conspiracy theories, but this one might actually be true. Which means we have to investigate that. But before that, you better order some room service. Mekiri is not the only one hungry, and we can't go to the restaurant because well, she is liable to attract unwanted attention."

"Okay, I will order." Alex stood up.

"Meanwhile, I'm going to take a bath," Sam said, pointing at both Alex and Kasumi, who stared at her with smiles plastered on their faces. It was funny to see how both reacted the same way to certain things. "Alone! And use it to meditate and maybe take a peek at how the magick is looking inside the Tempest to give me an idea of what we are facing."

"Spoilsport," Kasumi mumbled.

"I'm going to take a nap on the terrace," Yoko said, then he pointed to Mekiri. "Keep an eye on our Grace, she is liable to try to eat the wax fruit instead of the actual fruit."

"Wax goes up, wax goes down," Mekiri said, juggling two candle wax grapepears.

† † †

A knock on the door startled Alex awake. The warmth of the noon sun was relaxing, so much so he'd drifted off. Kasumi was playing a card game with Mekiri, communicating with her through hand signs. Kasumi had turned off her hearing aids, having she said she needed a reprieve from all the noise. Sam was still in the bathroom and Yoko was snoring on the terrace.

"It's open!" Alex yawned. "I just hope we can find the murcana soon, so I can take a real rest," Alex mumbled as the attendant entered the room.

At the mention of the word 'murcana', the attendant stopped dead in his tracks. He stared at Alex, then to Kasumi, then to Mekiri. His eyes widened, as if he recognized them, and then shoved the cart away and ran out of the room.

"Why is he running?" Mekiri asked. "Did he forget the mustard?"

Kasumi darted out of the door and after the attendant in a mad dash through the hotel.

As Kasumi ran after the man, Alex—still yawning—grabbed the bow and arrows decorating the wall and turned to his right, walking toward the open window. On his way he passed by the fruit bowl and stabbed two of the arrows into two medium size oranges. He then stood on the balcony, set one arrow on the floor and nocked the other, pulling back the bowstring. He glanced at the banners hanging from a flagpole from the next building. There was a swift breeze, which made him adjust the angle at which he was aiming the tip of the arrow. As Alex waited for a few seconds, the attendant came running out of the building and toward the empty mall between the hotel buildings.

He winked at Mekiri, who was looking at him with an amused smile.

Alex released the arrow and bent to pick up the second arrow, nocked it and released it in a quick, fluid sequence of movements. Both arrows spiraled in the air, as the oranges' weight shifted their balance. The fruit-tipped arrows descended from their ascending curve, hitting the attendant, one in the back of the head and the other in the back of the knee, knocking him to the ground. The oranges split from the impact, allowing the arrows to fall to the ground with a soft clang. Alex pumped his fist in a celebratory gesture. "Yes! I still got it."

"You know that could have seriously injured that guy," Yoko said from behind, his arms crossed as he rested against the frame of the balcony's door. He was clearly amused.

"To be fair I was aiming at the space between his shoulders, but he was slower than I expected."

Kasumi approached the prone attendant and looked back at Alex, signing in what could be politely translated as, "What the Pits were you thinking, dunderhead! You could have killed him."

She grabbed the arrows in one hand and picked up the guy with her other arm, using her full hand to balance him.

Alex went to the fruit bowl, grabbed an apple-lime and started to eat it, then said to Yoko, "Remind me to not piss off Kasumi again, I forgot that she is super strong for someone with her short stature."

As Kasumi returned with the half-conscious attendant, Sam came out of the bathroom. She wore only a bathrobe, her hair glowing lilac, and left a dripping trail as she joined them.

"I take the astral trip didn't go as planned," Alex observed.

"It is worse than I thought," Sam replied as she sat down on the sofa. Kasumi tied the attendant to a chair, using a bed sheet as an improvised rope.

"What did you see?" Alex asked Sam.

"The Tempest is in disarray."

"Wello," Yoko said, trying to break the tension. "That's why it's called the Tempest and not the Calm or the Relaxed."

Sam looked at him with a mix of amusement and annoyance.

Alex almost choked with the comment, so Kasumi had to hit him hard on the back—in fact a tad harder than necessary, making him spit out the piece of fruit he'd been chewing.

"Naming conventions aside," Sam continued. "The flow of magick is disrupted there. After floating around for a while, which felt like ages, the only thing I could find was a huge ball of energy, chained by some kind of mystical bonds that had akeleth sigils similar to those at the professor's house."

"What does that mean?" Alex asked. "You are the only one that can know right now, because well, Mekiri is in no condition to explain."

He pointed with his thumb to Mekiri who was on the bed, folding sheets of paper she found in the room's desk into silly paper hats.

"Truth is," Sam replied. "I don't know. So, yeah, we need to find the murcana and so she can recover her mind if we are gonna fix this."

"We will have to wait until that guy comes to his senses—hopefully without a concussion after the stunt you just pulled, Alex—to see why he ran away after hearing us talking about murcana."

"But it worked," Alex replied with his trademark goofy smile.

"That's not the point," Kasumi said, shaking her head, trying not to smile.

"I liked the arrow shooting spectacle," Mekiri said, without looking at them.

"What arrow shooting spectacle?" Sam asked Alex, tapping her foot on the floor, her arms crossed, and her fox ears wiggling in annoyance. "Care to explain?"

"Yes, Alex," Kasumi added, grinning. "Care to explain?"

"I..." he stammered, his face turning as red as the cherries in the fruit bowl.

† † †

The PA system in the Mystical Adventure Park blasted music from recent hits. Sam couldn't avoid smiling when she heard the lyrics of the song currently being played, and the voice in the recording:

A beautiful Game!
We are stuck in circles.
Can't break apart,

Can't stay with you.
Like chasing a ball
Swept by the winds.
Aimlessly.
A beautiful game.
Which is our future!

"She was angry at Fionn when she wrote that song, uh?" Alex said.

"I think they had an argument that week," Sam replied. "I don't want to think much about that."

"It's a weird situation," Kasumi added.

"I can think of weirder ones," Alex mumbled, looking at both women. "Anyway, the entrance should be here. If what the attendant said was right, we should find a service door in an empty building near the path that connects this park with the Movie Action Park."

"I suggest Yoko waits for us there," Sam said. "If you don't mind of course. I'm not sure how much space we will have inside to move around."

"Fine, take all the fun of discovery with you," Yoko complained.

"It's times like this when I see the resemblance to Sid," Alex mused.

†††

The corridor was pitch black. The sound of dripping broke the silence through which they moved. Alex led the way, Yaha's subdued light the only thing that kept them from tripping over one another or their surroundings. Sam was in the middle, on babysitter duty, leading Mekiri. Kasumi was in the back.

How did the attendant make his way through this place? Sam wondered.

"I can't believe we managed to enter what should

be the most secure place on the island, with such ease," Kasumi whispered.

"The invisibility spell works," Sam replied in hushed tones. Before they'd entered the passage, Sam had cast a modified version of the invisibility spell she had used to hide from the Creeping Chaos at the SkySpire. The spell didn't make them invisible to each other, or to someone standing really close. Rather, it obscured from any sensory organ of any creature or machine.

"Plus, the best way to keep something hidden, is to leave it in the open and don't attract attention with dozens of guards?"

"Or perhaps it is also because of those things," Alex said in low voice, pointing to twelve creatures made of ink resting inside alcoves on the walls. One resembled a large mantis with six legs and pincers. It was some sort of *predacor*. All of them were rhythmically swaying from side to side, half in trance, half asleep.

"Imagination is wonderful, but a trap as well," Mekiri whispered.

"That... is unnerving," Sam said.

"There is the door, we should move faster now," Alex suggested, pointing to the end of the corridor. Sam couldn't agree more. The whole place was making her nauseous. Maybe the curse was real after all.

The four of them approached a heavy metal door, barred by an ancient lock. Kasumi unsheathed Breaker and with a swift movement, she cut the lock in two. Alex caught the fragments, so as to not disturb the sleeping inky creatures. They entered the subterranean lab.

It was a small space. Smaller than what Sam had expected from Quentin's notes. It looked more like an ancient alchemist dungeon than a modern chemistry lab. There were glowing spineless cacti growing in flowerpots. Massive glass tubes with brass bands reinforcing them.

Inside, there were inky liquids Sam didn't dare to guess what they were made of, as well as a couple of floating bone fragments that didn't assuage her fears.

"We need to be careful," Alex said. He closed the lab door and barred it with a heavy metal girder. "This is not the best place to get caught in a fight. I'm of not much use."

"Worst case scenario, I'm here to protect you," Kasumi said to him with a wink.

"This smells funky and spunky," Mekiri said, pointing to a vial with an oily black liquid. "I don't want to drink it."

It was sitting on a desk next to a floating head in a large jar. The head seemed to be decades old, half rotten. The skull had been cracked open and the milky dead eyes were staring at the void. The face had a rictus of pain froze on it. Next to it was a framed photo of Wally Byne and an unknown man, whose staring eyes made Sam feel uneasy.

"What do you think, Alex?" Sam asked. Alex got closer to the desk and sniffed the vial.

"If you're asking about the smell, yes that's murcana. If you're asking about that," Alex replied, pointing to the jar, "I can't avoid feeling sad for him and wishing that this urban legend was nothing but a lie. What do you think really happened to him?"

"Maybe he wanted to retire and do his own thing, but his partners wouldn't let him," Kasumi suggested ruefully, an edge in her voice. "And I don't mean Ray Korben, but the guy that picture. Sherman Zay?"

BANG!

"What was that?" Kasumi asked.

BANG!

"I guess someone is at the door," Alex replied as he moved to the door in question.

BANG!

"The creatures?" Sam asked.

"Possibly. Or something worse," Alex replied as two

red dots appeared in the metal door's surface. The dots grew in size and the air filled with the smell of burning metal. "Aw, crap, they found us. In the creepiest, smallest room ever, below a theme park."

"We can't fight them here. Space is too tight," Kasumi declared, eyeing the back door. "Sam, do you have what we came for?"

"I think so," Sam replied, pocketing the vial. "Healing Mekiri will give us better odds against them. That is our priority right now."

"Then let's take this outside, heal her, and then we will fight," Kasumi replied, taking over the leadership role, clenching her fist around the hilt of Breaker.

"I will cover you, you get out first." Alex unsheathed Yaha as the others fled. As Alex turned to follow, he paused for a moment to take in the lab. The banging on the lab's door increased in intensity, the metal becoming taking on a red-hot glow as it warped under more and more by the second.

† † †

Yoko was standing idly beside the exit door to the tunnels, staring at his claws, bored out of his mind, as the same chirpy tune repeated over and over.

How that tune doesn't drive any visitor mad? he thought. *After the fiftieth loop, it is torture.*

The 'torture' was interrupted as one of the doors was blasted away by a spell, breaking Yokoyawa's train of thought. From the tunnel, Sam came running out, dragging Mekiri by the arm. Kasumi came second, her weapon unsheathed. Alex was nowhere to be seen. Yoko looked into the dark tunnel and saw a glowing blade approaching fast.

"Run!" Alex screamed as he bolted out the door. He skidded to a stop to close the door behind and followed

Sam, Mekiri, and Kasumi.

"What's going on?" Yoko asked as he ran after them.

"That!" Alex jerked his thumb over his shoulder. One of the creatures made of ink—a large one that resembled a mantis—and two acolytes blew up the door and chased after them. The five of them ran as fast as they could along the path that connected the two parks. Yoko noticed that the ink creature was reducing the distance between them. If this kept going on, they would be caught in a tough situation, so he made a decision.

"I will take the creature," Yoko said. "You four keep running, and I will catch up later!"

Yokoyawa stood back, growled at the creature and punched it in the head, dazing it. It roared in anger as the acolytes passed by. They seemed to be more concerned with catching the others.

The creatures roared a second time, straight into Yoko's face, the resulting gust of wind messing with his already messy hair.

"You could use some mints," Yoko said. "Damn! I'm speaking like Sid does. Human habits are contagious."

Yokoyawa ran toward the back lot between the parks, the creature hot on his heels.

Good thing I started wearing sneakers as Siddhartha suggested. Yokoyawa thought as he reached an open space with some abandoned warehouses. *This should be almost as easy as hunting hurgarths back home.*

Yokoyawa was counting on his years of experience hunting giant monsters. Ouslis was if anything, a continent full of dangerous creatures, some survivors from the original samoharo homeworld, some grown locally. And although they hunted them, they didn't kill said creatures, unless it was for food. Most of the time the samoharo just returned them to special locations where they could run free without hurting the population. This time, however,

Yoko would kill this thing without remorse.

Yokoyawa ran, luring the creature to an empty warehouse, far from any civilians. The inside of the warehouse was a large open space with wooden crates stacked haphazardly in piles around the room. Four large concrete pillars were spaced evenly in the warehouse to support the roof.

The creature stubbornly followed him. Once he had it inside, he unleashed the full force of the Stellar Ehécatl—the large, ancestral samoharo obsidian scimitar that was on par with a Tempest Blade—with well-placed slashes aimed at the creature's legs, hoping to slow the creature's movements. He ducked to almost floor level, evading the pincers from the creature. He ran toward one of the concrete pillars. With a single stroke he made a clean diagonal cut. The pillar began to slide under the weight.

Yoko then ran, sliding under the creature's tail and reached a second pillar, making a similar cut to the first. The tail swung back and Yoko jumped over it, landing on top of the tail and jumping from there toward the third pillar, cutting it as he came down. The creature's tail lashed again, knocking several crates his way. Yoko rolled to his side to avoid them, and he ran back to the front, where the creature's head was growling in anger. Yoko jumped again, dodging its pincer and with a backflip, which was on its own an amazing sight, seeing someone his height being able to do that with ease, cut the fourth pillar. He landed on the ground, placed his left hand on the pillar and gave it a gentle push. It slid down and that unbalanced the roof, making the other three pillars slide as well.

"Oops."

The roof collapsed on the creature as Yoko jumped backwards, avoiding the debris. The roof crushed the ink creature, leaving a large stain on the ground. Its head was still alive, so Yokoyawa pushed the Stellar Ehécatl into the skull through a gap between the neck plates. The head closed its eyes and dissolved in a puddle of ink as well. Yokoyawa pulled back the sword, swung it around a few times to get rid of the ink from the blade.

"Right, need to go back to help," Yoko said to himself, satisfied. He could only hope all the remaining fights, if any, were this easy.

I know, wishful thinking.

†††

"Keep moving! I will deal with this one!" Kasumi yelled as she stopped. Alex, Sam, and Mekiri kept running toward the entrance of the other park. They passed by a smoothie cart, from which Sam snatched one of the drinks as Alex threw a crumpled bill at the startled seller.

Kasumi twirled Breaker as one acolyte stopped in front of her. The path was empty of civilians, as many were already looking for a spot for the Eclipse Festival. That served her well, she could fight on her own terms against the creature. She knew Alex worried about her, more than necessary for being just friends. And part of that worry was because he had lost his powers, which fed his fear of losing her. Sam, despite what she said, acted the same, for exactly the same reason. Plus, she was the leader of this mission and that was adding extra pressure on her. After all, while Kasumi had defeated a Titan, her injuries had taken time to heal. And as much as Kasumi cared about those two on a deeper level, she had only admitted to herself their attitudes annoyed her. Even if they came from a place of love, the result wasn't too different from the jeers and jokes other demonhunters had played on her during training. And that made her blood boil like lava.

The acolyte took its sunglasses off and opened its eyes, unleashing the beam that had terrified Alex and Sam. Kasumi dodged it with alacrity. Focusing on her breathing and expanding the extra sense that every demonhunter trained to acquire, she could perceive the aura of the acolyte across the empty space. Kasumi noticed something, as she dodged beam after beam. The aura disappeared around the back area, as it was pushed forward to feed into the beam. It was a subtle thing that Alex could have noticed if he still had his powers, or Sam would have caught if she weren't so worried.

But that's why I'm here, to care for them, Kasumi thought with pride. Now, the matter was to get behind the acolyte, who aptly shot its beams to every spot Kasumi was trying to reach. Each impact left craters and scorch marks on the path and the walls. If Kasumi wasn't careful, that beam could punch through a wall and hit someone. She needed to stop it for a second or two.

I can stop it, a voice whispered into Kasumi's mind, and she smiled. The acolyte shot another beam and this time, Kasumi didn't dodge. Instead, she cut it with Breaker, which gave honor to its name by splitting the beam in two. That sent a forceful feedback to the acolyte, who lost its balance. It was in that split of a second in which Kasumi acted, jumping and running over the acolyte and landing behind it.

With a swift slash powered by a spin, Kasumi separated the head from the body.

One done, one more to go, she thought. Kasumi ran toward the park, trying to catch up with the rest and help them take down the remaining acolyte.

† † †

Alex, Sam, and Mekiri reached a small tent. They went inside to hide and to gain some time. Without losing a moment, Sam opened the flask with the murcana and poured its contents into the applelime smoothie, mixing everything with the bamboo straw.

"I hope the smoothie makes this taste better, Mekiri, so drink it now!"

"But it smells funky," Mekiri complained. "Like my brother's chamber after one of his parties."

"I don't want to know," Sam replied, forcing the drink into Mekiri's mouth. "This is for your own good, so forgive me, your grace."

"You better hurry up," Alex said from the tent's entrance. The acolyte had caught up to them and was taking its sunglasses off. "Aw, crap!" Alex exclaimed.

Alex saw the Acolyte's eyes charging, first as a tiny ember in a totally back eye. As the ember grew, each eye turned into pure light, ready to unleash their beams toward Sam and Mekiri. Alex ran to stand between the two women and the Acolyte, who unleashed its energy beams. By instinct, and truthfully, without any other option, Alex unsheathed Yaha and held the blade horizontally, the flat side of the blade taking the brunt of the attack.

To his surprise, as Alex had expected to be burnt to a crisp—or at the very least to have his chest perforated by that beam—Yaha held strong. The mystical nature of the oldest Tempest Blade in existence proved once more to be immutable, impervious to even time. If anything, the blade was getting hot as it glowed with the orange hue of metal being held in a fire.

Alex's grip on Yaha was white-knuckle. The flat side of the blade currently not receiving the blast was braced by his left forearm, covered by his bracer. The smell of burnt leather reached his nose. He dug his heels in to avoid being pushed back. Holding his ground against the acolyte, who kept advancing with a slow, deliberate pace, was proving to be as tough as or perhaps tougher than stopping a runaway train barehanded. Then again, back then he still had most of his Gift. Maybe Yaha would hold on without problem, but himself? That was a another story.

"Whatever you are doing, Sam!" he yelled. "Better hurry. I'm not sure how long I can hold on!"

"I'm working on it!" she replied. Alex saw through the corner of his eye Sam making Mekiri drink the murcana smoothie. The color was off-putting, but it was the only way to make the taste bearable. Mekiri struggled to finish the drink but kept chugging. As she did, realization dawned in her eyes. Her absent gaze was being replaced by some sort of recognition.

Alex was trying to come up with a plan to get out of his current situation. Every time he tried to push away or deflect the beam, the acolyte simply gave one more step and increased the strength of the surprising concussive force that the beam carried with it. The pain in his arm was getting worse and the smell of burnt leather and kinetic polymer from the bracer was flooding his nose. Yaha was almost white, and sparks were cascading away. They had a few seconds at best before he had to somehow be fast enough to dodge. And even then, there was no after. His mind was utterly dry of ideas. Alex whispered an old prayer from the Straits, to one of the messengers known to help you when you get into a pickle.

"*Santa patrona de los desamparados,*
Que nos guías incluso en los días más obscuros
Te pido auxilio y socorro
Para salir avante de este trance
Y... what was next?"

Alex couldn't remember the next part of the prayer. He couldn't remember when he had last spoken that prayer, probably the day he got the Gift. And while a part of him said that it was in poor taste to ask for help after all these years, unlike Fionn who did it every time before a battle, the dread invading his chest was strong enough to make him reconsider. It was the third time in his life he was this afraid.

"I heard you," Mekiri said as she stood up behind him, placing her right hand on his left shoulder. Mekiri then grabbed Sam by the arm with her left hand and three glowing circles of white light and floating runes encased them. "It will be alright."

The acolyte pushed even harder, the bream increasing its diameter and the pain and heat became unbearable. Alex closed his eyes and the next thing he knew was that his stomach was churning as he was thrown into the weird space that was the Tempest.

†††

Unlike Alex, Kasumi wasn't scared by the acolytes, even less so after killing one. Uncontrolled fear was the worst enemy for someone whose main job was to hunt demons and monsters, as well as exorcise evil spirits from mortal locations. Fear was useful to keep you grounded, but you couldn't let it run amok. She would take down all the acolytes chasing them on her own if needed, to keep her loved ones safe.

Tracking the last acolyte was easy, she just had to follow the fleeing civilians. But the cacophony of the screams mixed with the theme park noises was too distracting. She turned off her hearing aids and focused on her demon-hunter senses to "see" the spiritual energy of the beings around her. When she felt it the acolyte's energy sent goosebumps through her arms. The energy increased as she got closer. When Kasumi finally arrived, she saw Alex and the acolyte in front of a tent. Alex was pinned by the acolyte, holding off the beams with Yaha, straining under the assault. Behind Alex, Sam was trying to get Mekiri to drink what looked like a smoothie.

Kasumi darted toward the acolyte. Her options were limited, separating his head from his neck would cause the beams to carelessly shoot toward the unaware civilians or toward Sam and Mekiri. She quickly came up with an idea, after all, she was the wielder of the Tempest Blade famous for cutting anything and everything: Breaker. Jumping on a trashcan, Kasumi raised Breaker, and taking advantage of the reach offered by the naginata, descended with a fierce, keen slash that passed through the acolyte.

As Kasumi landed, she saw out of the corner of her eye Alex whispering something and Mekiri standing up, as a light engulfed her, Sam and Alex.

The acolyte's eyes flickered as the beam disappeared. The eyeballs turned black as a thin, string-like stream of black ichor ran from the top of its head, down its cheeks and chin. The acolyte's face then fell away, as Breaker had sliced its head from top to bottom, separating the face from the rest of the skull. The strike had been precise enough to sever whatever connected the eyes to the head and thus powered the beams. Without that connection, the beam ceased to exist as the face fell to the ground, followed by the brain. The body of the acolyte dropped to the ground and Kasumi stabbed it in the back, piercing the heart in one swift movement to end the threat.

"Gruesome cut," Yoko said as he arrived, gasping for air after crossing the whole park in a few minutes.

"The creature?" Kasumi asked.

"Dead, like the acolyte," Yoko replied as he turned to where Alex, Sam and Mekiri had been standing until a few seconds ago. "Where are they?"

"Do you think we were too late?" Kasumi asked as she ran toward the spot, followed by Yokoyawa. She clutched Breaker's hilt as a sour taste invaded her mouth.

"No," Yoko said, as he kneeled, examining the ground. "These marks are similar to Sam's teleportation spell. Except more precise. This wasn't Sam's doing."

"Mekiri?"

"It's a good bet."

"If she teleported them, where did they go?"

"I'm not sure," Yoko replied. "But I think they are far away from that."

Yokoyawa pointed toward the Haunted Clocktower, where Sherman Zay was just now walking onto stage for the inauguration of the Eclipse Festival.

"I dunno about you," Kasumi said, her blood boiling, "but I'm planning to stop that guy from hurting anyone else. Do you want in?"

Yoko sighed. "We have to stall him, at least."

"I'm planning to kill him," Kasumi replied as she tightened the cords of her sneakers. "I just hope that wherever Sam and Alex are, they're safe."

† † †

Alex vomited his guts out third time in less than a week. Wherever he was, he felt slightly lighter. The room smelled of age and dust, and was barely lit by a thin, far away light. He was disoriented but didn't feel like he was in danger. He grabbed Yaha, which was lying next to him, and stood up. Alex clutched his stomach with his left arm, still pulsing in pain, as he walked toward the light. It got brighter and he found Sam illuminated by a ring of light as she stared at a window.

"I think I will never get used to teleporting around, where are we?"

"I don't know, this doesn't make any sense," Sam replied as she pointed to the window.

"What doesn't make any sense?"

Through the window, Alex saw a view few humans in all of history had seen. A view that sent chills down his spine. Alex's eyes widened, and he leaned in closer to the window. Anything that he had gone through in the last days, including the sensation of nausea disappeared before the awe-inspiring view he was witnessing.

Through the window he saw a round, blue planet with brown and green landmasses, covered by white and grey clouds, through which lighting danced. The aurora was hitting the upper hemisphere of the globe. The planet was surrounded by dust rings, orbiting at leisurely pace in the void of outer space. Stars peppered the dark background. On the far side of the planet, the Round Moon was almost aligned with the star that humans called Sun and the free-folk, following akeleth tradition called Tawa Seridia.

"Sam, I've a feeling we're not in Theia anymore," Alex muttered.

"Welcome to my home," Mekiri said from the shadows.

Chapter 9
Wrong End of the Sword

*"**AND TO THE RIGHT, WE** have a magnificent painting by the master of the Renewal period, Buornotti the
Third,"* the Duke of Mon Caern chattered along, showing
off a large painting depicting a bucolic scene from the forest below the hills that surrounded ancient city.

The Duke had insisted, to the point of it being an
order, on giving them a private tour through his personal
chambers of the castle. Few people outside government
officials of the city-state had walked through these
hallowed halls in years. Sid, Viv and Joshua had excused
themselves, instead preferring to stay on the terrace, from
where they could watch the festival below the battlements
and admire the eclipse. Gaby found it odd how many
guards still followed them on every step of the tour.

Their steps echoed through the mostly empty rooms
and hallways. Gaby was listening as Harland discussed
the history of the castle with the Duke. Fionn was looking
around, absentminded. Livia was walking slowly behind
them, the gap between her and the rest increasing slowly
but surely. The castle had been built during the Age of
Strife, after the Fall of Umo, a century After the Death of
the Dragons. But it had been refurbished in more recent
times, with the baroque excess of the pre-Great War
period, placing marble floors and gold leaf cover on nearly

every surface. No wall was left empty, paintings from every classical era hung from them. There was no actual curation of the collection, but Gaby suspected that was the point, not a show of taste, but of financial and political power, for Mon Caern controlled one of the largest trade routes across the middle of the continent.

"A castle of cards," Fionn muttered, breaking her train of thought. Gaby knew exactly what he was referring to though, for financial or political power collapsed easily when times got tough. As they turned a corner after the bathrooms, Gaby slowed her pace, as she was receiving psychometric visions from the past, all the intrigues, betrayals and murders that had taken place in the castle. Like her sudden visions of the future, or her dreams, Gaby was beginning to understand that these psychometric readings activated as some sort of warning sense.

A vision from the recent past, earlier that day hit her so hard and out of the blue, that she had to stop for a second, to regain her composure.

"Something is wrong here," Gaby whispered to Fionn, who had stayed behind with her, and the ever-watchful guards keeping them company as Harland and the Duke continued with their talk.

"What do you mean?" Fionn replied, matching her whisper.

"I'm getting a vision from earlier today. Someone was here talking with the Duke. He is hiding something."

"I believe you," Fionn said. "But we need more evidence than a vision."

"What about a half-consumed cigar hidden in a flowerpot?" Gaby replied as she passed by the flowerpot and grabbed something from it without being noticed. She had recognized the cigar from her vision, but holding it in her hands confirmed it. The brand and the smell were familiar to her, for it had been part of her early childhood. Even the way the butt had been chewed was all too familiar. "That bastard," Gaby growled, narrowing her eyes. One guard looked at her, suspicious, but did nothing.

"So much for no smoking allowed in the premises." Fionn received the cigar butt offered by Gaby as proof. "These will kill you fast, though. Now, by your reaction, you know who left this behind."

"This is the brand my father likes to smoke. It's expensive and hard to buy, only subscribers to the maker's black book can get them. And with whom is dear papa working now?"

"Dewart, which means that he could be working as well for the Golden King. You were right. The bastard." Fionn clenched his fist with such force that he crushed the cigar butt. He leaned toward Gaby. "Look around discreetly, I think your former friend just bailed on us after we turned that corner near the bathrooms."

"So, you won the bet," Gaby sighed. She had to give it to Fionn, experience did make a difference. Since Doncelles mentioned he had sent an agent to search for the Crown, and said agent was a former Sister of Mercy, Fionn had suspected that said person might be a double-agent. It had been a tactic used during the Great War, one that even Fionn's squad had used. Sid had reached a similar conclusion and had tried to flush the truth to win the bet early, while Gaby wanted to give Livia the benefit of the doubt. Then again, her former friend had been the one that had taken her place and become the favorite of the Sisters when Gaby had refused to kill her and had been thrown into the chasm below the academy. The past kept reaching her, whether Gaby wanted to leave it behind or not. "What now? I doubt the Duke will allow us to search for the Crown."

"Harland and I will keep them distracted, while you search for it. Sound good?"

"Sounds like a plan," Gaby said with a shrug.

"Be careful," Fionn said, his tone betraying his usual concern. Gaby knew that in her case, said concern was tenfold. It was both sweet and annoying.

"I always am. Remind me, who is the one saving the others most of the time?" She gave him her trademark crooked smile.

Fionn stifled a laugh. "Point."

† † †

The Duke led Fionn, Harland, and Gaby into the depths of the castle, toward his office chambers. Gaby began to fall behind on purpose, examining a series of paintings that she had seen once in a textbook at school.

"Ahem… Your grace," Fionn said, clearing his throat. "I have to say that this is an impressive place. The woodwork, the carvings, the fatuousness of the place. Even the preparations for the festival, so detailed. I'm impressed."

Gaby knew that tone of voice. The edge there bordered between diplomatic and sarcastic. Except that Fionn wasn't being diplomatic. Harland and Fionn exchanged looks. Harland smiled.

"Thank you," The Duke replied. "I've tried my best to keep our city state as safe and fruitful as possible."

"More credit to you," Harland replied. "One would have a hard time considering that Mon Caern is so close to a conflict zone and all the trade routes have been disrupted in the region for quite some time."

"Indeed," Fionn continued. "One would think that being in that situation would wreck the economy of the place, and the gold leaf decors would have been gone long ago."

"What are you implying?" The Duke asked, his voice betraying annoyance at the direction the conversation was taking.

"What the Greywolf and I are implying," Harland replied, "is that there is something else going on here and you are just stalling for time."

"Stalling? Nonsense," the Duke defended himself.

"Maybe not stalling," Fionn said, raising his voice. The sudden volume startled the guards enough that they focused their sight on him, offering a small distraction for Gaby. "But hiding the fact that we are not the first guests you entertained today."

"Are you accusing me of something?" the Duke asked. His face burned in anger.

"I don't know," Fionn continued as he spotted Gaby slowly slipping around the corner. "Should I?"

"With what authority?" The Duke challenged, holding Fionn's gaze with a matched glare..

"I'm still a Justicar under Her Majesty's service," Fionn returned the stare, unflinching.

"Haven't you seen the news?" the Duke said, and smiled. He was mocking Fionn. "She just passed away, a true shame."

Fionn's hand went straight to Black Fang's hilt, but Harland placed his hand over his friend's.

"I think this is a discussion that would be better served by a glass of wine at your office, Your Grace."

"Yes, that's a good idea," Fionn replied. If he could, he strike the man's head from his shoulders in one slash.

† † †

Gaby slipped through an unguarded window, as the guards were busy keeping an eye on Fionn. That was not the kind of distraction she needed to slip away, but it would work. Under other circumstances she would be worried about the guards being ready to attack, but mostly because Fionn would trounce them, starting a diplomatic incident. But since Harland was with him, he would find a way to keep things from escalating. She had to give it to Livia: the way she had evaded everyone, only to be nowhere to be found, was most impressive. Of their generation at the Sisters of Mercy, Livia had always been number one when it came to stealth and disappearing. If Gaby didn't know better, it would seem like magick. But no, it was pure skill.

Gaby used the shadows covering the façade to walk over the ledge and reach a pipe that descended to the next level.

Child's play, Gaby thought. She then looked down.

"Dangerous child's play," she muttered as she started her descent, disappearing into the shadows of the night.

Number two when it came to stealth and disappearing, however, had been Gaby.

† † †

"I did meet with the envoys from the Golden King this morning, before your arrival," the Duke said matter-of-factly as he took a seat behind his desk.

Fionn did his best to keep his face impassive. He couldn't believe the Duke had met with the same people who'd created the Titans crisis *and* was behind the NLP party.

"And what did the envoys want?" asked Harland.

"They offered me a peace treaty," the Duke replied, his tone making it sound like the deal of the century. "They asked that Mon Caern remain neutral and allow their armies to use the roads that pass through the Northern Peaks."

Fionn realized that would allow their army to avoid the Longhorn Valley, which was now a fortified pass after a century of building and reinforcements.

"Neutral? You mean secede from the Free Alliance," Harland said.

"Yes, though we would not join the Confederacy."

"But that goes against the Alliance charter. And common sense," Fionn said, trying to keep the anger and incredulity from his voice. "Sooner or later that neutrality agreement won't keep you or your city safe. And you know it."

"The situation changes every moment, thus we can't be beholden to the status quo of a charter written a century ago," the Duke said.

That was what the old saying "The wrong end of the sword" usually meant, a chaotic situation where the changes were so sudden and unpredictable, that you ended up facing the wrong end of the sword, the pointy end, when you expected to be the one holding the sword. Fionn was used to seeing the situation change and how those holding the right end found the roles reversed by unforeseen events. Like your opponent managing to steal your sword from your hand. He had done that several times in the past. Maybe it could work this time as well.

"And you are considering it," Fionn said, knuckles white as his fist clenched in his lap.

"If this proposal aids with my end goal, yes!" the Duke replied, clearly annoyed. "I don't want war on my city."

"But you don't mind war passing by, do you? What of the northern city states? It's too much of a coincidence now that the Alliance is mourning the Queen's passing. Not even a week from that, Heavens!" Harland interjected, throwing up his hands. "And what is your main goal? To take the Golden King's offer so they leave this city alone? Do you realize how dumb that sounds? Once you let them in, they will never go. One day you will die from a mysterious illness, then, they will take over, and then one by one they will start going after your citizens, the freefolk first, if they are still here and you didn't expel them beforehand as a 'peace condition.' Later those that don't follow their religious beliefs, or their political alignments and so on and on, until your city is nothing but a graveyard. Peace of the graves."

"You can't be sure that will happen," the Duke said.

"He might, or might not," Fionn replied. "I have seen this scenario played out before. The problem with 'the ends justify the means' is that at some point said end will be used to justify bigger atrocities. There must be a line at some point. Otherwise, your cause is not just anymore, and you are no better than the bad guys you are trying to stop from destroying your city."

"You say that, but I have heard of your reputation," the Duke hissed at Fionn, his eyes full of anger and poison. "The One-Man Army. The Greywolf. How many have died at your hands for your end of protecting your people? Was not the so-called Withered King your friend? One of the Founders of the Alliance turned into a monster? Or that's what you told everyone?"

"Too many, unfortunately," Fionn replied with sadness, but holding the Duke's stare, unflinching. "And each one of them, including the Withered King, who had been my friend, is a heavy burden on my heart. I have never claimed to be a perfect paragon. I'm just telling you the history, so your people don't have to relive it."

"Fionn might not be perfect," Harland said, pushing his friend away and standing in front of him. Fionn recognized the act for what it was: Harland was shielding him from the verbal attack, the same way he protected Harland from physical harm. "He does have blood in his hands, and he is the first to admit and regret it. Yet, he is a good person, and the only thing I have seen from him in the past years is that when someone asks him for help, when someone needs to be defended, he does it without asking for anything in return."

"If that's the case, where are the two women that

entered this place with you?" the Duke asked. "Was this whole argument a ruse so they can go on a treasure hunt in search of that fictional stupid relic?"

"Maybe they are admiring your luxurious castle?" Fionn replied, his voice dripping with sarcasm.

"Enough with you two!" the Duke said, then turned to his guards. "Arrest them!"

The guards closed in to arrest Fionn and Harland. Fionn considered his options, how to get both of them out without seriously injuring the guards. His hand reached instinctively for Black Fang a second time, as he looked around for potential exits.

The castle rocked, shaking everyone in the chamber. BOOM!

"What was that?" the Duke asked, confused. The lights flickered with worrisome intensity.

Fionn recognized the sound. It was the booming noise of warning shots by energy cannons.

"Your peace treaty, Duke," Harland replied, "being broken."

†††

Gaby wasn't sure where Livia had gone, but if Harland's information was right, she was sure where the Crown might be. More than likely, she would find Livia there as well.

She moved through narrow alleys, evading the guards and using the arrival of guests to the castle for the festivities as cover to reach the small church near the castle's courtyard. It looked like an unimportant chapel, compared to the large cathedral at the top of the hill. But it made sense. It was open to the public enough to keep suspicions away, but not important enough to conjure conspiracy theories. The perfect hideout for a powerful object. She walked inside the old church, which had been annexed to the main castle complex in ancient times, trying not to make a sound. She couldn't shake the feeling that she was being observed.

The place was being illuminated by the fading moonlight entering through the stained glass on the left wall. The right wall of the nave had several shelves full of images and relics. There was also a glass casket set into the wall, containing mummified remains of what Gaby assumed the church passed off as belonging to saints.

Gaby walked toward the right wall. The moonlight pointed toward a faded painting on the wall, between the shelf with the relics and the casket. As she got closer, Gaby got a better look at the mummy inside.

"Pleased to meet you, Miss Braneh," Gaby whispered.

The mummy was shrouded in a white tunic with golden brocade covering the shriveled body, whose hands were holding a golden astrolabe. On an engraved plate, her name had faded, but a quote remained: 'Be humble and the truth reveals itself'.

Gaby examined the faded painting. It was composed of two lines, one above and one below, and between them a depiction of each of the phases of the moon, including an eclipse and what seemed to be dates recorded there long ago. Gaby noticed that the dates were not sequential but seemed to be registered at random, or at least in disorder, and below them, there was a second set of numbers, that seemed to be fractions of some kind. The moonlight coming in through the window hit each phase, except the eclipse. Each phase had a keyhole of different sizes. Gaby looked around the church and beneath the stained-glass window, saw a statue, holding an old bronze key ring with different keys that looked more like decoration than actual keys. Yet the statue's eyes were pointed at the casket.

Hiding in the open to keep it so obvious no one would suspect, Gaby mused.

Grabbing the keys from the statue, she returned to the wall and studied the keys. *This is where Harland would have been more useful than me,* she thought. *No, stop thinking that, I can do this. Let's see from another point of view: This is not a clue, but a code. The dates are not random, but probably important dates that coincided with these moon phases. I don't know what happened then, but I suspect the dates are not random.* She stopped at one that was familiar to her. One that she knew by heart and that caused her eyes to well up with unexplainable tears. The fact that she recognized the date, that it had made her cry and feel it as something personal, rather than as a random fact learned from her history lessons, created a knot at the bottom of her stomach. Her fears about who she was were being confirmed, piece by piece, during the whole ordeal.

It was the date when King Castlemartell had passed away. A significant date for Fionn and... Izia.

Focus Gaby! She thought. *This is not the time for that.*

Going by that date, it meant that the other ones were registers of when the previous wearers of the Crown had passed away. The oldest one coincided with Matthias death. And all the dates were in disorder. Gaby wondered if the keys would have to be turned in such a random way. But if it were that easy, someone would have already done it. And there were no apparent signs of someone having activated the mechanism.

How is it that the Crown returned here with no one knowing it was here after Castlemartell died? Unless the Crown has the mystical ability to teleport to its resting place once the wearer dies. No, that's a distraction right now, she thought. *The answer lies here but is not that obvious.*

Gaby gave another look to the corpse in the casket. Why would a corpse in a church have an astrolabe, an instrument for celestial measurements?

What did Harland say? That Sylvie Braneh had calculated the measurements of the Round and Long Moon and their distances with an.., she thought. Her eyes snapped open in realization and she smiled her crooked smile.

"Astrolabe," Gaby whispered to herself.

It makes sense now. The upper dates are there to distract you from the actual sequence to open the keyholes. The numbers below each date are the ratios of the Round and Long Moon with respect to the size of Theia. That's the real order. The only real use of the dates, besides keeping track of the people that had worn the Crown at some point, is to indicate if the order goes from large to small or the other way. And if I'm correct, it goes from small to large. Here goes nothing.

Gaby turned each key in order, going from the smallest ratio to the larger one. As she turned the last key, she heard a sound like the ticking of an old clock behind the wall. As the mechanism worked its way through centuries of disuse, she stared at the plate on the casket and the quote there. Nothing in this place had been built at random.

"Be humble and the truth reveals itself," Gaby whispered.

Gaby bowed and heard the squeak of hinges and rattle of relics echo through the empty church as something on the shelf above her opened. She almost straightened up to see what it was, but on bowing she noticed a container on the floor opening. She realized that whatever had opened above her was placed there to distract less humble thieves. She knelt to examine the container on the floor, expecting to see the fabled Crown of the Dead. Instead, it was empty. The fabric in it was depressed, as if something of considerable weight had been kept there. But the mark's shape didn't match a crown, rather, a single object, like a marble had been kept there and recently taken. And yet there were no signs that someone had disturbed the place. *Unless...* Gaby thought. *The Crown has never been here either. But I'm sure someone knows.*

"Where is the Crown?" Gaby asked aloud, hoping for a reply from the person she was sure was watching her.

"The Crown was never there," the familiar voice of Livia replied, coming out from the shadows of the altar. She was admiring a crystal gemstone that shone under the moonbeams. "Just the last gemstone you need to find its true location and activate it. And it has been in my possession for at least a century."

"Let me guess, you knew all this time where it was," Gaby replied as she turned around. "This whole charade has another purpose, am I right?"

"You don't sound too surprised," Livia said, tilting her head in a stiff, almost mechanical way.

"Why should I?" Gaby replied with her crooked smile. "It was a matter of time until you revealed yourself. I think I owe Fionn ten bucks."

"All of you suspected me and yet you allowed me to travel with you? What gave me away?" Livia asked, befuddled as she moved toward the entrance, placing several pews between her and Gaby.

"'Keep your enemies closer,' they said back at school, remember?" Gaby said, moving slowly toward Livia. "As for what gave you away... Oh I don't know? The sudden failure of the Figaro's engine—which, by the way, Sid fixed immediately. Or the way you appeared at the Tower of Salt. Perhaps it was the way your body subtly reacted at the word 'coward' when Harland explained his philosophy behind the creation of the tovainar."

"And the whole in fight between your group, the harsh words by the samoharo, making the traitor feel like he was the guilty party, all of it was a charade?"

"The fight, yeah. But knowing Sid, he meant every

word he said. He means well even if he lacks manners. And he knows how to read people. As for Joshua, he knows we trust him, so he played along."

"So, you have been keeping an eye on me since then," Livia mused, and nodded. "I admit that I underestimated your silly band."

"It was too much of a coincidence that of all people Doncelles—who is a traditionalist and too much of a careerist—hired to track the Crown, he went with a former Sister of Mercy who just happened to be my roommate back in that nightmare. A roommate I knew too well. You might have fooled him. But not me, nor my friends. And even if I didn't want to believe that you broke bad, I am a realist. Which is why you better tell me who you really are and what you did with Livia before-"

"Before what? You kill me?" Livia replied, her voice shifting with each word. It sounded as if two people, one male and one female, were speaking now. "You would be killing her as well. Like you and the stupid akeleth parasite infecting you, we are but one, but one, but so much superior to you."

"One of the tovainars," Gaby realized. "The one that Joshua has been tracking."

"Ah yes, the traitor. Good guess. Now let's see how fast you are." Livia bolted from the church at inhuman speed. Gaby went after her, but Livia managed to stay ahead of Gaby. They ran through the crowd and across the courtyard toward the Clocktower. Gaby could hear her name being mentioned but remained focused on catching Livia as she entered the Clocktower.

Blurry images struck her like a train and Gaby short at the threshold of the Clocktower.

I'm being baited, she thought. Having foresight was a curse, for while you could predict things about to happen, you couldn't always do something about it. And from that came despair, which was poison to the heart. *To the Pits with that. I will do something about that.* As she entered the Clocktower, the sound of guns being cocked reached her ears. She unsheathed Heartguard and Soulkeeper, the blades giving off a comforting red and blue glow. Taking a deep breath, she focused on the inner core of her Gift. Her irises glowed with an electric blue hue and energy ran across her body, burning through her muscles, giving her goosebumps.

"This is my song," Gaby whispered as she gazed at the stairs with thousands of steps she would have to climb. "Let's make some music."

The heavy door closed behind her with a loud thud, which deafened the booming sound coming from outside.

† † †

Sid, Vivienne and Joshua were on the castle terrace, waiting for Fionn, Gaby, Harland, and Livia to come out after the Duke's tour. Joshua was perched on a gargoyle on the battlements, staring at the city below. Trumpets signaled the start of the event and the three of them looked up toward the sky to witness the beginning of the Lunar Eclipse.

Sid was the first one to break the silence. "That's the Round Moon, correct?" Sid asked.

"Yes, why?" Vivi asked.

"This eclipse doesn't make any sense then," Sid mumbled.

"What do you mean?" Vivi asked this time.

Sid looked at them and moved his hands.

"If my calendar is right, and it is because we samoharo are nitpickers about celestial movements, there can't be a lunar eclipse tonight, because right now, on the other side of the Lirian Ocean, there is a solar eclipse taking place."

"Maybe that eclipse is caused by the Long Moon," Vivi

suggested.

"Nope," Sid countered. "In all history, there is no Long Moon caused eclipse registered, because its movements are too erratic to synchronize."

"Some sort of magickal mirage?" Joshua ventured. "After all this city has the legend of the Devil King and is said to possess some sort of mystical aura. I can see it as a miasma flowing from the ground."

"With the state of magick right now, I wouldn't bet on that," Vivi said. "I see where you are going, Sid; something else is happening."

"Well, this world is full of strange miracles and happenings, as we witnessed at the Tower of Salt, or even the Tempest Blades," Joshua replied, staring at the compressed version of Fury.

"I hope you are right, because right now I'm getting a bad feeling," Sid said.

"I have always wondered, who forged the Tempest Blades?" Vivi mused. "Not even Ravenstone had a register of that. There are no mentions of who made Yaha for example, or Black Fang, which is of more recent creation. It is as if any record has been erased from memory."

"No one knows for sure," Joshua replied. "In fact, no one really knows how many exist or were created and destroyed over ten millennia. My travels to obtain Fury didn't uncover much, as if someone, as you said, Vivienne, had erased everything on purpose. Yaha and Black Fang are the only well-known Tempest Blades throughout history. That's why it has been surprising to have so many blades—Heartguard, Soulkeeper, Breaker, and now Fury, resurfacing now."

"That's the thing," Vivi said. "There are millennia separating the creation of Yaha and Black Fang, and along that timespan, the others were made. So surely it can't be the work of a single person. A tribe, a family perhaps. Maybe an unknown demigod?"

"Somehow, I doubt it's the work of a demigod," Sid replied. "They wouldn't risk creating weapons that can hurt them, as we saw with Yaha and the Crawling Chaos. Though... the Stellar Ehécatl was created by the Prophet from a vision he had. Although it's not exactly a Tempest Blade, more like a prototype. Regardless, if I'm honest, any other alternative frightens me."

"I get you. What kind of being or beings can forge a weapon with a soul and the power, in the right hands, to cut down deities?" Joshua said, staring up at the stars.

BOOM!

"Is that Gaby running toward the clocktower?" Vivi pointed her out in the street below.

"Now what?" Sid asked.

"Problems," Joshua replied as he summoned Fury to his hand.

BOOM!

Chapter 10
Moonglow

BOOM!

A small steam explosion echoed through the otherwise empty rooms of the strange habitat.

Inside a well-lit laboratory, with equipment so advanced that it seemed like magick, those expensive tools lay around in a haphazard disarray. Complicated chemistry equipment was distilling a black liquid, emitting puffs of purple and green steam. There was a monitor, similar to an oscilloscope, with an all-black screen, except for the parallel thin lines being displayed. When a line got interrupted, after a few seconds it disappeared. A new one was created later. An ancient song, exalting the virtues of strange science experimentation, from a distant, bygone world played in what seemed to be a weird data cube music player. A man, who seemed to be working on several experiments at the same time, including the distillation and another that included hefty amounts of electricity, was dancing to the tune of the song. He seemed to be alone, as he broke into song about his intentions with his experiments. The man pirouetted and grabbed a cup, which he placed at the end of the distilling experiment to catch the black liquid that had started to fall from the burette. When the cup was full, he brought it to his nose and took a deep breath. He smiled as he inhaled the stringent, smoky smell coming from the black liquid.

"You can't get coffee of this quality on this side of the galaxy... well in any other place of the galactic local cluster anymore, really," the man mumbled with a gusty sigh.

As he was about to take a sip of this peculiar brew of coffee, the lights of the laboratory flickered, and a charging sound echoed from one of the darkened corridors. The man left his cup on the lab table and checked his energy experiment.

"I hope I didn't bring the station offline again. Mother will get angry at me. Again."

The readouts turned optimal, according to his quick check. The only strange thing was the detection of a sudden surge of energy somewhere on the station.

"This peak looks familiar," he said as he stroked his chin. "But it can't be, I haven't fixed her problem yet."

A second crash came from the same corridor, followed by the tell-tale sound of someone throwing up. Two voices spoke in a language that seemed familiar, but had words he couldn't recognize. A third voice joined in. That one, he recognized. Still, a cautious man by the nature of countless years of experience, he grabbed a device similar to a comms and put it in his ear. As he walked toward the corridor, he grabbed a large hammer, with glowing lines and runes all over its surface.

He walked across the dark corridor guided by the light emitted by his hammer. He entered the observation deck where it was possible to see Theia, as well as Tawa Seridia, through a huge window. By the star's light coming through the window, he could see three humanoid silhouettes, two female and one male. One of the female ones seemed to be familiar and her voice confirmed his suspicions. Still, he kept his guard up, as the male was holding a familiar sight, the very first thing he'd created. He knew that object's silhouette by heart, with the intricate gold and silver, polished guard, the handle covered in soft leather from a species now extinct. His brother had told him that it was too flamboyant for its purpose. But the man liked the design, It gave the object a mystical aura. How many swords had six wings as the hilt guard? He'd done it in memory of the true shape of his mother's people. Yaha was one of the few creations he was proud of. The fact that the sword, sans a few scratches, remained the same as it was when he made it several millennia ago, with only the sheath being the newest addition, brought warmth to his heart.

The three strangers had not noticed him and were talking, the comms in his ear translated their conversation.

"Your home? What do you mean by home?" the unknown woman asked.

"Yes, this is my home," the woman that he recognized replied. "What, did you expect me to spend all my time in the World Scar?"

"What about Ravenhall?" the first voice asked again.

"That's part of my mind. I can't stay there all the time. I'm not that crazy. I can't stand myself at the best of times," she replied. She then addressed the man, who seemed to be mesmerized as he looked through the window. "Alex, you are oddly quiet. You are never quiet."

"Judging by our relative position with regard to the sun, Theia, and the Round Moon, and the apparent altitude we are, plus the time of the year... Are we inside the Long Moon!?" the man called Alex exclaimed.

"That would make the Long Moon some sort of space fort or station, Alex," the first woman said, "which means that this must be of akeleth construction. Unless the samoharo are not telling us something."

"Trust me, Sam, Sid would not stop babbling about this if he actually knew. The Long Moon must be disguised by some sort of spell, or even built inside a hollowed out actual moon."

"Y'know," the familiar voice replied, in the peculiar accent she had adopted from the freefolk the man knew as Asherah, "I have always liked how quick you two come to conclusions. Sometimes you are wrong, but not this time. Yes, this is the Long Moon, this is a space station... well, what was left of it, built by the akeleth inside an actual moon... and we are not alone. You can come out, kid!"

The man, startled by being noticed—but of course she would have known he was there, she always knew—tripped over his feet and stumbled forward to land in front of the three people as the lights of the observation deck turned on.

"Are you alright, son?" Mekiri asked. Alex and Sam leaned in to help him stand up. They stared at him, as if they had recognized him. It happened at times, so he smiled.

"Stealth?" Sam asked. "What are you doing here?"

"Hello, mother-not-so-mother," the man waved at Mekiri.

"Mother?" Alex asked, then added "Stealth?"

"Oh, hi," the man replied with an affable smile. "You must be confusing me with my twin, Stealth. Used to happen a lot. My name is Forge. And I see you are carrying my very first creation."

"Your first creation?" Alex asked, confused.

"Yes. The sword. Yaha," Forge pointed at the Tempest Blade.

Alex and Sam glanced at each other with a mix of open confusion and bewilderment.

"Hello, son," Mekiri replied. "And yes, I'm still your mother, even if I'm trapped inside my avatar."

† † †

"So, let me get this straight," Alex said, as he took a

cup of coffee from Forge. The resemblance to his brother Stealth was uncanny, except for the eye color and the tribal markings. "Your brother... your twin brother is Stealth, the guy we met at the World Scar and helped us to fix the Figaro."

Sam looked around as their conversation echoed through the large hall where they were sitting. She had half-expected, based on the huge window of the observation deck where they'd arrived, that the place would be built like the interior of the Figaro, all metal, with screens and panels everywhere. But instead, it looked like the inner gardens of Ravenstone, before Byron blew the place to smithereens. Sam felt at ease here. She could feel her body feeding on the glowing energy coming from the walls, which created waves of warmth inside her, just like when she kissed Alex or fell asleep next to Kasumi.

The edges of the room's walls were decorated with runes and engravings that glowed with a faint blue light and emitted something similar to magickal energy. The same light ran through lines etched on the floor and walls. The lines stretched everywhere and got lost into the distance of the huge place. There was no sign that the runes had been carved with tools of any kind on the material that Forge had called 'morphocrete'. The air smelled of red oak, maple syrup, and incense.

Her train of thought was interrupted by the abrupt increase in the volume of Forge's voice.

"Helped?" Forge asked, taking a seat at the table of what seemed to be a much disorganized bachelor kitchen, next to the laboratory. "I'm surprised he did that. He is not fond of technology."

"He said he had a degree in engineering and high energy," Sam replied.

"That lying bastard," Forge replied. "He stole my degree! The only energy he likes is Late Energy cartoons!

You know, those ones about office people fighting monsters after leaving work late in the night."

"That 'lying bastard' is your brother, and right now he's busy trying to restart Ravenhall and re-empower the wards protecting the freefolk border," Mekiri replied, pinching the bridge of her nose. "Can't you clean this place now and then? And why are you still fighting with your brother? You haven't spoken to him in five millennia? Why did I have twins?"

Alex and Sam remained silent, staring at Mekiri, mouths open.

"What?" Mekiri said. "It's too hard to think about a goddess being a parent?"

Prompted, Sam was forced to find her voice. "We are not judging the issue of having twins, your grace," Sam replied. As she spoke with the most important deity of her people's pantheon, she was doing her damnedest to keep her cool. But deep down, she was about to crack. "We are just... confused."

"Like, how are you talking coherently right now?" Alex said. "Or how come that Forge, is the person who forged, pardon the repetition, Yaha. The sword is almost ten thousand years. Which means..."

"Ten thousand and one, I believe," Forge said. "I'm slightly younger. But we of freefolk stock age slower than humans."

"The timeline doesn't check," Alex frowned. "I mean how could you have sons after seeing what happened to Asherah and tried to understand the mortal life, but said sons, as adults, were there to forge Yaha as the first Tempest Blade?"

"I forgot that you mortals experience time in a different fashion to us, starting by the fact that from the Arrival to the Battle of the Life Tree, time passed. It wasn't just a week. That said, time for us is like a cyclical river we experience from the outside, we can jump in and out. You perceive it in a linear fashion because you are inside the river," Mekiri replied.

"But that wouldn't mean that every time that you jump in you change things. Can you predict the future, because if—"

"Is it this the moment to discuss temporal mechanics?" Sam interjected, annoyed. The entire chat was giving her a migraine. "But he did ask a good question about your mind being healed, your grace."

"Yeah, you are right, time travel sucks," Alex mumbled.

"I'm talking coherently," Mekiri said to Sam, "because you were right analyzing the clues left behind after my fight with that bastard. Murcana, as much as I despise the thing, helped to rearrange my mind, though it couldn't restore all my powers. That's why I could only teleport us three here. And to do so I had to draw power from your Gift, Sam, for which I apologize. But as of right now, this body is still a mortal humanoid."

"It's okay, your grace," Sam said. "I understand. I wouldn't have the Gift in first place if you hadn't decided I was worthy of it."

"Nonsense," Mekiri waved her hand. "You earned it, just like this space head next to us and his great-grandparent as well. Did you know I once suggested to Ywain to drink the murcana to try and fix his mind after Byron shattered it, but he refused because 'the thing causes more problems than is worth,' the goodie two shoes. I rather think he wanted to forget everything and start a new life with Zyanya. Then again, he was right about murcana. In fact, dealing with an old nahual, a shaman of sorts, that had enslaved a whole town with murcana is how the great-grandparents of this space head meat each other... am I boring you, Alex, with the story of your family?"

"Don't mind him," Sam said. "He is geeking out at being the first human, I assume, to set foot in the Long Moon. I mean, I'm still coming to terms with what they told me they saw in Ravenhall about the Three Species not being native to Theia, but arriving from other worlds. But that would explain the lack of fossils."

"What's that?" Alex asked as he stood up and examined the bizarre monitor. "Those lines... one of them starts on my day of birth. Same with the other and Sam's day of birth. The other one... it starts ten millennia ago, if I'm counting the markers right. I assume is your avatar's creation date?"

"That," Forge replied with a wide grin, appropriate given he probably invented it. "It's the Fate monitor. It doesn't generate fate, as that is created through sheer free will. It tracks the lifelines of living beings on the planet. Right now it's focusing on you three, but I can decrease its focus to see the whole Band of the Greywolf."

"Not that name again," Alex groaned.

"What's wrong with it?" Forge mused. "It sounded nice when I proposed it in the chat room after "Pack" got down voted. What? Why is he angry, Samantha?"

"Don't mind him," Sam said as she approached the monitor. She was curious at how tangled, erratic and changing the lines were. "Funny, for being about monitoring fate, one would think that you would like a single tidy line. I mean, isn't chaos an enemy, as in the Creeping Chaos?"

"You are getting it wrong, which of course was his plan," Mekiri said with a sigh that betrayed a deep-seated sorrow. "Not your fault though. Legends work like that, by being half-truths. No, no. The Creeping Chaos definition of chaos is a misnomer to confuse and fool mortals. It's version of chaos is in reality the absence of life, of thought, of freewill, the cessation of any movement beyond the occasional random quantum blip in a morass of nothingness, not unlike the Primordial Void from which we all come, before the times of the First Light and the First Darkness that break away free that gave birth to Kaan'a and to create the multilayered, cyclical universe. Order and Chaos, on the other hand, are essential aspects of Creation, like Life and Death. Two sides of the same coin, balanced to foster life, evolution, creativity, dreaming, change. And on the rim of the coin, the Tempest, from which you ultimately draw your abilities, because the Tempest is the result of the infinite number of souls that give reality its meaning. That monitor keeps tracks of the lives of the mortals, for they are not bound by Fate to a particular road. The more lines the better. More lines mean more possibilities. Infinite, endless possibilities. Growth, change, the hope of improvement. The occurrence of the impossible made feasible. That's what life is about. That's the actual Magick of Chaos. The opposite of the entropy they sell as 'chaos'. As long as those lines keep growing, I know there is still hope. For it means you are still alive. And if you are still alive, then we can win. That's what we, I, you are fighting for."

"I guess that's the advantage of avatars for deities and outer planar entities," Sam mused. "You can get a certain degree of freedom to nudge things certain way."

"Like, I assume, the warnings on the TV and the radio," Alex added.

"That, my dear child, is the gist of this. I can't tell you what to do, because I would violate Free Will, which is what made Shemazay angry at me. 'You are messing with the ancient plan,' he said. Stupid dunderhead. He doesn't know anything, like I do. I'm the one communing with the Universe. But can he follow a simple instruction? Noooo, he had to know best..." Mekiri ranted, banging her hand on the table.

"Who is Shemazay?" Sam asked. "Never heard of him.

Hunt said that he was from human folklore."

"He is one of my kind," Mekiri replied, "Just of a low-er rank. Usually under my orders of that of the Guardian. Was, until he betrayed us all."

"So, he attacked all of you?" Sam asked.

"I know he went after the Guardian and dispersed his essence on the whole of Theia's skies not long ago for me, but aeons in the past for you, and trapped the rest in a mortal body. I know he is going after Ben Erra, the Judge, because he really hates him. After all, this whole mess was his fault in the first place. And he tried to do the same to me, except that I'm used to being in this body, which I like a lot. I mean, I had kids with it just to experience the full range of mortal experiences. And no, you don't get to ask who's the father, Alex," Mekiri added with a pointed glance.

Alex had been about to say something, but he wisely closed his mouth.

"As I was saying, Shemazay is what you would call the god or the angel, depend on your tradition," Mekiri shrugged. "Of karmic retribution and ironically, for some-one so short-sighted and close-minded, creativity. He was the one sponsoring the creators of Korbyworld and the whole animated shebang, until he trapped one of them in that Pitlike underground of animated nightmares."

"So, he wants to take your place to start the end of the world or what?" Alex asked, taking a seat once more. "This coffee is really good. Where did you get it, Forge?"

"Old Earth, the plant is extinct now."

Alex stared at the coffee. Sam sighed, as getting con-firmation of Old Earth being real was bound to send Alex's mind racing through hundreds of thoughts.

"Don't overthink it, sweetie," Sam said to him. She kissed him on the forehead. "Just drink the coffee. Breathe. So, were you saying, your grace?"

"I'm afraid he is taking advantage of the Golden King's plans to start the end of the world, forcing the akeleth that are still around into a direct fight with the Lords of the Infinity Pits, just to go according to some prophecy he read once. Which is stupid because..."

"Prophecies are either self-fulfilling or after-the-fact interpretations of events, which for someone that can see outside the timeline but can't predict how the beings inside it will act due to free will is basically pointless," Alex finished. "But why now and not three and half years ago when we fought Byron? The Creeping Chaos was still around, would have make his plan easier."

Alex placed the cup on the table and stared at the darkness of the coffee. He pushed the cup away, his hand trembling. It hurt Sam seeing Alex like that. It wasn't as if she didn't have nightmares about that fight, about that being. Even after destroying his avatar, which sent his essence back to the deepest of the Pits, it seemed like Marius, the Creeping Chaos was still haunting them. Alex was still recovering from the beating of his life. In comparison, Sam got away relatively intact. She moved her chair next to him to give him a hug. Alex buried his face on her neck, and she could feel the tears rolling down it. Mekiri offered a sympathetic smile.

"I have to apologize. I never wanted you, or your friends and family, to go through this whole nightmare. I didn't foresee all that's happening now. It hurts me seeing you like this. I'm sorry for imposing on you."

"Nonsense," Alex replied, clearing his nose and wiping his tears. "Someone had to do it. It was my choice."

"Agree," Sam added. "Anyways, why didn't Shemazay act until now?"

"Because he is scared of you two in particular," Mekiri said, pointing at Sam and Alex. "He wasn't a fan of mortals to begin with. And as aeons passed by, he got more extreme in his views. It was rare the mortal he did like. Then you, and by you, I mean the Band of the Greywolf, come about and start messing with the tovainar prophecy, and you two kill the Creeping Chaos in what I admit was a spectacular fashion. It scared him shitless. Because he sees you as a threat to us. And with nine hundred million souls down there on Theia, the potential for more Gifted to be reborn is high. So, he wants to get rid of you, me, magick as the freefolk know it and force that confrontation. That's why he did this to me, and why he bound magick and rewrote its laws so only he and his acolytes could use it."

"Well," Alex replied. "You are here, you can reconnect with your other self and rearrange magick to what it was."

"That's not how it works," Forge interjected. "I know—I have been trying to reconnect Mother with her essential form, the aurora borealis you have been seeing, for the past three or four days, to no avail. Once the avatar is cut from the essential form, it can't be rejoined. It becomes a mortal body with a trapped spirit. For that spirit to rejoin the essential form, it must..."

"Destroy the body," Sam said somberly. "Right?"

"And that might not even work, she might end up becoming a wandering spirit. The same spirits that merged with you to bestow the Gift," Forge replied. He hugged his mother, surprising Mekiri.

"Don't be sad, they were my people that couldn't get beyond the barrier, the Gift is a way to keep them alive and protect the world they loved so much. But if that happens to me, I'm fine with my destiny," Meriki said, a maudlin undertone in her voice betraying the cheerful façade. Long gone was the freefolk elder that looked like a child with bunny ears and a green poncho covered with raven feathers. Instead, in its place, there was a worried, tired woman contemplating her own mortality.

In a way, Sam mused, she was indeed experiencing the

full range of mortal experiences. And yet, it was not fair. The universe was a cold, uncaring place for the most part. For many of the freefolk, and some humans as well, knowing that the Trickster Goddess was out there looking after them, even if her lessons were harsh at times or not clear at the start, was a source of comfort. What Shemazay had done to Mekiri made Sam's blood boil, to the point that her irises glowed lilac as her Gift activated involuntarily.

"You know what?" Sam said, standing up with such sudden motion that her chair screeched back. "Screw destiny. I'm pretty sure Alex can think of a different way to help you reconnect with your other self for sure. And then you will regenerate this avatar."

"What makes you so sure you can do it?" Forge asked.

"Because you just gave us a whole long winded infodump speech of what we are fighting for," Alex replied. "And Mekiri, the weird Freefolk librarian, helped me when I needed it the most. I owe that to my friend."

"You think of me as your friend?" Mekiri asked, taken aback, half-smiling, half-confused. "I think that is the first time since Asherah that someone has called me friend. But even if that was possible, I wouldn't be able to regenerate this avatar right away. I would ascend and would only be able to project an image. The first time it took me a lot of time to create Mekiri to avoid causing another Scar. And magick in the mortal realm is out of order and too instable for me to do that. Mekiri as you know it might not come back, or at least not for several years."

"It's better than nothing," Alex said. "Hey, Forge! Can some of this ancient equipment and mystical weaponry be used to collect, organize, and reroute energy into coherent particle beams? I need your help, because I have an idea, but I suck at the mechanical part."

"Yes, I think so, but I'm not sure if we will have enough time. I mean, the eclipse is about to start in a few hours and that was the deadline."

"I don't understand how an eclipse has any bearing on dimensional crossings, the fate of magick or anything really. It is just a planetary mechanic thing that happens all the time. There is nothing magickal about them. Is there?" Alex asked.

"The eclipse itself is not the reason," Mekiri replied. "What you call gods, my brethren and the ones from the Pits, are egomaniacs. We all are. And as I said before, we perceive time differently from you. The eclipse is a time mark to let you know that some god set up things to happen at that precise time, both as a reminder for us and to give our followers something to look for. It's also a show of power, for it means you can not only change the laws of celestial mechanics at will, but can alter probabilities within the mortal realm, alter and merge dimensions. In a way the eclipse it is mystical, because through it a deity is pushing their power to enact change."

"So, the eclipse and any other so called prophetic celestial phenomenon are nothing but a glorified colossal alarm clock and a flex?" Sam asked, crossing her arms.

"Yes."

"Geez, melodrama much?" Alex frowned.

"Told you, we deities are egomaniacs," Mekiri said. "Sometimes I wish we followed that old freefolk proverb about being kind, how does it go?"

"*It's cheaper to be nice than hateful.*

It's better to be kind than nice.

It's wiser to know when to be kind, when to speak, and when to remain quiet," Sam recited.

"That one." Mekiri bounced with delight. "Okay, I trust you. But while Alex and Forge work on his idea, Sam, I need to work with you on something else. Come with me."

Sam wondered what she could do to help the very goddess she prayed to so much when she was a little girl.

††† †

Mekiri led Sam to a room full of a huge variety of plants, pools of clear water, and tiny pollinizing insects. It was well lit, the air was fresh and filled with sweet fragrances. It was verdant with so many strange plants and flowers, none of which Sam had ever seen in her life. Not even in encyclopedias.

"These plants are not from Theia?" Sam asked.

"Very observant," Mekiri replied and smiled. "This garden is full of plants from worlds that are no more. I and my sons have tried to preserve them here through our technology, or your magick adapted arcanotech as you might call it. Unfortunately, this is the only place where they can survive. Their ecosystems no longer exist and are not easy to replicate. We had to repurpose Theia to allow the Three Species to live there and our experiments could only accommodate a few minor species. Still, I think these plants are worth preserving, if only so their memory doesn't fade. I was inspired by this place to make Ravenhall."

"I guess I will never get to visit Ravenhall a second time," Sam replied ruefully.

"Hey! Ravenhall is easier to fix than an avatar, so you will have a chance, I know."

"I'm not sure. I mean, I don't even know if I belong with the freefolk anymore."

"Why do you say that?" Mekiri asked, tilting her head. She gestured for Sam to take seat on the ground in front of her.

"Because I don't know who, or what am I anymore," Sam said with a sigh. "I always saw myself as freefolk, but after living for a while with my friends I reconnected with my human side. And I feel like I cheated my freefolk ancestry by doing that. And then the Gift. That changed me. My rebuilt heart is in constant arrhythmia so I dunno how I'm actually alive. It took me a long time to relearn to use my magick through the Gift, which is the only reason I can still cast spells while the rest of my people can't. And don't get me started with that other confusion about—"

"Oh, little one," Mekiri said interrupting Sam, as she caressed her hands. "You are overthinking things. You are who you are. And you are who you want to be. All those things you mentioned are part of what makes you, you. They are not in conflict, they are in beautiful, chaotic balance."

"I don't understand."

"You can choose, if you want, one particular aspect of yourself, but I suspect that will make you unhappy. So, the choice is clear. A third or fourth option if you like."

"You mean, not choosing anything at all? Just accept things as they are?"

"More than accepting, enjoying who you are and what you can do. Life, at the end of the day, has no other purpose than being lived. All the rest of mortal preoccupations are self-imposed. By society, by culture, by tradition. Forget about the rules imposed by tradition. Life only asks you one thing: to live it the best that you can, enjoying what you find along the way. That's the only thing that both mortals and gods can really do with the time we have in this realm. It took me years to make Asherah see that."

"What do you mean?"

"Let me explain it this way, okay? I will use the old storytelling tradition," Mekiri said, while with a flick of her hand, the lights dimmed, and a small bonfire appeared between them. Mekiri threw powder into the fire and the flames changed colors, portraying colorful yet simple images that matched her speech word for word. But unlike the Freefolk version that used creative metaphors and symbols, Mekiri's version actually created holographic images, as if it were a movie recreating her words. Even without her full powers, she remained the Trickster Goddess, and she was famous for telling stories.

"I love this storytelling technique, good to teach magick as well," Mekiri giggled. "Like watching a movie but with a better director: me. Anyway, just look at the fire and clear your mind. Follow my words." Images began to form in the fire as Mekiri spoke. The images changed in shape and color, following her words. It was like watching a holographic movie coming out from the flames.

"You, Samantha Ambers-Estel, use your Gift to perform magick and—" Mekiri began to say with solemn voice.

"I know that," Sam interrupted.

"Hush, this is my story," Mekiri said, waving Sam's words away. The images flickered for a moment and then began again. "Asherah was one of the only three who could face the First Demon..."

"Because you choose her," Sam interjected. Her shoulders slumped, as if a heavy weight pushed her against the floor. And that weight was the turmoil inside her own heart.

"No. Stop interrupting," Mekiri said, frowning. "I didn't choose her. She already had the innate talent to tap into magick. The first being in thousands of years to actually do it. And that was because she intuitively discovered, upon her arrival on Theia, which was flooded with magickal energies back then. When the First Demon attacked the Life Tree, she was, along with the Iskandar and the Samoharo Prophet, the one that had the means to defend the Tree." The images showed the three of them defending the Life Tree.

"But how did she learn those means? Intuition is good to cast spells under stressful circumstances, but only if you already know them. Back then there were no spells. How did she come up with them?"

"She made up everything along the way. I mean, I did give her a few ideas during the journey to the Tree, but mostly, she improvised." Mekiri shrugged. The movie showed Asherah creating magic. "There were a few spells I never considered before she tried them."

"What?" Sam said, raising her voice in surprise, the sound echoing through the room. "How's that possible? Magick is hard to use as it is, with the rules guiding us to avoid blowing up."

"Easy. What Asherah understood, as well as Queen Kary in her time, was that magick is chaotic by nature." The images showed Asherah and Queen Kary making up spells. "It's more than just an elemental force of the universe. It reflects the collective unconscious of everything and everyone that lives in the universe, and shapes it, mind over matter. Imagination made reality." The images showed the creation of magick from the minds of spell casters.

"Which is good if you manage to channel that chaos into a coherent way. But left on their own, that chaos takes a particular shape." The image became a chaotic jumble of images that Sam recognize.

"The Tempest," Sam said, her eyes opening in realization. "Any spell is possible within the Tempest, or if you channel it through... no, from within you, like I can do thanks to the Gift?"

"Exactly. But Shemazay, like the freefolk elders, doesn't understand that. He is too fixated with the old ways, the old customs." Mekiri's movie showed Shemazay and freefolk elders being stubborn and imperious. "He can inspire others, but has no clue how to be imaginative by himself." Mekiri smiled ruefully.

"So, he did what the elders did to Asherah, stifle the power flow to control what they really didn't understand. What freefolk do is just a fraction of what Asherah could, even under the codified rules. Neat, tidy, safe. And that's good in general. Keeps practitioners healthy and in one piece. But if you take that to the next level of restrictions, in such way that only Shemazay and his acolytes can use it to force dependence on him by the mortal species, and eroding Free Will, like Before the Fall. What he doesn't realize because his ego is too big, is that by doing that, magick will build pressure..."

"You don't stifle the flow, you block it in its entirety, like a dam," Sam replied.

"Now you are getting it," Mekiri said with a delighted clap. "And what happens when a dam faces a tempest of cosmological proportions?"

"It busts open, flooding and sweeping everything in its wake."

The image of a bursting dam exploded within the flames.

"Which in this case would be massive reality alterations, alterations that play right into the plans of the Golden King. Magick would be locked out, this time for good, after the eclipse finishes."

"But why he would do that?" Sam asked. "Why would a god—or akeleth, or whatever you actually are—do that?"

"Angels," Mekiri said quickly, avoiding Sam's gaze for a second. "Because like those old freefolk elders that are too stuck in their ancient ways, our kind tend to get stuck in our ways. And Shemazay is looking for a fight to prove his worth, his privilege. He is not fond of... well you, the Gifted. And since that was my idea..." The image in the flames showed Shemazay standing imperiously over the Band of the Greywolf and a chained Mekiri.

"He trapped you."

"And the others. Right now, you people are the last line of defense standing."

"But how do I beat him?" Sam's gaze fell. "How do I

beat a god if I can't cast reliable magick'?"

"Says the woman that helped kill the Creeping Chaos. You do it like you are doing now, drawing from within yourself and your connection with the Tempest thanks to the Gift. Just like Asherah did," Mekiri said matter-of-factly.

Sam's eyes widened, gawking.

"Don't look surprised," Mekiri said with a frown. "Of course, she was a Gifted like you. Nowadays freefolk rarely, if ever, become one because they learned from her to use magick, the same way humans learned from the Storm God, another Gifted that ascended, the ways of demon-hunting and titanfighting. Or the way your samoharo friends can invoke their ancestral blood pact with one of my siblings to empower themselves." The images showed the freefolk, humans, and samoharo all performing the tasks they had learned. "There are many ways to cook a soup. As you know firsthand, to become a Gifted it takes being in certain life or death circumstances. Freefolk magi rarely are in those situations thanks to magick. And if that fails, usually there is no body left so..."

"But I'm not Asherah, I don't have the knowledge nor the strength to do what you are asking me to do."

"Neither did Asherah back then. In the Tempest, there is no real difference."

"What?" Sam was taken aback.

"Asherah was the first mortal that I came to consider a friend," Mekiri said, a hint of sadness in her voice. "She was this young woman, who through the constant use of magick, had her body painfully changed from the milky gray skin, featureless face and the giant, colorful eyes of the shapeshifter Freefolk she was at first, to a young near-human woman with fiery orange hair, olive skin, and a tiny nose, and ended locked in that shape. Only her big turquoise eyes never changed. The whole ordeal scared her." The images in the flames showed Asherah's changes, ending in the image of a frightened freefolk woman.

"Why didn't you help her?"

"In my way, I did. But she had to realize on her own the same thing you have to right now: Who do you want to be? What do you choose to do? That's something only she could decide. Like you must do now."

"I... I'm not sure. I'm not sure if I want to choose between being a freefolk, or a human... I don't even—"

"You don't even know who of those two, Alex or Kasumi, you love enough to begin a serious relationship with instead of what you have been doing so far?"

"Yeah," Sam replied ruefully. Her eyes were welling up with tears that she struggled to hold back.

"Asherah took a husband and a wife, you know?" Mekiri winked at Sam. "That's where your tribe came from. Anyway, my point is: It is not magick, nor the Gift that grants you power. It is the ability to make your own path. It is scary, and not many go ahead with it, because it comes with responsibilities and risks. Asherah did it in the end, because that was who she chose to be. She could yearn to be what she was before the Change, or she could discard everything and move along. Can you guess what she elected?"

It then all clicked for Sam. The heavy weight she had felt pushing her down lifted all of a sudden as realization made her heart bounce lighter inside her.

"Nothing, she chose nothing," Sam replied, wiping the tears. "Rather she created a third option to feel complete: Own it all. She was the old freefolk as well as the new. There was no choice, only free will. And with that, she shaped things of her own accord. Which I guess the elders didn't like much."

"Now you are getting it." Mekiri smiled at Sam. The young woman reminded her a lot of Asherah. With a single difference that Sam hadn't realized yet: While Asherah had been in her position by happenstance, Sam chose to be there from the moment she joined the quest to stop Byron.

"Thing is, it took decades for Asherah to take the leap, and with it, finally be in the right mindset to learn what she needed to enter the Tempest and shape the magick flows, to codify the rules your people now use. The very same thing I'm asking you to do now." The images in the fire disappeared and the flames died down until nothing remained.

"But without Ravenhall to train with time running differently, I only have hours to learn everything I need before the eclipse finishes, and the dam explodes."

"Less I would say. I'm afraid your friends down below are at great risk by fighting him. As soon as Alex and Forge are done with the machine, you need to return. Thus, you need a crash course."

"How?"

"Do you trust me?" Mekiri asked, with a tone of voice that was as heavy as it was tough. She stared into Sam's eyes, unblinking.

To her credit, if blinking a bit herself, Sam held her gaze. "Yes," Sam replied, with a deep breath.

Choice. That was the key to all of this. And Sam was nothing but decisive.

"Then look into my eyes, for a deep trance is the only way I will be able to download all the knowledge you will need without frying your brain. For this is a training of the mind and soul rather than the body, which the Gift will take care of."

Sam stared into Mekiri's eyes as her irises glowed as if she possessed the Gift. Hers glowed white, like the moonglow in a warm, clear night. They were deep pools that sucked Sam's mind in. It was said that the eyes are the window to the soul. Sam was about to meet face to face with the soul of a god.

† † †

"This is your idea, then," Forge stared at the quick sketch that Alex had drawn in mere minutes.

"I'm not sure if it is actually possible," Alex replied. "In theory it should work, it is a conversion of matter into energy, like a star does. But in a controlled way to keep the information in a coherent stream aimed at the aurora borealis. I'm not sure I'm making any sense."

"No, no, no, it is actually a good idea. I was toying with something similar but didn't consider the magnetic field to keep the stream enclosed and focused. The older systems on this place should be able to do it with the right tinkering. We can use one of the hypersleep pods as collection chamber. If you help me, we can finish this before Mother finishes teaching your heartmate what she needs to do."

"She is not my heartmate," Alex replied, flustered. He rubbed the back of his neck with his left hand, showing the bracelet Gaby gave him a few days ago. "We are just... very complicated friends in a complicated situation."

"Oh, I'm sorry for assuming," Forge said. After a brief pause, he tried to change the topic. "That's a nice bracelet."

"Yeah, my best friend gave it to me," Alex explained, as he followed Forge to the hypersleep chamber. "Although it reminds me that I can't use my bow anymore."

"Why?" Forge asked, as he pulled some weird looking cables covered in a clear slime. Alex raised an eyebrow as he looked at the slime. "Don't mind the slime. The neuro quantum links use it to keep the interference to a minimum. It's used everywhere on the station. This ancient technology has its quirks."

Alex nodded skeptically at what Forge considered to be "ancient" technology and answered Forge's question.

"My bow was designed to work around my electro-magnetic abilities, but since I burned away most of the stored energy I had thanks to the Gift, I can't use it. I can barely keep up with the others as it is."

"Can you use a regular bow?" Forge asked.

"I can use a regular bow, but it doesn't make sense against the things we usually fight. I should know. Hence, I shifted to use Yaha," Alex replied. He began to help Forge with the cables on the hypersleep pod. "Man, I have so many questions about this place. If we weren't pressed for time, I could spend months here."

"I know! Pretty cool, innit? Anyway, if you don't mind me asking, why keep the bracelet if it reminds you of that?"

"Because it also symbolizes all the stuff we have gone through together."

"It must be nice to have friends," Forge said, rueful. "Be careful, those links are connected to the main power source and the electric shock could kill you."

"I know I'm not the right person to say this but keeping yourself cloistered here won't help making friends—*demonios*!" Alex exclaimed, as he received an electrical shock.

"Are you okay?" Forge asked. "That could have killed you. Unless your Gift is regenerating, and thus a..." Forge's eyes widened as a thought occurred to him.

Alex was finding out how annoying that was. "What?"

"Nevermind. To be honest, I prefer to remain here because that way I don't hurt others with my creations. Last time I created something, it was used for a terrible war. I don't want that, for I have become Death."

"You are not death," Alex said with a wave of his hand as the sensation came back to his fingers. "You created things that have been used for good, like Yaha. You are not responsible for our actions, only for yours. And right now, you, my friend—and I mean it—are the only being in the cosmos that can help me to save your mom... Mekiri. Because I have the idea, but I have no *pinche* idea of how to make it work."

"Leave that to me," Forge smiled.

† † †

"Okay, this is how it will work," Alex explained. "This machine will transform your avatar into coherent packages of energy and send it directly to Last Heaven by punching a hole through realities with a focused beam aimed at the aurora borealis. It will take time for that because we don't want to lose any part of you on the way."

Sam was dealing with a massive migraine and only understood half of what Alex was saying. Her head was heavy, her mind full of thoughts that her brain struggled to make sense of. The whole experience with Mekiri in the garden had been surreal. She suspected even murcana couldn't compete with the experience she'd just had. It was as if someone—a certain melodramatic goddess, to be precise—had downloaded half the aethernet directly into her head.

Alex and Forge stood next to the heavily modified hypersleep pod. There were cables, links and quite a hefty amount of slime all over the place. The cables and links connected to bigger ones that ran toward the dark recesses of the Long Moon.

"Like an incursion but in reverse," Sam mumbled.

"Exactly," Forge said.

"Now, I'm afraid we couldn't get around the whole keeping the avatar alive with so little time, but by converting the avatar into information, Mekiri won't be totally lost," Alex said, staring at his feet. Knowing him—and Sam knew him well by now—he was kicking himself for not finding a way to preserve the physical body. But given how fast he had come up with a plan *and* how fast Forge had made it a reality, plus the time constraints they were under, she had to admit it was nonetheless pretty impressive.

"Mortal creativity never ceases to surprise me," Mekiri said with a wide smile, hugging both Alex and Forge. "How did you come up with that?"

"You accessed a random memory back at Professor Hunt's house. You told us how your other you created Mekiri, in detail, by energy manipulation of subatomic particles. I figure the process should work the other way as well, you know, matter and energy being the same thing and all that stuff I fell asleep to at school," Alex replied.

"Okay," Mekiri said, getting ready to cast a teleportation spell. "I will start the procedure once I get you back to Theia. I fear that Kasumi and Yokoyawa, as strong as they are, might be in serious danger."

"Ahem, mother," Forge interrupted. "You will need every bit of your remaining power to do the procedure as intended. I suggest a different method that will get you two down there in no time. Relatively speaking of course. Follow me!"

Forge led them to a hangar, which had an open bay from which Theia could be seen, as well as the Round Moon getting closer to the point where the Eclipse would form. Standing in a neat row against one of the hangar's walls were three giant armored suits, each the size of a three-story building. They looked vaguely humanoid, covered in angular armor, with wide feet and long shoulder pads in the shape of diamonds. The helmet was in the shape of a raven's beak. They also had wings.

"Woah!" Alex exclaimed, getting close to one that was painted gold. "I thought these only existed in cartoons!"

"What are they?" Sam asked.

"These are ancient combat mecha-armor units, called Aditis. They are really, really ancient."

"That's why I'm wondering how they will be of any

help, son," Mekiri replied. "They are not coded for humans nor freefolk yet, and their batteries ran out millennia ago. I'm not sure the armor will withstand re-entry, especially with Theia's thick ionosphere. It was thinner back then."

"Trust me, mother," Forge said. "This is exactly what *Alex* and Sam need right now. I suggest they take the one specialized in collecting environmental energy to get through the ionosphere."

Sam noticed that Mekiri had the beginnings of a grin.

"You are right," Mekiri said. "Alex, this is your lucky day. You get to pilot one of these, with Sam as copilot."

"Really?" Alex asked, astonished. "I mean, I have some training on how to fly the Figaro, but I'm not sure that—"

"Trust me," Forge interrupted him. "This thing has more intuitive controls than a samoharo ship, by far. As long as you follow my instructions, you will be fine."

"What instructions?" Sam asked. Something was afoot, and she suspected it had to do with Alex. Mekiri had always been the Trickster Goddess to Sam, but after her time in the garden she was starting to trust Mekiri, and by extension Forge, more than she would have even a few hours ago.

"As the pilot, Alex, you can never, ever, let go of the controls, no matter what. If you do that, this Aditi will return you safely to Theia. Then it will disappear."

"Why? Why can't you lend us that thing to fight?" Alex asked.

"Because it won't survive anything after landfall. This thing is old—really old. And using it in free fall is not the same as using it in combat. Plus, you don't even have the organs to synch with it and make it work. These are linked to akeleth physiognomy. You only have their energy signature. That's why I can program it to take you back and nothing more."

"What a shame," Alex replied, rueful. "It would have

been cool to fight using a giant robot."

"Maybe someday," Sam said with a forced smile.

"Ready? We need to hurry."

"I want to thank you both, for all you have done," Mekiri said as she hugged Alex, then Sam. Mekiri broke the embrace and waved at both of them. "Now you go, time is of essence."

Alex took off his bracelet and offered it to Forge. "I really mean the friend thing."

"Thanks!" Forge said, admiring the bracelet.

As Sam and Alex climbed into the cockpit of the ancient machine, his hands trembled, but Sam wasn't sure if it was from excitement or fear.

"Are you okay?"

"I guess it's my turn to do a daring free fall jump, with you as copilot. From the Long Moon, to Theia. This should be fun," Alex said with monotone voice, as they stared at the golden combat mecha-armor.

"I really hate you right now," Sam muttered, amused.

"For what's worth, me too," Alex replied.

This was going to be quite the leap of faith.

Chapter 11
Against All Odds

HE IS JUST WAITING FOR something, but what? Kasumi thought. Her first instinct had been to attack right away. But as she and Yokoyawa headed toward the stage below the Haunted Clocktower, the number of visitors gathering around it made that more complicated than she'd expected. So far, the Eclipse festival activities around the stage had been oddly pleasant and subdued—normal, even. Too normal. But Kasumi had a bad feeling about the situation.

A drumroll announced the appearance of Sherman Zay onto the stage. From the back of the crowd Kasumi watched as a tall, bald man with a few days' worth of stubble that contrasted with a sharp business suit without a tie walk out. He waved to the crowd with a smarmy smile plastered on his face. He took the microphone from a stage aide and walked toward the center of the stage.

"Hello!" he exclaimed as the feedback from the microphone screeched through the surround sound. The electronic shriek made Yokoyawa wince, while it disoriented Kasumi. She reached for her hearing aids and pushed a small button to change the settings. The screeching subsided.

That wasn't a regular feedback noise, right? Kasumi hand-signaled to Yoko, who was still recovering from the noise. He nodded at her in agreement.

"Apologies for that," Sherman Zay said, his voice now muffled to Kasumi's ears. "Nothing that a few minor adjustments to our sound systems can't fix. So, let's begin. I'm..."

Kasumi and Yoko pushed their way through the gathering crowd, toward the stage where Sherman Zay was giving the speech. The eclipse was about to start. To his credit, while he saw them approaching the scaffolding, he kept talking to the audience, his smile never faltering.

"I see that we have both the former and the current champion of the Chivalry Games with us," he said, pointing at Kasumi and Yokoyawa. "Give them your applause, for their presence honors this event!"

A raucous round of applause ensued as everyone turned to acclaim them, much to Kasumi's embarrassment. Yokoyawa, however, never stopped looking at Sherman, who waved his hands to quiet the audience, who complied in synchronicity. Everyone but Yoko and Kasumi stood at attention, as if they were mesmerized by Zay. *Or maybe enthralled was a better word,* Kasumi thought.

"As you can see, KorbyWorld, of which my family has been a staunch supporter and investors for more time than you insects have been alive... than you good people could remember. Since the day we offered to crack open Byne's mind and sponsor his work with Korben, KorbyWorld has aimed to offer good entertainment. And now, at this Eclipse Festival, I tell you that new things will be offered to you smaller beings. Soon you will enter into a new era! Well, some of you anyways, most of you are only a burden to the plans I have in mind for the glory of my people."

The audience was unusually silent, not reacting at all to Zay's words. His body emitted an unusual amount of steam and heat. Red cracks were appearing on his face.

"That guy is losing it," Kasumi whispered to Yoko. "His

speech is a bit unhinged."

"I'm more concerned about what he is about to do," Yoko replied.

"Because today, you are both witness to and a part of the show," Sherman Zay said, opening his arms. A strong wind surged from him as the eclipse began.

"Everybody, run!" Yokoyawa boomed, his deep voice more felt than heard. The people gawked at him for a second, and then scrambled off as the wind picked up in strength and temperature, whatever spell they had been under finally broken.

Yoko darted in front of Kasumi to shield her as the wind became deadly steam. Unlike Kasumi, whose demonhunter garb offered little protection, Yoko had the advantage of a thick skin and being accustomed to the searing heat of the Hegemony lands. And yet, even he was struggling to remain on his feet as his arms took the brunt of the attack.

Kasumi twirled Breaker and cleaved it into the ground, releasing a wave of cold that countered the deadly steam, dissipating it. "Are you okay?" Kasumi asked.

"I will be fine," Yokoyawa replied with a grimace, which given that he was a samoharo, looked like a giant iguana trying to bite its lips. "That looks painful though," he pointed to Zay.

Sherman's skin had cracked open, falling to the ground in flakes. Underneath a red, orange, and grey being was struggling to break free, until what once had been a human exploded in a rain of viscera. In its place, stood a hulking behemoth of a demonic knight, whose grey skin steamed. He held a strange weapon, a mix between a scythe and a ball and chain.

"The human served well as conduit for the birth of my avatar," the being said, mostly to himself, but also to Yoko and Kasumi. "Now, to finish what I started when I took down Ishtaru."

His presence emitted an aura that sent chills down Yoko's spine and to the tip of his tail. This was the kind of being he had trained to kill. And yet, as Sid had told him once after a particularly dangerous mission, and again after the Titans crisis, no amount of training, no amount of somewhat friendly competition at the Chivalry Games could prepare someone to face a being that is way more powerful than a regular incursion. Not even a 'newborn' Gifted emitted such a terrifying aura during the merging of souls and the ensuing mental chaos. It was perhaps the first time Yoko felt absolute, abject fear. Now he understood why Alex and Sam still had nightmares after facing the Creeping Chaos, and why Alex had become more cautious and scared after barely surviving that encounter. For the being standing in front of Yokoyawa and Kasumi was not a run of the mill incursion. This was a god. Or at the very least, the avatar of one. The same one Professor Hunt had mentioned, a deity of karmic retribution. And no amount of training had prepared him to face one.

"Tell us your name, demon," Kasumi said.

"Demon? No. I am a god. Shemazay."

"Sherman Zay and Shemazay? Really? How original."

"His family served their purpose as hosts for me. Who cares about the name I gave them. You don't care about the names of ants."

"I do."

Kasumi approached Zay; Breaker tightly gripped in her hand. The Tempest Blade emitted waves of freezing air to protect them, glowing with an unusual intensity. Almost as bright as Yaha or Black Fang or Gaby's twin blades did with their respective wielders. But Kasumi was not a Gifted. A sudden realization came to Yokoyawa. This had the words 'bad omen' written all over it.

"Kasumi, wait," Yoko said.

But she didn't listen. She was already running toward Shemazay, Breaker held aloft to hit him in the face.

"Come to me if you dare," Shemazay taunted as he teleported himself and Kasumi to the top of the clocktower, from where an explosion could be heard.

Yoko looked at the top of the tower, unsheathed the Stellar Ehécatl and raced to reach Kasumi before it was too late. He clenched his jaw as he ran, with a single aim in his head: Protecting Kasumi from herself.

† † †

Yoko reached the top of the tower in record time. Then again, not many beings below a godly avatar could stop an enraged, two-meter-tall, and over two-hundred-kilogram mountain of muscle with tail, claws, fangs and an obsidian sword. Dragons might have gone extinct centuries ago, but the samoharo were more than able to fill the niche. Not for nothing were they considered mighty. Yoko may have decided to become a pacifist the day he left his clan and become a therapist, but that didn't mean that he had lost his edge.

And yet, Yoko couldn't shake the feeling that this had been too easy. If he were a seasoned warrior and pathfinder, he would not face the stronger member of a group of enemies, but rather get them alone by using another member of the group as bait. It was a trap. It seemed that Shemazay considered Yoko the biggest threat to his plan. If the situation hadn't felt as dire, Yoko would have chuckled. It was obvious to everyone who was the strongest of this team. And the second strongest.

There was a door on the back of the face of the giant clock on the top floor. Yoko crossed the threshold and saw Kasumi standing on a large dais floating outside the clocktower. There were six columns rising along the edge of the dias, following its diameter. A short stone bridge connected the clock face with the dais. Kasumi was struggling to keep Shemazay's attacks at bay. Yoko ran at her.

I only need to help Kasumi and hold long enough for Sam and Alex to get here, he thought. *Wherever you are, I hope you are on your way.*

Shemazay had several deep cuts in his body. While they were slowly closing, it was more than Yoko would have expected. He was limped on the right where Kasumi had cut the tendon. Being a godly avatar, he would heal in no time, but Yoko was sure he hadn't anticipated such fierce resistance from Kasumi, who was using Breaker's length to her advantage, keeping him at bay while cutting him with the glacial wind and the fluid movements of the Tempest Blade.

Then, to Yokoyawa's horror, Shemazay managed to wrap his chain around Breaker and pull Kasumi toward him, so fast that she didn't have time to let go of her weapon.

Shemazay struck her in the face with his right fist, sending her flying back, close to the entrance to where Yoko stood.

Kasumi hit the floor in a boneless sprawl, pieces of her white cat mask skittering away. Yet, Breaker remained tight in her grip.

The omen that Yokoyawa had seen was becoming a reality.

Shemazay closed in to finish her, but a flying kick by the samoharo sent him reeling to the other end of the dais.

"You want her? You have to go through me," Yokoyawa said. His blood boiled.

"I see you samoharo, and I pity you."

Yokoyawa crouched beside Kasumi, examining her injuries. She was unconscious, bleeding from the nose, but otherwise seemed to be breathing fine. Yoko was worried about the potential brain damage such blow could cause, but he didn't have the time nor the equipment to make a fair assessment. It would be better if he didn't move her until medical aid could arrive. Which meant that he would have to be careful while fighting Shemazay. Kasumi opened her eyes and groaned.

"Don't move," Yoko whispered to her. "You did fine. Let me take care of him now."

"Be careful," Kasumi mumbled.

"I pity you," Shemazay continued, "for you represent the embodiment of all that's wrong with the samoharo."

Yokoyawa stood up, stretching his back. At his full height, without hunching over to present a less menacing appearance, the *Meemech* samoharo was almost as tall as Shemazay. He held the Stellar Ehécatl at the ready. From under his T-shirt a dark purple substance began to flow, orichalcum-titanium nanoparticles, a special alloy known only to the samoharo. The nanoparticles quickly formed an armor chestplate with a detailed dragon motif.

"I don't see what's to pity, aside from your fall," Yoko replied. He looked straight at Shemazay's eyes. They were black as charcoal with orange pupils that reminded him of embers from a fireplace.

"Fall? Or finally opened my eyes? I was once like you and your people. The akeleth sacrificed so much to protect the masterwork of K'anna, only for it to be squandered by the mortal races. The samoharo stood proud among the stars, until you lizards threw it all away to protect lesser beings instead of using your might to defeat our common enemy. And that cost you your home planet, the technology that you wear so proudly. And for what? To play caretaker of a bunch of monkeys and grey shifters? Your so-called prophet Rhaperial was a traitor to the akelethand was a fool like Ishtaru for forcing you to put up with that."

"That's the problem with you, isn't?" Yoko replied, taking measure of his opponent. "You never understood the meaning of piety, which is a problem for a so-called god. Our prophet Quetzalcoatl—or Rapherial, because yes, we know his real name—didn't force us to do anything. We chose it. And yes, we could have destroyed half the universe to beat the orionians, the mestahlaep and the other servant species to the Pit Lords. But for what? To live in a desolated universe as the only survivors, toiling away until the end? Sacrificing other species before they could reach their potential, like the humans and the free-folk, for barely a victory in a long war? It wouldn't have been worthy. Even less if it meant following the belief of such a pitiful being like you."

"I see that unlike most of your kind, you actually know your history. The real history."

"And that's why I retired as fighter. Until now."

"You should have stayed retired, then."

"Oh, just shut up or I will gladly rip your jaw from your mouth."

"So be it, samoharo!"

Shemazay threw the ball from his chain. It turned into a meteor of fire as it shot toward Yoko, who expertly parried it with his giant sword. They exchanged blow after blow with their respective weapons. It felt as if the Stellar Ehécatl would break every time the impact, but it held strong, befitting the original prototype for the Tempest Blades.

I need to get closer to make him drop that thing, Yoko thought. *Time to make him feel some mortal pain.*

Yokoyawa backed away, forcing Shemazay to throw a long-range attack with the chain, an attack that made him lose his balance.

Yoko threw himself to the floor to dodge the chain. He bounced up and ran at full speed toward Shemazay, tackling him with enough momentum that they almost fell from the dais. Putting all his weight behind it, Yoko reeled back and punched Shemazay's. His blow connected just above the wrist with force that would've been bone-shattering on any other species, making Shemazay lose his grip on his weapon. The fallen god shoved Yoko away and stood up. Shemazay closed his fists and punched the air, as if he were reloading his arms. Both the samoharo and the fallen god ran at each other, throwing powerful haymakers to each other's face.

It was as if Yoko had been hit by a warptrain. Or a meteor. He blinked and had barely enough time to block another haymaker with his left arm. The impact sent a wave of pain through his skeleton. Yoko grimaced.

"You shouldn't have retired, champion," Shemazay taunted between punches, reducing Yoko to just blocking the attacks. "These years of content and rest have weakened you. So weak that that pitiful demonhunter now holds your title just because she managed to beat a Titan."

"Kasumi earned that title fair and square. You won't insult her while I'm here."

"That can be arranged."

Shemazay threw several punches at Yokoyawa. While not exactly faster that could be seen, they were fast enough that Yoko's defensive moves weren't able to catch them all. However, Shemazay was trading power for speed, and each blow was less painful than the previous one. Yoko soaked up a few more attacks and then countered with several of his own. Hitting Shemazay's body was like punching the Rock of Aeons back home, the gargantuan rock that stood in the middle of the continent of Ouslis. And yet, Yoko could feel that his last punch had broken several ribs.

Shemazay roared in fury at the counterattack. He redoubled his pummeling on Yoko. But as long as that kept him away from Kasumi until help could get there, it would be enough. He had made peace with his own mortality decades ago, around the time he had retired, around the time Sid had saved him from their last mission together. Yoko was not afraid of dying. As he had assured Sid, he wouldn't let any of these human-freefolk kids—for they were kids at their age—die on his watch. Not anymore. Yoko kept backing up, leading Shemazay away from Kasumi, who was struggling to her feet.

Yoko was taking the beating of his life. For every attack he blocked, Shemazay replied with a counter faster than before. It was dawning on him something that Sam and Alex had told him once, during the therapy sessions: When fighting such monsters, no matter how powerful the armor of a titanfighter was, or how hard a demonhunter had trained to use their spiritual energy to empower themselves, the difference was milliseconds. The difference between a regular incursion and beings like the Withered King, Joshua and his Beast, or a godly avatar was defined in milliseconds of extensive preparation as the ones the samoharo made to take down rogue Gifted. The time it took them to move and attack during a fight. And that was the only reason a Gifted was possibly the only being capable of matching them without prep time. It was not a difference of power. It was of perception.

Yoko fell back to his training and focused. He protected his head, leaving his abdomen exposed. The chest plate was degrading fast, and he could feel ribs break. His mouth filled with blood. It was enough.

The samoharo counterattacked. Pushing harder than ever, summoning the ancestral strength of the blood of Quetzalcoatl. He returned the blows with all that was left of his strength, almost breaking his own hands in the attack.

A shockwave exploded through the air above the tower. Gold and lilac lightning struck the tower, electrical arcs bouncing away from the impact, followed by the nearby sound of thunder crashing the ground below. As Shemazay pounded Yoko's body, the samoharo smiled, blood glistening in his sharp teeth.

"What are you smiling at?" Shemazay demanded.

"Did you hear that thunder?" Yokoyawa replied, swinging a right hook to the jaw that ended with a cracking noise. The punch nearly ripped away the jaw, making good on his promise. "That's the sound of your demise."

Shemazay fixed his dislocated jaw with sheer brute force. His eyes glowed like fire.

"You put too much faith in the human and the freefolk."

"I do because those two have proven time and time again that they can deal with the likes of you, against all odds. Just ask the Creeping Chaos," Yoko replied, spitting blood into the face of the fallen god. "Oh, that's right, you can't. He's *kimen*."

"Soon, you two will join him in death!"

Shemazay snatched Yoko by the arm and flung him, sending the samoharo crashing through the clock face and back into the tower.

"We will see," Shemazay muttered, as he walked to Kasumi—still dazed—his scythe rematerializing in his hand, emitting a dark miasma.

Yokoyawa struggled to stand, but his injuries made that difficult. Gasping for air, he could only watch in abject horror at how Shemazay hoisted the kneeling Kasumi and stabbed her in the gut.

Chapter 12
Crossroads

AS THE MECHA-ARMOR FLOATED in space, Alex pushed the controls forward trying to accelerate, though to no avail. The armor wasn't responding to his commands.

"So much for piloting experience," Sam mumbled.

"This is an akeleth giant robot," Alex said. "Must be programmed to reply only to Mekiri."

A scream echoed through the comms of the mecha, and an explosion of light blinded them. The mecha shook them by thrusting forward at increasing speed.

"What was that?" Sam asked.

"That," Alex replied, trying to keep the reins on the mecha, "must have been Mekiri converting her avatar into energy to rejoin her other self."

"So, is she dead?" Sam asked.

"I don't think that definition applies to her," Alex replied as the mecha approached the upper atmosphere of Theia. "Whatever she did, she gave us the push to reach the planet. Hold tight, this is gonna get bumpy and really hot."

"Define hot?"

"As hot as charred meat if I don't get the reentry angle right!"

"The what? If we die, I will kill you again in the Tempest!"

"Duly noted!"

Alex tried to remember the simulations Sid had made him practice since the Figaro became fully functional, in case he had to pilot it and for any reason he was in the upper atmosphere or above. The mecha's A.I. was doing most of the math work, but still required the pilot's input for the initial adjusts. It was clearly designed for a form of life that wasn't human or freefolk. Under any other circumstances, Alex would be delighted to fly outside the planet. Maybe in another world, in another time, this would be a televised event, a dream come true. But right now, he was just trying to get himself and Sam onto the planet alive, and near the Haunted Clocktower, without becoming a charred piece of junk or killing thousands with the impact. Through gritted teeth, Alex moved the control to aim for the spot they had to reach and the altitude the mecha-armor would have to start to decelerate to avoid becoming a meteor.

The mecha-armor reached terminal speed just above the ionosphere. It was descending faster than either Alex or Sam had expected, but stayed on course, just as Forge had told them it would once they had pinpointed the landing place, as long as the pilot didn't let go of the controls. Sam braced herself in the back seat as the g-forces made her feel like the skin would be ripped from her bones.

Without warning, two large needles appeared from the console and stabbed Alex in the arms. Alex cried out as excruciating pain seared through his arms, and it took all his effort just to keep his hands on the controls. As the armor passed through the ionosphere, it started to absorb all the electrical energy from the surrounding area, leaving behind it a two kilometer diameter hole. The mecha-armor channeled all that energy through the needles into Alex like live wires. The sensation was akin to every cell in his body bursting like a squall line, lightning cracking through his body as surely as it would the sky. A golden light flickered in his irises, dimmed for a bit, and then became steady.

"Now I get it, Mekiri," Sam whispered.

To his credit, Alex never let go of the controls. His fists clenched the controls so hard the ancient parts creaked so loudly they heard it even over the din around them. Forge hadn't warned them about this. Maybe that was why he had been so insistent that Alex had to be the pilot. Maybe he knew this would be a way to recharge his Gift. There was still only so much that Alex could shoulder, and he began to cry. Hallucinations crept in, and he saw a giant winged man standing on the planet's surface, extending his arms toward them in welcome.

"You are my sons," the hallucination said. Between the pain and the g-forces, Alex felt he was about to pass out.

Sam leaned forward and placed her hands on his shoulders, holding him tight. She whispered an enchantment that ran from Alex's shoulders into his arms, numbing them just enough to reduce the pain.

"I'm not letting you go if you don't let go those controls," Sam yelled at him to get through the noise of the shaking mecha-armor. "I have faith in you, I always have. You can do this! For both of us!"

The sound barrier was shattered.

†††

A shooting star could be seen across several regions, breaking the darkness of the eclipse. Gold and lilac lightning followed the shooting star as it approached the theme park. Many visitors, already scared by what had happened a few moments earlier, ran scared from this new threat. But the shooting star decelerated with the activation of retropropulsors. It looked like a giant suit of armor, similar to those of the Solarian Knights. It landed softly and in the precise spot Alex had aimed for, a few meters from the entrance to the clocktower.

The mecha-armor cockpit opened, surrounded by a cloud of steam. A few onlookers approached as Sam hurriedly unbuckled her belt and grabbed at Alex, trying to shake him back to consciousness. "Don't die on me, León," she said.

"I wouldn't dare, Ambers," Alex mumbled. "You are capable of kicking my ghost's ass for eternity."

"And don't forget it, now let's go."

"I need to get these needles from my arms first."

Right on cue, the needles retracted, leaving two seeping punctures in Alex's arms. Sam whispered a spell and the holes closed.

"You have been practicing your healing magick," Alex smiled as Sam helped him to get out of the mecha-armor.

"Just the basics," Sam replied. "To keep you with me longer."

"I feel weird," Alex said as he examined his arms and hands.

"You are weird," Sam replied, and she kissed him on the forehead. "That's what I love about you. Are you sure you want to go there and fight? You are not at one hundred percent. I can try to do this on my own."

"That's why I feel weird. Are my irises glowing?"

"Yes."

"Then I'm back," Alex said with a grin. He ran toward the clocktower, Sam on his heels. "Now, I thought the lesson last time was that we don't need to do things alone. Look, if this is my last fight…"

"Please tell me that you are not feeling down again."

"Let me finish," Alex interrupted her. "If this is meant to be my last fight as part of the team, I'm fine with that. I will go there, kick some ass, win and then I will gladly take a back seat and let you be the sole hero from now on.

I just want to end things on my own terms. And make you proud."

"You are risking your health again."

"For you, for Kasumi, for the rest. That's what friends... what family are for. Truth be told, you are my inspiration."

"What?"

"You are not a hero because of what you can do, Sam, but because of who you are. You tackle every challenge no matter how frightening it is or how exhausted you are. I wish I had half your courage," Alex explained. "And for the record, I don't think you have to choose to be either freefolk or human. Why can't you be both?"

"Now is not the time for this," Sam replied. Her face was turning as red as her hair had been pre-Gift activation.

Sam and Alex entered the clocktower. The entrance hall was burnt to a crisp, the smell of burned wood and charred metal filled the air.

"Here we go," Alex mumbled. "Ready?"

Sam looked at him and sighed. "About Kasumi... and you... and me... there is something we need to discuss the three of us... sort things out, clarify the situation, you know what I mean."

"Let's worry about that after we save her and Yoko," Alex said, and winked at her as they approached the first flight of stairs.

The stairs were full of armed soldiers and neither of them could identify what army they belonged to.

"This doesn't look like the interior of the ride we visited last time. The whole place has changed. And since when did it have armed soldiers?" Alex asked confused, walking up the first steps. The soldiers were getting ready to fight them.

"Something else is going on," Sam replied as flicks of light came from her fingertips. Her hair flowed lilac and her irises glowed in the same color.

"Anyway, here we go," Alex said, as he unsheathed Yaha, whose blade glowed golden. Electrical currents surged from his arms as his irises glowed with a golden hue.

"Agreed," Sam said, following him. One wind spell of hers blasted several soldiers away, opening a path through the stairs.

†††

Alex looked up. There was still another floor to go and there were too many soldiers in the way.

Where are these guys coming from? Alex wondered. Shemazay definitely wouldn't use them, and the notes they had on him didn't indicate a cult. Their uniforms, though, those looked like they belonged to the Golden King's army. But they were an ocean away. It didn't make sense.

"Stop daydreaming and focus!" Sam shouted as she knocked a guy with her staff.

Snapped out of his reverie, Alex tackled another one with the left shoulder, pushing him into the void, while with his right arm, swung Yaha to cut the arm of another axe-wielding guard. "Time is running out."

As they reached the last floor, they saw a long and seemingly endless corridor. At one end was the back side of a clockface, but outside it was clearly night. It was still daylight when he and Sam had entered the tower. Was time being affected? Then Alex looked at the other end of the corridor and saw the back of another clockface. Outside this clock it was still daylight with the shadow of the eclipse darkening part of the clock. Above them the clock's gears floated freely, rotating as if following some mysterious counter. And in the middle of the corridor stood Gaby, working her way through a mass of soldiers. A quick headcount by Alex indicated at least thirty still standing.

"Gaby?" Sam asked, confused, as Alex cut his way through the soldiers to reach her. The three of them stood in the middle, back-to-back, surrounded by the enemy. But which enemy?

"What are you doing here?" Gaby asked as she dodged an attack.

"We could ask the same question," Sam replied.

"Probably the place where you are and this one are connected during the eclipse, by some kind of weird dimensional magick," Alex added as he slashed through a rifle with Yaha. "The towers must be twins. I could try to explain, but as my boss just told me, we don't have time."

"Good," Gaby said dodging a shot coming from her left. "I like the new you. Still, what's going on?"

"Fallen god deposed Mekiri and altered magick," Sam replied, activating her True Spell to shield them from a rain of bullets.

"Kasumi and Yoko are fighting him, but they need reinforcements while Sam fixes magick, and you?" Alex asked Gaby.

"Trying to stop a tovainar that has hijacked the body of countless Sisters of Mercy—including an old friend—from claiming the Crown of the Death and deliver it to the Golden King, changing the future of the incoming war. These are their soldiers," Gaby explained with a grunt as she stabbed two with her twin blades. Soldiers kept coming up the stairs, but not many as before. "I'm not sure if these guys are actually human anymore."

"Stupid gods complicating our lives, who needs them?" Alex said, as he grabbed one soldier by the arm and threw him at another.

"Mekiri is our friend, remember?" Sam said, knocking one with her staff.

"She's the exception!" Alex replied, as he jumped on Sam's staff and made a back flip kick that pushed the head of a soldier through the floor. "We don't have time to play nice with these guys!"

Alex and Sam attention snapped to an opposing wall when Yokoyawa crashed through it, bits of rubble skittering across the floor. Shemazay stepped through the hole and strode toward Kasumi, picked her up by the neck like a rag doll, and slung the business end of his scythe into her. The gleaming tip protruded from Kasumi's back. Shemazay dropped her to the ground, leaving blood to pool around Kasumi's struggling form.

"Sam! Kasumi needs help!" Alex yelled.

"On it, make way!" Sam replied as she patted Alex on the back. "*Fasdn!*"

Sam called a lightning bolt that Alex caught with Yaha, then he cleaved the floor with the sword, sending a wave of energy that knocked every soldier in Sam's path to the floor with the shockwave. She ran toward Kasumi and used her staff to knock aside any stragglers.

† † †

Sam ran faster than she had ever done before, her Gift at full power without having to focus. As her irises glowed lilac and her silver fox tail grew anew, the adrenaline pumping through her veins fed her muscles to push beyond what was humanly possible, to cover the distance of the seemingly endless corridor to the dais. Shemazay had noticed her approach, for he threw a fire covered ball chain toward her. Sam didn't flinch or slow. With a flick of her hands, she cast a spell that froze the floor of the clocktower between her and Kasumi. Sam dropped and slid under the chained fireball. With a single thought, she cast her True Spell and used it to deflect the fireball. As she reached Kasumi, she gave a quick glance at the stab wound. It was bleeding profusely, and the edges blackened. But she was alive.

This is not good, Sam thought. "Don't worry, Kasumi, I got you."

Shemazay recalled his chained ball and approached, scythe held aloft to cleave Sam in two. However, the Bubble deflected the attack with a purple shimmer, as Sam closed her eyes, embraced Kasumi and cast the only card she had left, for running away was not possible. Rings of light surrounded them and as the scythe descended for a second time. The Bubble spell broke as Sam teleported them away, leaving only scorched marks on the ground.

"Run, pathetic ones, for I know where you are going," Shemazay roared. His body trembled, splitting into two copies. One of those copies opened a portal made of a ring of fire and entered it.

†††

"This is getting ridiculous and a waste of time," Gaby yelled at Alex, the both of them fighting back-to-back against twenty soldiers.

"Tell me about it! These guys are from your mission, not mine," Alex replied as he punched one soldier so hard that a crunching noise echoed through the room. "It's time to end this. I'm gonna try something I've always wanted to do."

The rest of the soldiers drew their guns and cocked them.

"Agreed," Gaby replied, knowing exactly what Alex was about to try. He had talked nonstop for years about that maneuver, and it seemed he had now both the knowledge and power to do it. She smiled at him. "Just line them up for me."

"Deal! Keep close!" Alex replied.

The soldiers shot a rain of bullets. Alex irises glowed with increased intensity as he extended his hands in front of him. All the bullets stopped in midair around them. Alex closed his hands and the bullets fell to the ground, filling the air with a noise remarkably similar to rain. He then opened and closed his hands a second time, in close succession, jamming the hammers of all the weapons. Alex then raised his hands, and all the soldiers were lifted from the ground and floated a meter above it.

"Now!" Alex yelled, as sweat beaded on his forehead. Gaby didn't waste a second—she turned, jumped on Alex's shoulders and then moved at superhuman speed, her Gift at its full output. She struck the nineteen soldiers with Heartguard and Soulkeeper, with such speed they seemed two blurs of red and blue light, jumping from one body floating midair to another in quick succession. She landed again at her initial position, at Alex's back, who then relaxed his hands. The soldiers dropped dead into the ground alongside several newly freed limbs from their previous owners.

"I never thought I would be able to pull this off," Alex said with a satisfied smile.

"After the train thing, this must be a piece of cake," Gaby replied, breathing hard.

"Don't mention food. I'm starving and I still have to put that asshole god wannabe in his place."

"Are you gonna be okay? Do you need help?" Gaby asked.

"Yes. Besides, you have your own mission."

"Sure?" Gaby was concerned about her best friend. She didn't know how but he seemed to have gotten his full Gift back, but he'd overused it before. Maybe there was a way to help him and then go after Livia.

No, there is not enough time, we have to trust each other, she thought.

"Sure." Alex smiled his goofy smile at her. "I'm the sixth man that comes from the bench to punch above his weight and win the game. Be careful, Team Mom. Love you!"

"Love you too, Bedhair. See you on the other side."

Arcs of electricity danced across Alex's body. He ran as fast as he'd done when he'd jumped from a balcony to land on a wyvern, leaving track marks behind. Gaby saw her best friend rushing to face a terrible monster and yet, she felt at ease. She ran in the opposite direction, toward the last set of stairs to reach the roof of the clocktower.

I kinda feel sorry for the guy that has him this pissed off, she thought. *Almost as sorry as I will feel for Livia after I beat her ass.*

Gaby reached the top of the tower. In other times, the mechanism that operated the clock was housed there. But now the roof was full of holes, the walls damaged, and gears floated around, as if gravity had said that it had had enough and decided to take a nice holiday somewhere else, leaving its younger, less powerful sibling in charge.

Livia knelt in the center of the room, moving tiles around like a slide puzzle until the correct combination activated a mechanism. She stood up and moved back as the floor opened and the Crown came floating out.

Gaby saw the Crown of the Dead for the first time, the fabled object that had changed the destiny of many battles, and had shaped history. It looked as it had in her vision at the Tower of Salt: a burnished, black bronze filigree circlet, the metalwork twisted into intricate threads to resemble a corpse's ribcage that had been crossed with protruding temple spires, and intertwined throughout with vines and thorns. The flowers, a strange mix between roses and carnations, had open-mouth skulls at their centers, where the rubies were placed. There were six red rubies and an empty seventh setting, waiting for a new soul to be caught. An aura of wintery sorrow emanated from the crown. For a second, Gaby swore that she could see shadows, souls running across the surface of the crown, lamenting their fates. The Crown floated in the middle of the room, but unlike the clock gears moving freely around the space, the Crown remained frozen in a single place. Livia was about to take it, but a cold white light pushed her hand away. She shook her hand, as if she had been stung.

"If I were you, I would walk away," Gaby said.

"Finally, the last key to solve the puzzle and obtain the Crown is here. Took you long enough."

"Had to take out the trash first. What do you mean by the last key?" Gaby said. Her eyes widened as the realization hit her like a ton of bricks, as every piece and event of the last couple of days fit to create a larger picture. "Oh, I see. You knew all the time the Crown was here. So why the whole charade when you knew I wasn't going to fall for that?"

"Because the part of the legend that you and your small friend ignore is that the Crown can only be summoned and be ordered to obey its new owner, not unlike the Tempest Blades," Livia said, "through trial by combat. The winner proving their worth to the warrior kings and queens of yore to use it for conquest as it was meant to be."

"And whoever you are inside Livia right now, used her as bait to lure me here, knowing that I wouldn't fight her at full strength? Like you dropped a hint when the Queen died, and you tried to steal her soul?"

"So many misconceptions. You never were the cleverest student. The Queen's soul," Livia showed a clear crystal, which she crushed with her bare hands. "would have been useful, like that of her trapped father. But I was more interested in her Gift, the ability to see the past of a person, of a place, of a soul. That was the actual bait, for you and the Greywolf, not Livia. She is my most recent and valuable possession: my host. And I don't care whatever hang ups and traumas you have that might affect this combat. Regardless of the result, I, and by extension, my King, will win. There is no other possible outcome."

"Yeah, we will see about that. You are wrong about one thing," Gaby replied as her Tempest Blades took on an intense glow. "These blades don't have an owner; they have a partner of their choosing."

"Partner?" Livia said, derision filling her voice. "They are weapons. Like us. They don't have a choice. We don't have a choice, don't delude yourself."

"Wrong again. The Blades have a choice, as we all do. Everyone has a choice. Even you. Let me help you to get rid of that tovainar inside you, Livia," Gaby pleaded.

"Get rid? Gavito and I are one now, we have been since we killed Madam Park after her failure," Livia said with a laugh, "and got this younger host in exchange."

"So it has a name," Gaby replied, her blood boiling. To think that the corrupt spirit of a coward was a serial body snatcher and had killed its previous hosts. All of them women. "Good, that way I know who I'm beating. Trial by combat? Fine, let's do this and when I defeat you, I will get Livia back."

"Hope will get you nowhere but the graveyard." Livia smiled. "I shall put you there like this host should have done years ago."

Chapter 13
Tears of Blood

BOOM!

The echoing sound of speakers being turned on attracted the attention of several guards, who raced to the terrace, where Sid, Vivi and Joshua were staring at the incoming army marching through the city across the river. Leading the army, on top of a large chariot with pyrotechnics and a large screen projecting his face, was man with the makeup of a mime and a garish fashion sense. Fionn and Harland came out from the castle as the man began to speak into a microphone.

"Is this thing on? Oh, it is! Ha ha ha ha! Listen to me, people of Mon Caern. Hear me! My humble personage has been ordered by our merciful liege, our beloved messiah, the Golden King, to deliver this city to him, as he wants to provide it with his grace. Rejoice to be among the beloved culled before the Void arrives! To be saved from the End of Times! But! We are open to offer you a mercy, if you chose to give us the Band of the Greywolf and the Crown of the Dead, currently hiding inside the walls of your inner city!"

"Who is that guy that keeps talking and talking and talking as if he were some kind of villain pastiche?" Sid asked, staring at the guy leading a battalion coming out from the town and closing in on the castle complex. "And why does his outfit seem to be composed of whatever clothes were available during laundry day?"

"The guy dressed as a clown is Edamane," Fionn replied. After the Chivalry Games had unveiled the Creeping Chaos it was only a matter of time before the Golden King revealed itself. As a result, Fionn had a few projects in hand just for that scenario: keeping tabs on the players of major developments after the southeastern city states split from the Alliance, fortify Skarabear in case a last retreat was needed, and polishing a special combat technique. It was the first project which had given him and Harland intel on who was working on the Golden King's side. "He is known for being crazy. As in bloodthirsty, mad genius crazy. If he is here, then for sure the Crown is here. Which means that they have someone on the inside already."

"And we know who," Sid chuckled, then looked at Fionn. "I think you won the bet. And that this castle might be already compromised."

"So much for achieving neutrality," Harland said, arid.

"It seems that the Duke was played for a fool by their envoys... until their army arrived here," Vivi replied, sarcasm heavy in her voice. "Where is he, by the way?"

"Last time Fionn and I saw him, he pushed us out of his office and closed the door with at least four locks," Harland replied. "I don't think he will be of any help."

"As my old man said," Fionn replied, "'If you don't fight for something, you will fall for anything and everything.' The Duke is proving that adage correct."

"There is something else you should know about Edamane," Joshua said. "I recall something about him from many years ago, when I still lived in Carpadocci, and became a tovainar. He is a twin."

"Many people are twins," Sid replied.

"Not many people are twin tovainar," Joshua explained. "Millennia old twin tovainar. They are older than me."

"Crap," Sid muttered under his breath. "Here we go again."

"Does he have the same abilities as Byron?" Fionn asked. He knelt to tie his shoelaces tight. He stood up and took two rolls of training bandages and started to wrap his hands.

"Not as far as I know," Joshua replied. "But he has something for sure."

"Then Edamane is mine," Fionn replied with such tonelessness that it inspired noticeable shivers in Sid and Harland. They were already acquainted with that attitude.

THUD!

A low frequency reverberation shook the walls.

THUD!

A second reverberation shook the ground. It was as if huge footfalls were hitting the ground.

THUD!

Some of the houses near the river, in front of the terrace, collapsed as if shaken by an earthquake.

"What was that?" Vivi asked.

"Their big guy." Harland pointed at the undead giant crushing buildings in its wake. "Question: If magick is not working properly, how were they able to use necromancy to raise that thing?"

"Not sure, maybe they are using a summoning of some spirit from the Pits to bypass that," Vivi replied. "It wouldn't be unheard off, but it would require a lot of summoning leverage."

"Which the Golden King has," Joshua said, staring at the giant. Its skin was blue, as if its blood had been congealed from being frozen under tons of ice. "Possession rather than necromancy?"

"I guess they didn't count with magick failing either," Vivi added.

"Is everybody inside the walls?" Fionn asked a female

guard, the badge on her right shoulder's pauldron marking her as a captain. The other guards were coming to the terrace armed with rifles.

"As far as we know," the captain replied. "What do you want us to do?"

"What about your boss, the Duke?" Harland asked. "Shouldn't you wait for his orders?"

"He is hiding inside, while our families are in danger. You are here, about to risk your lives to protect them. The choice is rather obvious," the captain answered, eliciting a smile from Fionn. He patted her on the shoulder.

"Good. Gather any remaining guards you might have inside the walls and follow Harland's orders, we will take care of the rest."

"What are you planning to do?" the captain asked.

"As I said, what we always do," Fionn said. The muscles along his neck knotted with tension as he stared down the battalion. Sid was to his right, next to Vivi, while Joshua was to his left.

"Just to be sure, are we in an agreement that what we are about to do is stupid?" Sid said as he twirled his tomahawks in his hands.

"When is something we do *not* stupid?" Fionn asked with a smile at his friend.

"Just wanted to be sure," Sid replied with a smile of his own.

"Are you afraid?" Joshua asked and laughed, still staring at the giant.

"Of fighting humans and incursions alike? As if," Sid replied with feigned aggravation. "Just let's end this battle quickly and with as little bloodshed as possible."

"You didn't peg me as a pacifist," Joshua said.

"I'm not. I'm just lazy and a long fight don't interest me."

"He is right. Let's end this quickly," Fionn added, ready

to jump down the battlements. The advantage of having the Gift is that he could afford to take the short route. "I will take the center. Straight to Edamane."

"I call dibs on the big guy there," Joshua nodded toward the giant.

"So, I guess I take the right," Sid said, then turned to Harland. "You better get their shooters to cover me, Harland."

"I'm going with you," Vivi said. Her tone left no room for argument. Fionn stifled a smile. Vivienne Ortiga was famous for being not only a tough teacher at Ravenstone, and a shrewd diplomat, but she had also faced hardship as a perimeter guard at a Freefolk settlement that the NLP party had constantly raided. Magick or not, he didn't fancy the odds of someone crossing her. Not even Sid.

Fionn jumped from the battlements to the surprise of the guards. Joshua followed suit, while Sid and Vivi took the more sensible route down the stairs.

"There they go: a living legend, the Titan of fire, a daring Freefolk, and the biggest cretin I've met who happens to be a superb fighter," Harland said to the guards. "Now, let's get ready to give them cover!"

† † †

A shadow moved in silence across the rooftops of Mon Caern, toward the giant corpse stomping through the city. Joshua used the Beast form as a shroud to obtain cover in the moonless night. He would assess his foe before unleashing any attack. A year and half of travels and experiences back to his city of birth and across the ocean and then through the Grasslands to obtain the Tempest Blade known as Fury, had allowed him to find a balance between himself, the Beast, and the Titan core they had absorbed. As the Shimizu clan had taught him, they'd become a single symbiotic organism—free from the Dark

Father's influence, free from being a tovainar, able to seek a new path in life.

All of that sounded nice and dandy. On paper.

The invasion of Mon Caern would be the first actual first test of this new balance, especially when it came to the fire powers, because no matter how good your intentions, fire was uncontrollable. A lesson he learned the hard way in the Grasslands.

This time, let's try and not burn this town to the ground, okay? Joshua thought.

The lumbering giant walked over the town, crushing houses that seemed to be empty. Joshua reached a nearby rooftop, one that the giant would soon pass. He couldn't avoid wondering how that thing was moving around, given that magick was out of service. Possession seemed the most likely option, but that meant that the being was basically a giant incursion, and that required cutting his head and destroying his heart in quick succession. Easier said than done with a creature this size. And unfortunately burning everything down, while faster, was not the best option.

Joshua waited patiently until the giant's left side was almost in front of him. His grip on Fury tightened and he jumped toward the giant, landing on its arm. Fury exploded into a column of fire that burned the giant's flesh, but not Joshua's, who ran toward the head at full speed. As he was about to reach the giant's neck, it quickly slapped at Joshua as if he were a mosquito, sending him crashing into a nearby building. As soon as he tried to stand up, the giant protruded sharp bone spikes from his hand and threw them at Joshua. One hit him on the side, impaling him on the rooftop of a half-collapsed building. His body hung, limp, lifeless. A similar attack would have killed a regular man, maimed a titanfighter or a demonhunter, and probably would have stopped a Gifted not called Fionn.

But Joshua was none of the above. He opened his eyes as blood came from his mouth. He was not in pain. He was grinding his teeth, his head tilting with jerky movements as he glared at the giant, baring his teeth, with two protruding fangs.

"For the record… I really, really tried to do this the right way," Joshua said to the moonless sky He stared for a moment as if he was waiting for an answer. He grunted as he pulled out the large bone staking him to the building. "But the right way and the effective way to keep those people alive are not matching."

No reply came.

"Frig it, no more Mister Nice Titan," Joshua muttered, realizing that for the first time he was accepting his status as the Titan of Fire, the only one on the good side.

The Beast receded into his back.

He saw the giant approaching a three-story house. Through one of the windows on the ground floor he could see a father hugging his family, trying to protect them from the attack, even if he knew was futile. It made Joshua's blood boil. His irises shifted from the pale color of a former tovainar into bright red as his body started to combust.

Joshua leaped and took to the air as the giant's hand split the roof. His flames spread out to form wings and a tail, like a royal phoenix, and he slammed into the giant's hand. The hand caught fire and the giant pulled it back. Joshua landed in front of the family, subduing the flames so as to not injure them.

"Leave now and find another place to hide. This section from here to the castle is not safe," Joshua said to the family.

"Tha… thank you," the father said.

"Thank me when I get rid of that thing," Joshua said. As soon as the family got away, he became engulfed in flames and jumped once more. He landed on the rooftop of another building, facing the giant.

"Am I interrupting your playtime, big guy?" Joshua sneered, unleashing a shower of sparks as he cracked his knuckles.

"You should be dead," a voice coming from the giant replied. It was clear that the giant was not the one speaking, but rather the spirit possessing him.

"Yeah, undying is my curse. You, on the other hand…"

The giant tried to slap Joshua, but its fingers flew in different directions as Fury cut them like a hot knife through butter. Joshua jumped onto the arm of the giant, leaving behind a trail of gore, ichor, flames and severed tissue. As if he was a shredder made of fire.

Redemption was a tough road to travel, but Joshua was well on his way.

† † †

"Who left this entrance unprotected?" Sid mumbled as he and Vivi ran downstairs through the poorly lit corridor of the ancient castle. It would lead them to the gardens near the main bridge entrance that Fionn was heading to defend.

"Someone not thinking about a fight," Viv replied. "Cut them some slack, would you? These are peaceful people. I bet the entrance on the other side must have been infiltrated already. Probably going after the Crown."

"Wello, that's why they have us here then."

Sid saw a shadow from the corner of his eyes.

A scout, Sid thought. *Thank the Prophet for low light vision.*

"Wait a sec, darling," he said.

Sid jumped over the rail and kicked the soldier in the chest, knocking him against the wall. He let loose a round of bullets that echoed through the depths of the corridor.

Vivi reached the soldier and punched him in the neck and below the shoulders, knocking him cold.

"Pressure points?" Sid asked.

"Good for therapeutic procedures, good for taking down someone without killing," Vivi replied. "Be more careful, those bullets ricocheting around could have hit someone. Like me."

More bullets came their way, this time from two more soldiers who were crossing the threshold to the stairs. Sid and Vivi took cover behind a statue in the corner where the stairs turned.

"That could work," Sid muttered, staring at the metal shields hanging on the wall of the corridor, while Vivi picked up the rifle from the soldier they had just taken out of service. Sid grabbed the shield and placed it on the ground, at the edge of the step he stood on. He got up onto it and balanced a bit, getting a better feeling of the weight. He smiled at Viv.

"I thought you hated surfing, and skating," Vivi said as she returned the smile.

"I do," Sid replied with a loud sigh. "But doesn't mean I'm bad at it."

Sid let gravity do its job and used it as a surfboard, sailing down the stairs at full speed. He lifted the shield as a new round of bullets came his way. Airborne, Sid flew across the entrance and into the yard, landing hard with the shield on the bodies of four soldiers, knocking them, as Vivi laid down covering fire to keep the oncoming soldiers from reaching him. Not wasting a second, Sid moved swiftly across the backyard, his samoharo obsidian tomahawks in hand, slicing several tendons in the legs of his opponents, leaving them prone on the ground, bleeding. Using the darkness of the lunar eclipse, he took cover behind the statues, as the soldiers shot. Using their muzzle flashes of lights, Sid calculated the distance he had to run and sped up to take down a new wave of assailants. A flood light turned on as he was finishing the last member of this squad. Two more squads approached. A rain of armor piercing arrows fell upon the soldiers, forcing them to retreat.

"You wanted cover? Here is your cover!" Harland shouted from the battlements above.

"Took you long enough!" Sid yelled. A soldier approached to his left, trying to take him by surprise.

Silly human trying to be stealthy, Sid smiled. He was getting ready to tackle the soldier when a well-placed shot hit the soldier in the neck, piercing the carotid with a spray of blood that arced through the night air.

Vivi strode toward him, keeping the incoming soldiers in her sights.

"Where did you learn to shoot like that?" Sid asked, amazed.

"Doing guard duty in a Freefolk refugee camp before Fionn got us back our lands. I might not have magick right now, but I know my way around these rifles."

"What happened to the medical oath of not doing harm?"

"You really want to debate that right now?" Vivi replied, taking aim at another soldier coming out from the gardens. The round hit home.

"No," Sid smiled. "Just wanted to tell you that I love you."

"Yeah, yeah, tell me that when our lives are not in danger," Vivi replied, winking.

† † †

It was pitch black at the front entrance of the castle as the mystical eclipse continued. The area was as quiet as a graveyard, the only noise coming from the river below the bridge. A squad of soldiers advanced slowly across the bridge, moving through the mist with the help of their night vision goggles.

"Keep moving," one of the soldiers said. "They have no guards here; we can take the entrance without problems."

"What's that, sergeant?" another soldier asked, pointing at a shadow in front of the castle gate. The wind blew, creating a chilling sound akin to the howling of a wolf. A very particular kind of wolf, rarely heard since the Dawn Age: the grey dragon wolf. It was the kind of howl that matrons used to create a frightening ambience when telling stories about werewolves that snatched children from their beds, lock your doors and pray to the gods, so the beast will not devour you and leave behind a bloody trail. But those were just silly children's tales that old ladies spun to make their grandchildren go to bed. They were urban legends, myths about wolves whose fangs glowed in the dark before striking.

"I... I'm not sure," the sergeant replied. Two glowing green eyes opened in the shadow. What the tales often got wrong was that there were no werewolves, not anymore at least. And dragon wolves lived far north of the Scar.

The wind howled a second time. Closer and with increased intensity, as a straight, green light broke the darkness. A man smiled what some would call the 'wolf's smile'—a predator's grin right before it closed its jaws around your throat—as the green light from a blade illuminated his face.

The wind howled a third time. Synchronized with the breathing coming from the man.

"Fire!" the sergeant gave a panicked yell. But it was too late. For the Greywolf, the One-Man-Army, was already on the hunt.

Fionn moved at lightning speed, using the full force of the Gift. He swung Black Fang with precision, deflecting each bullet with ease. Most people assumed that Fionn, being born a century ago, and a swordsman, wouldn't be used to fighting soldiers with guns. Most people were wrong. That was of little consolation as the sergeant fell into the cold waters of the river, struck down by a quick slash from Black Fang.

"Kill him! Kill him now!" another soldier screamed in terror, to no avail. Fionn jumped onto the rail of the bridge and from there into the midst of the squad. He cut down a soldier, splitting his rifle in two, as well as the statue behind him. One soldier got behind Fionn, trying to bash him in the head with the butt of his rifle, but Fionn reacted too fast, throwing a punch into the man's jaw, knocking him out with a sickening crunch. Bullets fired at him, but he either evaded or deflected them with Black Fang, as his reflexes were at their most efficient, and if by chance a stray bullet managed to graze him, he healed almost immediately. As he healed, the wounds released specks of green light flashing in the dark. Fionn kicked a soldier with such force that he knocked the man from the bridge. The soldier's body hit the waterway below with a large splash, with the noise distracting a couple of his companions. Spinning around, Fionn finished the squad with a few well-placed slashes and then walked across the bridge, leaving a trail of bodies behind him.

Fionn had never liked what he was good at, but right now, what he was good at was exactly what the inhabitants of Mon Caern, hidden inside the walls of the castle complex, needed in order to avoid death at the hands of the Golden King's army.

He hadn't fought like this in a century. Fionn unleashed pent-up anger, mixed with the tranquil fury needed to control the Gift, into the next two squadrons that were blocking his path toward his main objective. The soldiers threw everything they had at him, but it was for naught. The howling in the wind only became stronger, as did the screams.

At that moment, Fionn wasn't thinking of being nice, or a pacifist; he was pure, unbridled rage unleashed, and he released all the pain and sadness he had been keeping inside. A cold, focused machine with one main goal: Reach Edamane as soon as possible, and kill him to end this.

† † †

The Duke emerged from his place of refuge, trying to look like he had not been cowering in his room, and walked out onto the terrace. From the battlements the Duke looked at the destruction below.

To the left, the raging fire of Joshua taking down the giant zombie. To the right, the samoharo Sid and his freefolk companion had made short work of the soldiers trying to sneak into the castle through the gardens and were now trying to catch up to the frontlines in the center of the battlefield, where the most terrifying sight could be seen in the wake of what could only be described as a force of nature plowing through the invading battalion. One of the guards threw up after pointing the flood light toward the Greywolf.

"Oh, oh my," the Duke said, sounding like he might throw up as well.

Harland was looked on with mixed feelings. He knew what his friends were capable of, especially Fionn.

But using his full power and combat skills against regular troops, who admittedly had committed unspeakable atrocities already in this war, was stomach churning to say the least. At least a tovainar or a titan could have offered more resistance on an equal footing. This was not a battle. It was bloody curb-stomp fight.

The whole scene brought to mind the stories Sid told him of when Alex got the Gift and unleashed it on the cultists and the incursion creatures. Or of Gaby carving a path for them to escape Ravenstone. A mortal possessing the Gift, in action, was something to behold.

A pissed off, unrestrained mortal possessing the Gift, in action, was something to fear. Fionn was a force of nature painting the streets of Mon Caern crimson red. He now understood why the samoharo had their policy about culling them before they got out of hand. Harland still thought that policy was ethically and morally reprehensible, but he could see the point. And this time it was worse, because there was no Gaby or Sam to bring his friend back from the current maelstrom he had become. Even Joshua, the former Tovainar of the Shadows, now turned Titan of Fire was showing more restraint, showing a finer control of his flames and his shadow beast, as he battled, or rather minced the giant, piece by piece.

"I... I thought the legends of the Greywolf had been mere exaggerations, flights of fancy from surviving soldiers of the Great War that looked for a symbol to rally behind. But this... this is beyond any nightmare I could ever have had," the Duke said in hushed tones.

There was a long moment of silence before Harland spoke. "Few people can. You want to know the scary thing?" Harland asked. "Those stories are from before the Greywolf became empowered by the Gift, when he was a regular mortal."

"What will it take to stop him once he is done with them?" the Duke asked, trembling.

I wonder the same, Harland thought, reflecting upon the fact that if having taken Fionn out of retirement a few years ago had been a mistake. He could only pray to anyone listening—to maybe Mekiri, wherever she was—that Fionn came to his senses before it was too late.

"Fionn can handle himself," Harland said, reminding

the guards they still had a duty to perform. "Sid and Vivi, on the other hand, need our help. They are not afforded the advantages of being a Titan or a Gifted."

†††

Fionn approached Edamane, who appeared to be unconcerned by the tempest of destruction coming his way. His smile was infuriating Fionn more and more by the second. He could hear Sid and Vivi calling to him, but he paid their words no heed.

"My followers tell me that you three have created more casualties on our side than our whole campaign," Edamane said. "Wonderful display."

At that moment, the burned head of the giant bounced from building to building toward them. Its body collapsed as it turned into ashes, avoiding further destruction. Both Fionn and Edamane stared as the giant head rolled between them, like a burning tumbleweed. As it tumbled into the river with a thunderous hiss of steam, they turned to look at each other.

"And I'm happy to continue doing so," Fionn replied. In that same breath, he ripped a stone shield from one of the statues guarding the entrance of the bridge and kept walking.

The soldiers guarding Edamane opened fire on Fionn, who used the shield to deflect the bullets. He then ran at them, bashing them with the shield and finishing them with a well-placed kick. The crunch of broken bones echoed through the streets.

"What a nice sound," Edamane said. He grabbed a rifle and shot at Fionn. The bullets missed and Fionn closed the gap between them. He bashed the tovainar in the chest with the shield, the force of the impact shattering it into pebbles. Edamane staggered back from the impact, smiling even through the blood as his broken teeth grew back.

Fionn darted at him and made a slash aimed to cut the tovainar's neck in one swift movement. His irises glowed with such intensity that his eyes began to hurt for the first time in his life.

But the edge of the blade stopped less than a millimeter from Edamane, only superficially nicking the skin. That pinprick drew a drop of the black ichor that made up the tovainar's blood to the surface, but no more.

Joshua arrived at the spot where Fionn and Edamane were staring at each other, without moving a single muscle, like statues. Flames no longer enveloped Joshua's body, through thin tendrils of smoke rose here and there on his skin.

"Why did you stop?" Joshua demanded. "You have him dead to rights!"

"Look at what... he is holding in his... right hand," Sid interjected, trying to catch his breath as he and Vivi arrived at the same spot.

In Edamane's right hand, there was a small metallic sphere. Fionn took a few steps back and sheathed Black Fang.

"Is that a bomb?" Vivi asked.

"A worse version of one," Fionn replied, his irises returning to normal as he recognized the sphere. He had seen its blueprints once, on Byron's desk when he planned the attack at Longhorn Valley with the goal of capturing the devastating weapon that the Blood Horde had used to conquer most of the continent. The same blueprints that had made Fionn, Ywain and Izia go rogue and destroy the weapon before Byron could get his hands on it. "It's a thermobaric bomb, with the power of which can obliterate any living being in a kilometer radius. It's powered by the dark miasma and aura from the Pits. And it must have a dead hand's trigger."

"Which means that if you kill me, this goes kaboom!

I knew you would recognize it," Edamane gloated, as if he were the proud teacher of a slow student. "Yes, it is something similar to that Orb that played such a huge role in you acquiring the *Gift*." He sneered the last word. "Similar, but not identical. While the Orb was powered by the eternal struggle of an akeleth—the one you merged with—and one of us, this one draws power from the Pits itself, and is the perfect bomb. The same effect as at the Battle of Line, all in the palm of my hand."

"Where did you get it?" Fionn asked, his brain racing through scenarios to get rid of it. "This serves no purpose for you."

"Ha ha ha ha! It stopped you from taking my head off, so yes, it is being useful." Edamane replied between laughs, and he pointed at his left temple with his index finger. "I might be unhinged, as you would say, but I'm not stupid. Unlike Byron, I don't underestimate you. I'm well aware of your fame as the 'Greywolf,' the one-man army who can heal any injury in seconds. And samoharos are always hard to deal with. I even know what happened to that traitor to our side that currently prances around you like a lap dog, burning our giant. I know this is a battle that will last for longer than either of us want and can end with either of us losing their head. Which is why I brought this as insurance. And it worked."

"You could have used it before you lost so many soldiers," Joshua pointed out. "And the giant."

"Yes. Yes! And it would be glorious! The light, the heat, the muffled screams as the air leaves the lungs of everybody in this city!" Edamane screamed with unrestrained glee.

"But you are not sure if it would kill me... or that you or the Crown would survive," Fionn said.

"I'm pretty sure you would survive this, even at point blank range. Your Gift has grown to levels even you are not aware of. The traitor might survive as well, in his new shape. The samoharo might even survive if he is fast enough to get away. I can't say the same about the depowered Freefolk woman next to him. Nor any of the occupants of the castle for that matter. And for me, my humble personage yearns for the sacrifice it would be for the glory of my liege."

Fionn clenched his fists. He had experienced firsthand the full brunt of that kind of explosion. It had killed him. It took a true miracle and the Gift to keep him alive, and even then, he spent a month in bandages, recovering from the severe burns that covered his body. Fionn was sure he could survive this again, even if it would be painful. Same for Joshua. But he wouldn't risk everyone's lives to test that theory. He wouldn't give into the provocation. Taking a deep breath, Fionn slowed his heartbeat by thinking of Gaby, focusing his Gift's energy on his back up plan: the secret technique he had been working on for the past year. It would require a swift movement to pull this off and the technique still required quite some time and a lot of calmness and focus to charge. He kept his fist balled up, as tiny green spheres of energy popped in and out of existence on the surface of his hands. Fionn could feel the increasing heat of each new bubble. He just hoped that Edamane didn't notice.

"And that is a sacrifice your liege won't like. Not when you are so close to getting it… assuming your partner can beat Gaby," Fionn replied.

"And here I thought you were a simpleton, a brute in service of that pathetic excuse of a goddess," Edamane mused.

"Why does he have to talk like a thesaurus from last century?" Sid muttered to Vivi.

"Ego," was Vivi's short reply.

"Thus, I propose a cease fire from the proceedings,

while we find out how long it will take my partner to win their duel. And who knows, if your champion at the Clocktower wins—however unlikely that might be—you might convince me to let everyone go so we can play again in another siege, if you give me the Crown," Edamane said, offering his hand to Fionn to seal the deal.

"So, either way you get the Crown. And if we say no?" Joshua asked, looking with interest to Edamane. Fionn wondered if ancient memories had rushed to Joshua's mind.

"The wrath of my King won't reach me, for all of us will be dead and this place won't be more than ashes of sorrow."

"You are *not* planning to agree," Joshua said, aghast, and looked to Fionn.

"Right now, he is in a stronger bargaining position," Fionn replied. "We need to think about those people inside the castle."

"I can't believe this!" Joshua threw up his hands as Fionn sealed the deal.

"We will wait at the front gate of the castle," Edamane said. "I want to admire the craftsmanship of the gates. I've heard you have an interest in woodcraft. We might even have a nice talk about that, who knows? Ha ha ha ha ha."

"As long as your remaining soldiers stay back on this side of the bridge, in the city," Fionn countered. Keeping him distracted that way could give Fionn enough time to charge the technique.

If I get out of this one, I need to improve the charging speed of the thunderstrike, he thought.

"Are you not worried of having this beautiful trinket so close to the castle?" Edamane asked, clearly confused.

"What for? If that thing goes off the city is as good as gone, no matter where you are," Fionn replied with a shrug. "But at least this way, I can keep an eye on you in a place where I can contain you should your soldiers decide to get entrepreneurial."

"I always said that Byron was an utter fool for underestimating you," Edamane exclaimed with glee, dancing in place. "Lead the way, Greywolf."

As Fionn, Joshua, Sid, and Vivi went back to the castle gate, followed several meters behind by Edamane and his surviving soldiers, the band talked in whispers.

"I can't believe you agreed to this," Joshua said.

"I have to agree with him," Sid replied. "And that pains me a lot."

"We earned a few precious minutes while we figure out a way to take that bomb from him," Fionn replied.

"Precious minutes?" Joshua echoed, indignant. "You had Edamane right at hand to kill him. You know, if you'd just cut the dude's head off with your magic fangsword we wouldn't have to worry about this!"

"You are right," Fionn replied. "And then everything and everyone would have been obliterated by that bomb. No more worries at all."

"I take it you have a plan," Sid interjected.

"I do," Fionn replied. "But it will have to be enacted quickly, a hand amputation before anything else, the moment a window of opportunity opens."

"I don't mind doing an impromptu surgery," Sid mused. "Those were fun back in the day."

"And meanwhile... What?" Vivi asked.

"We trust that Gaby will win," Fionn replied.

Chapter 14
Bound To Survive

"That damned *skansen* wannabe god!" Sam exclaimed in frustration. She pressed her hands against Kasumi's wound. The deep gash stitched itself together through the spell Sam was focusing through her hands. But there was a dark aura, a miasma coming from the wound—it wasn't a physical injury, but a spiritual one. Some sort of ancient curse Sam wasn't familiar with. And all the knowledge that Mekiri had passed to her was focused on the task at hand: fix the problem with Magick.

"Do something, please!" Kasumi exclaimed, eyes locked on the still-bleeding wound. Then she the stared at Sam as realization of what was going on with the wound hit her. "Wait... why am I not bleeding to death? Not that I'm complaining."

Sam sat down on the ground, if it could even be said that there *was* a proper ground. Until now, they were inside the eye of some kind white whirlpool made of stars. But there was no wind, no water. She tried to draw a long breath to calm herself, then she remembered where she was and sighed in frustration. As soon as she exhaled, mostly by reflex, the whirlpool disappeared and transformed into an open space, which looked halfway between a mirror made of frozen water, and a luxurious bathroom floor. Above them, the sky—if you could call it that—was clear. A soft, warm breeze caressed them, and what seemed to be a few fey flew around like butterflies and fireflies. It was a relaxing place, the kind Sam usually visualized during her meditations to get the Gift under control, but with some aspects influenced by Kasumi's mind.

"We teleported here, far from the clocktower, where I managed to heal the physical wound the best I could, but it is just a temporary measure," Sam explained. "It will still hurt, though, because the curse remains active. And I have never seen a curse like that, so... No, I don't know how to remove it. But while you remain here, it's practically frozen in time. That gives us a chance to find a way to dispel it."

"Ugh, and I thought you've been practicing first aide spells," Kasumi said through gritted teeth as she sat down. "Where are we by the way?"

"I have been practicing, but I didn't have much time to think on a better spell thanks to my girlfriend getting stabbed because she was too damn hotheaded and went and fought a god. I had to get you out of there first. As for where we are, we are inside the Tempest," Sam said with a smile.

"Girlfriend? We are official now? And what about Alex? Because there is the issue of feelings going all around and I think he is a bit confused," Kasumi said. She blushed and bit her lower lip. And with that, the space echoed with the sound of an accelerated heartbeat."

"I think I found a solution for that issue, but the three of us really need to talk to see if all of us are onboard. That is, if the dunderhead survives his fight against the physical avatar of Shemazay," Sam replied. Even if she didn't need to breathe, for the Tempest was a place of the spirit and energy rather than the material, she was trying to anyway just to calm herself as she searched for what she'd come here seeking. And to pay attention in case *it* reached this place as well.

"What? But he is depowered! How can you be so relaxed?"

"I'm not relaxed; I'm trying to get in the right mindset for what I came here to do. Alex has his mission, and I have mine. As for Alex's Gift? Mekiri's parting present was to recharge it in full, I think a bit over it actually. And he was really angry with Shemazay. I'm trust him."

"Parting present? What happened to Mekiri? And Alex is angry? Angry as in when he loses a game, or angry as in when he barely utters a word for days and seems eerily calm?"

"The second. Seeing you being hurt didn't sit well with him. As for Mekiri, her avatar had to die for her to reconnect with her astral godly self, so she preloaded a teleportation spell to get me here inside the Tempest and fix what's wrong with magick, and I brought you along so I could have time to heal you."

"Which you can't because of the curse. I could try to lift it with a demonhunter purifying ritual at the Water Temple," Kasumi suggested, examining the wound. It had closed, but the edges around the impromptu scar were black.

"That's the thing, if you leave this place, the curse will reactivate and I don't know how much time you will have. At least here in the Tempest that's won't be an immediate concern." Sam grabbed Kasumi's left hand and caressed it. "I promise I will find a way to heal you once I fix magick. Maybe we could bring Vivienne here so she can do it. She was my healing teacher after all."

"So, I'm stuck here?" Kasumi looked around. "I expected more, you know, lightning and thunder, more ghosts and stuff floating around. This is actually quite peaceful," Kasumi pointed around.

"If Alex were here, your description would be apt. The Tempest reacts to your heart and your imagination. A mindscape of sorts that can connect with others, like having a shared dream. Of course, I'm summarizing a lot. Not sure which of us it's currently reacting to, maybe both, but I'll take this clear sky over the eclipse."

"Even the sun is shining," Kasumi added, pointing to the source of light. It was a ball of energy, wrapped by five thick chains that extended into nothingness. "Despite being chained. Is that a metaphor about our hearts?"

"That's no sun," Sam explained. "And no metaphor."

"Then what is it?"

"That, if what Mekiri downloaded in my brain is correct, should be the actual core concept of Magick, bound by what Shemazay did after severing Mekiri's connection with her divine self. We need to cut those bonds so Magick flows free again."

Bloodcurdling cries reached their ears. Correction: Reached their brains directly, skipping the whole process of being carried by sound waves through the inner ear and corresponding nerve.

"Well, I think the *skansen*, as you called it, is coming here because the sky is changing. And I think the not-sun is crying," Kasumi said.

"I guess his astral self finally detected us here. It was going to happen sooner or later," Sam said, grim. A knot formed in her stomach. She had to admit to herself that despite Alex's encouraging words, she did feel fear. And this time it was unlike any other fear she had ever felt. It was dread.

"So, we need to deal with that guy first." Kasumi replied. "How do we do that?"

"I have a plan," Sam muttered.

"You are sounding like Alex," Kasumi chuckled. "I like that. On both of you."

"I know; habits rub off after spending so much time with those that you care for. I got some habits from you too." Sam winked at her.

Kasumi offered a faint smile. "What's the plan?"

"A magick duel in the shape of an illusionist show full of tricks with lip-synch included," Sam replied as she stood up and offered Kasumi her hand to help her stand up.

"A... what? You can do that? And why a lip-synch?" Kasumi asked confused, as she took Sam's hand.

"Here? I guess, if I manage to take the initiative on how the duel will take place. He expects a traditional blast off magick duel with raw energy, and if I do that, I'm gonna lose. But with what I'm planning, something as mundane as an illusionist's show, hopefully will take Shemazay out of its comfort zone. And since you are here, you can help me."

"Count me it. I have a score to settle," Kasumi replied, wetting her lips in anticipation.

"You are not going to fight this one," Sam told her, releasing her hand. "Instead, I need you to do something else: use Breaker to cut those bindings and let magick flow free."

Kasumi took a second to reply. Sam hoped Kasumi would agree to help her on her terms rather than trying to fight Shemazay directly once more. Because what Sam needed to do would be easier having Breaker with them.

"Okay, this is your field, I trust you."

"Good, because the key to a good illusionist's trick is misdirection, and for that, I need a dance partner-slash-assistant," Sam said with a wry smile, for she knew very well how Kasumi felt about illusionist shows.

"Are you going to transform me into a rabbit?"

"I was thinking more on a panther." Sam winked at her.

"I like that," Kasumi replied with a forced smile as she

clutched her wound. It was clear that the poison, or curse, was beginning to hurt. "Shemazay is here."

The flapping of wings echoed through the Tempest, as a humanoid form descended from the clouds above Sam and Kasumi.

"Pathetic mortals," Shemazay scoffed. In the Tempest, his true form was revealed. A man with grey wings, the tips blackened. Twice as tall as Sam and with deep blue eyes. He walked around bare-chested, with only a loincloth covering him from the waist down. His head lacked hair, instead covered with runic embossing that protruded from the skin. Eyes watched them from his upturned palms. Shemazay didn't look like an akeleth, or how Freefolk depicted their deities, but rather how humans depicted the terrifying angels of Kaan'a. Harland was probably right, they were all the same and it was one's perception that changed based on the cultural context. But even then, Shemazay didn't look like a divine being, but more like an incursion mockery of one. This was how a fallen god looked.

"Hiding here in the Tempest, trying to stave off the curse I delivered to your foolish friend who dared to challenge me. And now you think you have an opportunity to stop me? You won't. My plan will continue, the mortal world will be invaded by the Pit Lords, and we will finally destroy them without having to be careful about not hurting Ishtaru's precious mortals. Kaan'a will thank me later."

"You don't care about what happened to us." Sam replied, standing up. "You talk about Kaan'a, but didn't Kaan'a create the universe? Us?"

"Why should I?" Shemazay said. "Ishtaru's... Mekiri— what a stupid name—her concern for you has hampered the efforts of our siblings to finish this endless war. Even Mikharemiel the Guardian was corrupted by those thoughts. And let's not talk about Luykerion the Judge, he thinks he can be redeemed by keeping you safe. Your continuous existence is what stops Kaan'a from ever awakening and defeating the Pit Lords, leaving us to do the dirty work. And to add insult to injury, Ishtaru has been forcing our people, our smaller siblings trapped as spirits in the mortal world to merge with you! Tainting their everlasting essences. Of course I don't care about you mortals, glorified monkeys, shapeless beings and lizards. I don't care about your precious worlds either. I hope the Golden King finally takes over yours. I want you gone so I can finally fight the Pit Lords as it was written."

"You are a monster," Kasumi said.

"No, I'm a god!" Shemazay replied as the Tempest rumbled with lightning and thunder. "And you are mere mortals that will soon die here. Heavens, it feels so good to finally be able to say that in the open."

"You know what?" Sam said as she strode toward Shemazay, visibly irritated. Her eyes were stone-cold, glaring at the so-called god. Sam wondered if this was what Alex felt when he faced the Creeping Chaos. She planted her feet wide, stretched her arms and cracked her knuckles. "You talk a lot, probably because you wanted someone to hear your rant. And yes, you are right, I am a mere mortal. But here, I'm as powerful as you. I respect those that wield Tempest Blades, for it takes skill and soul. But I don't need them because here, I'm the weapon."

"What are you trying to do? Threaten me?" Shemazay snorted, waving his hands with disdain. "Silly human. Fine. Have it your way. I will win, nonetheless. By the ancient rules of magick, I challenge thee to a duel."

Good, his ego is getting ahead of him, Sam thought. *As Mekiri said it would.*

Sam gave a disarming smile and took a deep breath. Warmth surged from her chest as her irregular heartbeat normalized.

"Sure, I'll agree to that. And I get to choose the form of the duel, according to the ancient rules of magick."

"Your beloved goddess tried that and failed." Shemazay shrugged his shoulders.

"That's because she wasn't trying to kill you, she was trying to save you from yourself," Sam replied. The warmth reached the tips of her fingers, which glowed with a faint light. "But me? I don't have that problem. I am a mighty Freefolk, and indomitable human. And I have the Gift. And I will fix what you broke even if I have to rewrite the rules of Magick itself while beating your sorry ass, you son of a cosmic bitch! Let's play the music!"

With a flourish, Sam extended her arms and flicked her hands. A guitar riff rumbled. Drums beat rhythmically. Gaby's voice echoed through the air, as one of her songs played from nowhere and everywhere all at once. Sam's favorite song. The one she had asked Gaby to write for her birthday, after talking about how Sam had been feeling after getting the Gift. After trying to understand how her heart had changed, both physically and spiritually, after meeting Alex and Kasumi. Gaby had written her a song to help her to lift her spirits, the best birthday present she had ever had. Gaby had captured that chat and had turned it into an amazing rock tune. It was a tune she'd once put on, thinking she was home alone one night. Alex and Kasumi arrived not long after to her carefree dancing, and Kasumi had jumped right in while Alex restarted the song and joined them in their silly dance. As Gaby's mantra used to say, this was her song. Sam's song. The one about the magick lights.

Oooohhh!

Oooohhh!

"What is this horrible sound?"

"That?" Sam smiled. "It's my favorite track from the album of one of my best friends."

"And stepmom," Kasumi whispered.

"And I will lip-synch you to death with it," Sam added as she pointed with her index finger toward Shemazay. From the tip of her fingers sparks of energy sprouted.

The Gift inside Sam activated as her irises started to glow lilac.

And the world around them changed.

† † †

The visage of Shemazay, the fallen god, in its real form, sent shivers down Alex's spine. A hulking behemoth of a humanoid shape, with a helmet that covered half of its face, the enflamed and twisted horns, a tattered cape made of smoke and brimstone covered the once upon a time golden armor, now a corrupted collection of random bits that Alex could swear were sucking the life of anything around. Beneath the helmet, long ash white hair stuck out. The fallen god had dark eyes like dying embers that made for a stark contrast with the grey-blue skin, tightly constraining the bulging muscles.

The eclipse in the background and the ominous ticking of the clocktower didn't help to lessen the already frightening aura.

So this is how it looks when a god falls and becomes a being from the Pits, Alex thought, as he moved toward Yokoyawa. Upon reaching the samoharo, who was taking shallow breaths, he placed a hand on his shoulder.

"Are you okay?" Alex asked him.

"I'm gonna live if that's what you are asking, but it will take me time to regenerate and heal," Yoko replied. "He just punched me silly until he broke my ribs, unlike what he did with Kasumi."

"He is not attacking," Alex observed.

"I don't think he considered me a threat anymore, which offends me, even if it's somewhat true. I think he is just flexing, waiting for a worthy challenger."

"Me?"

"Yes, because Sam got away with Kasumi. He screamed and split in two, the other one I guess went after the ladies. You know, gods and their dramatic personalities. I think he really hates you," Yoko replied.

"Yeah, I've been told that," Alex said, staring at the fallen god, measuring it. "Quick question: Power or speed?"

Yoko slowly looked up, as if he had realized what Alex was actually asking and why. "Power. Seems that he's new in that body. Can't shift gears. But still fast for a regular mortal."

"Good thing I'm nothing but a weird mortal then," Alex said with a sly smile at Yoko. "That's all I need. Get some cover, this will get messy."

"Are you sure you can deal with him? That Sam will?"

"Quoting the Twelve Swords oath," Alex replied with a smile. "'I believe we are bound to survive against all odds.' This is not gonna end here for me. Or Sam."

A thunderstorm could be heard in the distance. Yokoyawa smiled through the pain as he dragged himself to take cover behind the clock face and let himself slump to the floor, clutching the broken side of his chest plate.

Alex walked away from the clock and gingerly went up the few steps that led to the large dais that floated in front of the clocktower. He looked out toward the horizon. The sky was a maelstrom of clouds and energy, making everything look really wacky. Alex supposed that's what happened when magick went haywire during an astronomical phenomenon, it spilled the excess energy of the Tempest into the real world. *My first post-doctoral paper could be about the intercrossing of dimensions*, he thought. Fifty meters below him Alex could see the theme park and the now empty rides.

This is not the time to think about your fear of heights,

nor on the day job. Focus, he thought.

Shemazay, the fallen god, had his back to Alex. He turned slowly as soot blew across the dais.

Alex faced the giant muscle-bound avatar of Shemazay. Now that he was closer Alex thought its terrible visage resembled one of the ancient demon knights summoned by the fallen saurian empire in their fight against the silver riders. In his right hand he held a strange weapon, a combination of an axe-like scythe and a chain with a round weight on the end.

That weapon is made for reach and focused power, to compensate for his lack of speed, Alex surmised, as his brain developed a plan. *And that armor is more for showing off than for actual protection.*

The air smelled of the sulfurous scent of burned flesh. It was a walking cadaver dying and rebirthing. If dread needed a picture for its dictionary definition, this was it. For unlike the Lords of the Pits, this one had an objective that started with good intentions and ended in hatred of the very thing it was meant to protect. To think this was a former akeleth, but now it stood in direct contrast, and opposition of Mekiri, both in body and heart.

It was what a fallen god looked like in the real world. Purpose made flesh. Correction: Zealotry made flesh, consumed and recreated at the same time by its hatred. A walking nightmare of a different kind to the Dark Father. It reminded Alex of paintings by a certain classic artist that had depicted historical figures in terrible ways. In his hands a portrait of Fionn would have made the Greywolf seem like a nightmare.

Except that this was very real. This was not a horror movie monster, but a dark fantasy gone wrong by way of the mind of a deranged artist.

Alex noticed his left leg was shaking. Excitement and fear combined ran through his body.

Its booming voice resonated. "Who dares to challenge me now? For I am the mighty god Shemazay and my plan is infallible! Are you a god?"

Mekiri is better with the dramatic entrances. I give her that.

"Ah… no," Alex replied, as he stepped onto the dais. "I'm not a god. But I'm pretty special."

"It's you! I finally see myself face to face with the mortal that dared to raise his fist against a god, even if it was from the Pits, disturbing the divine designs." Shemazay stomped the floor. The dais trembled. "I shall teach you a lesson on staying in your place."

"Maybe I should have told him that I was a god. Too late for that," Alex mumbled to himself with a shrug.

The booming voice of Shemazay, the former god of heavenly arcana and karmic justice, rumbled through the open space of the dais once more. The behemoth looked down at the relatively small human in front of the clock face. The samoharo was nowhere to be seen. This human emanated energy from his body. Shemazay smiled. "You are nothing but a failed project of Ishtaru. Wasted potential of my kind's blood in such pitiful, flaccid, mortal coils."

"Hey!" Alex interrupted. "I know I'm out of shape, but no need to get personal. I was ill."

"You dare to talk back at me? You are brave, I give you that. Braver than the samoharo that's hiding. Let's see if you are smarter than the demonhunter I punished for the sin of defying me."

The sole mention of Kasumi brought to Alex's mind the critical injuries his friend had suffered. And calling Yoko a coward as a low blow. The samoharo had almost bested the god.

Now you are asking for it, Alex thought. Electrical currents surged across his legs and arms, as he unsheathed Yaha from his back scabbard. He held it in his left hand, the point aiming at the floor.

"You have one of those monstrosities as well?" Shemazay aimed a finger at Yaha. "I thought I had worked things to get rid of them all centuries ago, but they keep cropping up. I will get rid of it as well and then..."

"Okay, that's enough talk," Alex cut him off again. "Let's get this done with."

"You are anxious to die, I see."

"Look, I might not be a god. But I already killed one. I don't mind adding a second one to the list," Alex replied with a smirk. His irises glowed with a golden hue as he breathed, summoning the Gift to the forefront, its inner core exploding into a thunderstorm inside him.

Shemazay didn't utter another word. His own eyes glowed red as it hurled the metal sphere toward Alex. It became a fireball that rapidly increased in speed, which forced Alex to parry it with Yaha. Barely. The impact was stronger than expected and it flung Alex backwards, landing with a grunt as he slid towards the edge of the dais. A glance over the side showed it'd be a long fall.

I know this is my favorite attraction, but not that much of a favorite to die on it.

Alex rolled to the side, evading by millimeters the descending slash made by the scythe. It hit the dais with enough force to shoot a crack through stone.

No wonder Breaker had a tough time deflecting that thing.

He twisted just in time to parry a second slash aimed at his midsection, which rattled his bones. He got a kick to the chest for his troubles, knocking him against a pillar. Alex pushed away and parried a third attack. Every time the scythe and Yaha clashed, the latter glowed while the former released tiny balls of magma. The weapons were having their own mystical duel at the same time as their users.

Alex and Shemazay traded several blows, each one releasing a shockwave that rocked the dais, it was becoming harder and harder for Alex to defend himself as Shemazay pressed his advantage through sheer brute force. Three more attacks ensued, the last one hitting Alex so hard that it sent him once more into the air. He hit the dais hard enough that a tooth fell from his mouth. His irises ceased to glow.

The eclipse was halfway through.

Chapter 15
Make Destiny Our Own

"*THIS WON'T BE LIKE ANY* of your silly Sister of Mercy's test!" Livia exclaimed.

"Oh, I was hoping you'd say that. Bring it on." Gaby said.

Gaby brought Heartguard and Soulkeeper together, touching the pommels of each blade to the other. The hilts of both weapons shifted and changed under her hands, joining together into a long handle and creating a single, double-bladed sword. Gaby dashed forward, throwing the joined weapon at Livia as she was about to grab the Crown.

The blade spun through the air and forced Livia to jump away or lose her hand. Angered, Live drew her sword, which unfolded into a flexible, serpentine blade, giving it the qualities of a whip. Livia drew back the sword and flicked it toward Gaby just as her joined weapon returned to her hand like a mystical boomerang.

Gaby smiled at Livia's familiar attack. She deflected the blade and jumped onto one of the floating gears, splitting her weapon into two once more. Gaby jumped down, pushing with all her strength toward Livia, giving her no chance to recoil her blade and use it to parry the blow. Gaby landed behind Livia in a three-point stance, the force of her thrust making her slide across the floor.

"Park's metal extending technique?" Gaby said. "You really are milking that. Get something new."

"Like this?" Livia replied. She slashed at the air with her sword, sending energy shockwaves at Gaby. Livia ran right behind the attack toward Gaby.

"That's better," Gaby said, and she evaded the attacks with ease thanks to the Gift. Livia, on the other hand, was moving faster, no doubt empowered by Gavito, the tovainar possessing her body, pushing it to inhuman limits. Gaby knew that level of exertion by the tovainar would kill Livia, so Gaby needed to exorcise the tovainar and end this fight now to save Livia. That meant destroying the Crown. As long as it existed Gavito would keep fighting.

Gaby and Livia moved at lightning speed, their blows barely missing each other. Gaby dodged one suck attack aimed at her face by mere millimeters, though she was not as lucky with another. It drew blood on her left forearm, wet heat slicking her skin.

This was nothing like the test when they were kids. This was a hundred times worse. That first time, so long ago now, neither had been trying to hurt the other, despite what the Superior Mother had ordered. But now, controlled by Gavito, Livia was trying to kill Gaby, while she was still trying to save her friend. A second exchange of attacks ended with a clash so forceful that it sent them reeling back to opposite sides of the tower. Gaby had milliseconds to react as Livia raised her left hand. Countless energy daggers appeared in thin air, created from her body's spiritual energy.

Just like a shaman summoning their weapon, Gaby thought.

Gaby wasn't sure how she knew that, but Izia had been a shaman. It seemed that Livia-Gavito was able to use the abilities of each of her previous hosts.

Be careful with what you wish for, Gaby thought. *I*

wanted a challenge, and this is it. She evaded the energy daggers by jumping onto the floating gears and deflecting those that got close. Once the rain of daggers ended, Livia-Gavito went after Gaby, jumping on the floating gears, taking the conflict into the air. They continued to trade blows, jumping from gear to gear as they moved. As they reached the top, their swords clashed once more. Their faces less than a meter apart Gaby could feel Livia's breath, seeing swirling energies in her eyes.

Livia is still there, trying to fight back, Gaby thought. *I need to finish this!*

Gaby tried to push against Livia-Gavito's sword, but the tovainar possessing her pushed back. Livia-Gavito was stronger and sent Gaby careening into a gear, landing behind her and unleashing a second energy attack. Gaby gasped for air and parried the attack, but the force of it made her drop Heartguard. It clattered to the floor below. Livia-Gavito lifted her sword, then unleashed a powerful slash that forced Gaby to jump down. The gear split in two beneath her feet. Gaby allowed herself to free fall toward Heartguard, extending her hand to grab it. The Tempest Blade did something that it had never done before: It dematerialized into specks of light and reappeared in her hand.

So that's how Yaha reached Alex back then, uh? Nifty trick. Thanks, Heartguard.

Gaby rolled as she hit the ground, softening the impact. As she stood up, Livia-Gavito came right behind her, relentless in her attacks, forcing Gaby onto the defensive. Each blow rattled Gaby's bones. She bit her lips to focus on the attacks rather than on the pain. Livia-Gavito's eyes were now a terrifying combination of black sclera and red irises. Gaby had no clue what that was supposed to mean, but her instincts told her that it couldn't be any good. The brief distraction opened left an opening in Gaby's defenses, and Livia-Gavito grabbed the opportunity—and her—by the throat. The strength with which it threw her was inhuman, and she hit the gear with a sickening thud. The impact stole the breath from Gaby's lungs, making her cough as she struggled to her feet. A white light came from the Crown, and moving by its own volition, having chosen a side, it floated toward Livia-Gavito. Gaby ran as fast as her legs allowed, the burning sensation of the Gift empowering every fiber of her muscles to the straining point. She closed the gap at astonishing speed. It would be a race decided by millimeters.

Livia-Gavito grabbed the Crown at the same time that Soulkeeper struck it, Gaby hoping to cut it in two. At the moment they both touched the Crown time slowed to a crawl and then stopped, freezing them in midair.

What the Pits? was Gaby's last thought as even her thoughts froze in time. The Eclipse was halfway through its progression.

†††

Open your eyes.

What is this place? Gaby wondered as she looked around. It was a nice, sunny meadow, a stark contrast to the clock tower where she had been seconds ago. Her body felt lighter and at the same time stronger than before. A small pond next to her offered her a reflection of her current shape. She saw a skinny, braces-wearing, sixteen-year-old who had dyed her hair a dark shade, decked out in baggy jeans and an oversized stellar print hoodie.

"This is weird," Gaby said to herself. Not far from her were the ruins of an ancient Gamadash-Montsegur temple and inside it, a crystal statue of her. "And what's that statute of me?"

"This? It's like a mind space, generated by your subconscious and your soul and in some weird way, connected to the Tempest itself, given that the Tempest is created by the collective subconscious of every living and dead being in the universe, deities included. It's like a layer of reality if you like. The statue is your mental representation of the Ice State, that takes your place here when you use it," a female voice said in a friendly tone behind her. Gaby turned around and saw what appeared to be the ghost of a woman wearing garb that mixed elements from the Great War and the freefolk. The woman had faint olive skin and eyes that reminded Gaby of someone. She was smiling at Gaby like an old friend. But Gaby couldn't pinpoint from where she knew her or why she felt so familiar.

"And you are?" Gaby asked with reluctance.

"A part of you, of course," the ghost replied. Gaby was sure she had seen this woman in some old photos at a museum, the eyes were similar to those from Sam and... a realization dawned on Gaby, her heart sinking with the weight of knowledge. Confirmation of what she had feared all along.

"Izia," Gaby said.

"Yes and no," Izia replied. "Please, don't be disappointed."

"Well, your presence here doesn't help to assuage my..."

"Fears that all your life has been a lie because you are the reincarnation of someone else and thus all your choices seem to be preordained?" Izia replied as she sat on a white rock that used to be a column.

"Yeah, something like that," Gaby said, following suit.

"I can assure you that is not the case."

"And yet you are here."

"Yes, like they are here, too."

"Who's they?" Gaby asked, confused.

"The being that merged with you, years ago and became the Gift, your Gift," Izia explained, pointing above them. In the clear sky Gaby saw a familiar translucent humanoid silhouette, with wings on the back. It was the same being that had helped her on Manticore Island. "I think Alex is right, it's too crowded inside here," Gaby muttered, more to herself than to Izia.

"In reality, we are all different aspects of you," Izia explained. "Our personalities are the sum of several things, among others, your personal image, how you think others see you, your inner being, or soul if you want—and in the case of the Gifted, the being that merged with us. All of us are you, and you are all of us. I concede though that Alex is right, our minds can get a bit crowded at times. That's why many people have problems discovering who they are, some never do, or why some might develop mental health issues, as you saw with our friend last year. But in this case, we are not here for that. We are having a little chat to clear some things up before that thing finally breaks the defenses."

"What thing? The tovainar?" Gaby asked. A rumble could be heard in the distance, as the sky shifted into that of a grey sky with clouds that were more like penitent souls than rain clouds. It reminded Gaby of how Alex had described to her his mental landscape when suffering from depression.

"Yup," Izia replied, looking around. "Through the Tempest, it's trying to break the last defense inside you, since both of you are right now in a clash, too close, it's getting a better foothold to try and take over, hence the pounding you are hearing. We don't have much time."

Izia tried to take Gaby's hand, but she refused.

"Take over? Like you did when I started having those dreams about Fionn and the Professor?" Gaby asked, her blood boiling... or a similar sensation given that technically, they were inside her mind inside the Tempest inside. As Alex would say, it was *torta samohara* of reality, piles and piles of ingredients on top of each other. It shouldn't work, but the taste was good.

"Okay, you need to listen for once," Izia replied, snatching Gaby's hand. Gaby tried to pry herself free, but the ghost was by far stronger than she was. Izia had been as strong as Fionn in life and here, as a former shaman, now a spirit in her element... "I get it: You think I took over your body and all your choices so far, including who you fell in love with, are my doing."

"Am I right?"

"Far from it. Yes, you, we—sorry, the pronouns are getting complicated—are the reincarnation of Izia. Mekiri wanted to give her—past us—a second chance after sacrificing herself to save the world from that idiot Byron. But here is the thing. When someone dies most souls go back to the Life Tree to get cleansed and join Kaan'a or dwell in the Tempest. A few go back to the world at some point in time, to keep learning the lessons they need to learn. Others, go straight to the Pits if the Judge considers they deserve it, or, in case of heroes, to Last Heaven, which was the case for Izia, so they can wait to be reunited with their loved ones and take care of them, in a way. And while she was there, she was offered a second chance. Of course, she jumped at it, even after knowing what would happen to her."

"Which was?"

"Ceasing to exist as she knew it. Once you... we, Gaby were born, Izia as a consciousness ceased to exist. The moment a person is born; the soul is rebooted, if you like. Yes, there are memories from the past life, certain skills and proclivities that reappear after a while, but only when you are a kid. To a degree the person is the same. But only to a degree, the rest is decided by you, and you only, once you are born. But they are just echoes that you can choose to either listen to or ignore. Your feelings are yours alone."

"What about being destined to something by virtue of being a reincarnation of someone that earned a second chance?" Gaby asked once more, relaxing her hand. Izia smiled at her with sorrowful eyes. "You should listen to your own songs more. Destiny is what we are making of it and you know it. Just think about this: Instead of allowing father to take you to the Sisters of Mercy, you could have escaped before, which would have meant you never get the Gift in first place and thus you would never have met Fionn, or the others for that matter. Or you could have died in the same car crash as mom. Or decided to escape and leave Alex behind during the incursion at the Straits. You could have decided to pass the test, murdering a younger Livia in cold blood. You could have even refused the Gift and you wouldn't be here. There are many uncertainties depending on many factors that change how our life evolved. Some just happened without your input, others you actively decided what to do. Either way, you choose how to react and act in each instance."

"That means that the elections have always been..." Gaby mused.

"Yours. You always have had free will. All the choices that have taken you to this point have been yours... ours. And will always be ours. Yes, Izia is a part of us, like the Gift being is as well. But the sum of all is Gaby. You choose to fall in love with Fionn, not Izia, because for starters I'm just an echo of hers that is also part of you. You chose to start a singing career, like you chose to be a hero before that, or accepting the Gift. Gaby decided all of that. And you have been always Gaby."

"And now Gaby is at the crossroads of picking what I want to be from now on," she said, this time pulling Izia closer for a hug. "If I survive this."

"You sound disappointed."

"Concerned."

"You have been listening, but not understanding," Izia chastised Gaby, breaking the hug. "You can choose. Kaan'a gave mortals Free Will, and that can change the world the way they see fit. There are as many roads as you want them to be."

"So, I don't need to choose from one of two roads..."

"There is always a third option," Izia explained, lifting her left hand, with three fingers extended. "You don't have to follow the path of the warrior or the artist, you can choose to follow one that balances both. The same way you decided to break free from our father's influence, or from the Sisters of Mercy. The same way..."

"I got rid of the Ice State influence in my mind while keeping all its perks in combat. Battlebard."

"Now you are getting it." Izia winked at Gaby. "We are you and you have always been in charge. You can be whoever you want to be, because the choice is yours and only yours."

The rumbling evolved into clear and strong pounding, as if someone was not trying to knock a door, but to take down a wall.

"The pounding is increasing its strength," Gaby noted.

"The Gift won't be able to hold any longer," Izia noted, looking up at the cracks appearing in the sky. "This is going to be even more crowded."

"What will happen then?"

"That thing will come inside, and it will try to take over and take away our freedom and mind."

"Not if we face it together, as a single force," Gaby replied with a wink and her crooked smile. "And on our terms."

"I like that," Izia said, with a wide grin and her hands on her hips. "And we have them as support."

Two more humanoid silhouettes appeared in the meadows, walking in the middle of a thunderstorm, with a calm pace. They were holding hands.

"Who are they?" Gaby asked.

"The souls that reside in Heartguard and Soulkeeper?" Izia laughed. "What? Do you think your Blades won't fight for you after these many years of knowing you? We are in this together. In a weird way we are the one and the band at the same time."

"I wish I could have met you before," Gaby said ruefully. "I mean, when you were Izia."

"You have, we are one. And thank you," Izia said as she pressed her forehead on Gaby's. It was the Freefolk way to show affection, equivalent to a human kiss.

"For what?" Gaby asked.

"Being here," Izia replied, pointing to Gaby's heart.

† † †

Gaby waited, seated on a stool, in the middle of the mindscape, which morphed to resemble a concert hall. The one where Hildebrandtia had one of their few concerts before the conflicts put that to a halt. She grabbed... manifested a guitar.

An older man, dressed in what Gaby thought were robes from the priests of the Asurian Empire, if she recalled her history lessons, walked down the aisle of the concert hall. The man sported a goatee and a neatly coifed grey hair.

"I like it," Gavito said. "Nice architectural choice. Late Neoclassical style, I take it?"

"Yes. I know, it's my head. Now, get out of here."

"How rude, when we are such good friends." Gavito smiled. Not a friendly smile, but the kind that every woman got in their workplaces or in the streets when a man commented on their outfit. Gaby had been on the receiving end of many of those. It was the smile of a predator. "And this is such a great place to be. I was disappointed when

I didn't get to use you as my host. The most talented girl in the Sisterhood, thanks to the fact that you inherited the skills of one of the most powerful women in Theia. Plus, all the perks of having a body rebuilt by the Gift. Stupid Akeleths and their precious project."

"And I didn't get a puppy when I was a toddler. Life is full of disappointments," Gaby replied as she tuned the guitar.

"True," Gavito allowed. "But now I will get you."

"Yeah, I don't think that will happen. You are not welcome here."

"That's the thing. I don't have to be. I've always been here, lurking, every time you used the Ice State, every time you got angry or frenzied in battle."

"Oh, I know, until I kicked you out."

"An unfortunate consequence of you deciding to go back and help that stupid Greywolf. But not this time," Gavito said. "The statue is still here, which means you have never wanted to let go of the advantages offered by the Ice State, as it is so convenient to use when you fight."

"I'm willing to get rid of that as well. I don't need it." Gaby replied, as she stared at the ice sculpture of hers. Granted, being able to access that ability, so to speak, had helped her save not only herself, but her friends on several occasions. But it was a burden now, something that was like a weight on her soul. It was time to get rid of the crutch.

"Why do you fight this so hard? What do you have to fight for, when you could simply take a back seat and let me control things? I assure you, you will be fine under my command."

"I fight for those that can't do it. For my friends, my family. But more importantly, I fight for myself!" Gaby asserted, her voice reverberating through the acoustics of the concert hall.

"That's nice, very brave, but pointless. While we talked, I accessed this memory," Gavito replied. The mindspace shifted to the open gardens inside Ravenhall. Fionn was standing alone on one of the balconies overlooking the garden. The sky above the library was overcast, gray as if a winter storm was coming toward it. The air was moist and cold as snowflakes started to fall. And despite the lack of stars, it remained such a magical place. "The exact moment when you fell in love with the idiot. Now follow me, my beautiful Gaby."

Gavito-Fionn extended his hand toward Gaby, who took hold of it. He led Gaby toward the ice sculpture and placed her hand on it. The statue began to absorb Gaby, emitting sweet whispers with promises of peace and eternal love, or always being in this magical moment for eternity, once she was fully encased. Gavito-Fionn grinned.

A chord echoed through the air, a song coming from the deepest depths of the Tempest was blasting away, breaking the hold the sculpture had on Gaby. She recognized the song; it was one from her album. The one Sam had said was her favorite. Somehow Sam's battle had its own soundtrack and had made it to here, through the Tempest.

"So that's the trick, huh?" Gaby asked with a calm smile as she removed her hand from the sculpture version of herself, creating cracks on it. It was so simple and yet so logical. No wonder no Sister had been able to break it. Because it hit at the core of your very being until you were trapped of your own accord. Again, the question was choice. She was surprised that beating this monster would be easier than she expected at first. Paraphrasing Alex, she had a plan, and while it would take all her mental power to make it work, she decided it was the best option. For not every fight had to be won through trading blows. Not when it came to the mind, the heart, and the soul.

"You never actually possess someone. You just trap them inside their own head using what they love the most or their most precious memory, while you use their bodies until they burn out."

"Something that won't happen to a Gifted body. Clever girl," Gavito-Fionn said, rueful. "I see that the battle at the other corner of the Tempest is becoming too intense. It doesn't matter who wins that one either, the Freefolk or the god, at the end of the day all of them will succumb before my masters."

"You should focus on your own battle," Gaby said as her body changed into her present adult self and her clothes morphed into a brand new outfit: black leather pants with black leather boots, a blue top crop-top with a sheer fabric covered in rhinestones below the neck. Over that, a silver jacket. Both wrists were covered with diverse bracelets. But the most important one was the silver bracelet with dragonwolf and the pearl: her heartmate engagement bracelet. She gave it a brief look and smiled. A reminder that Fionn would always be with her, as she was always with him. Two beating hearts combined into one and as such, can't be torn apart. Certainly not by the monster in front of her trying to fool her by looking like her husband.

"Right. Now you die, then and I take over your body;" Gavito-Fionn said matter-of-factly.

"No. You already took away too many lives from innocent people for centuries. Now, you are the one who will finally die," Gaby said as she strummed the guitar strings.

The riff of a guitar echoed through the air, followed by an electronic keyboard playing the first notes of a song. A silver microphone stand appeared in front of her and she grabbed it, holding it by the mic.

"What is that sound?" Gavito-Fionn looked around confused.

"That? One of my favorite tracks from my album,"

Gaby replied as a microphone formed in her hand. "I'm very proud of it." Behind her, three energy silhouettes appeared, two women and one large man, holding musical instruments.

"You have a band inside your head?" Gavito asked, incredulity showing in his face.

"Like any musician, yes. How do you think we compose music? And I will sing you to death to keep you out of it," Gaby replied with her trademark crooked smile.

"If you do that you would destroy me, Gaby!" Gavito-Fionn screamed with a supplicant face, bursting into tears.

"Stop being such a drama king. I know Fionn. You are not Fionn. I wrote this song for us, based on this very moment, as a present for him when we decided to become a family. So, I will take my precious memory back, thank you. One, two, three!"

The chords reverberated inside the mind space as spectral images of the memory when Fionn and Gaby almost kissed for the first time three years ago at Ravenhall, floated in the air. It was as if she was creating her own music video.

"Open your heart, Fionn.
We are here,
The roads are open,
Take my hand.
The limit is only the sky.
Come into my heart,
When it's dark,
To make it warm again.
Take my hand.
Hold on tight.
There is no fear,
'cause I wanna be with you
And make Destiny our own!
And dream, dream with you, my love

'cause, I wanna be with you
And make Destiny our own!
And dream, dream with you, my love
Always."

Gavito-Fionn shrieked in rage and, manifesting a sword, launched himself in the air, spinning, and attacked Gaby with a series of rapid slashes and thrusts, all while insulting her.

"Do you think you are so important as to reject me? Who do you think you are? Just a scared woman whose father never wanted anything more than a tool to use for power! You should be happy I paid attention to you and have been watching every step in your life. You should thank me for thinking you deserve to be with me, instead of choosing to reject me! Who was nice to you? Me! Who gave you your skills? Me! But no, you prefer to be with that pathetic loser half-blooded freefolk! Once I take over your body, I will stab him! And when he heals, I will do it again and again and again until he pleads to be put out of his misery, all while he looks confused as why you are the one murdering him. I will break your bond and then you will be only mine!"

Gaby dodged and deflected with swift movements, every single blow, using her seemingly unbreakable mic stand as an improvised weapon, without losing her concentration or missing a beat of the song. Each verse, each chord was wearing out the form of Gavito, who shifted from Fionn, to Livia, to Gaby's own mother, and to forms of people she never knew but were probably related to previous hosts. The shapeless forms of Gavito tried to attack the rest of the musicians, but the music had created a barrier around them. That barrier effortlessly deflected the onslaught. He returned his focus to Gaby and tried to punch her in the face, but she merely sidestepped.

"There is snow

Falling upon us.
Remember when we first kissed,
Setting everything in motion?
You took my hands
And asked me to run with you.
Am I here in vain?
Hold on against the dark
There will be only our mark
'cause, I wanna be with you,
And make Destiny our own!
And dream, dream with you, my love
'cause, I wanna be with you
And make Destiny our own, Fionn!
And dream, dream with you, my love
Always."

Her voice grew in strength, filling every corner of the place with an energy very similar to the ripple effects caused by Sam's magick. If this is what Harland had referred to as the 'music of the spheres' that allowed the legendary battlebards of yore to inspire and alter the battlefield to their favor, then it was a powerful thing. So powerful that Gaby could see how the mental representation of the Ice State, that ice sculpture of hers cracked more and more with every single note. It would mean that she would lose that ability forever, but she would also be free from Gavito. And now, she had something much better to replace it. Her own voice.

"When it's cold
And dark
Love sustains.
Hold on tight,
Let's beat the night.
There will be no fear
'cause, I wanna be with you
And make Destiny our own!

And dream, dream with you, my love
'cause, I wanna be with you
And make Destiny our own!
And dream, dream with you, my love
Always, I wanna be with you
And make Destiny our own!"

As the song ended, the sculpture exploded into millions of fragments which immediately evaporated as the sky cleared into that of a warm summer day. As Gavito's shape turned into that of a frail old man, he tried to throw a final punch toward Gaby, but she simply sidestepped it again.

"You are nothing but a pathetic being," Gaby noted. "Always taking from others, never creating anything of worth."

"I created the Sisters of Mercy."

"Correction, you stole them from the women that actually created the order. You know what? I don't have more time or energy to deal with you. *Begone!*" Gaby screamed the last word, sending a shockwave that hit Gavito with full force, turning him into dust. "My body, my choice!"

Gaby breathed a sigh of relief. She couldn't sense the tovainar anywhere in her mind. For that matter, there was no sign of the always present sore from the Ice State. Finally, she was free. She allowed herself to smile.

The place shook and cracks appeared in the surrounding mindspace.

"I knew it was too soon to signal victory. What's happening?"

"I think the stasis spell is about to dispel, which means that your fight in the physical world will resume in a few seconds. You will have to react fast, because he is still around somewhere and your body is in danger," Izia warned.

"Thanks for the heads up. As usual." Gaby winked at

the other part of herself before she closed her eyes, and the world around her went dark.

†††

As the stasis spell broke and time resumed, Gaby went back to real world. Everything still moved at a slow pace, which allowed her to see Livia trying to stab her in the belly with the sharp edges of the crown. Before Gaby could think, Soulkeeper shone with intensity and moved on its own volition to block the attack. The impact released a powerful concussive force and blinding light that sent both women flying into the air.

Gaby hit the ground with enough force that all breath left her body in a pained wheeze. Momentarily dazed, she shook her head. With some effort, Gaby pushed herself up. The vest had taken the brunt of the impact, as the special kinetic gel inside it had exploded. That meant that she might have only suffered a broken rib or two and not an internal injury.

Thank Kaan'a. I will have to ask Alex for a new one, she thought as she grabbed Heartguard. *Now, where is my other Blade?*

Gaby looked around until she saw Soulkeeper a couple of meters away. The room was filling with spectral fireflies, leftovers from the Tempest. Gaby walked slowly, as the broken ribs were a tad painful. She grabbed Soulkeeper and the sight of it worried her, for the Blade was cracked. Destroying the crown had taken its toll on one of her twin blades... on one of her friends. She could only hope that the forge Fionn had shown her during her last visit at Skarabear could repair it.

But that still leaves the question of who could repair it, she thought. But Gaby pushed that thought aside. Livia was a few meters away from her. She lay in a pool of blood with the broken crown next to her, the blood rubies' glow fading away. Gaby moved toward her former friend. She kneeled and cradled Livia into her arms, as tears ran down Gaby's cheeks.

"Thank you," Livia mouthed. Her eyes were no long red and black but had returned to their normal color. With her last breath she said: "I'm sorry."

"Don't be, it was not your fault, please hold on!" Gaby pleaded as she held her friend, finally free from the tovainar.

But it was already too late, for Livia had stopped breathing.

Gaby cried into Livia's chest. With care, she laid Livia on the floor. Exhausted, and flooded with sadness, Gaby sank down next to Livia. Gaby extended her arms as her breathing slowed. She stared at the night sky through the gaping holes in the rooftop. The moon and the stars were shining once more as the strange eclipse came to an end. Funny how an seemingly random astronomical event caused so much chaos.

Gaby broke and began to sob, wrenching ones that tore from her chest. She wondered if Fionn had felt the same after his fight with Byron.

No, Byron was well aware of what he was doing. Livia was a hostage acting against her will, she thought. *Regardless, the result is the same: My friend died at my hands. So me refusing to fight back at the test, refusing to kill my friend so I could graduate as a Sister of Mercy echelon, was for nothing?*

"I don't think so," her inner Izia-voice replied. *"Choosing that made you worthy of the Gift. Which led you to this path. And in that way, you have helped a lot of people."*

With the tovainar dead, she, the other Sisters of Mercy, and even Livia for a brief moment, were finally free. And yet, a sense of dread filled Gaby's chest, making her heart beat like a drum out of pace. It wasn't over yet.

With barely a whisper of a voice, Gaby began to sing her song once more.

A firefly flew and rested on her nose and covered her with its light as her ears and nose began to bleed.

† † †

"How long has she been up there? The eclipse is over," Sid whispered to Fionn. The wait was sending Fionn to the edge, his finger itching to grab Black Fang and end the stalemate. He felt a hand placed on his shoulder.

"I think she is coming out," Vivi said in a whisper. "Also, something just changed in the environment, I can feel it in the tips of my fingers."

Gaby emerged from the clocktower, walking slowly. Fionn walked toward Gaby. He could see dried blood under her nose and from her ears. Her arms were covered in bruises. And her eyes, they looked different, with a sadness flooding them.

"Gaby, are you okay?" Fionn asked as he got closer to her. In reply, he only felt a sharp pain coming from his abdomen. Clutching at the source, he saw blood flowing from a wound. The damaged blade of Soulkeeper covered in blood, resting on his hand. Gaby looked at him directly in the eyes. And it dawned on him.

"Shut up, or next time I will lodge this into your heart. The only reason I don't kill you is because our king might want to do it personally," Gaby said, and she pushed Fionn to the ground. He fell on his knees as Vivi and Sid moved closer to examine the injury, confused.

"What's going on?" Sid asked, staring at Gaby. Fionn saw from the corner of his eye how Joshua clenched his fist around Fury's hilt and the blades starting to heat up. Fionn just shook his head, mouthing 'No.'

"What is happening, samoharo," Edamane said, with his chilling, screeching, mocking voice, "is that my champion won, for not only they took over her body and mind, they also have the Crown."

"Unfortunately, in two pieces," Gaby replied, showing the broken pieces of the Crown, the rubies devoid of color. "The woman put up more of a fight than expected. I liked my previous host, it was a good body. But this one is far better, with the power of the Gift."

"How long until you have total control of her body?" Edamane asked.

"Not much brother, not much," Gaby replied.

"Bring the crown to me," Edamane said. He juggled the thermobaric bomb. "Then we will blow up this city."

"To send a message?" Gaby asked as she got closer to the tovainar.

"To teach you and your friends to not mess with us," Edamane replied as his voice dropped an octave, showing his bizarre nature, as no mortal could do that.

"I'm not that good liar, am I?" Gaby said, and smiled.

"I knew someone would best my twin sooner or later. Now give me the Crown!"

"Take it!" Gaby said as she threw both halves of the crown into the air. "Catch!"

"Sid, the hand!" Fionn exclaimed.

As the tovainar stared at the flying pieces of the crown, Sid whipped into motion and cut Edamane's right hand, the one holding the bomb. At the same time, Gaby pierced his chest with Heartguard. For a moment, Edamane stared at the bleeding stab wound as Gaby tried to pull back Heartguard. But Edamane grabbed the blade with his left hand, keeping it in place, as his teeth morphed into rows and rows of shark-like fangs, and his mouth opened wide—wide enough that he could bite her head off.

"Gaby, duck! Fionn yelled.

It took mere seconds. As Fionn stood up, put his hands together, both palms facing out with the tiny green energy bubbles coalescing in front of his palms that took shape of green whirlwinds. An explosion of light followed as a gust of wind energy, glowing green, came from Fionn's hands, unleashing enough shock force that it generated a sonic boom.

When the flash of light dispersed, Edamane's head was gone, leaving behind only a charred neck stump and part of his lower jaw. His body collapsed as it disintegrated into a mound of dust.

"Mental note," Fionn mumbled, looking at his hands. The burns were extensive, his palms and fingers comparable to raw meat. "It's easier to do it focusing the energy on a weapon than with the bare hands. And less painful."

"The bomb!" Sid said, breaking the sudden calm. "Where is the bomb? I cut the hand but I couldn't see where it fell with that bright light!"

"What bomb?" Gaby asked, startled.

"This one?" Vivi replied as she looked up, making hand gestures to keep it floating in the air. Trapped inside a bubble, the thermobaric bomb was cradled in a hand that actively rotted away.

"Nice catch, Vivi," Fionn said.

"I better teleport this to somewhere it can't hurt anyone. For some reason I think the teleportation spell got easier to cast," Vivi replied. With a snap the bomb disappeared.

Fionn nodded to Joshua, who smiled. Fury turned into a weapon made of pure fire, as Sid got his small ax ready, and from the battlements above, Harland got the guards ready once more. Fionn stared at the soldiers of Edamane's battalion.

"You can leave now by your own feet," Fionn said to the soldiers. "Or with them in front of you, though not necessarily attached to the rest of you."

The members of the battalion looked at each other,

dropped their weapons and ran away.

"Wise choice," Fionn continued. "And tell your so-called Golden King that he is next!"

† † †

"I guess the change I sensed," Vivi said, "was whatever Sam just did to fix magick."

"I love you so much right now," Sid said. "I might even invite you to dinner."

"You better not be saying that because I just saved our skins," Vivi said with a laugh, her cheeks flushed.

Fionn picked up Heartguard and the damaged Soulkeeper, and knelt next to Gaby. He gave her back the twin blades and embraced her.

"For a moment you had me worried," he said, the tension in shoulders finally relaxing. It was as if a heavy weight had been lifted from them, and his heart stopped hurting. At that moment, the mere thought of losing her was his only real weakness.

"I was worried, too. I'm so sorry for hurting you," Gaby replied, sobbing into his chest.

"Can't say I haven't done something to deserve it," Fionn said. "Besides, it was a mere flesh wound. Most of the blood was from that cut in your hand. I guess the crown had very sharp edges. But it did cause enough shock to let you get close to Edamane. Though, as you said, you are not a good liar."

"Don't say that," Gaby replied. "You haven't done anything wrong. Annoying, perhaps, but that's all."

Fionn broke the hug, but couldn't stay apart from her for long. He cradled Gaby in his arms. "Is... is that thing inside you?" Fionn asked, examining her.

She laughed. "No. The Gift took care of whatever I didn't destroy before. I do have an incredibly huge and painful migraine. Plus, my eardrums got damaged; never a good thing for a musician."

"I can fix that," Vivi said, placing her hands on Gaby's ears. "Unlike my favorite student, I *do* know how to cast healing spells." And magick is flowing freer this time."

As Vivi healed Gaby, Fionn stood up, wobbling. There were small burn scars on his palms, which began to heal over as specks of light came from the wounds.

Joshua stepped up to him. "Two questions: How... how did you do that? Blowing up his head with that green energy beam? It looked familiar."

"Because it is," Fionn replied after taking a deep, long breath. "It's a special technique I've been working on for the past couple of years, since Alex used a similar thing on an arrow to punch a hole through the Creeping Chaos' chest. I'm trying to make it work without burning the Gift, but it seems I still need to work out a few issues. What's the second question?"

"You knew Gaby was lying to get closer," Joshua said as matter-of-factly. "Without knowing if she was truly her."

"It was the best chance to get rid of that bomb," Fionn replied. "I know her eyes. I trust her implicitly. Someone very wise recently told me that a good leader has to do that, same as a partner."

"And you are telling me this for...?" Joshua waved his hand, urging Fionn to continue.

"If you are serious about helping so-called monsters to redeem themselves, you will have to learn to lead them and trust them," Fionn explained.

"Sorry to interrupt this very important lesson," Sid interjected. "But now that I think about it. Gaby has two tovainar and titan kills under her belt, Alex has a god..."

"Probably two by now," Gaby added as Vivi finished with the spell. Everyone looked at her and Gabby just shrugged. "Long story."

"And defeated a tovainar to turn it to our side. Fionn

only has one tovainar and one titan. You are falling behind Greywolf."

"I'm not keeping a tally, this is not a competition," Fionn replied. "Also, you only have half a titan."

"I thought you weren't keeping the score," Sid said, rueful.

"I could use rest, but first I need to go to one more place to finish some business," Gaby replied.

"Where?" Fionn asked. But he already knew the answer. He had been expecting this for quite some time. Closing circles and all of that, which Yokoyawa kept saying when he got into therapist mode.

"Manticore Island," Gaby said.

Chapter 16
Magick Lights

"I REFUSE TO DO SOMETHING so human as... lip synch." Nothing less than disgust dripped from the words. "But you... you created this domain in the Tempest and thus you set the conditions. It matters not. I will abide by the ancient rules, for my victory is assured," Shemazay said.

Mekiri was right, gods are egomaniacs, Sam thought.

Sam walked toward Shemazay as the surroundings morphed into a stage in an open park, with the lights of a city in the background. Shemazay moved toward the center of their encounter, making gestures with his hand to generate a fireball that he threw at Sam.

He is so obtuse that he is going for basic elemental spells, Sam thought. *I will teach him how to put a good show then.*

Sam mouthed the first lines in perfect lip-synch as the fireball approached.

For long enough
I've been waiting for you like crazy.
I'm in isolation
As the world goes empty.

A metal ring appeared around Sam's feet as she mouthed the words, from which a red drape hung. Sam tossed it upwards, letting the dramatic whoosh of fabric obscure her form. The fireball struck the drape with no noticeable effect. A second later, the ring and drape fell to the ground and dissolved, to reveal Sam wearing a new outfit. She now wore a glimmering magenta short, tight-fitting dress with long sleeves with integrated gloves covering her hands. Her irises now glowed lilac, and a brilliant lilac seeped through her red hair like spilled ink with the shift. The color of the dress combined well with her silver fox tail, which swayed as she walked.

So let's go-oh on.

Light them up!

We can find us a new world.

Shemazay created hundreds of ice needles in the middle of the air, and sent them barreling toward Sam. With a flick of her left hand, she transformed most of them into a rain of metallic confetti.

When the confetti disappeared, another quick change took place, and now, over the body suit, she wore monochrome silver: Pauldrons on her shoulders, a chunky belt attached to the sleek dress, and knee-high boots which were made of a flexible metallic material.

You have to do just one word.

Shine!

As she stood in front of Shemazay she closed her eyes for a moment, smiling. The Gift grew inside her, sending energy coursing through her body, giving her goosebumps on her arms.

"Confetti? Is that all you've got? Should I be intimidated?"

"I haven't started yet."

"I know what you are trying to do, and I should warn you: It won't work. You can duel me or you can free the magick. You can't do both in the time you have," Shemazay smiled. "The eclipse will be over soon, and I will be the new god of magick and not a subaltern."

Alex is right, Sam thought, *these 'gods' like to talk a lot.* "You're right, let's speed up this," she said.

My love I say ooohhh
I have a passion foooor
the magick lights
In your eyes.

Sam extended her right arm. Kasumi took her hand. Sam looked into her eyes and kept mouthing the song. She pulled Kasumi toward an embrace, with the spin transforming her clothes into a royal blue haori printed with white sakuras, with long, flowing sleeves, a sky blue obi with a pink rope belt, over black latex legging and white ankle boots. A pink flower with hanging golden rings and charms decorated her black hair. An outfit proper for a magician's assistant. With another spin, Sam seated Kasumi in a big chair that grew from the ground, as Shemazay hurled a ball of fire toward Kasumi. Sam covered Kasumi with a red cloth and then pulled it away as the fireball destroyed the chair. But Kasumi had already disappeared.

Behind the fight, Kasumi found herself being hurled into the air, with Breaker in hand, toward the bound ball of energy. With one swift cut, she sliced one of the heavy chains, before disappearing again in a puff of smoke.

My love I say ooohhh
And I just wanna feel you so much.

Sam then pulled Kasumi from a top hat, as if she were a rabbit. However, she now had black panther ears on top of her head and a long, black tail. Shemazay transformed his fingers into arrows that flew toward both women. With a smile Sam pushed Kasumi into a large red cabinet. She shut the door and stepped behind the cabinet, giving it a spin. The arrows pierced the cabinet, but Sam was unconcerned as she tapped the cabinet with a flourish of her hands. The cabinet's four sides fell away revealing nothing, Kasumi had disappeared again.

For a second time Kasumi found herself being hurled into the air with Breaker in hand toward the ball of energy. With another swift stroke, she cut one of the chains and landed. Shemazay turned around to attack her with lightning, but as it was about to strike her, her body became stiff as a board as Sam put Kasumi into a sleepy trance. Sam snapped her fingers and a large red cloth appeared and deflected the lighting. Sam threw the red cloth over Kasumi and with a gesture, sent Kasumi floating into the Tempest before disappearing again.

For long enough
We've run out of time.
I see the sun setting in your heart
The moon sleepless over the night sky.

Kasumi opened her eyes and found herself falling toward the ball of energy. During her fall, she managed to slice a third chain. She again disappeared in a puff of smoke and appeared next to Same who stood next to a large cage. Shemazay hurled a giant seed from which vines and tree branches sprouted. Sam got Kasumi out of the way by pushing her into the cage. Once Kasumi was inside, Sam spun the cage as the vines covered the sides of the cage completely. Sam deftly leapt over the tree branches and landed on top of the cage. She lifted the lid and out from the cage came Kasumi, transformed into a black panther. Not wasting a second, Kasumi jumped around the vines and the tree branches, reaching the core. With her new-found claws, Kasumi tore through a fourth binding before returning to Sam's side.

My love I say ooohhh
I have a passion foooor
the magick lights
In your eyes.
My love I say ooohhh
And I just wanna feel you so much.

Sam pet Kasumi-panther and then threw the red drape over her. The cloth collapsed and Sam picked up a playing card from the ground, the Queen of Spades. On it, there was a drawing of Kasumi wearing a fancy dress, while holding Breaker in her right hand and she was sporting a wide grin. Sam picked up the Queen of Spades and with a flourish with her left hand, conjured a deck of cards. She put the Queen of Spades in the deck and made them fly from one hand to another in a perfect arc.

Shemazay, annoyed, summoned several swords and aimed them at Sam. Unconcerned, she flicked the cards from the top of the deck toward the swords, intercepting each one of them. Every time a card hit a sword, the weapon morphed into a rose that landed on the floor, forming a small garden. Without more cards in hand, Sam knelt to pick up one of the roses and set it on fire, transforming it with a flourish into the Queen of Spades card.

Ooohhh!
Ooohhh!
Ooohhh!
Ooohhh!

Sam flung the Queen of Spades card toward the last chain binding the energy ball. Shemazay cast a flaming arrow to burn it before it reached its target, but the roses below sent up jets of water, as if they were a fountain, extinguishing the flames from the arrow just in time. The Queen of Spades sliced through the final chain.

I'm sinking in your eyes
As you drive me to a surprise.
We're running out of time
Don't let them fade away!

Sam and Kasumi stood side-by-side, defiant.

"Let's see if you like these foolish parlor tricks when used against you," Shemazay said. He formed a crystal cube and hurled it toward the women. Sam pushed

Kasumi away, as the cube hit Sam square in chest. A flash of light momentarily blinded them. When it subdued, Sam found herself trapped by Shemazay inside a crystal box full of water. Strong chains wrapped tight around Sam's arms and legs.

Kasumi dashed over, ready to use Breaker to destroy the box, but Sam smiled and nodded her head, pointing. Kasumi leaped and did several back flips as she dodged an attack and grabbed the red drape that had just appeared. She ran and jumped, leaping over the box, letting the cloth fall to cover it. Shemazay growled in anger and prepared to cast another spell at the box, ice crystals forming in his outstretched hands. But as the red drape slid off the box, Sam was nowhere to be seen.

My love I say ooohhh
I have a passion foooor

Sam was suddenly standing atop an amplifier that was blasting Gaby's song right next to the ball of energy. Water dripped from her body, the chains still around her arms and legs. But with a slight flex of her arms, like she was going to burst free through sheer strength, they turned into glimmering white doves that flew away.

All of the chains had been cut away.

Shemazay seemed to realize this and ran toward the ball.

Sam clapped hard and a cloud of smoke covered her. When the smoke dissipated Sam disappeared from the top of the amplifier and reappeared right in front of the energy ball.

As Sam stepped up to the ball of energy that was the core concept of Magick itself, her tail multiplied into nine, like the fable nine-tailed silver foxes from myth. For the first time ever, Sam enjoyed having the tails. They gave her confidence as she continued to lip-synch to the song.

the magick lights

In your eyes.

Sam placed her hands on the core, at the same time as Shemazay. The half on Sam's side turned lilac and gold, like everything about her, with soft sparks of light floating around like fey. Shemazay's side was black with lightning crackling on its surface. With the core of magick itself finally free, the toughest part of the duel was about to start. The core was composed of layers upon layers engraved with runes in combinations that 'programmed' into the fabric of reality the rules that governed magick. Fixing them wouldn't be a contest of raw power, but of pure will and mind. Mekiri had entrusted this mission to her, in part because the Gift gave her the power needed to do so, and in part, because Mekiri had faith in her.

My love I say ooohhh
And I just wanna feel you so much.

But Sam realized she had a problem: Gifted or not, she was still mortal, with a mortal mind. She wouldn't be able to rewrite all the complicated rules of magick as fast as she needed to during this contest of wills. Shemazay pushed with renewed force, as he increased in size, towering above Sam. His will was increasing in strength.

Hey! Hey! Hey! Hey!

Magick had so many rules. And Shemazay had rewritten them all with his own. There were thousands and thousands of runes one on each layer of the energy ball, each one combining with others in weird ways that Sam's mind couldn't even begin to understand. Sam tried to rewrite a simple rule, like the range of a spell, by rearranging the runes on one of the upper layers. But Sam needed to divide her focus on what Shemazay was doing, to keep pushing him away with her willpower, so she missed a couple of components in the spell and the new line scrambled away. As things stood, it would be impossible to crack the code. With Shemazay pushing harder and harder, the black side of the energy ball grew like cancer.

As the song entered the long guitar bridge where Gaby was showing off her prowess with the instrument, Sam tried to push back, to regain control of the energy ball. Her whole body felt the strain of the effort, the muscles in her arms burning. If she didn't find a way to rearrange the runes while keeping control in the struggle of wills, she would lose, which meant if she was lucky, an immediate death, but that would leave Kasumi at the mercy of the deranged god. And all the effort Alex surely was going through to destroy the god's avatar would be for nothing.

Biting her the inside of her lip, she tried to stand firm, but her legs began to shake. All that Sam wanted now was to not be there, to somehow be at the other end of these events with everything magically fixed.

There should be a third option.

It dawned on her. And Sam smiled as a fluttering in her chest appeared, the muscles in her legs tightening up.

Sam recalled what Asherah had done before. How and why she had performed actual, real magick for the first time in the universe's history: She had just hoped for the best to save everyone. And the universe had responded to her request. Sam hoped that asking the universe itself would work.

Sam had an idea on how she would rewrite the rules. For what's Magick in the end if not faith in things changing for the better?

Hey! Hey! Hey! Hey! I say!

Shemazay had the upper hand. His terrible wings cast a shadow over the ball, the darkness covering all but a small source of light. Sam still held on, but the black had almost reached Sam's fingertips.

Sam focused on One. Single. Rule. As long as hope is in your heart, you can use magick to change the world.

Millions of minds, billions of hearts, all with the power to shape things if they so desired it. Mekiri would have to fix some control later, but for now this should suffice. The Universe would take care of the rest. The ball of energy changed. Her side of the energy ball wasn't just white light anymore, instead, it emitted every light from every color of the spectrum, like a rainbow.

Sam was unleashing what Mekiri had called the Magick of Chaos, the power of choice. No prophecy could withstand that. Her side of the energy ball began to overcome the black side of Shemazay's, forcing him to focus all his will on his hands, reducing his size to that of a regular human. His wings began to wither as he drained them of energy to counter Sam's Magick of Chaos. The runes scrambled in ways neither of the opponents could understand, jumping between layers, replacing lines for clouds of probability.

Hey! Hey! Hey! Hey! I say!

With a last push, Sam gained control of the entire core of Magick and instead of trying to contain it, she just let it loose in all the glorious Magick of Chaos that exploded in an infinity of colors as it reacted to what she had that Shemazay didn't: Hope. Shemazay's body became weaker, emaciated. He fell to his knees. Steam sizzled on his skin as he screamed in realization.

I say, I'm entranced by your smile.
I say, I'm sinking in your eyes.
I'm entranced by your smile,
I won't sleep until you show me
The magick lights
In your heart.

Sam finished lip-synching the last lines of the song, as part of her mantra to cast her chaos spells. Sam walked toward the fallen god and placed her left hand on his forehead and the right in his chest. Light emanated from his mouth and eyes, which the Tempest promptly absorbed.

"And that's how it's done," Sam said to Shemazay as her tails disappeared. She had finally learned how to summon and dispel them at will.

"Are you okay, Sam?" Kasumi asked, as she approached Sam. Her outfit had returned to that of the assistant instead of the Queen of Spades. Kasumi placed a hand on Sam's right shoulder, but the pauldron on it was too hot and she pulled it back. "What are you doing to him?"

"It's time the being in charge of karmic retribution gets a bit of karma himself. I'm trapping him in the worst kind of prison, the one he despises the most. I trapped him in a mortal form, where he will be trapped forever if Alex manages to destroy his avatar in the mortal realm."

"Remind me to never make you that angry," Kasumi muttered as she grabbed Sam's hand. Her grip was tight, and her knees buckled.

Sam lurched to catch her. "Kasumi, are you okay?" she asked, worried. The pain of her injury seemed to have overcome her.

"You might have won this, mortal," Shemazay chuckled. "But at the cost of your love. For I'm the only one that knows how to break the curse. And while the Tempest would have prevented it from progressing, by helping you she lost focus on keeping it at bay."

Sam clenched her jaw in realization, as she saw Kasumi growing weaker.

"I'm sorry, Kasumi, I didn't know," Sam replied, stress in her voice. She then turned to Shemazay, her irises glowing intensely. Sam lifted him by the neck. The weakened body was easy to lift now, and Sam's anger only fueled her physical strength. "Break the curse or I will break you with my bare hands!"

"I can't. You took away the powers that would have enabled me to do so. Karma."

"You *skansen!*"

"Sammy... I don't feel that well," Kasumi said with short breaths and a weak smile. Ultimately, she gave up on standing and knelt.. "I thought we had time."

"We still have as long as you keep focusing your will. We are in the Tempest; you can do this! Kasumi!" Sam exclaimed as she threw Shemazay away.

† † †

You are letting your opponent dictate the terms of combat, Alex could hear Fionn's voice in his head. *Did I teach you anything? If you have a plan, stick to it.*

"Yeah, I know, I know," Alex murmured. The metallic taste of blood filled his mouth as he struggled to get up, using Yaha as support. The silvery surface of the blade was now glowing with maximum intensity as Shemazay approached.

"You are nothing but ants trying to harness the power of my brethren forcibly injected into your veins," Shemazay growled. "But I will end that, starting with you!"

Alex stood up and stared at the horrifying visage that was Shemazay. Recovering his breath, he channeled the Gift once more, and his irises glowed.

"You insist on fighting me, child?"

"For someone that supposedly knows all about mortals, you don't know how stubborn we can be," Alex replied, spitting blood to the ground.

Shemazay didn't waste a second and hurled the fireball chain toward Alex once more, but this time, Alex didn't parry, he simply stopped being there.

He could feel the Gift send electrical currents into every fiber of his legs' muscles, which coupled with the adrenaline, allowed him to move faster than he ever had. He ran toward Shemazay and slashed at his leg. By the time the fallen god reacted, Alex wasn't there anymore.

Another cut appeared on Shemazay's left side, and a third one on the right bicep.

The plan wasn't to match him strength with strength. The plan was to debilitate Shemazay with fast attacks until an opening appeared and Alex could strike him hard in the chest as he'd done with the Dark Father. Except that this time he didn't have the assistance of Sam, so he would have to do it all by himself. His lungs screamed from the effort, as Alex wasn't one for running and speed attacks, unlike Gaby or Fionn. But he was enjoying this. It brought up the same elation he had during that last hoops game, as he cut, dodged and ran around Shemazay.

The fallen god, irritated, launched a series of rapid attacks, catching Alex unguarded, breaking the cadence of his attacks.

Now he is going for speed. He is fast but is not putting much strength in the attacks this time. He doesn't know how to use a physical body.

Alex had an easier time parrying the attacks, as they were weaker than before. As he deflected slash after slash, he used those small openings to make more swift cuts on the exposed skin.

Enraged, Shemazay threw a slash aimed at Alex's legs. Alex leaped, evading the attack that left a groove in the dais. As he landed, Alex aimed his own slashing attack at the shaft of the scythe-axe, below where it joined the blade. Both weapons were locked together, Alex holding down the scythe-axe, as Yaha generated enough energy to heat the shaft into red, then white. He released the shaft, making Shemazay pull it away with enough strength that he lost balance, and stumbled. Shemazay recovered and launched a new attack, this time aimed at Alex's neck, but he expected as much and instead of parrying, Alex countered with his own slash at the same spot Yaha had just heated, cutting it cleanly and sending the scythe blade flying away. It skittered away, falling from the dais and the top of the Clocktower.

Alex didn't get a chance to celebrate. Shemazay punched him in the side and sent him flying back once more, creating a gap between them. This time, Alex landed on his feet and readied himself as the attacks came as fast as a meteor storm.

Alex was pressed back as he blocked the barrage of attacks. In the last one, the chain snared Yaha's blade, and before Alex could react he found himself in the air, being pulled toward Shemazay. The fallen god generated a ball of fire in his right hand, cranking back to punch Alex. It would all be over in seconds.

Alex breathed and closed his eyes, bracing for the impact. He was about to try the only combat maneuver that Sid had never been successful in teaching him.

By now, the connection with Yaha, as Fionn had taught him, was second nature. He had done something like this before, but not this extreme. The blade dematerialized and shrunk to the size of a kitchen knife, freeing itself—and Alex—from the grasp of the chain. Alex pulled up his legs and arms toward his chest, focusing his weight and momentum toward the floor, hitting it with force and rolling away, dodging the fiery punch aimed at his chest by mere millimeters.

Alex sprang into the air from his roll without losing momentum, changing Yaha into a reverse grip. Speckles of light, followed by lightning, crackled across the blade as it rematerialized into its full length, stabbing Shemazay in the back, right where the heart should be in the avatars of deities. The blade came out of his chest, glowing as if it were made of light, as black ichor and flames burst from the wound. Alex fell to the ground and pulled Yaha out. Shemazay staggered, then collapsed onto his knees and then to the floor. Flames continued to lick at the air from the wound. It was hard to breathe, and Alex felt a pain in his ribs from where he'd landed, but as he struggled to his feet Alex was relieved to have won.

And yet I think I forgot something, Alex thought.

Shemazay slowly rose behind him, growling. His body engulfed in fiery, magma like blood was decomposing quickly. Shemazay let out a guttural scream no mortal being could have produced, its infrasound frequencies inspiring nausea in Alex and an ache in his bones.

"Dodge!" Yoko yelled from behind.

Alex sidestepped as he saw the Stellar Ehécatl flying across the room, from where Yoko stood at the clockface. The weapon struck Shemazay in the head, cleaving it in two with a clean cut. The scimitar lodged itself into one of the columns, part of the fallen god's head stuck to it. Shemazay's body collapsed backwards, finally dead. The magma-like blood pouring from the wounds finished consuming the remains of the avatar's body.

"Always go for the head," Yoko said, lumbering toward Alex and pulling his scimitar from the column. Yoko shook scraps of tissue and ichor off the blade. "Head and heart. Did the Greywolf not teach you anything?"

"Gross," Alex replied, staring at the lifeless eyes of the avatar. He then looked up at Yoko. "I didn't know that throwing a sword that way was actually possible in real life, even less that you could do it with such force as to do that."

"I didn't know either," Yoko smiled. "Worth the try though. So, your tally is two dead gods now?"

"With assistance, to be honest. I didn't do it alone," Alex replied.

"And yet I wouldn't be surprised if you start being called 'Godkiller' in the chat rooms."

"Ugh, no please," Alex said. "Don't give them ideas. Though, it beats 'The Pack.'"

"It certainly does." Yoko replied. "How do you think Sam and Kasumi are doing?"

"I hope better than we did," Alex said, rueful.

Yaha glowed once more with intensity as a circle of energy opened in front of them, creating a pathway to the chaotic multicolored streams of the Tempest. Sounds of combat could be heard at the end of the pathway.

"Sam?" Yoko whispered.

"No. That portal opened from this side. And the special effects," Alex said as he moved his hands around in a circle, "are not from her magick. It was someone else."

Alex looked up as a beam of light, like a comet, crossed the sky from the direction of the Long Moon and into the portal. The eclipse was ending at the same time.

"That was fast," Yoko said.

"At least this time she didn't break the world," Alex replied. "I think we should follow."

Both entered the portal, following the beam.

"I knew I should have taken my nausea medications," Alex muttered as the portal closed behind them and the eclipse came to an end, lifting the shadow that covered the world.

Chapter 17
Who I'm Meant To Be

"Kasumi!" Alex yelled at seeing Kasumi kneeling, clutching her abdomen, while Sam was holding her hand. Several meters away, Shemazay lay unconscious.

"I'm… glad to see that you beat… him," Kasumi said between labored breaths, trying to smile. "It really hurts, Sam."

"Is she going to be okay?" Yokoyawa asked. "Is he dead?"

"He won't be a problem anymore, but the bastard placed a really complex curse on her and it's becoming really painful. How did you get here?" Sam asked, surprised at seeing them inside the Tempest.

"We followed that," Alex said and pointed to the ball of energy floating above them. The energy ball morphed into a winged humanoid, a tall woman, taller than any human, freefolk or samoharo, at least three meters in height. As the form became tangible—to an extent, as the light gave her an ethereal quality—Sam could distinguish the trademark features that Harland had related to them after his encounter with Her: Long hair with fiery red and jet-black strands framed a face with olive skin and freckles. Two large raven wings emerged from her back. She sported a friendly smile, which made her big turquoise eyes shine brighter than the moonglow. When you looked into them, they pulled you into a timeless pool that betrayed the fact that this entity was a walking timeless abyss. Just the sight of her caused goosebumps to prickle at their skin. *For it was said that their actual forms were so alien and bizarre, so full of wings, eyes, and mouths than the mere sight of them could drive someone crazy,* Sam recalled from Mekiri's memories. The goddess was clad in black and silver armor that was made of small metallic feathers. The shiny helm resembled a raven's silhouette. On her left wrist was a silver bracelet with a jade stone set in it.

"I know it's awe inspiring to see a god," Ishtaru Ghavreel, the Trickster Goddess and holder of the Horn, said as she extended a hand toward Yokoyawa and Alex. Their more visible injuries were healed in a flash of light. "But we already know each other."

"No offense but... would you fucking shut up and help me save Kasumi!" Sam replied indignantly. After all they had done for her, was she so callous of their current plight? At that moment, Sam wanted to punch her as badly as she had Shemazay.

"Right, sorry about that. Let me fix it," Ishtaru cracked her knuckles. Then she stopped. "On second thought, I can give you something slightly better, if more painful, for a while, if you choose to. Which given that you are not gonna stop picking fights with beings larger than you, could be handy in the long run."

"Are you... implying what I think you are?" Kasumi struggled to ask.

"Yes, but it has to be consensual. You know, Free Will above all," Ishtaru said as she approached Shemazay's unconscious form. "Well, not for him, not anymore. This *skansen*... hopefully, he will learn a bit of empathy by being trapped as a mortal. However, sending him back with you, with his spark of power, it's a terrible idea. So, what I'm going to do is to give this spark of power to someone that earned it and who I know will make better use of it."

Ishtaru placed her hand over the chest of the unconscious Shemazay and tendrils of energy flowed from her fingers and dug into his chest. Alex grimaced at what he was seeing. Ishtaru pulled a ball of energy, which pulsated as rhythmically as a heartbeat.

"Can you see energy flows again?" Sam whispered.

"Yes, and what she is doing to him is not pretty. Remind me to never get on her bad side," Alex whispered back. "It's kinda like what we did with Joshua's Beast but more painful."

Ishtaru returned and kneeled next to Kasumi. The goddess placed her free hand on Kasumi's wound, and the latter's face relaxed as the pain subsided.

"If I say no, will I die?" Kasumi asked. She wasn't keen to have the divine spark that granted the Gift, sourced from Shemazay.

"No," Ishtaru smiled, but her eyes betrayed a sudden surge of sadness. "Because I will do my best to heal you and break the curse. But to do so I would have to put you in a special trance and keep you frozen inside the Tempest till I do it, because Shemazay did it so complex and layered that it will take me time to remove the curse."

"That doesn't sound that bad," Kasumi replied.

"Be aware that choosing that option, time will run differently for you," Ishtaru warned in a stern voice. "By the time I'm done, several decades, perhaps a century will have passed. Your loved ones might not be alive by then. It's up to you."

Kasumi stared at Sam and Alex, grappling with that idea. She grabbed Sam's left hand and Alex's right. Kasumi took a long breath. "I... I'm not sure how to say this but... I love you both. With all my heart. Alex, I've loved you since we were children. Sam, you are the person that makes my heart jump when we hold hands. I can't choose only one of you. But I can choose to spend the rest of my life trying to figure out our relationship. No life is worth living without you, even if we remain only friends."

Kasumi turned to Ishtaru. "Do it," Kasumi said with resolve, not letting go of Alex and Sam's hands. Kasumi took a few moments to think. She stared at Sam and Alex. Both smiled at her, their faces the perfect portraits of contentedness. "I accept the Gift."

"What about the voices... the feedback during the merge?" Alex asked.

"I trust you both will help me with that. I trust you with my life," Kasumi replied.

"Okay. Get ready, because it will hurt. Badly," Ishtaru said.

Kasumi braced herself. Ishtaru lifted her hand from the wound and a choking pain seized Kasumi's body. It felt as though every muscle in her body were rioting. She couldn't breathe. Could barely even string a thought together. The convulsions worsened. Her back arched under the force of them with a strangled gasp. Her jaw clenched against the pain.

"We are here for you," Sam whispered in her ear.

But Kasumi couldn't respond. Her heart stopped.

"Now!" Ishtaru exclaimed as she pushed the energy ball of the divine spark into Kasumi's chest. All it took was the brief moment between the tick and the tock of a clock.

Kasumi's body convulsed with the jolt of divine energy, and her irises glowed with a light whose color was similar to the icy blue of an iceberg or the foam of the sea. Of what she saw in the astral trip, she wouldn't remember.

†††

"In hindsight, that looks even more painful from the outside," Alex said.

"That's because we were almost dead when we got

ours. Your mind was busy with other concerns," Sam replied. "Technically, she is still conscious."

"Good point," Alex conceded, then he turned to Ishtaru. "Why don't the samoharo get the Gift, or the Freefolk? Other than Fionn and Sam."

"Because Freefolk have their magick abilities, which humans don't," Ishtaru replied, her eyes closed. Her wings were covering the four of them, while Yoko stared at the process with peculiar interest. "And Samoharo… they have a particular deal with a friend of mine that even I don't know how it works. But trust me, Sid and our friend here can fight you without a problem, if he actually focuses."

Ishtaru opened her eyes at the same time that Kasumi did. "How are you feeling?"

"Tired. Weird," Kasumi replied, hoarse. She was still having trouble breathing. "My aids are fixed too, but the quality of sound is vastly improved. And that feels odd."

"Why is her hearing not healed?" Alex asked.

"One," Ishtaru explained, raising a finger to count. "The Gift can only heal mortal wounds just before the merger, and her hearing issues come from an illness from her childhood. Two, the Gift can only heal what she wants to get healed."

"My aids are part of who I am," Kasumi said, and smiled at Alex as he helped her up. She closed her eyes against the throbbing pain. "Why is my head hurting?"

"It will ease with time," Ishtaru replied. There was sadness in her voice. "Now, I must return to Last Heaven as there are things I need to fix there and here, while you need to go back to the land of the living. I shall give you a warning though, be aware that things will only get tougher, and I won't be around to help you. This will probably be the last time we see each other in a long time. Your best option is to stick together and support each other. And I mean the whole band."

"What do you mean by this is last time we'll see you?" Sam said.

"Reforming my avatar without breaking the world or using some extreme measures will take time, from your perspective that is. Also, I need to rearrange some of the changes Sam made on that," Ishtaru said as she pointed to the core of all Magick.

"Sorry 'bout that," Sam replied sheepishly.

"Don't be. It had to be done. Magick had to be freed, to add the mortal element of chaos. I'm proud of you." Ishtaru smiled at Sam. It felt as reassuring as the smile her mom used to give her when she was a toddler. "While I need to get some parts of it back to where it was, I might leave some of the changes you made, as a back door. But before I send you back, I want to give you something else, a parting present: My blessing. Kneel, my children."

The four exhausted fighters knelt before the goddess. Every muscle in Sam's body was ached, the adrenaline fading. Ishtaru placed her hands on top of them, growing two more arms to place a hand on each one. Her wings opened to their full span, which seemed to expand into infinity. The goddess closed her eyes and recited in a language that seemed similar to the one of the Straits, but more ancient.

Sam could make out a few words, something about blood of the dragons, protection, breaking limitations, miracles. And even then, she wasn't sure she got the translation right.

Ishtaru opened her eyes, her wings closed, and the extra pair of arms dissolved in the air.

"Now, seriously, you need to get back. Otherwise by the time you return, centuries might have passed."

"What about dad, Gaby, and the rest?" Sam asked. Somehow it felt unfair to her that they were not there for the blessing.

"I will give them my blessing too, don't worry," Ishtaru replied as she opened a portal, on the other side of it, KorbyWorld was waiting. The four of them stood up and walked toward the portal, Yoko first, followed by Kasumi. Sam and Alex were the last.

"Oh right! I almost forgot. Hey, Alex, catch," Ishtaru said. She threw a bracelet to Alex. It was the same as he had given to Forge earlier, but it glowed with orbs of golden light running across it. "Something from my son. As thank you for calling him your friend. You will find out how it works."

† † †

Sam, Alex, Kasumi, and Yokoyawa found themselves in the middle of a pathway, near the lake and on the opposite side to the clocktower. People looked at them with a great deal of confusion, thanks to Sam and Kasumi's flattering but out of place outfits.

"I'm hungry," Alex said, trying to break the awkward tension. "I forgot how having my powers back made me hungry all the time."

"We still need to change, these outfits are not that comfortable," Sam said. "And I would *like* to eat without everyone staring at us. I mean, they get like that because of these outfits and not because of the two dudes with swords?"

"Maybe because it is a theme park? And I was about to ask what's with them," Alex replied, indicating the outfits.

"A crazy idea I had. It seems your bad habits are rubbing off on me," Sam explained with a coy smile.

"Both of you look really pretty, if I can say so," Alex bumbled, rubbing the back of his neck.

"You can," Sam replied, reddening. She didn't mind the compliment.

Kasumi fell behind them and stopped. Her gaze got

lost into infinity as her hands trembled. She fell to the ground, dropping Breaker and grabbing her head with both hands and mumbled incoherently.

Sam noticed that something was wrong and hurried back to her friend. "Kasumi, are you okay?" Sam asked, about to kneel down to help her.

Alex stopped her. "Sam, look at her eyes. I think you better step back," Alex warned, placing himself between both women.

"Arghhhhh!" Kasumi screamed. Her irises glowed with a white-blue light. "Go away or I will kill you!"

"What's wrong?" Yokoyawa asked.

"It's the period of personality settlement. Kasumi must be dealing with the remains of the thoughts of Shemazay, residuals in the energy Mekiri used to give her the Gift," Alex replied. Sam had been lucky, her personality settlement period had been short and was almost painless—aside for the heart problem thing—without a major incident. But Gaby had told her once how Alex had gone through a huge breakdown and it took him days to recover.

"No," Sam said. "We won't leave you. We are on this together, remember? We love each other. You can fight this."

"I will kill you!" Kasumi screamed, the ground frosting over with a thin layer of ice. Her voice had pitched in a strange, otherworldly quality. "Please, go."

"Sam is right," Alex replied as he walked behind Kasumi. He lifted her in a hug and held her tight to keep her from grabbing Breaker, which rested only a few steps to her left. The Tempest Blade trembled as if it were about to be activated. Yokoyawa placed himself between them and Breaker as an addition barrier. "We won't leave you. We are here for you. Remember? You told us that you trusted us with your life. So, listen to me: This is not you. Don't let the voices control you. You are the one in charge.

Just breathe and calm down."

Kasumi struggled against the hug, frost creeping over Alex's arms.

"Geez, that hurts," Alex mumbled.

Sam shifted closer to Kasumi and looked her in the eyes. They looked so beautiful with the glow of the Gift. She wanted to kiss her. But that would have to wait.

"You need to stop," Sam begged. "You are hurting Alex. I know you are inside there, Kasumi. You can fight this. You have the strongest will I have ever seen. That's part of what I love about you."

"You and I have so many memories together," Alex said. "But we can add more with Sam if you fight this. You control the Gift; it doesn't control you."

"I will freeze you to death. Sooner or later, you will choose, and you will discard me like everyone did when I lost my hearing. I better kill you now!" Kasumi growled as she struggled.

"I won't fight you, Kasumi," Alex said, loosening his grip. "I won't leave you. And certainly, I won't choose between either of you. Can't live without either of you. So, do what you must."

Kasumi broke free from the hug and turned to Alex, who braced for the strike, closing his eyes.

"Kasumi, don't do it," Sam grabbed her left hand. Kasumi didn't refuse, nor did she pull away. "Truth is; we are not just friends that pass time together or do things. We are practically family. We'll become a real family if you want. But you need to regain control. We know you can do it."

Kasumi raised her right fist, surrounded by freezing air, ready to strike Alex, but after a prolonged moment, she dropped it. Alex opened his eyes, as Kasumi started to cry. The glow of her Gift faded from irises and Breaker deactivated.

"I... I... I'm sorry. I dunno what happened," Kasumi said, sobbing, hugging Alex.

"It's okay, it happens when you get the Gift," Alex replied. "Luckily, you do have an iron will. I'm sorry for holding you so tight."

"It's okay, Alex," Kasumi mumbled, her face in his chest. "You were trying to help."

Sam walked toward them, and joined the hug, kissing both.

"I'm sorry for hurting you both." Kasumi took turns looking at both of them. "You know I really love you both, right? I don't want to choose either, I want to be with you both, if you want to."

"Love you, too, Kasumi. We are just glad that you are back," Sam replied, holding tighter Kasumi's hand. "And I want that too with both of you. Alex?"

"Of course," Alex said, grabbing Sam's hand and pulling Kasumi closer.

"Can I join the group hug?" Yokoyawa asked.

Sam shook her head. "Obviously. Come here!"

Yokoyawa grabbed the three of them and lifted them with ease in a bone crushing hug.

"You know, this does remind me of an old tv show, just gender reversed," Alex mumbled from within Yokoyawa's bear hug.

"Alex, don't ruin the moment with your random references, please?" Sam said sharply, pushing to get out from the hug. Yoko set them back on their feet before he let them go, and the three of them could finally breathe properly.

"What now?" Kasumi asked, rubbing the back of her neck and fidgeting with her feet. It was clear for Sam that she was still embarrassed by what had just happened.

"I could use a vacation, and since we are here already..." Alex shrugged his shoulders. He was scraping the frost from his arms.

"Again?" Sam rolled her eyes. But she couldn't stop herself from smiling. "What's with you and this place? Besides, do you think they will let us stay after all of this?"

"I think we just gave them the best show ever for free, so maybe they will. And I suspect they would be glad to have someone clean out that underground lair from inky animated critters."

"They are not good for business," Kasumi nodded.

"As long as we are together," Sam replied, waving her hands in defeat. And yet, she beamed with happiness. "That's the silver lining."

Sam was just happy to have her friends... correction, her family with her. Their particular quirks just made them how they were, just like hers made Sam who she was. And they loved each other just as they were. If the question was about choice, Sam realized one thing: Whatever she chose, as long as it made her happy and didn't hurt others, was the right option. She didn't have to choose between her human and her freefolk heritage. They both were part of who she was, and that was fine. She didn't have to choose to follow a particular path to impress her dad. Fionn would be proud of her anyway. And she would make things work so her heart didn't have to choose between the two people she cared about the most in the whole world.

Because as Asherah had realized millennia ago, and now Sam did, she could choose who she was and who she was meant to be, marching to the beat of her own drum without apologizing or following orders, and that was glorious freedom.

† † †

The Figaro arrived at the shores of Manticore Island early in the morning.

On the water below the fishing boats set sail for the

day's catch. In the gardens of the Sisters of Mercy's academy, all the students and the teaching body were gathered. The Figaro's crew could see a small fight break out and then be quickly quenched. The Figaro flew twice in circles above them, grabbing their attention. Gaby, Vivi, Fionn, Harland, and Joshua looked at the students and teachers from the open hatch of the cargo bay.

"They don't look happy," Harland observed. At least a hundred well-trained, deadly women were staring at them. Gaby noticed that was making him nervous. Not that she couldn't blame him. The feeling of emptiness at the bottom of her stomach told her how dangerous this looked. For a brief moment Gaby considered activating the Gift, just to be sure, but decided against it. If what she was about to say was to affect some changes, she had to do it with open hands and without a showcase of power. As equals rather than enemies.

"Good," Gaby replied. "It means that it worked. They all felt the change of the Ice State gone for good."

"Do you need backup?" Fionn whispered.

"No offense, honey," Gaby said as she handed him her Tempest Blades, neatly sheathed, "but the last thing they need is four guys setting foot on the island to tell them what to do. Sid, just lower the ship, but keep it hovering. This is my responsibility; I will go alone."

"Fuel is not cheap!" Sid replied through the comms.

"I'm going with you," Vivi said. "I'm not a guy, and I'm older than you, so you can't send me to my chambers."

"I wouldn't dare," Gaby replied with a smile. It made her relax somewhat to have the Freefolk magus at her side. Vivi was not Sam, who could coordinate with Gaby almost if they were reading each other's minds. But Vivi had experience. And that was valuable as well. It seemed then that the so-called 'Band of the Greywolf', the renewed tribe of the Wind, had gained a new member.

Gaby and Vivi jumped from the cargo bay. Fionn and Joshua stood there, as requested, but knowing them, Gaby was sure they were making calculations on how to beat everyone without seriously injuring them in case it was needed. Gaby hoped that it wouldn't be. She was not doing this for herself. She was doing this for Livia.

Nobody moved as Gaby and Vivi landed. They walked side by side toward the center of the garden, as the elder Sisters approached them. Three older women, with grey hair and aged faces walked to their encounter with angry, stern looks on their faces.

"I take it those are your former teachers," Vivi whispered to Gaby.

"What tipped you off?" Gaby asked with a smirk.

"Oh, you know, the weary, disappointed looks of those working in academia," Vivi replied with a knowing smile.

The women indeed had been her teachers of history, spycraft and table manners, and lastly, combat and tactics. They were the upper echelons after the Superior Mother, who was nowhere to be seen. Maybe she had fallen sick due to losing her connection with Gavito. But at this point, it didn't matter. For Gaby the choice was not hers anymore, but of the students.

"I used to look at Sam the same way when she blew a spell while singing alongside the radio," Vivi replied. "If you need help, just wink. I want to try my spells, now that magick feels different."

"I don't think it will be needed," Gaby assured her, but mostly, was trying to assure herself. "But thank you, just keep an eye on the ones on the rooftop, those are the ones that worry me the most. I will handle the teachers."

Gaby stood in the middle of the garden, with Vivi a few meters behind, waiting for the welcome committee.

"Superior Mothers, how are you?" Gaby asked with a smile. A sincere one. She hadn't come here to gloat, but to fix things.

"You… you destroyed what held us together," one of them shouted at Gaby, the one that taught her combat. "You must be punished. I shall challenge you!"

Why I am not surprised? Gaby thought.

"One. You can challenge me, and I assure you, you will lose," Gaby replied, holding up a finger for each point. "Two. I destroyed the chains that held us down under the orders of a being that took advantage of the founders. But not anymore."

"You took away our edge. You left us defenseless," the spycraft teacher snapped.

"That's the biggest lie you need to unlearn," Gaby replied, raising her voice to be heard by everyone in attendance. Even with the Figaro's engines making noise, her voice was being amplified. Gaby wasn't sure if by the Gift or if Vivi had subtly cast a spell. Nonetheless, she smiled. "We never needed the Ice State or any of those things. We never needed to become spies and assassins to carve a space in this world. We only need whatever talent we already have, to change the world into what we want."

"Easy for you to say," the history teacher said. "You have those special abilities that you stole from this island more than a decade ago."

"I didn't steal anything," Gaby stated. "It was freely given to me after I freed the being that gave me those abilities, like I freed myself from your teachings, from your rules. And yeah, perhaps it might look like it is easy for me to stand here, in front of you, telling you all of this. But it took me a long road to get here. Nothing can be achieved with ease, especially those worth fighting for. Otherwise, we lose respect for them. We must relearn the value of strength, through compassion."

A heavy silence befell the place as Gaby's words sank in with the audience.

A student broke the silence. "How? What will happened to us now?" It was a small girl with freckles on her face. She looked scared. "Will you stay here with us to lead us?"

"No. You don't need someone to lead you," Gaby said to the girl with her crooked smile. "But I will be around if you need help, advice, or just someone to talk with. We are Sisters, in the real sense of the word. If my recent ordeal has taught me something, it is that the only person responsible for my choices, for my own happiness is myself. So, I'm telling you that you have the same freedom of choice. But you have to take it. With all the responsibilities it entails."

Another heavy silence befell the gathering. But this time it was quickly broken as the students whispered among themselves. One with long, raven-black hair moved toward Gaby and extended her hand.

"I'll take your offer, Sister. I want you to help me get out of here and have a normal life of my choosing."

Many others approached Gaby, pushing the elder teachers away.

"Cool!" Gaby replied, taking the student's hand. "It might take a bit to get all of you out of here, because the Figaro can only carry a few, but let me get in touch with the people that aided me to escape this place and I will get you sorted."

"I think you will need a name for this new Sisterhood," Vivi said.

"Maybe. But right now, we have work to do."

"Nice speech," Fionn whispered to Gaby through the ear comms.

"I had a good teacher," she replied.

"Me?"

"Of course not. Harland."

"That hurts. Where now?"

"My home. After helping these girls, we have earned a rest and a good meal."

† † †

"This place is huge," Joshua said, his eyes wide, as he descended from the Figaro, which had landed outside the entrance to the Galfano estate, in what seemed to be its designated space. The façade was at least a hundred meters long, full of windows with stone frames, each one with a sculpted dog's head carved from limestone. A large oak door was in front of them with the Galfano coat of arms engraved on it: A dog running toward the visitor, with a hawkdove flying above, as the sun rose from the horizon.

Gaby led a dozen of the girls from the Sisters of Mercy academy, followed by Fionn, Harland, Sid, Vivi, Joshua. The girls had nowhere else to go for the time being. And Gaby being Gaby had offered them a place to stay until they could figure out what to do next. There was no hurry.

"Welcome!" Gaby's grandpa exclaimed as he opened the doors. "Everyone, welcome to our home!"

"Thank you, grandpa for receiving us this late without notice, and with so many in tow," Gaby said, hugging him. This was her home. One of them, at least. The other was with her found family, her friends, who were now by right and union, her clan. Gaby then realized that she hadn't told the Galfano family that she was now the matriarch of the reformed Wind tribe of the Freefolk, made from the most varied members. But that was a talk for another time.

"Nonsense, this is your home," Grandpa replied. "You can come here anytime you want. As well as your friends. It's good to see you again, Fionn. And you too, Sid! Harland!"

Grandpa gave them strong hugs that lifted them from the ground.

"Thank you, sir," Harland wheezed.

"I didn't know she had this much money," Vivi whispered to Sid, who was coughing after the bear hug.

"That's the way she has always liked it," Sid replied. Then he turned to Grandpa. "What's for dinner?"

"Where are your manners?" Harland whispered.

"I left them at Mon Caern," Sid replied, making Joshua laugh. "Oh! The brooding man knows how to laugh. I need to take a picture of that, or Alex won't believe me."

"Shut up, lizard," Joshua mumbled.

"We were having a small family dinner, but come inside please, there is always room for more guests." Grandpa took them all to the garden, where large tables had been set. Dozens of kids, all having a similar semblance, were running all over the place.

"This is a 'small family dinner?'" Joshua asked.

"Gaby has a lot of younger cousins," Fionn replied.

"And people from Montsegur don't know how to cook small quantities," Sid added, glee in his voice.

"I need to teach you some manners," Vivi said, playfully punching him in the shoulder.

† † †

"Have to admit that it is funny to see Sid with Vivienne," Fionn said from their vantage point. Both he and Gaby were sitting on the terrace rooftop, away from the bustling noise of Gaby's younger cousins playing with some of the girls from the academy. Harland was talking with Gaby's grandparents, probably about some obscure fact about Montsegur wine. Joshua, as usual, was sulking in a corner of the garden, until a girl asked him to come and dance with her, all but dragging him away from the shadows. Not that Gaby could blame the girl. Joshua was handsome, if in a classic rugged movie star kind of way.

Gaby turned to see what had caught Fionn's eyes: Sid eating as much as he could, all while Vivi chided him to slow down because he had to keep his triglycerides in check. They were acting as if they were a married couple. Gaby wondered if they talked about kids.

Can samoharo and freefolk have kids? Gaby wondered. But that was a question she would keep to herself for years to come.

She did ask Fionn, "Why?"

"Height difference," Fionn pointed out. "She must be the one reaching for the cereal on the top shelf."

"The same happens with Sam and Alex," Gaby replied. "Have you noticed she stopped wearing high heels since Alex got out of the hospital? Unless he or Kasumi ask her to."

"Why?"

"To reduce the height difference between them."

Fionn growled under his breath, which made Gaby stifle a laugh.

"It was nice of your family to allow us to stay here to rest before returning to Saint Lucy," Fionn said, clearly eager to change topics.

"My grandparents have always made a point of welcoming visitors," Gaby replied. "And family."

"Like the other girls that escaped Manticore Island after you did? Or the new ones you are bringing here to stay for a time?" Fionn asked.

"Grandpa says that there is no point in having the company if its earnings can't help people even a little," Gaby said with a shrug as Fionn put an arm over her shoulders.

"I think he might be the only company owner to think that in the whole history of the universe," Fionn laughed.

"Alex said something similar to me, after grandpa paid for his university tuition in full," Gaby said "And when he helped him to move out from the Straits after all his problems there." Maybe Fionn's father had been right, the problem in the world was that no one wanted to help each other. Gaby was proud that her family agreed to be the change—as much as Fionn was through his actions, or Harland through the Foundation.

She took a deep breath of the cold afternoon air, her chest filling with happiness.

"Did you manage to get in touch with Sam?" Gaby asked.

"Kinda," Fionn replied. "Communication lines are still failing after that big energy explosion in space that damaged whatever system the Figaro used for long range communication. But they somehow fixed what was causing the problems with magick and helped Mekiri. Apparently a fallen god messed up things and Sam and Alex had to, you know, get rid of him. Before the call got cut Sam did mention two things that have left me worried thought."

"What?"

"The big explosion was result of something that happened to Mekiri, so we won't see her anymore in a long time, maybe never, something about her avatar."

"That's not good."

"And Kasumi is one of us now."

"One of us?" Gaby asked, before realization hit her like a ton of bricks. "Oh! That's not good, either. I hope it wasn't that painful. How is she doing?"

"Can't say, that's when the call got cut," Fionn replied. "I can't help but shudder. I mean Kasumi was already freakishly strong before. Now? As a Gifted? It will be like the sheer power of the ocean itself."

"The bright side is that she is with Sam and Alex, and they already went through the process, so they will look after her," Gaby said. "Which they would do anyway. I'm trying to wrap my head around how their relationship will work now. Is throuple the right word?"

"Well, most Freefolk are pansexual, which includes Sam," Fionn said with a loose wave of his hand. "And

Kasumi seems to love both of them, who were already entering into a relationship, so... they are adults, they will have time to talk and figure out what to do next. My main worry is that Alex and Sam tend to argue quite a bit, but my hope is that with Kasumi in the mix balancing things, they will talk and smooth things over. It's not uncommon for my people, after all, Asherah had two partners. I was raised by a dad and two mothers."

"I just hope no one gets hurt. Relationships are complicated by rule of thumb."

"You are sounding like a concerned mom." Fionn laughed at his own dad joke.

"I guess it's inevitable," Gaby replied ruefully.

"Did you find the answer to that question?" Fionn looked into her eyes. That calm look he always gave her that made her feel butterflies in her stomach at the same time that put her at ease. The best place in the world for Gaby right now was next to him. For many reasons.

"Which question?" Gaby asked in turn.

"I might be dumb, but I'm not *that* dumb," Fionn replied with a wry smile. "You have been musing about the whole reincarnation thing since we started traveling together. And you talk in your sleep. A lot. Even sing from time to time"

"Does it matter to you? The answer, I mean."

"Only if it makes you unhappy." Fionn held her closer to him. He had used the aftershave she had given him months ago, after the shower they took before dinner. It smelled nice. "As long as you are happy, I'm happy."

"Sure?"

"One hundred percent," Fionn replied. "But I get that you don't want to talk much about it."

"Not now. Maybe in a few days after I process everything," Gaby explained. She was still thinking about the talk she'd had inside the mindscape, reflecting on how she got to that point and what she wanted to do next. One thing she was sure of, though, was that she didn't have to choose a single path, as life was always in a state of wonderful chaotic change. She didn't have to hide what or who she was like she'd tried to in high school, nor run away from the painful memories or her fear that she was not the master of her own destiny. It didn't matter who she had been in a previous life, Izia or someone else, that was just a part of who she was now, but not the main part. Yet she could still love that side of herself, as she loved all she was. Beneath the bruises, the broken bones and accelerated healing, underneath the sprained muscles, there was a brave woman who from an early age had decided to choose who she wanted to be: A singer, an adventuring hero, a friend, a life partner, a leader. All of them were possible, and she could elect, without making any apology, who she was meant to be, as long as she was in charge of her own happiness.

After a moment, Gaby chuckled. "But, so you can be at ease, I will tell you: Everything is fine. I realized some things and I feel like a heavy weight was lifted off my shoulders. And I think I'm happier than I have been in a long time."

Gaby's wide grin beamed with a sense of freedom. The hawkdove was expanding her wings into the uncertain but exciting great beyond.

"Knowing that you are happy is the only thing I need." Fionn smiled at her once more, tightening the hug. "Changing topics, how do you feel after leading your first successful mission? Easier than giving a concert or not?"

"Exhausting. And it was barely a success. The concert is less scary," Gaby replied.

"Any mission from where you come out alive is a success," Fionn explained. "This line of work... I never wanted it for you or the others. It is too risky. But here we are."

"I know, but if you really think about it, no one—including you—must want to live forever," Gaby said. "The only thing we truly own is the time we have, the choices we make, and the lessons we learn from them."

"And what lesson did you learn this time?" Fionn asked.

"That we can choose who we want to be, and with whom to share that," Gaby replied.

"That's a good lesson," Fionn said. A bright light caught her eyes, and his as well. They looked up to the sky, as Fionn pointed to the dozens of stars falling across the sky. "Hey, look, a rain of falling stars! Make a wish."

Gaby closed her eyes and thought of one thing: *You can choose who you are. And this is who I want to be.*

Chapter 18
Bonus Track: Twenty Stitches

THE WOMAN HAD BEEN RUNNING all night. But, in spite of all efforts, her attempt to get across the forest was to no avail. The black *huargo* hound caught her just when she reached the shores of the sacred lake, a sharp cry escaping her. It dragged her back to the edge of the forest and mauled the woman, leaving a bloody trail behind on the snowy field. As the beast was about to rip out her throat, something frightened it. The hound stopped short, hackles rising with a growl at the shadows of the forest; the *huargo* was ready to defend its prey. It was the smell of sulfur that made it stop growling. But it was the red eyes burning as embers, staring at him from the darkness that sent it whimpering away.

A man in a tattered cape and old, purple armor walked from the darkness and toward the body of the woman. He knelt next to her and checked her wounds. She looked to be over forty and her breathing was uneven, fast. It was clear that she was in pain. And that there was not much the man, in his current situation, could do. He took off his cape, revealing his armor. It had rubies set in it, and in better times would have been resplendent. But the armor had been cracked and damaged, the rubies chipped. The man placed his worn-thin cape over the woman, and his left hand on her brow. He closed his eyes for a second then he smiled at her.

The woman's eyes widened when she recognized the red eyes of the being in front of her. Panic inspired her thrashed in a futile attempt to escape, making her already terrible wounds bleed worse. The snow was pink around her.

"Don't take me to the Pits!" she pleaded.

"Don't worry, little mortal," Ben Erra said. "Your soul will go straight to Last Heaven, pending a detour to the Life Tree as things are preordained."

"I… don't… want to die," the woman managed to get out amidst gasps for air.

"None of you mortals want to die, but I'm afraid that I can't do much to stop it now. My fortunes, like yours, have suffered a tremendous setback. The only thing I can do for you now is to ease your pain. Because the key for the painful alternative is unavailable to me."

"I don't understand."

"I know," Ben Erra said in his charming voice. "Don't trouble your last moments with the ramblings of an ancient being."

The woman gasped for air, and unleashed a scream, pushing him away. Ben Erra was about to place his hand on her head once more when a blast of blue fire sent him flying backwards into a tree.

He surged to his feet. His body might be mortal now, but that didn't mean that it was weak… yet. He stared at his attacker and saw a familiar sight. The one that was always tagging along with his sibling. The momma's boy.

"What did you do to her?" Stealth demanded, summoning a second blue fireball, holding it at the ready.

Ben Erra cursed his luck. Leave it to Ishtaru's pets to make it easier for her people to cast magick. And of course, he had to come across his 'nephew'. Stealth hated his guts and he—Ben Erra, Judge and Jailer of the Underworld—

was in the unfortunate situation of being without most of his powers, trapped in his avatar. He was practically mortal. He had been fighting against the escapees from the Pits for the past week, trying to reach the sacred lake deep into the Mistlands to commune with Ishtaru. But no, he had to find Stealth. At least his brother was more amicable.

"I did nothing. A Pit spirit infused *huargo* hound got her before I arrived. If you haven't noticed, one hundred and eight escaped last week during the falling stars rain. They are initiating their attack."

Stealth didn't reply. He had the gall to ignore the powerful Ben Erra. These new generations lacked respect for their elders. And they later complained when the spirits of their planets decided to punish them with floods and hurricanes for not showing them the respect that they routinely denied others. Ben Erra saw Stealth kneeling next to the dead body and examining it. The injuries were many and deep. The woman wouldn't have survived without a magus with a healing spell.

"What do you want her body for? Isn't the custom of the freefolk to bury their dead with a tree seed?"

"Not in this case," Stealth said as he left a crystal on the body's chest and prayed in silence. "She didn't deserve this."

Ben Erra walked toward Stealth, closing the gap between them. He put a hand to his forehead. A large gash had been opened by the impact and was bleeding profusely.

"I didn't deserve this either. I will need... how did that woman say it in her song? Twenty Stitches to close this wound."

"If you don't tell me what your purpose is here in this sacred land, you will need more than what Gaby sang about to hold your avatar's body together," Stealth replied, putting himself between the dead woman and the Judge of the Underworld.

"Yes, her. I admit, it's a good song. I love a soulful blues-rock song. But let's get something clear, boy." His voice got an octave deeper. "The only reason I'm not turning you into ashes is because you are *technically* my family and I have an alliance with your mother."

"You don't scare me," Stealth said, standing his ground in front of the body, pointing his staff at Ben Erra.

"Don't push your luck, or—" Ben Erra threatened.

"Or what?" a third voice said. The dead woman stood up, her body still broken, bloodied. Her eyes glowed with the same colors as the aurora borealis. The body began to levitate. "You are in no position to make threats."

Ben Erra looked at the woman. He recognized the aura emanating from her body. An all too familiar one, from the being he had been trying to contact.

"So that's why Stealth conveniently knew when and where to appear and retrieve the body, am I right, sister? You're not planning on becoming one of your Gifted and surrender yourself to that mortal's soul, are you?"

"No. For starters it can't be done because her soul has already crossed the Celestial River, given that the Judge gave her his blessing to do so," Ishtaru explained. "I never planned to become a Gifted. I'm using this empty vessel to communicate with you, and stop you from hurting my son."

"You could have spoken to my mind. That doesn't break the world, if that's your concern. Unless you are planning to use that body for something else, like let's say, reshape it into a new avatar to save time," Ben Erra said, enjoying the irony. "Isn't that desecration akin to possession?"

Ishtaru remained silent, only staring at him with a look he knew well. He always got a rise from provoking his sibling.

"I didn't know you had it in you to be this ruthless,"

Ben Erra pressed on.

"What part of 'Trickster' do you not understand? Or has being trapped in your avatar made you dumber?" Ishtaru replied. Long gone was the playful, calm voice. What came from the body was nothing like the woman's original voice. "She was one of my devotees. I asked her soul for consent, which she gladly gave. I'm not a bastard like you."

"Oh my, my, someone is mad," Ben Erra said with an open laugh.

"Of course, I'm mad, I lost my avatar. And I really loved that part of me," Ishtaru said. Ben Erra noticed some subtle changes in the woman's body. It started to look a bit more like Mekiri. But just a little. "All because one of our own decided to follow your example."

"How is this my fault? I got trapped in my avatar because of your second in command. Stupid zealot, I hope he rots in hell once he gets there after your punishment. Which, by the way, has been left in a precarious position only guarded by my loyal devils—"

"Because every now and then someone decides to follow your example, and that's how we lost three planets ten thousand years ago!" Ishtaru said, her voice raising with each word. The aurora borealis roiled at a frenetic cadence, reacting to her emotions.

"You can't blame me for teaching our people to think for themselves," Ben Erra replied. A weird sensation ran across his body, his blood boiling at the familiar accusations. Anger. That was what he was feeling in an actual body for the first time in a long, long, really long time. "You are a prime example of that. Now they accept it as the law ruling over mortal beings."

"I'm not blaming you for that," Ishtaru explained. "I do blame you for not showing them to be responsible, for letting their egos get the best of them, for thinking mortals are beneath us. Which I hope you have learned, is not the case. Like some of them have done by merging with them."

"So... you don't blame me for rebelling?" Ben Erra asked, confused. He hated to admit he was hopeful. Such annoying things emotions were.

"You really need to clean your ears. What I blame you for is for being a selfish *skansen* that derailed the original plan and forced us to improvise for the past thirteen point eight billion years," Ishtaru replied, clearly annoyed. "And your stupid experiment that let those things into Creation."

"Thank you," Ben Erra said. And for the first time in his eternal existence, he meant it. Maybe redemption wasn't off the table for him as well. He thought of Joshua and chuckled. Humanity was indeed contagious.

"You are still an idiot," Ishtaru rolled her eyes. "I don't know how *Diosamadre* Kaan'a puts up with you."

"Says the one breaking rules all the time. Yet the answer is obvious, you are a mother too. You tell me," Ben Erra replied with a half-smile.

Ishtaru remained silent for a moment, gazing at Stealth. She sighed.

"Now, if this heart-to-heart talk is done, we need deal with the mess upstairs," Ishtaru said, extending her hand. "Come with me, brother, we have things to do. First stop, the Tempest."

"What about your precious world and your beloved mortals?" Ben Erra replied, looking around. "I admit that after a dozen millennia, this place grows on you, like a fungus you want to care for."

"They will be ready for what's next, but right now, you and I have to deal with some unruly, upstart minor gods," Ishtaru explained, while waving her new hand in a circle, opening a portal to a tunnel whose walls were full of bright lights and moving blurred images: The Tempest.

"While I leave my new Mekiri avatar incubating."

A ball of energy came out from the body, leaving a trail of light into the portal in front of Ben Erra and Stealth. On the other side Ishtaru manifested once more into her winged warrior shape. Ben Erra strode toward the portal as Stealth walked over to the woman's body. It was still engulfed in light and rabbit ears grew on the top of her head. An amber cocoon appeared from thin air, encasing the body. Stealth picked up the cocoon and headed to the lake, to drop the cocoon there until it was ready to blossom.

"I take it we will pick up our other disembodied brother on the way up?" Ben Erra mused aloud.

"Of course, the chronic hero moron gave one of my guy's hallucinations. Just to make me notice him." Ishtaru turned her gaze on Stealth. There was a tenderness in her expression. "Be safe, Stealth. And take care of your brother."

"I will, mo…mo… my lady," Stealth replied with a bow.

"What is your plan?" Ben Erra asked as the portal closed behind them. Now that he was in the Tempest his armor began to repair itself. He could also sense his powers coming back, as black wings grew on his back.

"What's next is to be fought for at multiple levels, as you told me once when you asked for an alliance," Ishtaru replied as both flew into the maelstrom of spiritual and quantum foam energies that was the Tempest. "Our pieces are almost set on the board and each one will have a role to play against the common threat."

"And the endgame?"

"Hope for a future."

About the Author

Ricardo is a Mexican writer and lives in Toluca, Mexico. He studied Industrial Design at the School of Architecture & Design of the Autonomous University of the State of Mexico, where he currently works as a lecturer focused on sustainability. He has a Ph.D. in Design from Loughborough University. He's a founding member of Inklings Press, an indie publisher of short story anthologies of science fiction, fantasy, alternate history, and horror. His short story "Twilight of the Mesozoic Moon", co-written with Brent A. Harris, was nominated for the 2016 Sidewise Awards for Alternate History. His horror stories "Bone Peyote" and "The Sound of Madness" were featured at The Wicked Library Podcast. Other short stories have been featured in anthologies by Inklings Press, Rivenstone Press, and Aradia Publishing. He co-authored a chapter on world-building and system thinking in the book "Worlds Apart: Worldbuilding in Fantasy and Science Fiction" from Luna Press Publishing which won a British Science Fiction Award.

He is a fan of anime, the 80s' Saturday morning cartoons, Japanese RPG videogames, toys, and mythology, which clearly influences his writing. He also likes dogs.